UNKINDNESS OF OLD GIANTS

Kelly Virens

Port Fireflirt
Bindery

Copyright © 2025 Kelly Virens

All rights reserved. No part of this book may be reproduced or used in any manner without the prior written permission of the copyright owner, except for the use of brief quotations in a book review.

To request permissions, contact the publisher at Portfireflirt@gmail.com

Do not use any part of this book for AI purposes. It is seriously damaging to the environment and the creative industry.

Hardcover: 979-8-9883382-3-9
Paperback: 979-8-9883382-4-6
Ebook: 979-8-9883382-5-3

First paperback and hardback edition June 2025.

Edited by Brittany Gossin & Kai Yee Goh
Cover art, map, interior art and layout by Kelly Virens

Printed by IngramSpark in the USA.

Port FIreflirt Bindery
P. O. Box 278083
Sacramento, Ca 95827

linktr.ee/portfireflirt

<u>Short Stories & Novellas</u>
Beacon

~

<u>Old Giants novellas</u>
Swift of Storm

<u>Old Giants</u>
Secrets of Old Giants
Unkindness of Old Giants

~

<u>Enchanted Senses</u>
An Inspection So Sweet

Author's Note

Unkindness of Old Giants is not a romantasy. It is a fantasy with romance but we are not focusing on that. This is the story of Elodie and Cyrus finding their way. Cyrus was a character we never got to really know in book one but he certainly does have a side of the story worth sharing. The idea for this started with his apology to Elodie. I got to thinking what their dynamic might look like going forward. What might she be like now, after what she becomes, what does being the Earth Blessed really mean? In turn this lead to how the high estates might behave now too.

In book two of the Old Giants trilogy we are dealing with some heavy themes that may be a lot for some readers. While this book features no spice it does have a few fade to black moments. I have not noted all of these occurrences in the chapters but I did list the very heavy ones.

That said, the other trigger warnings listed below have been noted to the best of my ability. Please be advised.

<u>Trigger Warnings:</u>
- Profanity.

- Brief occurrences of injury and blood – Not graphic.

- Moments anxiety.

- Interrogation and humiliation tactics.

- Moments of isolation.

- Episodes of PTSD and night terrors.

- Brief sedation via injection. (Chapter: 9, 28, 35)

- Off page sexual assault – Not to or by FMC, not by MMC. (Chapters: 15, 25)

To anyone who feels like a stranger; not because your surroundings changed, but you have.

Unkindness of Old Giants Playlist

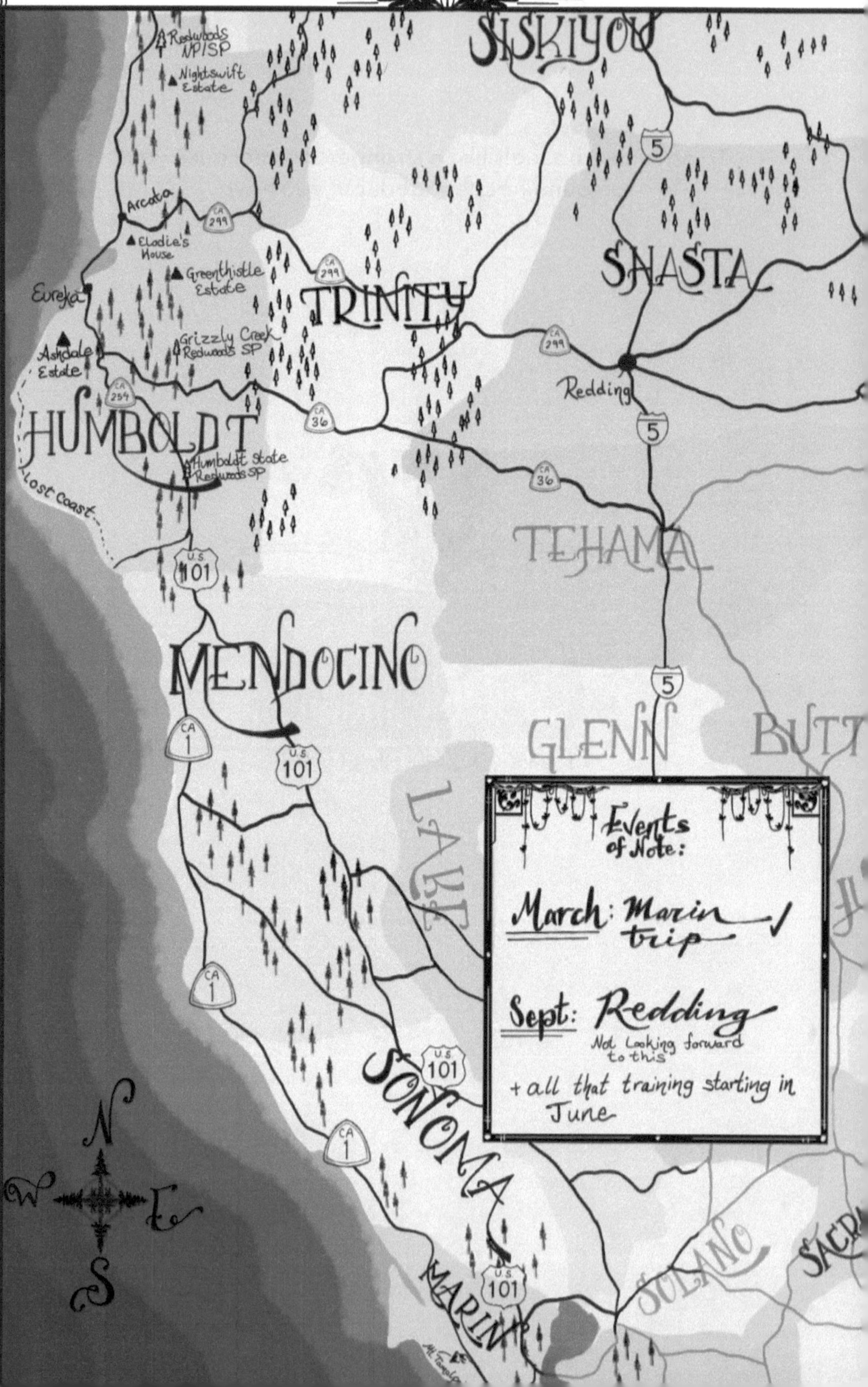

SISKIYOU
SHASTA
TRINITY
HUMBOLDT
MENDOCINO
TEHAMA
GLENN
BUTT
LAKE
SONOMA
MARIN
SOLANO
SACR
Redwoods NP/SP
Nightswift Estate
Arcata
CA 299
Elodie's House
Greenthistle Estate
Eureka
CA 299
Grizzly Creek Redwoods SP
Ashdale Estate
CA 254
CA 36
Humboldt State Redwoods SP
Lost Coast
CA 299
Redding
I-5
CA 36
U.S. 101
CA 1
U.S. 101
I-5
CA 1
CA 1
U.S. 101
U.S. 101
Mt. Tamalpais
N
S
E
W
Events of Note:
March: Marin trip ✓
Sept: Redding
Not looking forward to this
+ all that training starting in June

All he wanted right now was to roll on his side, yet his limbs were locked in place. Trying to focus, his senses ripped a cry from his already hoarse throat.

"I'm sorry!" he screamed.

The room shifted from the stark white void he had been chained up in to the cold metal of the restraint cell...to his room? The soft surface underneath him was a sensation he could not wrap his head around. Yet people were shouting, and rushed movements flickered all around him. Why couldn't he move his limbs? Slowly, his vision cleared. He was in his room. Nightswift Estate. Not the cell. How he got here was a blank spot in his mind. Hadn't he just been in the hold? He flinched, recalling the needles injected into him, the sensation of his body being restrained. What had he done to end up in the hold?

Trevin's cries, the absolute despair on his face as he looked up at the Old Giants, saying he was sorry. The arrows sticking out of him.

"Trevin!" he called out. "No!" Then he realized he was holding a crossbow. Autumn wept beside her brother, why did he lock her in a bargain to marry him? He hadn't thought of Autumn that way in years.

A sinister laugh raked up his spine like claws. His heart pounded and he spun around. "No! Not again!" he cried out, facing that stark white void again.

Once more it laughed as he turned to run and chains wrapped around his body, dragging him down to the ground. "No!" he screamed and struggled to get free.

Somewhere far away a beep was going off rapidly. "What is happening to him?" someone angrily asked.

"Help me. Please," he begged. He tugged again, more frantic.

"You are safe," a soft voice told him. It was full of sorrow and pleading.

"I'm sorry. I didn't want to do this," he cried.

"They are alright, just breathe," the sad voice replied.

Suddenly, he saw her. *Elodie.* She stood over him, glowing teal blood oozing from open wounds all over her, as she ripped those chains off him. As soon as he could, he ran and the void was gone. Now he was in a cold dark ruin. No, he had been thrown in restraints and dragged to the hold. He could feel the blood on his body—it was her blood.

"No! I'm sorry, Elodie!" he cried.

"She is safe." The sad voice was growing weepy. "You are safe."

The soft feeling of a bed under his trembling body brought him back to his room. He went to curl up on his side but the restraints tightened. "No!"

"Cyrus!" the stressed voice declared. "You are alright."

His room. His parents were there, standing over him. He tried to move again but they tightened.

"Just relax," the sad voice soothed. His mom.

Elodie had freed him from that horrible spirit. Their Earth Blessed had woken up and they brought him home. After all that he had done. Once more he wanted to curl up but he was held down. He tugged more. Why couldn't he move? Elodie had freed him, he was home but restrained? Trevin's blood pooled around his body. Elodie's blood on him. He was a monster. "No! I'm sorry. I don't want to be a monster!"

"Fine, just do it!" the angry voice said. It was his dad.

Something pinched his neck, causing him to cry out.

Then everything went black and still for Cyrus Nightswift.

Chapter 1

"It appears you are making good progress, Lady Elodie."

"Thank you, Lord Greenthistle, sir," Elodie replied then glanced away from the screen, as though something caught her attention on the coffee table.

Lord Greenthistle watched her.

"El, we can resume those drills tomorrow," Trevin soothed.

"I know. I just feel like I should be getting it. This is just memory stuff," Elodie groaned.

Trevin laughed and rubbed her back. "They were never my favorite drills to do either."

He could see Elodie and Trevin were on the couch in her living room in her home, the one she had recently purchased in the neighborhood of Sunny Brae. The wall behind them had been painted sage green, the perfect backdrop for her and Trevin.

He had to hand it to her, for as unsure as she had seemed after the ruins and the weeks that followed, she was finding her footing quicker than he expected. He did not miss her doubts and nerves though. In fact, they were hard to miss.

In the days and weeks since the ruins had occurred he had gotten to know this new version of Elodie Santiago. The mortal female that had run through the darkness of night only to emerge as some new and foreign, their Earth Blessed. She was one of their folk tales come to life. The redwoods had chosen her at eight years old and screamed so desperately for her to return to them because they all needed her, the Old Giants and fae alike.

She had saved not only all three of his cubs' lives, but the heirs of the three high estates as well. Elodie Santiago was aligned with Greenthistle Estate, and properly vowed to his firstborn, Trevin. She had chosen them all, and while they all knew the road ahead was not without growing pains, Lord Greenthistle knew he would always be grateful for her ever curious tenacity. He just hoped it would be enough.

So little was known of the Earth Blessed and they would all have to learn alongside her. She was the only known of her kind, chosen to be an extension of their entity, the coast redwoods, to and carry their knowledge, mending their land when it was needed. She had also become immortal and tied to the earth itself through the coast redwoods.

Lord Greenthistle smiled watching them interact. Trevin was so doting on her, and the two supported each other in everything. It was bittersweet to watch them for he thought of Trevin's mother, Selene a lot, but after she had passed he had sworn off anything long term or serious for himself.

"Maybe we proceed to the next phase of drills now?" he asked.

Trevin scoffed. "Like Cedar or Quinn trying to run them? Not yet."

"Like it or not, Trevin, she will be running drills with all of Nightswift and Ashdale very soon," Lord Greenthistle maintained.

"I know."

Lord Greenthistle heard an uneasy exhale escape Elodie. "Lord Greenthsitle, sir, I thought about what you said as far as addressing you all, but I still would rather address you all as your proper titles instead of your first names. Calling Lord Nightswift, Bracken, feels weird, as does calling Lord Ashdale, Miles. I know you said it was alright if I used your first name, but it feels weird to call you Echo."

"It is alright, Lady Elodie. We understand, but one day you will hold the same power as our entity, as you are an extension of the Old Giants and you will outrank us. That is why we offered you the option. Plus, giving you our names is a sign of trust." He smiled and brought his hands together. "However, for now rest assured you will be safe while at our estates. No one means you any harm."

"Yes, sir." She looked at the screen as if she were going to say something then stopped herself.

"Lady Elodie, please speak freely. We desperately need to ensure you trust us as well. Especially to voice any concerns you have."

"I know. I do trust you, I'm just not sure I trust myself. I am worried I might mess up or hurt one of you by accident. That first lesson with you, I got scared and lashed the vines out. It has been weeks of working on it, but now I will be put in front of Quinn and Cyrus. I haven't seen Quinn as much as I thought I would and Cyrus—"

"El." Trevin's voice was soft as he took her hand. "You will not hurt anyone. Even if they act like the biggest assholes, you wouldn't hurt them. Besides, they know their drills and courses."

"That is true, Lady Elodie. You will make mistakes and you are allowed to be scared. None of us are immune to fear either, but it is better you make mistakes in a controlled environment before something happens out there. We're all very attuned to our physical and mental abilities. We want to help you do the same."

"Yes sir. I want to master this. I want to be ready for anything," Elodie said.

"You will, of that I have no doubt, but ease your own doubts first." Echo made a few notes and looked at the door beyond his screen. "Enjoy your evening. Oh, and Trevin, leave her side tonight, just to show Quinn and Cedar you trust them. To show everyone else you are a normal mortal and not a territorial fae obsessed with his girlfriend."

After they finished the call up, Echo let out a slow exhale and glanced to the window looking at the redwoods in the yard. They had chosen Elodie for who she was, she was the perfect embodiment of all three high estates wrapped up in one anxious bundle. Ever since early March, when that night in the ruins occurred, they had scoured what they could researching Earth Blessed and found little. The tome sat on its podium as it had for weeks, with little more understood on it. The Greenthistle family had been so busy ensuring Elodie was settled that translating the tome was proving difficult. Echo and all three of his children had worked on it but they hadn't managed to decipher much of the old language the tome was written in.

Even after Elodie had visited with the Marin County high estates, who had actually had one of the last known Earth Blessed, little was learned. Only two of their high estates had any encounters with the forest sprite stating that she just went off into the forest one day and was never seen again. Mount Tamalpais was Marin County's entity, a prominent mountain seen from far across the Bay Area.

As they racked their brains as to what this all meant for Elodie, it proved difficult since the entity was so different. All they had discovered was that she was now immortal and could talk with the redwoods. Her body would emit a teal glow and sometimes her eyes pulsed a teal light, usually before she was going to use the illuminated vines that came out of her hands.

Greenthistle Estate had done a decent amount of training with the vines; they could be used to restrain, soothe, or lash out like a weapon. She still had not mastered being able to extend it through her dagger again as she had done on the night of the ruins. Cedar and Quinn remained the only two who saw her do that. Greenthistle had also worked on her conditioning over the last few months after he noticed how tired she would get after using her power.

When the doors of the study opened for the other two estate lords, he motioned for them to take a seat.

"Echo, how are things at Greenthistle?" Miles asked with a perturbed tone.

"Things are well, I suppose. Lady Elodie and Trev are at her place tonight. They will be back here in a few days," Echo replied.

"How is her training going? Anything of note, before she begins her week at Ashdale?" Miles asked.

"She is doing well. I think I would put her at our heirs' level when they were around ten. Able to run our course with minimal error, reactions are quick, stamina is good. However, she appears to get a certain level of bewilderment that Trev can't pinpoint the cause of." Echo went on to express the concerns she had tonight then looked to Bracken, who remained exhausted. He usually appeared so put together, but it was no secret that Nightswift Estate was struggling as of late. Cyrus was not making much progress in his recovery. Echo had visited a few times, and encouraged Cedar and even Trevin to try, but neither one had yet. "Is Cyrus still as I last saw him?"

Bracken leaned forward and dropped his head into his hands. "Yes. He manages three hours of sleep when he has nothing left to fight but it is usually ripped away from him with screams. He hasn't been sedated in a few weeks but it's obvious the strain this is all taking on him. He will not talk to us and curls up on himself. His three months are going to be up soon and he has to leave the house but the precedent has been set, I fear." Bracken sat up and leaned back in his chair. "Poppy is becoming withdrawn. Delia is growing angry. And Ari is just so distraught for our boy. She spends more time with him after he sleeps. She is much more nurturing, a mother's love I suppose."

"He will be alright. I hope Quinn will help calm her enough since she is starting the rotation within a week at Ashdale," Echo said.

"I sure hope so. Quinn has not been around as much, I went over her stamina drills he has been tasked with running, and the feral communication lessons his younger brother will do with her. Naturally Quinn acts as though it will be a walk in the park and I sure hope his confidence is not misplaced. The times I have seen her would indicate this is going to be a challenging summer. She has got to get over her mental block."

Echo nodded. "This gives her one week at Ashdale, and one week at Greenthistle, Bracken. Trevin has scheduled night shifts starting so he will have days and nights where they are apart during her Greenthistle week too. Getting assigned an intern I think works in our favor."

Bracken looked at Echo and gave a tight-lipped smile. "I heard Ari beg those Old Giants to make Elodie strong, to not forget about Cyrus, but I do not know how I am going to sit them in a room together. I hoped he would be better. I can deal with an arrogant and pompous Cyrus. I don't know what to do with him in such a fragile state."

"None of our boys have been in this state," Miles added.

"Trevin did mention she feels Quinn's notable absence and that she thinks she did something wrong for him to not be very present for her. I think it is fear in her with Cyrus, not knowing what to expect from him. She never got to know the real him. But true to her nature she fears hurting them more than anything."

Bracken tilted his head as if a thought occurred to him. "He weeps to himself that he is sorry to her the most. I think he wants to tell her a lot."

"I suppose he needs to feel just as safe to do so as she does," Echo offered.

"Well, we have until September." Defeat crept into Lord Ashdale's tone. "That is not much time to prepare her for that conference. I just hope our heirs have the foresight to work together despite each other's recent actions."

There was silence in the room with the weight of the task at hand and Echo gave one more quick glance to the trees before turning back to Miles.

"I think you should take the tome. You can translate far better than I can. We have too much to try to learn about her and I am hoping the tome has something more. There was nothing in the Falk book. Trevin, she, and I have all read it and stared at the pages for hours. Lady Elodie will bring the tome when she starts her Ashdale week."

"Are you sure Ashdale was not the retrieving estate? It was your firstborn and his vowed who found a way to get it," Miles said, bowing his head slightly out of respect.

Echo understood the gesture. He too knew the weight having the tome held. It was a prized artifact retrieved at great risk. The knowledge was likely invaluable. For Trevin and Elodie to do what they had done to get it was nothing short of extraordinary. Sending it to another estate, even one he considered a brother was a sign of great honor and respect.

"It is doing little here and unless Bracken has an objection, It is best kept at Ashdale," Echo explained then looked at Bracken who agreed. They shook on it with a smile and firm handshake.

"We will get through this. Cyrus will pull through, Bracken."

"I sure hope so, every ticking second feels as though a pendulum ax is creeping closer."

"We always stand together," Echo affirmed.

The three reviewed lesson plans for the upcoming weeks and it felt as though that pendulum was looming overhead.

Chapter 2

Elodie parked her car and glanced at the rearview just as Trevin turned towards her. She looked at him with a bashful grin.

"There is a lot of affection and endearment in your eyes," Trevin noted.

"I remember the first time I parked here and checked that my ears were still on correctly. I almost felt foolish for going as a fae, knowing everyone would assume I was an elf. I guess a few people knew what I was trying to be though," Elodie laughed.

Trevin took her hand. "That night I looked at you and acted like a complete creep to my Earth Blessed. Little did I know how important you would become to me and our home." He leaned in and kissed her.

"So, are we going to break away from each other at some point tonight? For appearance's sake?" Elodie asked.

"Yes, as much as I don't want to. This vowed bond makes it hard to leave your side still, but it's not the first time and it's just to keep up appearances. Despite Quinn being so occupied with Justine, I know he is keeping watch over you, as are Cedar and Autumn."

Elodie frowned and cut her eyes down for a moment before bringing them back to meet his. She feigned a smile.

"El. What is it?"

"I shouldn't go down this thought process, not here or tonight."

"I know well enough by now that you will venture down the thought process later and I'd prefer you not be on that path alone. Where the doubts could root."

Elodie's smile turned bashful and she gave his hand a squeeze. "I know you chose this just as I did, but what if there was more for you? My choice essentially affected yours."

"What more could I ask for? Heir apparent the oldest ruling estate of Humboldt, vowed to an Earth Blessed who fought her way through hell time and time again to save me? Maybe Quinn is right and I didn't deserve you but I'd be a damned greedy fool to ask for more. I have more than I could have ever dreamed of. Never ever doubt this is what I want. That I will continue to fight for this." His smile faded and he looked more reserved. "Do you feel as though there was more for you, that you could have had more? I would not fault you if you are unsure. You made a big choice with so many unknown variables, we know so little of what Earth Blessed are."

Elodie brought her other hand to cup his cheek. "This is more than I could have ever dreamed of too, Trev. You, this place, your family, even with the unknowns, what more could I have asked for? Moving somewhere new? Moving back to Marin? This is where I belong," Elodie said with a hint of proclamation.

Trevin moved her hand and kissed the faint scar on her palm under her thumb. He had one that matched it. They had been made with each other's daggers the night after the ruins when they had properly vowed themselves to each other when they joined their hands and sealed their intent.

"Then know that we chose this life and we fight for it, always." He then kissed her once more.

"Always." Elodie smiled widely and with one more endearing gaze at each other, they got out of the car and made their way inside Cora's house.

Elodie knew she was wrestling with her own doubts and despite her trusting him, she was not entirely sure how things could be right when she looked at all that had changed. It certainly had crossed her mind many nights since the ruins. Her presence had changed so much here and while she understood they had needed an Earth Blessed to stop that spirit that held Cyrus prisoner, she couldn't help but wonder what would have happened if she never moved up here. She felt greedy for wanting this, worried she might not be enough to keep it together.

The thoughts had always been there, confidence hadn't been her strong suit, but somehow she had preserved. When she reflected on the last three months, she found herself overwhelmed with all the thoughts. She just had to remind herself to worry about this summer and the conference in September.

The very thought of that conference formed a pit in her stomach. She was dreading the upcoming weeks of making a fool of herself, of not being ready come September, because while she doubted herself, she did not doubt the three high estates were putting a lot of faith in her to be ready. She had to be ready for them.

Trevin's grip tightening on her hand ever so slightly pulled her out of her thoughts before the words did.

"Hey, how's the week been?" Cora asked, walking around the corner from the kitchen.

Elodie fell into an easy smile. Two months of practice and at least this part was becoming easier for her. Trevin's need to protect was still prevalent and she appreciated the comfort of knowing he was near.

"It's been good, yours?" Elodie's voice was relaxed.

"Good, and how about yours, Trev?"

"It was good. I'm getting a dumb intern at work," he scoffed.

"That could be fun, no? Have you met them yet?" Cora asked. Trevin just shook his head. "You should come to the café next week, since you didn't this week. Both of you."

"Said intern is assigned to some graves, meaning I am assigned to some graves. So I might be a bit scarce."

Cora looked at Elodie.

"I will try. I promise. This upcoming week."

Cora smiled widely. "Everyone's outside. I was just on my way out there."

They followed behind Cora and Trevin leaned into Elodie's ear. "You seem distracted."

"Just worried about the summer," she replied softly.

"You will be fine. You can always talk to me about it too. I'm here to listen."

Elodie gave a quick squeeze to his hand and the two walked out to the yard where she saw Charles, Autumn, Quinn, and Justine. She was met with mostly warm greetings, and an eye roll from Justine.

Ever since March she had to reacclimate to the mortal world and contain her teal pulses from her Earth Blessed magic. It was a lot for her. Now though, she felt as if she had mastered that too. Lord Greenthistle had given her a lot of lessons over the months to ensure there were no slip ups. Even going as far as to pit Cedar against her in a few unexpected drills.

Every time after these drills Cedar held his head in shame at dinner and apologized countless times. He told her after the third surprise drill he refused to do any more. And that was the end of those. She figured that Greenthistle scaring her now was a lost cause, and besides, she was almost certain there would be plenty of chances to gauge her control at Ashdale and Nightswift.

Her ears refocused on the conversations that her friends were having. Various talks of hikes, that Oregon trip they had gone on during the Spring Equinox week when Elodie had been in Marin. Elodie spoke at times but again her thoughts went back to the trees. Her gaze drifted to the trees she could see, just the few redwoods in the yards nearby. It was quiet tonight but she could feel them watching from afar. It had been some time since she had walked among them alone. Usually Trevin or Autumn were always nearby.

Next week. She imagined herself projecting the silent words out to the trees.

When Elodie turned back to the conversation, she felt Trevin cup her hand with both of his as he moved closer. She knew he had noticed. His mountain lion-like focus was always hyperaware. The gaze she did not expect, however, was from Justine.

Chapter 3

Elodie offered her best smile to Justine but it wasn't returned. Instead, Justine glanced up to the trees and then back towards Cora who was talking about the place they stayed at in Oregon. Elodie glanced back at the trees briefly but didn't notice anything.

"It was a fun trip. Crater Lake was beautiful," Charles followed up. "You've been there right, Elodie?"

"Yes. It is pretty. I did the Watchman Tower hike which was a bit scary with all the snow and ice, despite it being July." Elodie shook her head in astonishment. "I think I was still on an adrenaline rush from doing that when I went to sleep."

Charles gave a soft laugh and she noticed Trevin, Autumn, and Quinn look at her with concern.

"Yet there is no fear out there with those redwoods?" Justine asked.

Elodie noticed Quinn's expression changed to confusion.

"Snow isn't my thing? Plus, if I slip, I'm on soft soil here, not jagged rocks. I'm alert here too," Elodie offered, then she noticed Quinn put a hand on Justine's knee, no doubt working his calming abilities on her. She recalled that Quinn's calming gifts felt different from Trevin's. Trevin sent a calming wave over her; he could pull emotions as well as send them outward. Quinn's abilities acted more like a weighted blanket.

"I could see that hike being wild with snow," Charles noted.

"No switchbacks, just straight up and following footprints." Elodie turned to Charles.

"He invited us on that hike, but no way was I doing that. We took the van and drove around the lake," Cora explained.

The conversation continued on about other national and state parks. After a little longer Elodie leaned into Trevin and said she was going to get a drink. He nodded and gave her a kiss before she went inside. She could feel her insides cringe as the conversation fell silent, knowing more than just Trevin's eyes were on her. She could probably guess eyes were on him too. With a shake of her head, she continued towards the kitchen walking by people.

Suddenly she stopped short, more grateful than ever for all the training she had had to contain her teal pulse. Quinn's younger brother locked eyes with her but seemed uneasy. They hadn't spoken, and had only been introduced once at Winter Solstice despite being in his house for the spring equinox. It was where Quinn had made quite the show of dancing with her for the opening dance.

Quinn's actions that night had dampened her spirits and she wasn't sure why. He had asked her to dance and she hesitated for a moment before taking his hand. Lord Ashdale had informed her later that it was for show, to assert she was under Ashdale's protection, but Quinn had told her it was also to get Trevin riled up so everyone could see the vowed bond. Then he had not spoken to her the rest of the night. She could only imagine the summer solstice was going to be much the same, only this revelry it would be Cyrus opening the celeration. One more thing to dread in these upcoming weeks.

She recalled the youngest Ashdale's mortal name.

"Connor. Hi." Elodie swallowed hard.

He bowed his head slightly and his voice was low. "Hello Elodie."

She wasn't sure what to do. Greenthistle had taught her all about rank among the fae. She was not required to bow to any of them for what she had done, but they could understand that she wanted to with the high estate lords and ladies. It was explained that Cyrus, Quinn, and Trevin bowed to those above them, and they should bow to Elodie since she was something else entirely. However it made her uncomfortable so she insisted that none of them bow to her. Plus they were in the mortal lands.

"I wanted to introduce myself properly. Given the week after next and all. I thought it might make it a little easier since you have met my parents and know my brother well. He speaks highly of you."

"Oh," Elodie marveled. "I appreciate it. If I am being honest, I'm a bit nervous for this summer."

"I am sure you will do fine." He leaned closer. "No one at Ashdale, fae, or bear means you harm," he said in a hushed tone.

"Understood." Elodie paused. "I haven't seen you at Cora's before."

Connor laughed. "This is my first time. I was going to stay home and read tonight but figured I'd say hi to you after my brother offered me the invite."

"He's outside with everyone."

"I will head out there. Make myself known to Trev too."

"Is that something you are supposed to do?" she asked, confused.

"From what I have seen and heard, it is certainly wise. I respect Trev a lot, but the level of fierceness he has now that he's with you is something else."

Elodie watched Connor for a moment and realized she sensed his unease wane. She wasn't sure if she had just become more aware of his tension relax or how she even picked up on that. All the fae she knew were usually really good at schooling themselves. Unless all hell was breaking loose in ruins of course.

Someone walked up behind Conner and her attention shifted with the movement.

"Look who is hanging with the big kids tonight. Connor." Cedar walked up and put his hand on Connor's shoulder giving what appeared to be a fairly hard squeeze. Connor rolled his eyes. "Hey El." Cedar grinned.

"Hi." Elodie laughed lightly with a slight step back at Cedar's big energy. She was learning how different all the estate kids really were. Quinn was laid back and Trevin was more reserved. Cedar had so much big energy and Connor seemed quiet. Autumn had so much charisma that everyone loved the middle Greenthistle. When she thought of Cyrus she paused. He had been so confident and arrogant, Trevin and Quinn both described him as that. That thought scared her now though. One of his sisters had seemed unimpressed and the youngest Nightswift child had appeared shy. She knew so little about Nightswift, and had asked so little about them.

"I was just heading outside, so your brother doesn't rip my head off for talking to her."

Cedar laughed. "The most he is going is glare. Besides, I bet you could take him."

"I don't want to have to though," Connor groaned.

"I was just grabbing a drink," Elodie followed up.

"Well come out when you're done. It will put Connor and Trev at ease, I'm sure." Cedar laughed once again. Elodie gave him a smile then watched them walk off with Cedar's arm draped over Connor's shoulders. She tried to focus on the tension or anything that would reveal Connor's feelings but she didn't see any. Tilting her head in confusion, she was not sure how to describe what she sensed in Connor but shrugged it off and went to the kitchen.

After pouring some rum into a cup she grabbed the cap and heard someone walk into the kitchen.

"Why do you look for the redwoods so much?" Justine's words caught her so off guard she flinched and saw her hand pulse as she balled it into a fist over the metal cap, causing a painful sting on her palm and fingers. She had to take a deep breath for a moment. Her heart was pounding. If she had just shown something it was all over for all of them.

"And you have gotten so jumpy. Why?" Justine asked. "This place doesn't seem very good for you."

"I—I was just caught off guard. You scared me," she said, still not turning around. The last time she had her back to someone in this kitchen like this was with Quinn, when this power was going haywire in her.

Breathe, you know how to control this. No one saw. Ignore the pain.

"Okay. What is it with those trees then?"

"I like them," Elodie said, finally catching her breath.

"Obviously, but why?" Justine prodded again.

"They're neat." Elodie felt stupid the second the answer left her mouth.

Justine sighed loudly. "Are you even going to look at me or just avoid eye contact like you do?"

Elodie closed her eyes trying to center her nerves and clamp down on the pain of the burn from metal in her hand then turned around.

"I really like coast redwoods specifically. I am not sure I can say it's one reason over another but I do. They are old, solid. They have been around for centuries and the only remaining natural groves are a narrow stretch along the coastline. Not too close to the ocean but not too far. They need the fog to survive and their crowns have their own ecosystems that we hardly understand. Together they remain strong, holding each other up." Elodie found she had calmed down talking about them, about her entity. Her lifeline. "I can go on."

She knew she could but not about how they chose her, and gave her a home. They chose her for Trevin and him for her, they gave her Greenthistle and this amazing power even if she didn't fully understand it. She was an extension of them in the form of a mortal woman who always believed magic was out there.

"No. I probably wouldn't get it if you gave me a hundred more reasons," Justine said and leaned against the cabinet door. "But that's the danger with places like this. You create a magic that's not really there in your head and you just hope it's going to embrace you right back. All that does is keep you from finding new places."

"We all make a place what we want to an extent, Justine. I did find the magic out there. Why would I leave it now?"

Elodie watched her and once again felt a shift in Justine. Her posture had softened for sure, but it felt more than just a change in body language. Justine's eyes shifted to nervous now.

"It's just, I don't know. You act like you look for them, the trees. What do you feel when you see them? Do you get the sense they look back at you?"

Elodie wasn't sure how to answer the question but it did increase her heart rate slightly. Did Justine know? Did she sense it?

"It's hard to explain. But I have always thought about this place ever since I was up here when I was eight. I like the redwoods, it's a small comfort to know they are near."

"You have bad memories here too though. Like March?"

"Was every day in New York good? I had bad days in San Diego, in Joshua Tree, I had plenty of bad weeks in Marin. I have good ones too from those places, but it's hard to explain," Elodie said. The stinging sensation in her hand sent a throbbing pain up her arm.

That lingering guilt crept in too. She did have bad memories here and so much had changed within her circle that she wanted to fix but didn't know how. Marin's leaders certainly had expressed their concern with her emotional range. She knew Lord Greenthistle saw it too.

Autumn's scent grew closer and she saw her and Charles walk in. Autumn was easy smiles and all, just as one would expect.

"Just getting a refill," Autumn chimed in, standing next to Elodie. Charles opened a cooler nearby.

"I was just heading back outside." Elodie's hand was still on the cap and she dreaded prying her fingers off it. In a desperate attempt to get out of the situation and get to Trevin, she took a sip of the rum straight and felt the burn. With another feigned smile, Elodie turned and hurried out towards the patio. Using her arm to open the sliding glass door, she clumsily made her way outside.

Trevin's eyes were locked on her in a second as he moved towards her.

"El?" he asked, concerned.

She didn't know what to do or say since Cora was sitting right there. "I'm alright." She leaned into him and spoke softly. "I slipped. I'm sorry."

Chapter 4

"Just breathe, we'll step inside," Trevin offered. Elodie agreed and followed him, not looking at anyone as he led her to the bathroom and closed the door. "What happened? You slipped and fell or you pulsed?"

"I saw the flash but I was looking at the counter, my back to everyone." She went on to explain then pulled her hand out of her pocket and began to unclench her fist as tears formed.

"Elodie. I'm sorry." Trevin cradled her hand in his.

"I don't know why she startled it out of me, Connor didn't."

"In a contest of least abrasive personalities, Connor wins every single time out of all of us," Trevin said softly as he did his best to remove the cap and avoid the blood that had formed. He grabbed tissue and started to wipe it.

"Let me do it, I don't want to hurt you." Elodie took her trembling hand away.

"I can handle the minor burn. It's faint on my skin. I think it just stung on the vowed bond so much because it was open wound to open wound."

Elodie continued to rinse her hand and Trevin found some antiseptic. She braced herself, knowing it was going to sting.

"Deep breaths. I will try to be quick. Dad is making me make up healing lessons on our off days since I missed a few." He laughed.

"Do you think Justine knows? Senses anything? Is she part fae?"

"I can tell you she isn't even a 16th, I get no traces from her. Quinn would have said something if he sensed it."

"Does proximity make it easier to sense the faeness of someone?" Elodie asked

"Yea it certainly does help, but if they are an 8th or more it's so obvious to us," he explained and then tossed the tissue. Gently, he cupped her hand and healed it.

"We should ask Autumn if Justine said anything about my pulse or if anyone else did," Elodie suggested.

Trevin agreed and once he was done with healing her hand, he pulled his cellphone out. "Are you ready to go back outside or do you want to go home? I have to tell my dad tonight though regardless."

Elodie deflated. "I thought I could do it. I haven't had a slip up yet, so why now after almost three months?"

"It has only been three months." He held her close now. "We all have had to learn a lot." Trevin pulled back slightly and tilted her chin up. Elodie cut her eyes away. "El. You don't need to be frustrated or scared. My dad isn't going to be upset with you, nothing seemed amiss in the house. I cannot imagine if they saw someone illuminate teal they wouldn't say anything. Hell, it took us all by surprise the first time too. It was a slip up."

"I know." Elodie wrapped her arms around him.

"If I may be honest, you have seemed a bit distracted for a while now. I'm not going to ask you to tell me every thought you have, but I do hope you know you can talk to me about it, about anything. I'm here however you need me. Vowed, overseer, friend, mentor, whatever you need."

"I know, Trevin. I'm grateful you are so understanding and so patient. I just hope your dad isn't going to be disappointed in me."

"He isn't, at all. Trust me, I know my dad's disappointed face and he has never once directed it at you," Trevin laughed softly. "Cedar and Autumn would agree."

When his phone vibrated, Trevin grabbed it and relayed the message. "Autumn asked if you were alright. She noticed you just drank straight rum and could see the burn." He glanced at the cup with the dark liquid.

"I didn't know how to pour the mixer in with a near scalding metal cap in one hand and I was getting nervous."

"I felt the tension in the air and was honestly going to give you five more minutes before I went inside. Nothing is amiss per Autumn."

Elodie pulled back from embracing him and exhaled. "Okay, let's go back out there. I think I'm done drinking tonight."

"I don't blame you," Trevin chuckled and dumped the rest of the cup in the sink then tossed it. "Let me know if it still hurts at any point. Deep breaths. We are all right beside you."

"You wouldn't have attacked Connor right? You weren't mad at him for talking to me?"

Trevin took her hand and smiled softly. "No, Connor is the epitome of respect, like they just forgot any ounce of reserve in Quinn and then doubled up for Connor. It's just this vowed bond sets me into high alert when we see someone new. We have to assess the threat. I might have questioned why he was here tonight given how little interaction you and him have had, but he explained it. Dee is his usual preferred company so he is seldom around. But I commend him for introducing himself to you and making an effort to welcome you. I know you will be fine at Ashdale."

"Okay, good. I don't want you to be mad at your friends," Elodie pressed.

"Everything will be alright, Little Mink," he assured, then motioned towards the door with his hand.

Once back outside Elodie felt everyone's eyes on her and she forced herself to take deep slow breaths and the nerves subsided.

"Are you alright?" Cora asked with concern.

Elodie nodded before Cora had finished asking the question. "Yes, I just nicked myself on a bottle cap. It felt worse than it was." *All lies.* She had seared metal into her palm.

"It was an easy clean up, but I tossed the cap, figured it wouldn't be needed much longer anyways," Trevin replied confidently.

Elodie noticed Justine narrow her eyes on Trevin and she found herself watching, sensing that Justine wasn't impressed with Trevin at all. Justine was still convinced Trevin had cheated and it certainly would appear that way to a mortal who could never possibly know the truth.

"Happy to help with the rum," Cedar also laughed, relieving the awkwardness.

"Justine was just asking if Arcata Community forest had anything different than Sequoia Park," Charles explained. "I haven't hiked it much, just a few trails. Have you had a chance to hike it a lot, El? It is close to your house."

Elodie gave a nod. "I have hiked it a fair amount. There's some neat spots there. A small waterfall, fun sculptures carved, though not sure the history of them. I like it."

"Go on a hike with us sometime Justine? We can do an easier trail, I promise. Elodie is probably a pro at that area," Charles suggested.

"Yea, it's a great place, you get that forest feel but you are not far from civilization, plus we can just go to El's afterwords, her house is right there," Cora said.

The deep breaths took over Elodie again then Trevin's hand around her waist shifted slightly so his palm pressed into her. Her heart rate slowed as that calming wave washed causing her shoulders to relax. She noticed the fae among her group looking at her with concern, they had no idea what had happened, she realized.

"Maybe, but I'm not doing that at night or even sunset," Justine insisted.

"It will be fun. I bet you will love it," Cora said.

Then the conversation resumed. Connor remained quiet, occasionally watching Elodie and Trevin, offering her a small smile.

When Justine brought up Lake Tahoe and Calaveras County, Elodie felt confused. She also did not miss the shock in Quinn's gaze or the unease Trevin and his siblings got. "What's the Eastern Sierra like? Since we all know at least half this group hasn't been there."

Quinn looked slightly hurt at the statement.

What is happening to Justine? she asked herself then spoke up. "Pretty in a different way. Warmer in the summers, heavy snow in the winters. Depending on where you are talking in the general vicinity you might be in a town smaller than Orick, or you could be surrounded by way too many tourists and traffic in South Lake Tahoe. But it all has its small town feel," Elodie explained. "South Lake isn't far from Sacramento plus the state line with Nevada."

"You'd honestly be more likely to run into a bear over there than here I think," Charles laughed. Elodie did not miss the slight slump in Quinn's shoulders. "El is right, some areas get crazy around holidays. The lake is lovely and there is a ton of hiking around there too. Alpine County is small but has Hope Valley which I hear is lovely in the fall for colors. Calaveras County has really big trees, a different type of Sequoia than here, right?" He looked at her.

Elodie wasn't sure what she saw in Quinn now. In her peripheral vision she caught Trevin glance at him then to herself.

"Yes." Elodie swallowed hard. "They are related but different species. Sempervirens, the ones here, draw from the fog, hence those ecosystems I mentioned. The Gigantea tend to like dryer mountain air and pull from the snowpack. Standing next to both of them makes you feel small in different ways."

Well explained. You will carry our knowledge well already.

Elodie felt her cheeks heat when she heard that voice in her head. It was from the Old Giants. They were watching. The fae in the group were all looking at her now she realized. She kept her expression neutral.

"Of course Elodie would know all about the trees," Justine laughed.

As soon as Elodie heard the words, her insides shriveled up from embarrassment despite Justine's laugh and she wasn't sure why.

"You asked about a place known for outdoorsy stuff, Justine. No need to roll your eyes," Cedar defended.

Elodie couldn't bring herself to look up. She was feeling as though she certainly could use the rest of that rum now. *Am I ever going to find my Greenthistle valor?* she asked herself.

You have plenty of it. All of Greenthistle knows this.

Elodie's shoulders slumped the moment they glanced at her. Trevin pulled her close and leaned his head against hers.

"Breathe," he whispered.

Elodie took a deep breath and remained quiet. A few moments later her phone vibrated and she noticed Trevin reach into his pocket to check his own phone. Her heart sank when Trevin held it for her to see it was his dad asking if everything was alright. She glanced at him, not sure what was going to happen but she realized he must have seen her fear when his soft smile formed and he wrapped his arm back around her.

"I will take care of it later," he said softly and then replied to his dad that everything was alright and he'd talk to him tonight.

Elodie wondered what her fate would be if someone had seen her hand or eyes pulse with that teal light that came from her power. She almost wanted to ask, that anxious curiosity that never seemed to be satiated.

Part of her wanted to continue to shrivel up and cry, but she had done that plenty in the last few months. Part of her knew she needed to maintain her sanity and prove she was safe here to the mortals. Then there was the fact that she needed to actually believe she was safe here because it was her home now. Even if she wasn't doing a very good job of fixing anything, the Old Giants hadn't lied, and the fae couldn't lie. They would keep her safe. They wanted her. *She* wanted this.

With a deep inhale she finally brought her eyes back to the group and met their gazes. The conversation had shifted to various movies and TV shows Elodie was familiar with but it wasn't her usual pastime to partake in. Luckily Charles kept the conversation going like he always did. It really was no wonder he and Autumn had gravitated towards each other with how charismatic they both were. Once again Elodie joined in when she could and tried to ignore the glances from everyone.

Chapter 5

Later that evening after Bracken had gotten off a call with Echo to review lesson plans for Elodie's Nightswift week, he sat back in his chair and stared up at the ceiling.

"This is not going to be pleasant for anyone," he huffed out to himself before pushing himself to stand.

Truth was Bracken was exhausted and had no idea how to handle any of the obstacles he was faced with. He had worked hard; he had proven himself time and time again as worthy of maintaining the role of Nightswift's high estate ruler. He had ensured he kept his kids strong and fully capable of maintaining Nightswift rank as second in command of the land they were appointed. His youngest daughter, Poppy, was still growing and while she was behind her older brother and sister, Bracken chalked it up to her being so young. It had taken him and Ari some time to have their third. They had almost given up. The rest of the high estate children were all relatively close in age. Where their firstborns were only two or three years apart, Autumn and Cedar easily filled in the gaps while Connor and Delia helped them transition into the mortal world. He did fear for Poppy being so alone.

When he reached the door of the study, he glanced back at the trees and realized there was an Earth Blessed here now. One who was an elementary school teacher. In three weeks' time she would be staying at the Nightswift estate. He wondered if it was wrong to ask that of her too. On top of training her and dealing with her and Cyrus learning to trust each other, could he ask Lady Elodie to help Poppy as well?

Fixing on the trees for a moment longer he turned and walked out of the study. He headed for the stairs and towards Cyrus's room. It was quiet. A rarity in the Nightswift estate as of late that always sent a small twinge of fear through him that something was wrong. He could not wrap his head around what Cyrus was capable of, not that he wanted to fully comprehend it either. His steps were slow and he faltered before knocking. Sometimes the very act would send Cyrus into a screaming fit.

After two months he still could hardly approach his own son without knowing what might set him off. Echo nor Miles had much help to offer. Quinn and Trevin were angry for different reasons and so Miles and Echo handled their firstborns differently. Even when Trevin's mother had passed, Trevin had a different way of processing his grief given his empathic abilities to pull emotions. It was a very different situation than Cyrus was in now. Cyrus had been a very different boy before the situation he was in.

Bracken noticed the door was slightly cracked. His vowed and Cyrus's mother, Ariyanna always left it slightly ajar. She feared Cyrus would put a ward on it one of these nights and lock himself in. Of course, Bracken or Ari could break the ward but it would be one more hurdle they did not want to deal with. He could hear Cyrus crying softly.

"Elodie. I'm sorry." His voice was hoarse even in its softness. "Trevin—" He faltered.

Bracken stepped closer ready to knock when he heard Cyrus gasp and sniff hard. He didn't bother knocking, Cyrus was aware of his presence now.

Cyrus's eyes rose slowly and Bracken hated seeing his son this way. Time was running out faster than ever it felt.

"Cyrus. Your house arrest is nearly up," Bracken said calmly.

"No. I don't want to go back outside. Please."

"You cannot stay in your bed. You hardly even get up as it is. You have to be going stir crazy. You are not locked up here, you have access to the house. Your mother and I told you that weeks ago."

"No," Cyrus said, trembling.

Bracken watched him drop his head and bring his hands to the back of his neck as he curled forward.

"You are my firstborn, heir apparent to the Nightswift ravens. You cannot rule while trembling in your bed. Trevin and Quinn have been back to drills and their mortal jobs for weeks now."

"I'm not ready. I need more time. Please," Cyrus begged, not looking up.

"Do you understand the precedent this will set if you do not return? You are telling Humboldt and eventually the council that my firstborn is giving up."

Cyrus remained silent save for a sniff.

Bracken took note of how frail his son appeared. "Is that what you wish? To renounce your title as my heir?" A small whimper escaped Cyrus and he shook his head. "Speak up. Tell me you want it still. Otherwise, I need to start preparing your sister to be heir."

"No," Cyrus cried out. "Please."

"Cyrus, I don't even know what you are begging for at this rate. You keep saying you need more time. You say it when we ask you about what happened. The night of the mountain lion attack, the times you got close to Lady Elodie, the night of the ruins. You will not talk about any of it. She talked about it. Lord Greenthistle knows all of it. Trevin knows all of it. What we do not know is your experience with it. She can't tell us all of it because she didn't see it all," Bracken explained. Cyrus still did not look up. "You say no when we try to get you out of your room, you say no when we try to ask you about it. All you can tell us you want is a sedative. You don't even ask for food or drink." Bracken began to pace.

"I'm sorry."

"Do you still want to be heir apparent or not?" Bracken stopped pacing and looked at him. Cyrus remained quiet. "You can't even answer that. If you need more time I think your answer is clear. We cannot help you if you refuse to help yourself."

"Yes." Cyrus swallowed hard.

"Yes what? Do you still want this or is the assumption I draw from your actions correct?" Bracken demanded now.

Cyrus slowly sat up and looked at his dad with tear-stained cheeks. "Yes. I still want to be heir. But I need more time. This is terrifying. What I saw, What I did."

"Then tell us, Cyrus. That girl bled for you. She ran into absolute and utter hell for Trev and she pulled you out too. Then she looked all three high estate lords of Humboldt in the eyes and told us she wanted this. She would serve all three of our estates, as our Earth Blessed. She didn't need time to hold her head high that night either."

Cyrus cut his eyes down and looked away. "That's because she's not a monster. She is a good person. She didn't hurt anyone."

"She told us what happened to you. That much we know. What we do not know, nor does she, was why you lost power. If you are passing judgment on yourself for your actions, fine, but do not think that will be enough come that conference. If we do not know how to defend you, we cannot defend you. I want to, son. Let us help you."

Cyrus shook his head and remained silent. Bracken sighed. "How are you going to show them you still want to be heir apparent if you can't even tell me?"

"I need more time."

"Your time is running out!" Bracken snapped out of frustration and Cyrus curled back up repeating how sorry he was. Bracken resumed his pacing. "I'm sorry. I know yelling doesn't help but I don't know what to do. I tried. We all have short of allowing Trev in here."

"Please don't. No," Cyrus begged, "I'm not ready to see him."

Bracken remained silent for a moment longer. "You told me you chose to remain my heir. You need to prove it now. If the regional council does not deem you fit, you may not have a choice in what happens to you. Do you understand?"

"Yes, sir," quavered Cyrus.

"Things are going to change soon. You can start acclimating to them now or you learn them as they arise. I am giving you a choice, giving you a chance to tell me what you prefer. Do you wish to know the changes so you can prepare for them, or be surprised?"

Cyrus looked at his dad again finally but was unsure.

"Know that you are not going to get a choice to not do the tasks we give you. To not do them tells us while you may want to remain heir, you simply are not cut out for it. Do you want to know what you will have to do?"

"Go outside?"

"That is the first step, yes, because what comes after could be very easy or very difficult."

"What is the next step?" Cyrus asked apprehensively.

Bracken explained that Cyrus would be expected to make appearances back in the fae world. He would conduct one-on-one drills with Cyrus in preparation for Elodie's stay and he would be confronting Elodie on Sunday afternoon after Trevin left. He stressed the importance of this that as long as he remained in this house, he would talk to Lady Elodie and she was to be treated like any other member of the high estates, with respect and kindness. Cyrus would be expected to conduct lessons with her as well.

Unfortunately it was not a surprise to Bracken when he finished, all Cyrus could muster was a 'Please, I need more time.' He did not say anything else to his son before he left the room, feeling his frustration build.

Chapter 6

When Monday morning rolled around, Trevin left Elodie's in the morning. Next Sunday she would be off to Ashdale for six days and he wasn't to see her unless it was an absolute emergency only he could respond to. Trevin felt as though there was never enough time in her presence until he realized he had forever with her. Then he'd have to take a moment and acknowledge the vowed bond was literally pulling him towards her. It certainly didn't help that she was so anxious and Friday night was an extra hard tug on that tether. He hated seeing her in distress, it was in his very core to want to nurture her.

But they both had responsibilities and lives they needed to uphold and his dad was not wrong. She absolutely needed to trust all three high estates if she was going to remain their Earth Blessed.

So after getting up to grab breakfast together at the bagel shop in the city of Arcata, and reassuring her she would be alright, Trevin took off on the trail back towards Greenthistle Estate.

"How was she the rest of the weekend?" Echo asked, walking into the training room.

"She was good. We went overnight in Redwoods National Park and I showed her some trails she didn't know about. I quizzed her on stuff as we hiked to our campsite, and had her show me how to navigate some parts of the trail. It's amazing to see her adapt to this. I can tell she is still distracted at times though."

"Did you find out what has her so distracted?"

Trevin scoffed. "Everything? Justine? Her power? Us?"

"Are you mad about it?"

"No!" he muttered, then took a deep inhale. "I just want to help her but I don't know what else to do. I can calm her down but I don't want her to get dependent on my abilities, and she doesn't want to either. At times she pulls her hands away and it hurts," he groaned and dragged his hand down his face. "I sound pathetic."

His dad gave a grim smile. "That is the vowed bond, Trev. But you know you cannot protect her from everything. She has got to trust in herself. Unless Quinn's mortal saw anything, there has been no talk of her teal glow."

"Justine is blunt, she'd have said something if she saw it. Plus, Quinn would have mentioned it if she said anything to him. I don't think she could keep her mouth shut if she saw it. Guess we will see how today goes. They're hanging out. At least Autumn will be there with our other mortal friends."

"Well that will help. She seems to trust Autumn and your sister loves her." Echo gave an endearing smile at the thought.

"I'm glad Autumn was always there for her," Trevin said, relieved.

"Autumn is wise. Next Monday, while she is at Ashdale we are doing drills here again. The plan is to have her join our Monday drills starting with her next rotation. But I do expect you to act as you do on any other drill day. Work hard and give it your all. Do not coddle her."

"I will do my best but the bond, right?"

"Yes. If she struggles or gets frustrated, do not offer her comfort. I know it's going to be hard, but she has to know she can do this by herself. Miles, Bracken, and I will assess over the next three weeks."

Echo gave Trevin a small smile and patted his back. He wanted Trevin to talk everything out. He seldom did despite taking on everyone's grief.

"What do you think is going to happen at the conference this year?" Trevin asked, finally looking at his dad. When his dad didn't respond, Trevin instinctively began to see the emotions his dad felt. The silence said he did not know, and the fear hovered just in the peripheral. It made Trevin's heart sink.

"We prepare as best we can. She may have stopped the fires burning here, but we need to be ready to walk into anything. The last thing I want is for her to be pulled away from us."

Trevin's eyes narrowed. Just as he was about to speak, he heard Quinn walk in. Both heirs had a scowl on their face. Lord Ashdale followed.

"We work together, remember. We never work against each other. Lady Elodie needs to see how Humboldt stands strong," Echo said. Quinn scoffed and his dad narrowed his eyes at him.

"Understood, sir," Trevin said, fighting a snarky retort towards Quinn.

Quinn's anger was more than obvious. "Where is El?" His tone was laced with annoyance.

"Off. Living her life as a mortal, or what she has left of it."

"You two just disappeared all weekend."

Trevin shrugged. "We went camping up in Redwoods."

Quinn rolled his eyes. "Justine was pretty pissed she bailed out on the bonfire. This is going to be difficult to cover up in the next few weeks."

Trevin gave him a sharp glare. "Justine is my responsibility? Last I checked she hated me. Figure it out. I'm not looking forward to next week."

Quinn leveled his gaze at Trevin.

"Work together. Not against each other. Figure out how to cover up her absence together. This is both your responsibility to your Earth Blessed," Echo chastised. "Run the course to warm up. Think of excuses you can tell."

They set off to run the course, Trevin in feral and Quinn in fae. Quinn got over the river using stepping stones as Trevin navigated a downed tree effortlessly.

"You are such a prick," Quinn snapped, navigating the small cliff side. He was usually slower at this part, given that it was designed for a mountain lion.

"Whatever stick you have up your ass should promptly be removed. Justine is just stressing Elodie out. I thought she was her friend," Trevin growled back.

"She's her friend, that's why she is so concerned," Quinn retorted.

They ran through obstacles as their frustration was mounting, causing foolish errors in them both. It made tension rise to the point where Quinn would lunge for Trevin and pin him when they were both in feral form. Trevin would fight back with an angry wave of emotion just as hard.

"Knock it off," Miles warned.

At his dad's words, Quinn pushed down on Trevin to get off him and walked a few yards away. Trevin let out a low growl and got up.

"Stop being a dick. Why are you so angry as of late? Every Monday it's the same shit. You come over here almost looking to fight," Trevin demanded.

"Because you just let that lie fester and you let Cedar and Cyrus plant those seeds of doubt in her. She's not the same as she was before and Justine is worried."

"Obviously she isn't the same. She saw everything she wanted burn to ash that night and she became Earth Blessed. You saw it before I did. Did you expect her to just brush it off?" Trevin stalked closer.

"I expected my first in command to not be such a coward. I didn't expect to have my mortal interest so damned hung up on trying to get her to move away from here," Quinn argued.

The mountain lion let out a low rumble of a growl. "I fixed it. Figure it out with Justine. I have my hands full. Don't you dare direct any of this at El next week."

"Some fine job you have done with fixing it." Quinn went back on his hind legs.

Trevin growled, arching his back.

"Stop!" Echo snapped. "Breathe. Focus. Now change back to fae form. Both of you."

Quinn and Trevin stared at each other for a moment before relaxing their bodies and changing. The bear and the mountain lion retreated and with an exhale, they were fae again. A smooth near instant transition from beast to fae.

"What are you both going to tell the mortals about where she is?" Miles asked.

After a few moments of silence Quinn spoke first.

"What if we say she is traveling for the week, since she is off, and Trev doesn't have the time to take vacation with his intern," Quinn suggested. "Or she just wanted time away from this overbearing asshole."

Trevin tensed and felt his anger build.

"*Quinn*," Miles reprimanded.

"It's not a bad scenario to say. It might ease the notion that we locked her up. She will be away from her house and Greenthistle. Traveling to other parts of the county," Echo replied, glancing at Trevin.

"You're such a jackass!" Trevin heaved.

"And you are stupid if you think I can just say she didn't want her overbearing asshole boyfriend around," Quinn lashed out. "But you should probably cut that shit out. It really doesn't look good for Justine."

"I don't care what Justine thinks. She doesn't believe El or Cedar, and she obviously doesn't believe you," Trevin retorted.

Quinn balled his fist up seething in rage.

"Stop!" Echo snapped again. "When asked we say she's traveling for a few days since she's off for the summer. Do not mention her stays at Nightswift or Ashdale. Instead you both just say she will tell them since she can lie. We will inform Bracken and we expect you both to act professional in the office this week. Whatever this is needs to be out of your systems."

"It has also been decided that since Cyrus's house arrest is up at the end of her week at Ashdale Estate, he will be resuming Monday drills after she concludes her first week at Nightswift. So I expect you to drop this shit attitude you both have when he returns," Miles explained.

"Great," Trevin muttered.

Quinn let out an obnoxious laugh. "Monday will be a waste of time with him back. Then with Elodie around him?"

"This is why it is imperative that you two start by fixing this. We cannot be divided. Certainly not with an Earth Blessed to protect. We want to make this as easy as possible for her," Echo said.

Trevin took a deep inhale and looked at Quinn. "Fine, I will do my best," he muttered.

"Fine," Quinn replied, then glanced at Trevin. "Enjoy suffocating her."

Trevin took a very deep audible inhale and fought the urge to change in his feral form. He wanted to lunge at Quinn so badly after today but he reminded himself to be better. He had to be. Attacking his third in command provoked or not was not what made a good high estate lord, and it certainly was not what Elodie wanted either.

With an equally deep exhale, Trevin spoke. "Are we excused?"

"Yes." Echo watched Trevin very intently.

Trevin turned without a word and walked inside. He heard Quinn run off.

"Tomorrow?" Echo asked, grinning.

"Tomorrow," Miles replied in an exhausted voice and then took off in his bear form.

"Where did this obsession with the Eastern Sierra come from all of a sudden?" Charles asked, looking at Justine.

Elodie glanced over at them, she was sitting next to Autumn at Cora's house.

"I haven't been there before. It was just a thought. What if we took a trip there? You and Elodie have been there. Cora, you could let the café run itself."

"That is a long drive from here. I don't know if I trust the café to run itself that long. I was stressed on the Crater Lake trip and South Lake is further than that. That kind of thing is maybe once a year for me. I don't have that kind of flexibility," Cora replied.

Justine looked at Charles then to Elodie. "We can go. We should. You guys are on summer break and I can work anywhere with Wi-Fi."

"Maybe, we can think about it but I still have some lessons in the area," Charles replied.

Elodie tensed, waiting for the scathing glare or snide comment.

"Well, I highly doubt just Elodie is willing to go with that recent large purchase she made," Justine sighed and took a sip of her wine. "It just looks pretty, the mountains, the lake being so blue. I want to see it and thought it would be a fun trip."

Elodie watched Justine and for some reason thought of the longing in her tone. She realized she didn't even feel hurt or bothered by the comments about the house she bought. It actually worked to her benefit at this point to let Justine assume she would always be busy with that, especially given how this summer was expected to go. There would be no vacations, and no trips for Elodie for some time. Except that one to Redding for the conference that worried her more than a week-long stay at each of the estates.

Almost on muscle memory her eyes went to the window and spotted the lone redwood in the yard. If Elodie had made a different choice that night, she might have been able to go. If she had chosen to remain mortal or even to forget her memory of them all, she might have even opted for the trip, possibly would even have looked for a job over there.

Then again, she had moved plenty for jobs, and every time it went back to those Old Giants. They wanted her and chose her. *They didn't choose wrong, did they?* Elodie knew she wanted this place and part of that left her feeling selfish for it.

"Step outside with me real quick?" Autumn asked, leaning into her. Elodie tensed for a second and looked at her hands to ensure she was not showing the teal glow. "I just wanted to enjoy the air. It's so nice out." Autumn smiled and took Elodie's hand.

Elodie smiled, relieved that Autumn was here. That she was nearly as good at Trevin at knowing what she needed.

Once outside the two sat down next to each other on one of the benches facing the dark fire pit and the pool. Their backs faced the house.

"Try not to worry too much about Justine's feelings. I know it's easier said than done but you are not doing anything wrong."

"I know I shouldn't. I just hate the opinion she has of your brothers. I have to lie to her and let her believe that Trev shackled me down here because it's almost easier than trying to convince her I want this. I hate that Trev looks like the villain." Elodie ran her fingers over the scar that formed a thin line under her thumb.

Autumn leaned against Elodie with a small laugh. "That's your need to keep him safe too. It's funny how differently it shows in you and him yet it's clear as day to all of us how much you two love each other. I am glad Trev has you as his vowed. Our dad is so proud of who he is becoming too."

"Has he told Trev that?" Elodie asked with a smile.

"Dad is Dad. Stern and strong, not one for a lot of emotions."

"Kind of terrifying? His gaze is just as intense as his mountain lion." Elodie laughed, and Autumn followed along. "Trev is trying so hard to balance his vowed instinct to protect me and manage all his responsibilities as heir apparent. Even before I knew what he was he wanted to make his dad proud."

"That has always been Trev. He never needed to be told what was expected of him, he just did it. Never talked back, and seldom ever failed at anything," Autumn said, looking at the water in the pool.

Elodie leaned forward, resting her arms on her knees as she too fixed her eyes on the water. "Have you been to the conference?"

"Never the annual one, but I have had to stand before the regional council. When I was younger, my dad, brothers, and I had to go to the deliberations between Humboldt and Everoak."

Elodie thought about what that must have been like, how difficult and scary it must have been for them all.

As Autumn continued explaining that during the delegations it was established that as the second born she was to stand in if her dad and Trev were compromised or away. Usually it would fall to the spouse of the high estate leader, in lieu of them it would be next of kin. Elodie learned that as a result of the determination, their dad had ramped up training for all three of his kids. It was one reason the Greenthistle children were much closer knit than Nightswift and Ashdale had been. Autumn and Cedar had nearly as much responsibility as Trevin did.

"So you usually run the estate when they are at the annual conference?" Elodie asked.

"Yeah. I have lessons once a week with Lady Nightswift and Lady Ashdale to help me learn. Though as of late it's been twice a week with Ashdale. I usually go over there or she comes over to Greenthistle. You get to start sitting in those lessons with us," Autumn added.

"Because one day I will be expected to run Greenthistle when Trev is called away. That's a weird and terrifying thought."

Autumn laughed, "Not trying to add to the pressure but I think you are expected at the conference going forward. So Greenthistle is still mine for a bit longer and even when you are our high estate lady, I will still be there. So will Ashdale and Nightswift. They each have a century or two of experience on us."

Elodie felt a sense of bewilderment at the thought. It hollowed something in her core and an overwhelming current threatened to drag her under. "What about when you meet your vowed? What if they are the heir to a high estate somewhere else? You'll have to leave then." Elodie felt sadness grip her now. "I know that is selfish to think. This all feels wrong."

She paused when Autumn took her hand. "Worry about one thing at a time, Elodie. I'm not planning on leaving Greenthistle, ever. I, just like my brothers, have a responsibility to it and my vowed would have to understand that, whoever they may be. I want to be there for you and for Trev."

Elodie took a deep inhale, forcing the calm once again as she sat back.

"I'm always here for you, El. Quinn is too. You will be fine next week." Autumn leaned into Elodie again and gave her a hug.

"Thanks. I'm so happy we're sisters."

"Always. Ready to go back inside and maintain appearances? Trev and Quinn are probably going to get antsy soon. Drills are surely done by now."

Elodie put on her best smile and stood up. Together her and Autumn rejoined the house where she found it easier to brush off the annoyance at Justine.

Despite Trevin messaging her first, Elodie waited until after Justine left for Quinn's call to head home where Trevin was eagerly awaiting her.

CHAPTER 7

Elodie had been on her own since Tuesday morning. Trevin left her place for work after they made breakfast and as she went through the motions of various chores around the house, she was in a daze. Grocery shopping and cleaning hadn't been enough of a distraction of the damning thoughts. So she took to trying to draw, read, and even nap but they persisted.

Since summer had begun two weeks ago, she found she had trouble adjusting to him not being around and felt dumb about it. It wasn't as bad when she had work and that responsibility to the classroom but the lack of things to fill her day with gave her too much time to think. She always hated having so much time and usually filled her summers with hikes and travels. It was why she started going to cafés to draw and people-watch or just sitting in her hatch somewhere to read. Somehow she justified it as giving her a goal. Drive or hike somewhere, relax, return home.

Echo had advised her not to leave the county alone until he deemed it was safe, at least not until after her second set of rotations. That meant any day trips to surrounding counties was not an option. She wasn't sure how safe she felt out there alone yet. So she stewed in the events that had led her here.

On Wednesday after sleeping in, making breakfast and cleaning the kitchen again, she knew she needed to leave the house. Staying inside never helped her anxiety, so she gathered her sketchbook, pencil pouch, and a novel from her shelf then set off towards the coast. Something pulled her towards the spot of that first bonfire she had with everyone. The one where she met Cyrus and told Trevin about the book on Falk. That book resided at Greenthistle where she would still look through it occasionally. They were still working on decoding things in it. The tome sat with little progress made, but Echo had mentioned she was to take it to Ashdale next week since he could translate it.

When she got to the beach, the first thing she did was to let her senses take in the salty ocean air and the cool breeze. The sun was out and there were no clouds in the sky, but the fog the marine layer created was rolling through in patches. Her eyes scanned the fire pit they usually claimed and the bathrooms off in the distance. It made her heart sink, recalling how Cyrus had grinned at her, how fast he had moved and placed a hand on her back. The gazes he gave her all night.

Some weeks after the ruins Cedar and Trevin told her about the conversation. They were astonished that neither of them saw it or questioned his behavior. Elodie couldn't help but wonder if it was a form of shame that they didn't. She hadn't asked them and at the time wasn't even sure why she thought it.

As she walked along a short trail she let her thoughts process, still no closer to any sort of clarity. Elodie knew she should talk to Trevin. It wasn't fair to not tell him. *Do I even understand what I am feeling?* she thought to herself as she came to a good viewpoint with an empty bench.

Her mind tried to narrow down the feelings as she watched the whitewash form and break on the waves rolling in. The tide pulled it ever closer up the shore. She was overwhelmed and nervous for next week. That much was true and while she couldn't shake it, she accepted it. Trevin and his dad had told her it was alright to feel that way. There had been enough trust gained from everyone that she believed them when they told her she was safe. The three high estates would not harm their Earth Blessed, since fae couldn't lie after all. Even if Cyrus was still a stranger to her and Quinn had sort of become one, she doubted either of them wanted her harmed.

Her safety never really had been the issue though. It was their safety that concerned her. It always had been.

Humboldt was her home, she affirmed that to Marin's leaders when she had met with them in March. The intent of the trip was to close out her dad's estate and ask for alliance with Marin's leaders. To ask that they agreed Elodie belonged in Humboldt and they supported her choice to move and become one of Humboldt's when they all faced the regional conference. It was hard to argue with a vowed bond but Elodie wasn't an average mortal or fae now. She was a living folktale, there was no saying who would demand what of her. Who would try to bargain with her for something.

It sat heavy on her that Mt. Tamalpais had never wanted her. *Why did it matter though?* she asked herself again for the millionth time. Maybe she had rejected Marin in a way, every single time she moved for so many reasons. Humboldt wanted her, and she wanted Humboldt.

Elodie realized that's what made this scary for her, made it hard to believe it was right for everyone. This was the home she wanted, the family she found along the way. They might all be in danger. So many eyes would be on them all now. Everyone at the conference would see the heirs so divided and her not having done anything to fix it.

She hadn't voiced all of these thoughts to Trevin or his dad. It didn't feel right to voice the 'what ifs' and 'whys' about Marin's claim to her or even wanting her to Trevin. It would hurt him to do so, and she knew it.

Yet it felt wrong to not tell him something that sat so heavy on her shoulders.

Focus on one worry at a time.

Sit with us at the Ashdale Estate.

We have knowledge to share.

Ashdale Estate, next week. The silent affirmation in her mind set the intention with a nod to the Old Giants. No one around her would know about the voices in her head from the towering redwoods nearby. They were her lifeline after all, she was tied to them.

She figured she should read up on the bears and the Wiyot history of them. Maybe even some anatomy of them couldn't hurt if she was expected to run with them.

With an exhale she got up to head back to her car. She would be back right before sunset and watch it from her hatch then she would head back home to start research.

Plenty of cars came and went while she watched the sun's descent. It was a common spot to pull off the highway and see the ocean. Once it was dark, she exhaled and made her way to the driver's side door.

A slight gust of wind sent a prickling sensation up her spine as she noticed the only other car that was directly facing hers. It was closer than comfortable too. What really made her insides twist in knots was the figure sitting on the hood looking right at her.

He grinned as he took a hit of his vape. She could hear his inhale and the small rush of air through the vape. "Nice view." His voice was smooth and confident despite the exhale of smoke. Elodie remained frozen. She didn't know what to do.

The moment he jumped off the hood though, Elodie jumped in her car and locked her doors. He remained grinning at her for a few more moments before he got in his car. Elodie remained watching him as she felt for her cell phone and pulled up Trevin's number. It would take him at least forty minutes to get here if he was at home. Quinn would take even longer. She didn't know where Cedar or Autumn were.

What should I do? she pleaded. Her heart was pounding.

Go to a light populated area. Eureka. Not home.

With the Old Giants' advice in mind, she started her ignition then felt her heart stop when his headlights flashed on, illuminating her cab. A second later the car moved forward, flipping in a U-turn back on the highway, the same direction she needed to go to Eureka. She sat there in the twilight blue of dusk alone for another fifteen minutes. She watched cars pass along with a few semi trucks. After another handful of vehicles went south, she put her foot on the gas and drove, looking for the red sedan with every car she passed.

CHAPTER 8

R elief hit her when she saw there was a spot right in front of the café and she scanned the area for the car or him. There was only about two hours until closing and Elodie figured she could stay until then.

Quickly she ran inside and looked to the counter to see Cora smiling.

"Happy to see you again."

"Yea, I missed it here," Elodie laughed somewhat nervously.

"I assume Trev will be here shortly?"

"No, actually he is working on stuff."

"Oh, so, just you tonight?"

"Yes," Elodie replied, finally calming down.

Cora smiled. "Well, just like old times then."

Elodie nodded then took a seat after ordering. Taking in her surroundings again, she made a mental note of everyone in the café, then took out her sketchbook and pen pouch. As she tried to draw a bear, every sound and movement grabbed at her attention. The scents and the lighting pulled at her. This was another new environment for her senses to adjust to.

The door opened and she looked up at the customer that walked in. They ordered, got their drink and left. No cause for alarm.

Someone walked up to her table and it took everything in her to steady her breathing and her power. She met Cora's startled gaze, setting down her order.

With a sigh Cora sat down across from her. "Are you sure you are safe? I know, you have said it a million times, but Trev has always been within earshot of you. You are so jumpy tonight."

Elodie took a deep inhale. "I am fine, perfectly safe. I promise you."

Cora sighed. "You certainly don't seem like it."

Elodie shook her head. "I was on the beach watching the sunset and some creepy guy was watching me. He left before I did but I didn't want to go home just yet."

"Oh of course not. Stay here until closing or stay at my place if you want."

"Thanks, Cora." Elodie smiled.

"I am sure if you told Trev he would absolutely put that guy in his place. He's been so protective over you. Honestly he's been like that since that Halloween party. It sure is something else to see him so attached."

"I feel safe with him. But I am sure it was just a creepy encounter. Certainly not going back to that spot alone for a while," Elodie laughed with some unease.

"I don't blame you," Cora said then got up to go back behind the counter tending to some dishes.

The café door opened about thirty minutes later and a loud sigh came from Cora. Elodie fought the urge to look up but couldn't help it. She found Justine smiling at her then Elodie looked back to Cora who had an almost warning glance. This made Elodie tense. *Deep breaths, deep breaths. Don't pulse, please don't pulse.*

She kept her head down and listened to her friends' hushed voices as she traced her drawing from earlier darkening the pencil lines.

"Justine, don't stress her out by asking. Please?" Cora pleaded.

Justine didn't respond, instead took the seat across from Elodie.

"Hey, I was just grabbing a drink before hanging out with my brother," Justine said in a cheery tone. "Nice to see you. Alone." Now her tone had a hint of jest, but Elodie got a feeling of suspicion.

A slow exhale left Elodie. "Hi, Justine." She fought the urge to ask where Quinn was.

"How are things?"

"Good, and how about you?" Elodie asked, unsure. If there were any fae around, surely they would hear her heart rate increase right now.

"Good. Consider the Tahoe trip please," Justine blurted out.

"I will?" Elodie was not sure where that came from.

"I looked at a few places we could stay. We could go for the summer?"

"What? Justine, I—can't," Elodie stuttered in shock.

"Why not? Nothing is keeping you here, let's go," Justine pleaded.

"I can't just drop everything." Elodie suddenly felt as though she were backed up against a wall. "What about your apartment? Your stuff? You are going to pay rent on a place you won't be in for three months? Plus a stay that long in South Lake is going to cost so much money." Elodie began listing off reasons this was absurd.

Justine rolled her eyes. "I'm just asking you to weigh your options. You have the summer off, go travel and then come back in August. I'm sure Trev would watch your house. Or is it that you don't trust him to not invite someone into your bed?" Justine gave a pursed lipped smile and raised an eyebrow.

"That's—no. He would never. He didn't," Elodie asserted as best she could.

Cora walked up looking very unamused and handed Justine her drink. "Your drink. Your brother is probably waiting," she said with a curt tone.

"Thanks." With that Justine got up and left without a backwards glance.

Elodie felt her eyes water and quickly wiped them. She had not thought about that photo since the night of the ruins but now it was stuck in her head. Alena's snide comments at Spring Equinox played in her head too.

'Your sister obviously tried her best, but pretty dresses and fancy jewelry on trash are still trash.' She knew Alena talked poorly about all of them. Trevin showed it day in and day out how much he loved Elodie, and the absolute rage in his eyes at that comment would tell her enough. Still the words hurt and she had to remind her that not everyone was going to like her regardless of what she had done.

"I'm sorry. I told her not to say anything, she's been going on about how dangerous this place is for you ever since that night," Cora explained.

"I just want her to drop it. Why does she have to bring up bad memories? And why does she want me to leave this place so much? If it wasn't family telling me what I should do, or my shitty ex, now it's her? Am I not allowed to like a place? To want to stay somewhere?" Elodie looked down at her things.

"Of course you are. I am glad you found home here. It's just that it was an odd situation that night. It was such an extreme move from you. But I am glad you worked it out and are happy."

Elodie feigned a smile but that word left her exhausted. Odd. Everything was odd, because she was the oddity. The Earth Blessed, the chosen one. She couldn't shake the feeling that things were still falling apart and she wasn't sure how to fix it. Her fear was she might not figure it out in time. She had just barely pieced everything together last time.

"I know it looks weird. It was, but I know now more than ever that Trev and I are better together. I want to stay here." Elodie started to pack her things up.

"Elodie, I don't want the café to be a sad place for you. Stay?"

"I will stay longer next time, I promise. I am a bit tired though. It's been a weird night."

Cora let out a sigh and accepted Elodie's response.

As Elodie hurried out she caught a familiar scent right before she bumped into someone. "I'm sorry!" she nearly whimpered. A gentle hand came to rest on her shoulder.

"El. Relax. It's okay," Cedar said softly. Elodie looked up at him and saw his shocked look contort to concern. He was in his police officer uniform. His ears were rounded, and his face markings were gone; he was glamoured to look mortal as required on this side of the boundary. "What's wrong? What happened?"

"I'm okay. I was just going home."

"Are you sure? Do you want an escort? I will keep my distance in the cruiser if you like?"

Elodie nervously shook her head and her breathing got heavier. She was fighting to contain her energy pulse.

"Breathe. You are okay. I know Trev is like a million times better at this but you are okay."

Elodie swallowed and slowed her breathing. She looked at him again. "Thank you."

"Anytime, El." He removed his hands.

She couldn't stand to look back and see all the curious eyes on her so she hurried back to her car. When she looked up she could see Cedar watching. He gave her a nod and then went inside.

Once home she changed then crawled right into bed. Her phone buzzed. It was a message from Cedar.

Don't be mad but I told Trev.

Did I show anything? I thought I could handle it. I'm sorry.

No, you didn't. Cora told me what Justine said. Trev would keep that place spotless for you and ward it only to allow you two to enter it if you were to travel. For centuries if you asked.

Thank you for that and calming me down tonight.

Anytime. I serve you. I am glad you are part of the family, El.

Then she received a message from Trevin asking if she wanted him to be there.

She let out a loud exhale and replied with a 'yes' followed by a 'sorry'. Curling into a ball, she tried not to let the disappointment swallow her.

She laid there thinking too heavily on the day and thirty minutes later, Trevin unlocked the door and she rolled over and went to get the light.

"I don't need the light. Lie back down," he said, removing his boots and pants. Then he crawled into bed, spooning her close.

"I'm sorry. I don't know what's happening. I thought I could handle all of this."

"I told you I would be here every step of the way however you needed me. You can do this, I know you can. It's just going to take time. Cedar told me you looked terrified."

"He was really kind. Gentle. I wasn't sure he knew how to be."

Trevin laughed. "You and me both, Little Mink."

Elodie mentioned the encounter with the guy and Trevin held her closer.

"A raven is the easiest way to monitor the areas. Lord Nightswift is more than happy to post one near you. He hasn't been barred from any since the ruins."

"No! Please. I need to do this. I want to do this."

"I know. The ravens are not there to watch any of us, they are just there in case there is danger. We don't have them around us all the time, just occasionally they fly over."

"No."

"Alright, no ravens. Try to get some rest. We will be at Greenthistle tomorrow night." He rubbed her head and soothed her into slumber.

Back at Greenthistle, Echo sat in his study and sighed. He made notes on what he had gained from his sons tonight, then called Bracken and Miles.

"The clock is ticking, but at least she didn't show anything. Next week is going to be rough on her," Miles faltered.

"I know. Any progress on Cyrus?" Echo asked.

Bracken shook his head then pinched the bridge of his nose. "I don't know what to do about him either. I hear his screams day and night. I guess if you call getting five hours of sleep progress between screaming fits. How's the relationship between Trev and Quinn? Lady Elodie and Cedar?"

"She trusts Cedar obviously. He has been very admirable and respectful of her. Trev and Quinn however—" Echo shook his head.

"Get them near each other and they act like petulant little cubs. Quinn just can't help but prod Trev. He is lucky Trev has enough sense of self-preservation to control his temper."

"Part of me wants Elodie to see Trevin's loyalty when Quinn prods him, but I also fear Trevin is going to snap at him, and then there is the part that knows it will hinder Elodie's view of Quinn." Echo hesitated. "That night shattered everything between our boys."

"Her lessons will need to start with teaching her to trust, I guess," Miles suggested.

"Then self-defense and feral communication alongside endurance?" Echo followed.

"Is that all?" Bracken replied wearily.

All three exhaled in defeat and wrapped up the call a short while later.

Chapter 9

Somewhere deep in slumber, Cyrus was struggling to rouse. His vision was filled with all the horrors he had seen for weeks. When he slept, he could not distinguish between reality and dreams. The chains certainly felt real, the cuts, and bruises all felt real too. Alena looked real, the spirit looked real.

No matter how loud he screamed, nor how hard he tugged, he was trapped again.

"No one cares about you, Cyrus," Alena sneered in his head. "No one wants you."

"Please!" Cyrus screamed. "Elodie. Please. Trevin, just figure it out. Just wake up!" He continued to scream. "Just wake up!"

Was he telling Elodie to wake up or himself? He didn't know anymore. For months, he had to be stuck in this nightmare. His friends couldn't leave him like this. Had he seriously been this much of an asshole, that no one had thought his behavior odd? Then again, he tried to tell them but that spirit would attack him and take over his body every time he tried.

"Please. I'm sorry. I don't want to be a monster." Then, he heard a growl in his ear, this was no mountain lion or bear though. It was something otherworldly. He trembled.

"No one is coming for you, little blackbird. No one cares. The mountain lion is so angry with you, the bear is too. You scared the wee little Earth Blessed so badly that she will never come near you. She is so young and fresh, these old giants can't tell her everything yet. She isn't strong enough."

"Please! Stop," he screamed through his sobs.

"Poor Cyrus, you are going to lose your title, you can see how disappointed daddy is in you. The disappointment in your mother too, for treating your sisters so poorly. They worked so hard to raise you right and now you are going to cost Nightswift rank."

"Please! Please stop." He tugged hard at the chains.

"Look at those ravens falling out of the sky, their estate failed them. You failed them."

Cyrus whimpered again.

"We could still get to the Earth Blessed, let her spill more blood for you, you loved it didn't you. It was on your feathers, and your bill. We can do it again."

"No!" His body jolted but he was restrained.

"Cyrus!" a voice shouted. "Wake up. Please," the stressed male voice hissed. He heard the spirit laugh. Alena's laugh echoed too.

"Please!" Cyrus screamed.

"Cyrus! Wake up," the male voice pleaded louder this time.

He felt someone hold his head—someone else had his ankles pinned in the bed. Then palms pressed his chest down.

"No!" Cyrus shrieked and somehow felt the ravens that had fallen by his own hand. Some strength was building inside him but he wasn't sure what it was. Though, if he hesitated, this power surge would be gone. He ripped the chains back and opened his eyes. Someone was looking at him, bracing his head.

He met his dad's wide-eyed stare. The stress and fear in his dad's expression made Cyrus retreat back. Shaking his head free, he pulled back and screamed again. They were holding him down as though they too were going to cut into him, or throw him in the hold. "No. Please! Please stop!" Cyrus screamed.

"You are safe. They are safe," his dad said through gritted teeth.

Cyrus trembled again. His chest was rising and falling frantically. "Please let me go. Please." He begged as his tears fell. "Please."

"Calm down," his dad repeated.

"Please, Cyrus. You are safe." His mom's voice broke.

His eyes fixed on the ceiling and his body went near catatonic.

"It was just a nightmare. You are safe and free of that thing."

Cyrus remained still and tense save for his chest rapidly rising and falling.

"Calm your breathing."

He swallowed hard and tried to relax but he kept seeing that thing grinning wide at him, holding the chains and a tremble started to take over his body. He could vaguely hear his parents arguing about a sedative as that spirit and him stared at each other. Then, before he realized it, a small pinch went into his arm and slowly everything went still and quiet for him.

As his body went limp and his head slumped to the side, Bracken threw the syringe against the wall and stormed out of the room. Ariyanna rubbed Cyrus's head and wiped her tears.

"Let him go and leave us please," she snapped out at the sentries. They nodded and left in haste. "Cyrus. I am so sorry. I should have seen it. Your father should have seen it. We were so blind and so stupid to let this happen," she cried and looked at the trees. "Please help him. Please do not forget about him. Make our Earth Blessed strong like you are, like the Greenthistle she is."

She looked at her son's body locked in slumber. "I hope it is quiet for you now, Cyrus. I hope I am doing the right thing by giving you the sedation. Your body is so battered down and you are so exhausted. I hope you know none of us care about the power shift. We just want you back. I'd give anything to have you back to your old self." She gripped his hand and cried for a few more moments then began to tend to him.

Ariyanna had smoothed out his hair and wiped his face down with a cool rag. "Your Earth Blessed will help you. She has to." Her tears fell when she looked at the trees. "Please," she begged them once again then gave his hand a small squeeze before she dimmed the light and left the room.

When she walked downstairs, she stopped upon seeing her vowed hug their youngest, who was crying.

"It is going to be alright, Poppy. We are going to find our way."

"I just feel lonely," she cried. "His screams were so jarring. And everyone was shouting and running towards his room."

"I know. I am sorry. It is better to keep your distance right now. We just want him to heal and not overload him with more," Bracken sniveled.

Ariyanna could hear it; his voice was breaking. Her shoulders slumped with a sigh and he met her eyes, still holding Poppy.

She offered her vowed a small smile and walked to the kitchen where she sunk into the chair. A short while later, he walked in and sat next to her.

"We should try to have dinner with the girls soon. Maybe we can both get through a meal with them."

"While our son is too terrified to even breathe?!" she snapped.

"I know you heard Poppy; she is lonely. The more I force Dee to watch her, the more annoyed Dee gets. Poppy and Cyrus were so close. Ari, I hate that our boy is up there trapped all over again in his own bed, but we have two other kids who need us right now more than ever."

"I want him at the table too."

"You know he is just not ready."

"I know. He is hardly eating as it is. I don't want Dee or Poppy to see their older brother like this. It's bad enough that they have seen what they have." She sighed and looked at him finally. "I'm so tempted to just ask the girl to help him now. Three more weeks of this? And then what?"

"We can't. She has her Ashdale week first. We need to get him up and prepare for going outside again. I had hoped he would be by now. That he would be more than ready to be out of the house," he exhaled in exhaustion. "I'm terrified to put him back in drills with Trev. If Trevin attacked Cyrus, Greenthistle, and Nightswift would be done as allies. Trev and Q can hardly look at each other without arguing as it is."

Ariyanna sat back. "Trevin has never been this angry. It's been so long since I have even seen him be loud and obnoxious. I hope he calms down."

"I do too. Echo knows the situation and assured me he is working on it. Trevin has been taking his overseer responsibility so seriously. Paired with the vowed bond and he's still so young."

"Selene would be so proud to see him with her. I feel like she knew, or had a hunch he would be okay. But I still miss her. I curse Echo sometimes for his shitty choices. As if what she did in response was any better." Ariyanna wiped her eyes.

"Echo was never supposed to raise three cubs on his own. He is great at his job, but he can be such a cold bastard to Trevin. Mother above if that boy ever found out what happened."

"He won't. You know exactly why Selene did what she did. The sentiment she left was loud and clear. He was not to become a Hazelthorn or go to Everoak's territory. Selene wanted him to be a Greenthistle and remain in Humboldt from the moment I met her, and right now it is imperative that they all know how to stand their ground despite the oncoming flood."

"I know. I know." Another loud sigh. "Let's try tomorrow night, to have dinner at the table with Dee and Poppy." Her voice was affirmative.

Chapter 10

On Thursday Elodie was seated at the dining table at Greenthistle. She looked at the Greenthistle family and realized how she still felt like she was an outsider to them. In a way she supposed she was, but she also felt at home here. There was still tension and she never fully relaxed, but she had hardly fully relaxed anywhere since the ruins happened.

Here she was, having a meal with Echo Greenthistle, and his three children, his firstborn was her vowed and they were bonded now officially. She recalled the night they had actually completed the bond, completed with removing diadems and the blood bond done by the small incision on the palm made by each other's daggers. The words and the intent had been sealed.

Autumn and Cedar were seated across from her. Cedar had given both her and Trevin so much space the first week. Even after she had been ready for his formal apology he kept his distance. Autumn too had always been there when she needed, often opting to stay in when Trevin had to work. The two had gone on hikes and swam in the pool. Still, Elodie felt weird about keeping Autumn from Charles and encouraged her to go.

She had not yet reached that level with Cedar and had only been alone with him briefly when she was between the kitchen or Trevin's room.

This was her family now, there had been numerous dinners exactly like this since the night of the ruins with the five of them. And she cherished them.

"Lady Elodie," Echo said, snapping her back to her thoughts.

She swallowed hard. "Yes, sir?"

"Please ensure you are eating enough," he urged. "Olive is going to certainly have bigger portions than we do, your appetite is best suited for Nightswift at this rate."

"They literally just eat charcuterie board stuff. She is going to starve by the end of her Nightswift week," Cedar laughed.

"Ariyanna knows how to feed guests," Echo chided. "She just doesn't need to be eaten out of house and home by you."

"You know you just need to ask both Nightswift or Ashdale for anything right? They will see to it you have whatever you need. Just like here," Trevin said softly, placing a hand on her leg.

"Yes," Elodie responded. In her mind she reminded herself this was her family again. Greenthistle wanted her. With an exhale she shoved another bite of the prime rib in her mouth. It was cooked to perfection and the flavor was amazing. Regardless of how mouthwatering it was, her stomach was still in knots.

"Is there anything I can say or do to assure that next week will be alright? I am not going to say it will be easy, but I do know that you will be safe and will do fine," Echo offered in a reassuring tone.

"No, sir. I do believe you. I just hope I don't disappoint you or any of Ashdale."

"The only way you could disappoint us is to simply refuse to try. Even if you try and fail, none of us will be disappointed."

She glanced at the window then towards Echo and thought about the question resting on her mind.

"Do Ashdale and Nightswift see me as a Greenthistle? Consider me one?"

Echo leaned back in his chair and swirled his wine glass as he fixed on her. She maintained eye contact with him until she felt her face heat. He would do this often and she assumed it was to test her nerves just as Lord Oakstone had in Marin. Trevin's hand tensing on her leg was evidence enough it grated on him.

"Would you believe me if I told you that they do? I do too. Bracken, Miles, and I know you are a Greenthistle, as well as a Nightswift and an Ashdale. Our intent this summer is to hone each of those traits in you so you know when to be which one. Only Nightswift can teach you how to watch as diligently as they do, and only Ashdale can teach you where your loyalty needs to stand and when. Do not doubt your valor has shown time and time again every time you've run into hell itself for all three of my children, for Cyrus, and Quinn."

"Yes, sir." Elodie felt the heat on her cheeks. Her thoughts flipped to what Lillyleaf stood for, Wisdom & Protection. Oakstone stood for Acuity and Direction. She hadn't exactly remembered the other three high estates in Marin's territory.

One question lingered as she met Echo's eyes again.

"Ask your question, Lady Elodie," Echo prompted.

"Do you know if Mt. Tamalpais could have claimed me after the Old Giants did? When I returned to Marin, after that camping trip when I was eight, did it know or see me any differently?" she asked and noticed Trevin's eyes widened then he too looked at his dad, who now tilted his head as if pondering her question.

"That certainly is an interesting question. How long has that been on your mind?" Echo asked.

Elodie broke eye contact to look at the trees, who remained silent. They had an answer but she hadn't asked them, she had asked Lord Greenthistle. Shame overtook her because she knew they were the ones she should be asking these questions too. Instead, she was being a bundle of nerves around this family who had spent months being there for her. It had felt wrong to not have this conversation with Trevin or Echo, but they couldn't give her the answers to the questions that gnawed at her.

She hadn't done a solo hike since before the ruins because she had been too scared to.

"A few months," she mumbled.

"Elodie." Trevin took her hand acting on his need to comfort her.

"Honestly, I have no idea. You are better off asking the Old Giants. I have been to Marin County six times since you've been born and paid my respects to their entity as is custom. Had I known one of its own would become one of ours, I'd have certainly paid more respect but I never got any notion back from it. Nor have I from any territory I have visited." He took a sip of his wine then set the glass down before continuing.

"We used to do a high estate leader exchange with Del Norte, you know? I felt the same presence from their Old Giants as I did Mt. Tamalpais. Bracken was the last to go, when he met Ariyanna. Trying as that all went, we ended the exchange given the mutual bloodline they would eventually have with Cyrus. Ariyanna can pass freely as can the Nightswift children, Bracken is allowed to pass as long as he is escorted by her or his children, though he and Ariyanna's father, Lord Stormbriar, kind of hate each other." Echo finished the story with a laugh. "You will have to ask Bracken about it. He nearly punched me and Miles in the face for being too close to Ariyanna for months."

Elodie looked at him, stunned, then glanced at Trevin.

"Yes, Trevin has wanted to punch all of us many times, but I know my boy wouldn't dare snap at anyone. Right?" He fixed on Trevin.

"No sir," Trevin grumbled.

"But back to your concerns, again, we simply do not know enough about the Earth Blessed. They are chosen but we are not sure what that all entails aside from spilling blood," Echo followed up, looking back at Elodie.

"Understood, sir."

"Eat some more please," he urged. And Elodie did, feeling more at ease. She glanced at the trees once more, vowing to talk to them at Ashdale.

Once they finished dinner, Trevin and Elodie took their plates to the kitchen where staff was quick to insist on cleaning their dishes. He took her hand and they headed towards the stairs where Echo greeted them with a knowing smile.

"Would you care to step into the study for a moment?" he asked, looking at Elodie.

She felt a sense of bewilderment and gripped Trevin's hand tighter, feeling him grip hers back.

"Both of you."

Trevin exhaled and they both followed him into the study where they took a seat across from Echo, who sat behind the desk as usual.

"I've heard a few accounts of what happened on your last visit to Marin, but not yours, Lady Elodie. Your questions tonight got me curious. Something happened and we need you to trust us as much as we trust you. Now I have Trevin's account, and I have Lady Lillyleaf's account of what happened, but I do not have yours. Would you mind sharing your experience of meeting Marin's high estates?"

Elodie looked at him, then at Trevin. She let out a long exhale and began to speak of what happened.

When Elodie parked her car at the Marin Headlands parking lot, she was greeted by Tanya Lillyleaf and another male. He was as tall and muscular as Cedar was and had a California State Parks jacket on.

"Trev, great to see ya, and look at her," he said and bowed before Elodie. "I am Jared Oakstone, heir apparent to the Oakstone Estate, second longest ruling in Marin. We are Tule Elk."

"Jared and I sometimes cross paths when training takes me down here or he goes up there. It's basically like going to work with Cedar," Trevin groaned.

"It also is not helping that Jared is a big flirt and Trevin is extra temperamental given that he's a kept and vowed male now," Tanya added.

"Oh. Nice to meet you, Jared? And see you again Tanya. Is my car safe here?" Elodie asked.

"It's why I brought the work truck and why I met you here. I got the keys. Unlike Humboldt's state parks we gotta lock our gates, more people and all," Jared explained.

Once at the meeting place, Elodie stood a few miles off trails she had hiked dozens of times. She took in the feeling of it all. The flashing lights of the Golden Gate Bridge peering through the fog, the cool breeze, and the sounds of the ocean. Marin Headlands was one of her go-to spots. Mt. Tamalpais sat watching behind her.

When her eyes caught sight of a hawk watching her, Elodie gasped. Trevin knelt down on one knee. A voice in Elodie's head stopped her just as she went to kneel.

"You need not kneel, Earth Blessed. He does though."

Elodie's eyes widened and she looked at Trevin.

"They speak true, El. Good control though," he said quietly, keeping his head down. Then, Elodie saw him tense.

"From overseer with a plaything, to vowed and ready to snap. My, my, little cub, you have come a long way since you last knelt before us and lied." A huge stag walked out of the trees.

"I told no lies, I can't," Trevin maintained.

"No, he was just very careful with his words. A wise choice in effort to protect his vowed." A large female mountain lion appeared, musing. Elodie forced her breathing to remain steady.

She looked at the Marin high estate lords and ladies gathered before them. Five of them, including a hawk, elk, mountain lion, raven, and a coyote. All fixed on her intently. Her heart rate increased as she stepped closer to Trevin who was still kneeling.

"Deep breaths, Little Mink," Trevin said softly.

"So it is true, an Earth Blessed stands before us," the raven said.

"How did we miss this?" The coyote followed up.

"Her vowed certainly didn't," the stag said. She saw his smirk and noticed Jared watching her intently. She then looked at the raven and the hawk, who watched from the tree. Tanya stood by the tree in fae form, as did the other heirs, two other males and one female.

"What might we call you other than Earth Blessed?" the mountain lion asked.

"Elodie is fine, Miss—Ma'am—Lady—I'm sorry," Elodie stuttered. She heard a sly little laugh from one of the heirs, no doubt questioning how she was a Greenthistle.

"You are in no position to glare, Trev," one of the males said. Elodie was taken aback at the comment, then glanced at Trevin who was gritting his teeth.

She recalled when Cedar had apologized to her and knelt in front of her. Lord Greenthistle had told her that he could not rise until she told him to, as a sign of showing respect. Now Trevin could not rise until Marin told him he could. She saw Tanya shove the male.

"Master Greenthistle." The hawk spoke and Trevin dropped his head. "Trevin Greenthistle, you are under order not to speak unless directly spoken to by a Marin high estate leader. Do you understand?"

"Yes, Lady Lillyleaf."

"He is going to writhe here shortly," Jared laughed and stepped towards her. His light brown hair was styled with a side part and his eyes were a rich brown. "Lady Elodie," he purred and walked closer. "Forgive us, none of us heirs are vowed, it is fascinating to see him like this." Elodie stepped closer to Trevin and a few of them laughed. "He is bound to remain just like that, and silent. He can do little to help you and it's driving him mad."

Elodie looked to see Trevin's fingers clutching the dirt and his eyes focused on the ground. "Trevin," she whispered and saw his body tremble slightly before he exhaled a breath and heaved.

"Interesting," the coyote said. "The bond is so loud between them."

Elodie felt Jared step closer to her, too close. She noticed the mountain lion and coyote approach close behind him. With every beat of her heart, their grins grew wider and she noticed the elk watching her carefully.

"How did I miss your presence all these years? Makes me wonder why our groves and Mt. Tam missed that thing in you and Humboldt saw it," Jared said. "Why did they let you tether them with your blood?"

"I didn't! I tripped and fell as a child. I belong there. Not here." Elodie's voice wavered. She told herself to hold her head high, to show them she was a Greenthistle.

"The fun we could have had, if I had seen you, I'd have changed your mind about where home was. You might have said it was here all along." Jared gave her a smug smile as he walked behind her and laughed softly in her ear. "Oh I see his claws trying to rip out of him. He can feel your little heart pounding—we all can. We can all see your fear too. And now there is nothing your mountain lion can do. I can show you all kinds of places you've missed while he remains bound right here."

Elodie clenched her hands into fist and took deep breaths. All the tests that Lord Greenthistle had done to control her nerves came back to her. Her power usually went haywire with her nerves in shambles. Then all the pieces clicked into place to reveal this was a test. These were fae that wanted to prod and poke her so her power flared. The elk was watching as diligently as the hawk and the raven. His son played the flirt and the coyote and mountain lion were there to protect him, not to touch her. Jared hadn't touched her, because he couldn't. Especially not with Trevin here.

Focusing on Jared's steps, Elodie waited for him to walk in front of her. When she looked right in his eyes, she saw the flash of teal and brought up her hand, illuminating teal. Fear washed over his face for a split second and all the heirs gasped. Except Tanya, who smirked. Elodie let her vines slip out and gave Jared a soft shove back.

"This is not my home. Humboldt is," she said, then abruptly pulled it back, feeling it getting too potent. Her body sagged as a wave of exhaustion washed over her.

"That too is unexpected. She's already exhausted from that little bit? Impressive as it was," the raven said.

"She is still young. New to this." The hawk flew down and changed. Elodie's eyes widened. Lady Lillyleaf was stunning, with deep rich brown eyes with a hint of purple to them. Her tan skin and black hair reminded her of Lord and Lady Ashdale and Elodie wondered if Lillyleaf had Coastal Miwok in their bloodline just as she had from her mom. She couldn't help but bow her head in respect. *"Tell me Lady Elodie, were you taught your good graces or did Lord Greenthistle's intimidation instill them?"*

"Umm, both, Lady Lillyleaf."

The woman smiled and gave a nod. *"You are well suited for Greenthistle."* Elodie's jaw gaped slightly for a second before she closed it. *"Now, let us ask you some questions. First, a question for our lie detector. Master Greenthistle, have you fabricated a story to work in your favor with Lady Elodie?"*

Still kneeling, Trevin lifted his head to meet her eyes. *"No, I have not, Lady Lillyleaf,"* Trevin said, then lowered his head.

"Excellent." Lady Lillyleaf and the other leaders of the Marin high estates peppered them with questions, from how they met to how she found out he was fae to how she awoke. Some held shocked, grave faces when she spoke of the night in the ruins. They also went on to say what they knew of their Earth Blessed, who was very kind and nurtured all the areas of Marin. She tended to many plants and animals. Only Lady Lillyleaf and Lord Oakstone had met her; they were young when she vanished. Prior to her absence, they had sensed a shift in the land, an unease that things were beginning to change in the 1400's. It was a ripple that started far away from the east and worked its way west. Over the years some of the Marin leaders had traveled to the Rockies and north to Canada and yet no one had reported an Earth Blessed.

They were not sure why the Earth Blessed disappeared. The conclusion Lady Lillyleaf came to was possibly that it could be how the land was to be treated, but heavy development still wouldn't start for a few more centuries, becoming what they all knew it was today. Heavy logging, especially in Humboldt when so many of the Old Giants had been wiped out to build San Francisco, didn't come about until the 1800's.

As Elodie listened, her mind began to work through all the possibilities for the disappearance. She had learned Marin's Earth Blessed had been a forest sprite born in Marin, chosen by Mt. Tamalpais. Deep in thought, Elodie turned to glance in the direction of the mountain. Muir Woods, the nearest grove to them, stood just on the other side where the fog could linger. She looked at her hand then back North. Her Old Giants were far away. Yet, here they stood near an old grove too. Never had they spoken to her and she was not sure why.

It wasn't that she wanted Marin; she knew she wanted Humboldt, was so grateful they had chosen her when she was little, even though she remembered the pain from the cut, the sadness when the trip was cut short as a result. She wondered if the Old Giants had let out that sigh then as they did now. Still though, Muir Woods nor any of the old groves she hiked elsewhere had spoken to her. Marin had let her go without so much of a hint. Thoughts started dropping, soon becoming downpour.

Why hadn't they talked to her? Why did she care? She loved Humboldt, loved the life she found up there. She didn't want this place. Humboldt chose her. Marin hadn't and five high estates had never detected anything in her, nor crossed her path. If they had, would she have stayed? Would she have missed Humboldt all her life? There was nothing left for her there and yet, some streak of sadness grabbed hold of her. They had never bothered to talk to her. She was from here and Mt. Tamalpais had watched her for years. The mountain was noticeable even from nearby counties, so it had seen her but never spoke to her. Never reached for her as those Old Giants in Humboldt did. Why?

What if Mt. Tamalpais knew what she'd bring upon Marin? Her energy was odd, bad enough to shatter three ancient estates. What if she were responsible for five of them right now? They didn't need that, Mt. Tamalpais didn't want her bringing that upon them. What if those Old Giants didn't realize it until it was too late? Sure, she saved them but she hadn't fixed anything. Hadn't even really made an effort to.

She looked at Trevin who was still kneeling. In the final wave of the downpour, she thought about what Greenthistle could have lost. Nightswift and Ashdale too could have lost their firstborns that night. Her eyes welled up.

"The doubt written all over you—your emotions range so much, so fast. You absolutely must get them under control before the conference," Lord Oakstone said with urgency.

Elodie gasped and looked at them, then saw the flash of teal. All of them, and their heirs watched her. Various expressions cover their faces. Tanya and even Jared, to her surprise, were concerned. Confusion or fear cascaded on the rest of the heirs' faces. These emotions were clear to her and she took a step back. "I'm sorry," she whimpered, breathing heavily now.

"You are free of your order, Trevin, consider it rescinded. Rise," Lady Lillyleaf said.

In the blink of an eye, Trevin embraced Elodie. She wrapped her arms around him tightly and buried her face into the crook of his neck.

He rubbed her head softly. "It's okay, El. You are alright. Just breathe, Little Mink."

"I'm sorry," Elodie repeated, trying to keep her voice quiet. "I got overwhelmed. I'm sorry."

"Nothing to apologize for. You never have to do this alone. I'm here, however you need me. I promise."

"And that, heir apparent, is what a vowed bond will do. It will rekindle the fire you lost," the elk said, his tone evident of a smile. "I could see you fighting that order with everything in you, Master Greenthistle. Even knowing how futile it was."

"If you are able to, may we ask that you walk in Muir Woods, or even Samuel P. Taylor Park or any of our groves to see how they react to you now that you have fully awoken? Tanya and Jared can accompany you," Lady Lillyleaf asked.

Trevin cut his eyes to Jared and glared.

"Mother above, calm down, dude. You know it was a test. I'm not trying to cost my estate power. You know why they're sending me."

Trevin let out an audible exhale.

Tanya laughed. "It will be a fun hike."

Elodie let Trevin lead the rest of the conversation but she did explain what she could. That the Old Giants hadn't told her much yet of her responsibilities but she planned to sit with them and listen. Trevin shared some of what they had managed to translate in the tome as well.

Chapter 11

Elodie had recounted the Marin County visit to Echo and Trevin, and now she waited for their reactions.

"El? That's what has got you so distracted? That Mt. Tamalpais might not have wanted you?" Trevin asked, concerned as always.

"I looked like an idiot in front of all of Marin. And I was scared I would disappoint you because I know it shouldn't bother me that Mt. Tam didn't want me."

"Maybe it didn't realize what you were because none of Marin's estates are like us. Maybe once you are claimed, you are off the table for any other entity," Trevin suggested. Elodie could see the worry in him. This wasn't a hunch, his body language was telling her everything.

"Once again, I am not disappointed in how the meeting with Marin went. They told me exactly how they would test you and they wanted their heirs to see a fresh vowed bond. They wanted to see Trevin's sense of control, because I assure you, that too will be tested at that conference."

"They are going to be absolute dicks about it too. Don't be surprised if I end up sedated," Trevin scoffed and crossed his arms.

"This is why you have tests this summer too. I need you at the top of your game, that includes your attitude with Quinn and how you act with Cyrus." Echo narrowed his eyes on his son.

"Tell them that then. Test them as well. All you do is tell Quinn and I to knock it off. I listen, but Quinn just keeps prodding, keeps snapping out his retorts," Trevin seethed.

Elodie looked at him shocked at how angry he was now. *The things you haven't fixed. Haven't even noticed.*

"You're angry at Quinn?" she asked in a pensive tone.

"El, if you heard how bad his attitude has been I think you might be upset with him too."

"I haven't talked to him much. Justine likely isn't helping the situation. I feel like this is my fault."

"No, it's not."

"He is right, Lady Elodie. It's not your fault. You braved hell to drag them out, it's up to them to work together. All the things Bracken, Miles, and I have been through, admittedly don't compare to any of this, but we had to work through it. I assure you there were times we all made mistakes, but it was up to us to fix it. Not Olive, not Ariyanna, and not Selene. It was our mess, and this is theirs. All you need to do is prepare for that conference."

"But I'm your Earth Blessed and I haven't even tried to help the high estate heirs."

"It's hardly been three months and you had a school year to finish out, a house in Marin to sell, a house here to buy, and an entirely new world to adjust to. A new body to get used to. Trevin, Cyrus, nor Quinn expect you to hold their hand through being friends again. They serve you. Remember that," Echo insisted then he looked at Trevin. "Let this be your motivation to fix it with Quinn and Cyrus. Do not make this another thing she has to do."

"I don't want it to be her responsibility. Quinn needs to take things more seriously for once and Cyrus needs to talk. What am I supposed to do, order them to behave?"

"Absolutely not. First-in-commands do not order their second and third, but you can work with them," Echo explained.

"I can keep it professional. Quinn is the one who seems to think everything is a joke."

Elodie frowned. The next week was going to be rough and despite what Echo had just told Trevin, she knew the three heirs needed help.

"I want to try to help them." She spoke up. "If Trevin is not to see me for a week while I am at Ashdale, I can try talking to Quinn."

"El, please don't think you have to help Quinn and I. You have so much to tackle already," Trevin said.

"But it feels like this is something I should be doing. You all serve me, let me serve you."

"It might take longer than a week unfortunately. Then it will be that on top of having to figure out how to even look at Cyrus. That damned grin and look of pure malice in his eyes haunts me." A chill passed over Trevin.

"That wasn't really Cyrus though. You know it wasn't. I know it wasn't and I hardly know him," Elodie retorted

Echo laced his fingers together on the desk. "I think the concern is, if they still act as divided as they are now, it will feel like you failed them. Correct me if I am wrong, Lady Elodie."

All she could do was slump back in her seat. "No, sir. You are not wrong."

"It isn't your responsibility, El," Trevin offered.

"Make a bargain with me, Lady Elodie." Echo leaned back with a grin.

"Seriously?" Trevin gawked.

Elodie swallowed hard. "What is the bargain?"

"You may try to help as you see fit, but only if you swear you will not take it as a failure if Trev and Quinn continue to act like petulant little cubs. If you try and fail, all your lessons with Trevin will be solo lessons with Cedar from then on. Or you can simply not say anything and let them figure it out. I will ask both Quinn and Trevin if you tried and are disappointed next week."

"No. What the hell kind of bargain is that?" Trevin muttered.

"Do not speak for her, Trevin. Not with me, and never in front of that council," Echo said with reverence.

Elodie looked at Trevin as he acknowledged his dad's request. Then she considered the bargain. They may have said it wasn't her responsibility and while it wasn't solely hers, she owed it to her high estates to try.

That was what Echo had asked of her after all. To simply try. So she would.

"I accept your bargain, Lord Greenthistle. I will try."

Echo gave her a knowing smile. "Wonderful."

"El. None of us deserve you." Trevin sighed in acceptance and took her hand in his.

"Enjoy the rest of the evening." Echo smiled at them.

Once they left the study Trevin took her hand and led her to their room. He closed the door and leaned against it but didn't let her hand go.

Elodie turned and looked at him. "Are you upset with me?"

He grinned and pulled her closer. "No. Are you upset with me?"

"No. What would I have to be upset with you about?"

"Let's see, that I'm annoyed with Quinn, that I spoke for you, that I'm so easily rendered helpless by my superiors when it comes to you? That my dad is my dad?"

"No. It just feels like I need to do more. Your dad is right, we have a lot to do and not a lot of time to do it. I didn't want to tell you about my feelings on Mt. Tamalpais because I didn't want you to think I wanted Marin still. I don't but sometimes, I get scared they chose wrong, that you all got stuck with someone who might let you down."

Trevin pulled her close. "I know they didn't. My dad agrees. I trust him, and I trust you. Trust in yourself, alright? We do have a lot to do, but I know you know what you are doing. I will try with Quinn."

Elodie smiled and pressed her forehead to his. He brought his arms to rest on her shoulders. "I'm going to try. I want to try."

"I know you will. I know you want to." Trevin kissed her as his arms embraced her body. "An entire week away from you will be torture," he purred as he walked her back to the bed.

"Good thing Greenthistle's rotation falls right between," she laughed and proceeded to tug his shirt off as soon as he laid her down.

Chapter 12

Sunday brought her arrival to Ashdale Estate. Trevin had shown her the way and the doors opened upon their arrival as they were warded for him, given that he was a high estate heir. Trevin had a hand on her lower back leading her into the house. The high estate lords would set their houses to recognize her and open the doors automatically.

She clutched the tome in her arms securely.

"Welcome to Ashdale Estate, Lady Elodie. You are looking well. As are you, Master Greenthistle. I assure you both, no harm will come to her. Lady Elodie will be treated with the utmost care and respect." Miles spoke with all the confidence one would expect from a high estate lord. Lady Olive Ashdale was standing next to him.

It was easy to see why Quinn was so laid-back with his parents being much the same. Though they both took things much more seriously than Quinn often did.

"Remember my requests. I expect to see her Saturday and Greenthistle must be notified if she is injured in any way," Trevin reminded them.

"Of course. No harm will come from any of Ashdale or outside of it," Miles affirmed.

Trevin nodded and noticed Quinn sitting on the couch with a challenging grin. He glared.

"Pay attention when you are running lessons with her."

Quinn laughed. "Cool your jets. I know how to run lessons, Trevy."

"Good." Trevin relaxed his shoulders, then glanced at Connor.

"Of course, Master Greenthistle. I will work with her as instructed. Mom and Dad are in charge of sparring, Quinn and I are there for endurance and communication with bears."

Trevin nodded and heard the uneasy exhale from Elodie. He gently placed his hand on her arm. "El. You are going to do great. They will take care of you and I will be here at two o'clock on Saturday. You can always text or call me, too."

Elodie looked at him and gave a quick nod in affirmation then looked at Lord and Lady Ashdale. "I'm going to do this."

Trevin could see her doubts and uncertainty. He could also see her pushing her way through them just as she always did. "You have no reason to doubt yourself. Watch your steps and work hard. Your mountain lion will be counting down the days." Trevin pulled her into a firm embrace. "I love you," he said softly in her ear.

"I love you too."

He pulled back from the embrace and gave Miles a nod then smiled at her one last time before heading out the doors. He forced down the urge to run back to her, to hold her longer. *Six days, try for her. Be better for her,* he reminded himself.

Just like that Elodie watched as the doors closed. She was to stay here on the estate grounds for six days, only leaving to run out in the wilds with them. There would be no going to the café, no wine nights with Cora, even just enjoying her house.

Six days every month until late August, she would be with one of the three high estates. They would give her two weeks to rest before the school year started.

"Lady Elodie. We encourage you to make yourself at home. Your home, not Greenthistle Estate," Miles said.

Elodie turned to face him. "Yes, sir," she responded. "Thank you, sir."

"That begins with relaxing as you would at home too, El," Quinn said with a small laugh. Elodie felt her face heat. She had known her response to Miles was formal. None of them expected her to be prim and proper but for some reason she felt she needed to.

"Quinn," Olive hissed. "That's not helping, even with your gift."

Connor, who now stood to one side, remained quiet but she could feel his eyes on her.

"Let's get the tome in the study and then I can show you to your quarters. I hope you will find them comfortable, but if you need or want anything, please let me know. Our staff is ready to serve you too. If you encounter any issue with anyone, let us know immediately." Olive spoke with a soft warm voice and stepped towards her.

"Thank you, Lady Ashdale. I hope to not be a burden or cause any undue stress while I'm here." Elodie tensed when she heard Quinn fail to keep in a laugh. She knew he wasn't laughing at her, but at how ridiculous she was being. She had been rigid at Greenthistle for a long time, and she still was at times. The only time she had been to Ashdale estate was for the spring equinox.

"Quinn! Can you please just take something seriously for once! You said she was your friend, so act like one to her," his mom scolded.

"I've seen El do extraordinary things as a mortal. As our Earth Blessed, she is unstoppable. I doubt I'm going to cripple her. She's getting her footing just fine."

Elodie swallowed and felt her face heat. Being the center of attention was never something Elodie craved but she knew she would be in the spotlight indefinitely now as the Earth Blessed.

Connor glanced at his brother, somewhat shocked.

"I am sure this is overwhelming. You forget how anxious you got when you started to integrate at school and you had Cyrus and Trevin there. I have no doubt Lady Elodie will be fine once she gets settled. But being in a strange place away from her vowed so soon is scary for anyone. After your mother and I were vowed, I didn't leave her side for months."

"Come now, let's get settled," Olive said, carefully putting her hand on Elodie's back.

Elodie did not look at anyone as she followed Miles and Olive into the office.

"Just right on the stand please. And if you could open it?" Olive nodded at the tome in her hands, motioning to the stand.

Elodie cringed then looked at her and Miles, recalling what happened last time she opened this book.

"What is it?" Olive asked.

"I—I only opened it once and it was a lot."

"Ahh that would be a predicament, it was closed to transport it." Miles rubbed his head and stepped forward. "Would it help if Quinn were in here? Maybe he can calm you down. We have medical staff on the premises. Echo mentioned you were just exhausted that weekend. Have you eaten and are you hydrated? Maybe we can wait until after dinner or tomorrow?"

"It was a stressful weekend. Sir." She looked intently at the tome recalling that day she first opened it. Would they give her another omen, she wondered.

"I will at least get Quinn to be here." Olive rushed out of the study.

Elodie set it down gently and unwrapped it from the cloth it had been in.

"Did you look through it much at Greenthistle?" Miles asked.

"A bit, but language has never been my strong suit, and this one is complicated to say the least."

Just then Quinn walked in. "What do you need me to do, El?"

Her eyes shifted to the window, seeing the trees. They were quiet.

"Last time I got riddles that should have been so obvious. The boy is trapped. He will be the first to fall. Never clear until I am facing the danger head on. Cyrus was trapped and Trevin would be the first to fall." A chill passed over her. "I didn't even think about having to open it again when I picked it up," she groaned.

Quinn stepped near her. "I'm going to give you a calming touch. I wil subdue the feeling then pull away slowly because if I don't the feeling might crash into you like a tidal wave," he said softly. "Think of it like a weighted blanket."

Elodie nodded. "Is yours dependent on touch like Trevin's?" She felt his palm come to her shoulder blade. It felt secure.

"It is always stronger with physical contact but generally my gift works within proximity. It is usually why just being near people mellows them out, unless you have nerves of steel like Justine."

"I see why you always have a hand on her when I arrive now?"

"One reason." His soft laugh vibrated through Elodie.

Breathing came slow and deep to her as she placed her fingers on the dial.

You all must tread lightly.

You can't grip sand.

Once again a tremble shot through her hand and she lowered it. She looked at Miles. "You would know if that spirit got out right? It's monitored?"

Miles looked confused. "Yes, it is monitored round the clock. We would know now. There was something off about that mountain lion that night, we all sensed it, we just didn't know what it was at the time, but now we do, thanks to you."

With a nod she lifted her hand again and began to move the dial. Once again as the mechanism slid and released a pin, Elodie felt the hum of power coming from the tome.

This is your home.

Stay with them.

Be there for them. All of them.

Her body started to tense until a mellow feeling washed over her and she took an inhale.

"Relax, El," Quinn said. "Breathe."

Watch just as much as the ravens do.

Do not leave any of them behind.

Be the Nightswift you are.

Her hand was trembling as she lined up the last symbol of the combination she had memorized.

"Elodie," Quinn called out to her but she kept going, now following that thrill of power. "Elodie! She's burning up." She heard and felt Quinn pull his hand away. She was running across rocks, no redwoods or ferns in sight, the air was hot and the sun burned.

As the last pin slipped into place, the warnings crashed into her. A pulse of teal flashed in her vision.

Those out there with bad intentions are waiting.

One overlooks and is overlooked.

One lost and altered.

One taken as bait for the true target.

Do not leave them.

Then she felt that familiar pulse hit her right in her core, seizing her body up as she stumbled back into something hard. Quinn caught her as her body went limp, yet her breathing was frantic.

"Elodie! Breathe. Calm down," Quinn said as composed as possible.

"Get her in the window seat," Miles called out.

A weightless sensation took over her body—she was being carried and set on a soft surface. Light from the sky led her eyes to the trees. Her breathing started to balance out. Gently, her head was turned, where Quinn and Olive came into view. A cool rag was being pressed to her face. It felt nice, and she realized now how hot she was.

"El?" Quinn asked.

Her eyes focused on him and her breathing slowed for a moment until the overwhelming sensation hit her hard. As she went to get up in haste Quinn held her down gently by the shoulders.

"Woah. Not until you relax. Your heart is racing."

"Well it's opened. So that's taken care of. I will inform Greenthistle so Trevin doesn't break our doors down."

"Don't. Please don't," Elodie pleaded. Quinn looked at her shocked. "I need to do this on my own. I want to do this. I'm fine, really."

"No one questions your dedication but it is an order from Echo," Miles informed. "I cannot override it."

"Please don't tell Trevin." She panicked and her eyes welled up in frustration. That overwhelming feeling came over her again and she hated it. This was another setback for her.

Her breathing slowed and she felt better. Quinn watched her carefully as he slowly removed his hands from her shoulders. "You're okay, El. Breathe."

A loud exhale escaped Elodie and she nodded.

"Do you feel well enough to sit up?" Miles asked.

Elodie nodded and pushed herself up slowly. She looked at Quinn. "Thanks for helping me."

"No problem. Go get settled." Quinn smiled and stood back watching her stand up. He stood near as she took a few slow steps.

"I will show you to your quarters," Olive said and Elodie followed. It was a good thing that their staff had already taken her backpack to her room, since she could hardly carry anything right now.

Chapter 13

"Now once you are upstairs, just head to your left. You're the first door on the right overlooking the backyard, a few doors away from Quinn and Connor. We are at the end of the hall. Lady Autumn was very helpful in sending options and sizes over for some clothes for you. I am not sure how much you brought with you but there is plenty of closet space and drawers." Olive led her into a large room and motioned to the closet and dresser.

"I tend to pack light. I thank you for the accommodation and amenities. This was not needed." Elodie awkwardly stumbled through good graces.

"Nonsense. These are your quarters indefinitely." Elodie flinched and looked at the door. Olive walked up to Elodie and placed a hand on her back. "We consider you one of our cubs and want you to know that. We are not keeping you hostage. Next week you will be back at Greenthistle. But any time you need anything, or if you are in the southern part of the territory, the estate is open to you."

Elodie met Lady Ashdale's olive-colored eyes. She was stunning. She certainly looked younger than 305 years old. Elodie knew Miles was a lot older and then thought of the age gap, which was still hard to wrap her mind around at times. Not that Miles looked anywhere near 397 and that she was younger than Miles.

Elodie knew Olive worked with the Department of Fish and Wildlife but wasn't sure what she did exactly. She just found it fitting for a bear.

"I will let you get settled. I'll send Quinn up before dinner to give you a grand tour and then Miles would like to go over your schedule for the week in the study. As a member of Ashdale, you always have a seat at our table too, so if you'd like, it would be an honor if you would have dinner with us. Of course, you are welcome to eat up here or in the backyard on your own. Just let us know."

"Thank you, Lady Ashdale. I appreciate it greatly."

"We are grateful for what you did, and to be able to serve you. To know the Earth Blessed is real is amazing, to actually work with one is truly a gift." Olive smiled and left the room.

Elodie closed the door then flopped down on the bed. Trevin was right, it was cozy like a cabin. An incoming call lit her phone up and she grabbed it. It was Trevin. With a sigh she sat up and answered it.

"Elodie. Are you alright?" Trevin asked. She could see he was in the study with Echo.

"Yes. I'm alright. Opening the tome was less stressful this time at least."

"Lord Ashdale told us what happened. I felt something was off but didn't feel the intense pulse like we did last time," Echo explained.

"Quinn used his gift, but it was weird. I heard him call for me but he sounded so far away even though his hand was on my shoulder. My body got hot but I couldn't help it, it lured me in."

"Did they tell you anything?" Echo asked.

Elodie sighed and looked down. "Yes." Her eyes slowly drifted back to the screen, seeing them both concerned. Then she repeated the warnings and the images.

"Well that doesn't sound promising," Lord Greenthistle said and both he and Trevin assured her they would do their due diligence to ensure everything would be alright.

For a few moments after the call ended, she tried to figure out where she had been in those images. It looked like so many places she had been to. Lassen? Trinity? Shasta? Eastern Sierra?

A knock sounded and she rushed to open the door to find Quinn standing there with a smile. "Would you like the grand tour of Ashdale Estate?"

Elodie recalled the night of the ruins and thought back to the injuries he had gotten for her.

"You are welcome to explore the house on your own if you'd be more comfortable. Mom just suggested I offer," Quinn offered after an awkward silence.

"No. I don't want to get lost here."

Quinn laughed and nodded. As they walked through the house she saw his room. It was large and lavish with some clothes scattered on the floor. A damaged firefighter helmet rested on a dresser and a plaque for the nearest CalFire station was on the wall. She then saw Connor's room, the grand suite, and his mom's office. The training room was also large and had bigger equipment, less things to climb up and more barricade type stuff. She could also see harnesses attached to large weights.

"I'm not expected to move that stuff, am I? It's so different from Greenthistle's." Elodie cringed.

Again, Quinn laughed. "No, we don't expect you to drag a tractor tire, but you will get some weight training in."

"I'm not the fastest at getting up to the platforms or the agility course."

"We are bears; agility isn't our specialty. Just wait until you see Nightswift's."

"What are your drills like then, if you all have to train at each other's houses?"

"Cyrus and Trev are expected to do what they can in fae form, whereas I run it in feral. We learn how to adapt and work with each other in mixed forms. Them fae, me feral, and so on. We have offsite drill days where we are all in fae, or all in feral. They set up challenges or games and we run them against our sentries, or sometimes even our parents lead them. Other times we are given scenarios and we have to strategize to tackle them."

Elodie nodded, thinking about how much all of them had to adjust to her. He continued to show her the backyard and the kitchen, before eventually leading her to the library.

"Do you usually call him Trevy?" Elodie asked, causing Quinn to laugh.

"We all do—did. It's a nickname he got. He usually scowls and rolls his eyes. The night you and him first kissed, we were all sitting at Greenthistle estate and I got the impression he was deep in thought about it when Autumn walked in. She and Cedar started commenting how Justine was back. I wanted the attention off me and naturally Trevy was the perfect way out."

"You guys talked about that night?" Elodie looked surprised.

"Autumn came back after us, obviously made quick work of Charles. She was eager to hear about our night. Then Trev nearly bit our heads off asserting his dominance. That vowed bond snagged him real good. I saw the kiss, Cedar did too. Never in a million years did I think I would see that dumbass act like he did with you. Every time you were brought up he was ready to snap. When he found out about the bonfire incident, I thought he was literally going to lunge for Cyrus at drills. Long gone are the days of apathetic Trevin," Quinn laughed again.

"Are you mad at Trevin or Cyrus?" She hesitated.

Quinn was silent for a few moments that soon seeped into awkwardness.

"That night changed a lot of things. It complicated a lot of things."

Elodie wanted to ask more but just nodded instead. Quinn led her to the study where Lord Ashdale was waiting, stopping her right in her tracks.

"Lady Elodie. Please relax. Have a seat. I just want to go over the plan for the week. If you have any concerns please let me know and we will accommodate."

"See ya later, El," Quinn said then left the study, closing the door behind him.

Elodie's heart felt as though it faltered when she saw him leave. She knew he had no reason to stay by her side. Trevin would have, but then again Trevin was her vowed, Quinn wasn't. It would be weird if he stayed. That was what she told herself. She looked at Miles who motioned towards the seat and sat down.

He showed her the schedule and explained a little bit about what each one entailed. Later that evening she sat at their table. They had a large spread and Elodie savored the food but remained quiet, only speaking when spoken to. Miles and Olive were relaxed and asked her questions about her life in Marin County and places she had traveled to. They talked about various things with her and each other. Connor remained quiet and Quinn acted as though it were any other night.

After dinner, she sat by the firepit with her sketchbook and started drawing. Quinn came and sat next to her where she felt a little bit more at ease. She wanted to ask him about why he was upset with Trevin but she also felt exhausted from her wide range of emotions. They had five more days she figured and let it go for the night. Eventually she went to her room and spoke to Trevin until she went to sleep, hoping she would be ready for the week.

Chapter 14

The week began and she ran various lessons and went to various locations in the southern region. She ran Russ Park again in a much quicker time and there were lessons in the southeastern part of the county in areas she had never been to before. It felt like a different place entirely, reminding her more of the central part of the state.

As she walked this area, she took in the stark differences between this side of the territory and the part she lived in. The soil was lighter and dryer, the air warmer, especially in these summer months. The trees were sugar pines and firs. Other types of conifers that behaved differently from the sequoia. Often between her drills and tasks, she would stop to press her hand to the soil, trees, and rocks. Life pulsed in everything she touched but nothing ever talked to her or connected with her as the Old Giants did. It always left her a bit bewildered.

This was part of the home she had chosen but it wouldn't connect with her. All she could assume was that she was stressed and overwhelmed enough as it was, or maybe it was that she was aligned with Greenthistle and she was here in Ashdale's jurisdiction. Despite all the perfectly logical reasons she came up with, worry formed in her that the land didn't want to talk to her. She would notice Miles and Olive watching her do this at times but they never pried and she never voiced her worry.

Quinn had left Monday morning for drills and she hadn't seen them until their first lesson on Tuesday midday. So he hadn't been around Monday. He also wasn't around Tuesday after the lesson, or Wednesday. The exact thing Lord Greenthistle didn't want her to do was happening. She was growing disappointed in herself.

Even as she chastised herself for not talking to him Sunday night, she never did express this to Trevin on their nightly calls. Nor had she asked Quinn to stay either. He was either working a night shift with CalFire or staying with Justine. The dejection grew, and it wasn't even that she might be running lessons with Cedar. It was that she still had yet to try to help the heirs.

In the evening after dinner she would sit outside on Ashdale's luxurious patio. Olive usually sent out some boozy beverages and a charcuterie board for her to enjoy. Insisting they didn't need to but Elodie appreciated it all the same.

After she finished her wine one evening, Elodie walked off the deck and passed the clearing that made up the rest of the official backyard. There were no fence lines so it just opened up to the forest. She found a spot and sat down on the ground, the ferns nearly towering over her. Her eyes traveled up the trunk of an Old Giant and she exhaled slow and deep.

This is normal to doubt yourself but you needn't. You are learning a lot and a fresh vowed bond is also adding to the emotions. You miss the cub, and he misses you.

The Old Giant's voice flowed into her mind. Elodie's curiosity was grand and she learned a lot. They had wanted her to sit with them and expected it so she affirmed she would sit with them at least twice a week. Tonight, however, she had learned that not every territory had an Earth Blessed. Humboldt never had one, and so much of the old lore was accounts from other areas. They explained that the county was her land as much as it was the mortals and the fae. She was to protect it along with the three high estates. There were many things she wanted to ask, but it overwhelmed her trying to prioritize them all.

You have time. As long as you stay safe. In time you will travel again but right now it is important to settle into your new home. There is a lot to do, but remember your high estates serve you. They want to.

Elodie simply bowed her head and thanked them before getting up and brushing off what dirt she could. Upon getting back to the deck she tensed and took a step back. Connor looked at her with caution from where he was sitting at the table reading and taking notes.

"Sorry," Elodie softly.

"You say that a lot," he said, relaxing now.

"Sor—" She stopped herself and saw him smirk. She smiled back. "Hello Connor. I'm sure the other night didn't set the right impression of your Earth Blessed. I hope to set it right one day."

"I will admit I wasn't sure what to expect. I guess I didn't expect my brother's mortal interest to be so—snippy either. Autumn's interest seems nice though."

"Yea. Charles is a really nice person. Justine is too. Was. I can't blame her though. I left a very bad impression on everyone on the night of the ruins. I have a lot to fix."

"Well, guess we are all going to figure it out together, right?" he laughed. Elodie did too. "So the trees talk to you? Actually speak to you?"

"Yes," Elodie said and then took a seat across from him as she told him about how it all started. As she spoke she noticed Connor's curiosity grew. He was inquisitive. She learned that he was learning some of the language at the tome. His dad had started teaching him after the ruins and he would be looking at it too. He and Dee were pretty close and of all the estate kids, he was the most studious. The two usually hung out at the college parties.

"Cedar usually always hung out with the firstborns despite being closer in age to us but no one wants a cop hanging out at the college parties," Connor mused.

"That makes sense," Elodie responded. She was about to ask about Quinn's elusiveness but Connor spoke first.

"Don't worry about the bears, you will get the hang of communicating with them. Have you tried mountain lions yet?" Connor asked. Elodie just shook her head.

"I feel like I should have but Trev, nor his dad brought it up."

"There is a lot to learn, I am sure they are saving it for next week. The bears are curious about you. After you walked into the yard I saw two cubs trot towards you, before their mom called them back." Connor smiled.

"What?" Elodie gasped.

"In due time, I am sure you will have a lot of cubs following you. The ones that hang around the house will all welcome you soon enough."

After talking with him for a few more hours they both headed back to their rooms. Tomorrow she would work with him on communication with bears then she would have another endurance lesson with Quinn.

On Friday Elodie had just finished a lesson on high estate life when she saw the text from Cora asking her again to go to the bonfire. Declining, Elodie just replied with a 'next time' and headed off to another endurance lesson with Quinn. This was followed by a lesson with Connor and by the time that was over making the trek to Eureka then to the beach to have to socialize sounded exhausting.

She had trouble keeping up with Quinn but he kept pushing her, which led her to struggling in the communication lesson. Her frustration was growing but after Connor told her to breathe, she managed to get the bears to respond. She even got to pet one and hold one of the cubs while the mom sat nearby. She was hesitant at first but Connor assured her that the mom trusted her, and knew that Elodie was an Ashdale and their Earth Blessed. It was a much needed morale boost.

After the lessons were done for the day, she had showered then went to the study. There she met Connor and Miles to look at the tome. They worked on translating and decoding the alphabet together, but Elodie was baffled by the alphabet which was an enigma to her. Still, she tried to translate a page but often got distracted with the small illustrations and diagrams on the margins.

When dinner time rolled around, she sat at the table and noticed that Quinn was not there. He had likely already left for Justine's place and Elodie felt dejected once more.

Once back in her room waiting for Trevin's call, sadness crept over her. She couldn't pinpoint if it was how behind she was, or that the other trees wouldn't connect to her, or maybe that she had hardly seen Quinn. Tomorrow though she would be at her house for the evening. Trevin and her planned to get dinner with

Charles and Autumn before walking around Old Eureka for their arts festival. A small pop of excitement came when Trevin's call came.

"Hey, how was today?"

"Good. I got to hold a bear cub, it was cute. And I was able to call on them," she said with some excitement.

"That's really good to hear. Hopefully you can hold a mountain lion cub next week."

"I get to curl up next to my own mountain lion," she laughed.

Trevin smiled. "You do have your very own mountain lion that wants nothing more than to remain by your side."

She smiled wide and felt her cheeks heat. "How was your day?"

"I met my intern today. He already seems annoying." Trevin rolled his eyes. "His name is Austin, goes to the university and moved here from Shasta County. I prefer doing my trail maintenance alone, instead I have to monitor the camp sites while he shadows me."

"He is mortal? Not fae?"

"Yep, just a mortal."

Elodie nodded then a frown formed. "Are you going to the bonfire?"

"I was debating on it. Autumn and Cedar are going. They said I should too, but I don't know. It would be weird being there and knowing you are on the other side of the boundary. Is Quinn going tonight? Or is he going to hang out with you?" Elodie felt overcome with sadness at his question. "El?" he asked, concerned.

"He's going tonight I think."

"Are you sad about being there alone tonight?"

"No. I'm used to it I guess." Her voice was still sad.

"Being alone there?"

"Connor and I talked on Wednesday night, and we worked on the tome today," Elodie said in a small voice.

"How many nights has Quinn hung out with you?" Trevin inquired.

"Umm. Sunday night."

"That's it? He hasn't just hung out with you? Like at all?"

Elodie felt her voice shrivel up. "He was at breakfast and dinner a few nights this week."

"What the fuck? Has he even offered?"

"No, I didn't ask. I'm sorry, I know I said I'd try. I just, it feels like he's avoiding me."

"Little Mink, these weeks are so you can learn from our estates but also so you can feel comfortable with them. So you know you can rely on them. If he hasn't even been there for you to try, that's on him. Not you."

"But now I feel like I made it worse. You're mad at him. Besides, I will have days where I am by myself."

"Not these weeks though. Not right now. You know you are not going to be alone next week at Greenthistle. Autumn and Cedar will be there when I have my dumb graveyard shift."

"Are you upset?"

Trevin sighed. "No. He didn't even give you a chance to try. As we told you before, it's our responsibility. I will try this week at work. I promise."

"Alright. I know Justine is probably a handful for him to deal with. She would flip if she knew I was at Ashdale estate."

Trevin sighed. "Regardless of Justine, he should be there as your friend. You are the priority for all three high estates. Quinn has always been a bit oblivious at times. He doesn't take things seriously enough and then falls back on the Ashdale name because basically any grievance had to go through the three high estates. It is a privilege we all get. We all have our faults though."

"What is your fault? Cyrus?" Elodie asked, curious.

Trevin laughed softly to himself. "I'm too aloof or now, too emotional at times. Dad says all the emotions I seldom showed before are greater with the vowed bond. He is worried that if I show too much I could suffocate the room as an empathic seeker. He added a lesson every week just in case. Cyrus is an arrogant and cocky bastard and I'd be surprised if he hasn't broken a heart or two on both sides. At least he used to be."

Elodie nodded, thinking about what it was going to be like meeting Cyrus for the first time.

"Is he mad at me?" she asked with some hesitation.

"Who? Cyrus? I honestly don't know. I haven't spoken to him since he is still on house arrest. I'm not sure why he would be mad at you. He owes you a massive debt for saving his life. I hope you never have to do something like that again. He should grovel at your feet when you're there."

"No, that would be too much." She shook her head. "You should head to the bonfire, it's getting late."

"I'm not going. It'd be too suspicious anyways with us all there but you aren't?"

"I'm sure Quinn has his hands full tonight with Justine anyways."

"I knew she could be snippy but damn she needs to cool it, Quinn needs to take the situation with her more seriously too," Trevin noted.

Elodie and him continued to talk until sleep became a losing battle.

The next day Trevin arrived at two pm just as Elodie was heading downstairs with her backpack. Quinn was not present and Elodie had accepted the defeat.

Chapter 15

When Elodie had finished her first week at Ashdale Estate, the heir apparent of Nightswift Estate had stepped out of the confines of the house. It was the first time Cyrus had done so in three months. The first half of his sentence was over.

Cyrus had not wanted to go out. He could not escape the chains it seemed. Under the crowns of the Old Giants and the stars, both watched the raven with immense sorrow for what had transpired tonight.

A sob formed in his chest, making breathing a battle. The sensation of his lungs and throat constricting while gasping for air made him beg silently to himself. Something else was swirling under the sobs and the screams. It had been something he tried to ignore, too scared to face it just like everything else. He had held it all in. Yet this thing under the pain and despair the night had brought on him brimmed with his emotions. It scared him.

Through blurry eyes he looked at the stars. *Please,* he begged silently to any greater force out there. His voice could not form words. *Make it stop.*

The sensations all over his body coiled around him like serpents. He couldn't get this out of his head. *I'd take the chains. The beatings, the blood. Please.* Yet this feeling made him want to vomit. It slid under his shirt and pants. *Make her stop.*

"No!" Finally it boiled over. The screams and sobs were hardly comprehensible in his ears when he could feel it inside his ribs and down his spine. Her hands coiled around his neck now and Elodie wouldn't save him this time, *could not* save him. He hadn't gone to the tavern for this. He just wanted to know he wasn't a monster. But monsters certainly were out for him tonight.

Alena had found him mid panic attack in the alley behind the tavern. She pulled him away from town to a dark secluded area. Her hands and touch had become serpents that slid over his skin. Up and down they traveled all over him. It felt as though one had remained around his neck.

He scratched at it but he could not get it off. Of course he couldn't grab it, because it was not real. The serpents were not real. Alena's hands were though. What she had done was real.

Then she left him there in the dirt half undressed. He had gone catatonic, unable to move. Her parting gift was a slap and nails across his cheek. The pain registered but he didn't care. His raven didn't care. The only thing he cared about now was getting this sensation off him. The dirt and malice off him.

So he flew. Fast and hard.

He hadn't wanted his lockdown to be over, he hadn't wanted to go out of the house. His mom gently coaxed him, after his dad told him he had to. It had turned into yelling at him.

"My heir will not be reduced to being a caged bird," his dad hissed.

"Please, you need to move, your raven has been cooped up for months," his mom pleaded.

So Cyrus had sat in the trees, tucked away. Then for whatever stupid reason he decided to go into town and visit the tavern. He owed Alena closure and an apology. He couldn't imagine being intimate with anyone. And he didn't want to be seen as the one who tried to kill the Earth Blessed, or Trevin. He wanted to start by apologizing to Alena. Yet he had heard all their whispers and felt all their stares. The pressure of it all was one more set of chains he could not break free from.

Then a scent of sage and fuschia caught his attention, somehow telling him he was going to be okay as long as he followed it. If only he followed that scent instead of running from it. He was trembling and terrified all while the owner of that scent saw him near a mental breakdown.

His vowed was here, watching him. So he ran for the alley. Why now? Why was his vowed here now? Seeing him like this. Probably appalled they were vowed to such disappointment.

Then Alena had found him. Her touch made him writhe. It always had. The spirit had wanted her, not him. He tried explaining that but then she started to run her hands on his body, her lips on his skin. His mind had gone numb, he had blocked it out but was afraid to push her away for fear he'd hurt her. He screamed 'no' and 'stop' but the serpents didn't listen. She said she'd drag him into a trial, reminding him how he'd have to tell everyone what they were doing. Relive it with so many eyes. For a moment, he had to remind himself that Elodie *did* seal the spirit up. It had not gone into Alena; this was just who she was. Someone with greed and malice who thought she was entitled to whatever she wanted. The high estates and their heirs included.

His vowed would hear about him, thinking he wanted it. He had dated Alena after all, of course that would get asked during the trial. They would ask about all the things he had been forced to do, and the things he dared not speak.

All those serpents constricted on his wings and around his neck. He cawed in absolute despair just trying to make it home, to his room. The harder he fought the memory of her touch, the more he struggled. This was not comforting and soothing like Elodie's vines had been that night in the ruins. No, these were oozing with such malevolence.

Harder he flew, finally seeing the doors to Nightswift open upon his arrival.

He was going too fast to land, breathing too hard and flying too frantically to make anything but a stumbling crash landing in the entryway of the house. Still on the floor, he changed then pushed himself up on his hands and knees, trying to catch his breath.

Something metal hit the ground behind him and he leapt to his feet spinning around, heaving.

Poppy, his youngest sister, stood petrified. She had dropped her water flask, likely in shock at the sight of him.

"Cyrus," she whimpered, backing against the wall. He hadn't seen her in literally three months even though her room was a few doors down from his. This was what he had become in her eyes, a monster that terrified her. He wanted to tell her he was sorry, for all the things he had done, for the things he had not. The sight of her tears running down her cheeks, her fair skin turning red broke him. He ran upstairs without a word.

"Horrible, disappointing, monster." He fell to his knees. Elodie's blood on his hands, Alena grabbing at him. All of it was too much for him to carry. He didn't want to feel any of it, hated feeling all of it. Cyrus forced himself up into the shower and turned the lever all the way to hot. Once he had ripped his clothes off, he got under the scalding hot water and started scrubbing his skin furiously. Then he repeated it, not even acknowledging the burning of the hot water. Again he scrubbed, turning skin red and raw. He reached for the mouth wash to rinse his mouth and repeated that.

"Fuck," he screamed again then sank to the floor. "Fuck!" He was so exhausted from this torment that he didn't even care that he was curled up in the shower. His sobs made his voice raw.

A memory of that scent, that figure sulking away, the teal and white hair. "Why?" He curled in on himself even more. "Why now?" Cyrus knew he couldn't seek her out now. He didn't want to leave his room ever again. The thought of his parents finding out, or them threatening to take Alena to trial for this, if she didn't first. His parents, Greenthistle, Ashdale, Elodie, his vowed, they would know he was no Nightswift Raven worthy of the high estate lord status. The thought ripped another scream from him.

"Cyrus! Cyrus, hun." He heard his mom call from the room. He didn't bother getting up. He didn't care anymore. "Cyrus! The water is scalding hot!" She panicked and turned it off. His mom rubbed his head and he shivered away. "Cyrus." The hurt in her tone was obvious.

"What happened?" his dad demanded and Cyrus fought another scream but couldn't stop the tears. He felt humiliated. "His skin is so red. What happened?"

"Don't use that tone," his mom hissed out. Cyrus could not bring himself to look at his dad. He felt so pathetic. "What happened?" she asked softly, setting a towel over him.

"I'm a monster. No one trusts me. No one will see me as anything different. Just a monster. Not worthy of being heir," Cyrus cried.

"You will remain my heir, Cyrus. I did not raise you to be weak. You are strong." His dad's tone was stern.

"No, I'm not. I'm pathetic. I'm sorry. I'm sorry I let that thing do all of that. If I was strong enough I'd have been able to fight it. I hurt them all, I hurt Quinn and Cedar, I assaulted Autumn, I was going to force them to watch Trevin die." He paused, trying to breathe. "I made her bleed. I made the Earth Blessed bleed! They all hate me, they *should* hate me. I shouldn't be here anymore. I should have died with it. Why didn't Lord Greenthistle just let me die?" he sobbed.

"Cyrus. Please don't say those things. That is not true. I know it's not. You never wanted to hurt them." Ariyanna wiped her eyes.

"You will remain heir, because our entity deems it so. Do not give this up, do not let that girl's blood spill for nothing. She chose this. Now tell me what happened tonight. I assume it was not Trevin or Quinn?"

"No! I haven't talked to either of them in months." He pushed himself to sit up. "I will get up and go to bed."

"What happened?" Bracken's tone was stern causing Cyrus to flinch again.

"I—I went out tonight to the tavern. I just thought, I just wanted someone to see me as something other than a monster but they all said I was a monster, unstable. Trevin should have killed me, I should be stripped as heir. Disappointment, monster."

"They're only words. This is why you need to tell them what happened, this is why you need to talk to someone. Anyone," Bracken demanded.

"I will go to bed." Cyrus pushed himself up, feeling even more humiliated as he picked himself up off the shower floor.

"But you will not sleep, you will scream and cry."

"Can I have a sedative then?"

"No!" his dad shouted, causing him to stumble back against the wall. He saw his mom glare at his dad. "Cyrus, a sedative, just puts a band-aid over a festering wound that cannot ever breathe."

Cyrus swallowed hard and nodded. "Okay. I will get into bed. I will be quiet." He walked forward.

"Cyrus, I order you to not put a sound barrier up either." Cyrus dropped his head at his dad's command. "I know how to read you. Lady Elodie will be here next Sunday evening. You will apologize to her and you will talk to her that first night. She fought for you. She wanted to. I will not lose my heir to some night terrors, not when we have an Earth Blessed who swore her alliance to us. Who spilled blood for you. Do you understand?"

"Yes, sir." Cyrus's voice was so small he could barely hear himself.

"I will send a meal up. Just try to get through the night without sedation," his mom said with a smile but Cyrus could hear the pleading in her voice.

He nodded and walked into his closet. When he heard his parents leave, he cried as silently as he could. "I'm sorry." His body leaned back against the wall. "I'm sorry."

Once he was back in bed fidgeting with the blankets and wiping his eyes, he thought of his vowed, not that he had even seen their face. "I don't know how to be better for you. Whoever you are."

The door opening caused him to tense. His mom set a tray of food down on the bed and smiled at him. He could tell she had cried. He hated being the cause of his mom's stress. She was so regal and strong, and he was causing her to fracture because he was such a disappointment. If only he could just grab hold of something, anything to get himself out of this pit he had fallen into.

"I knew the tavern was a bad idea, it was too much too soon. I'm sorry."

"You know they are just words. They said similar things about Trevin too." She paused and all Cyrus could do was nod. "You father is sorry for his tone. He sometimes isn't the best at being soft. At times I think he sees the way Echo handled Trevin and feels it was best. But I'm not sure it was the best for Trev to be raised that way. Luckily I see enough of his mom in him still, and Lady Elodie will guide him through the rest. I think she will want to help you, I don't think leaving you behind was ever her intention. And I am sorry you have been so isolated here. I am nervous with how Quinn acted though, that it isn't going to help."

"It's ok. I am not ready to see them either." Cyrus sighed then looked at his mom. "May I—can I see Poppy tomorrow? I want to apologize to her. I know she is terrified of me. I didn't want to make her cry or be mean to her. I was just scared that thing would go for them too." With his mom's silence his shoulders slumped. "I don't mind if it's supervised. Stick every single sentry in there."

"I think she would like that. I will ask her tomorrow?"

Cyrus nodded and his mom stood up. She hugged him and for a second he tensed. He wanted to tell her. He should tell her. She wouldn't be mad at him for this, she had never once been mad at him during this time, but she was under so much stress because of him. He knew as well as she did he could not approach his vowed like this, so why bother telling her.

"You're going to be alright, Cyrus. Your father nor I care about the powershift. We just want you to be alright. We hope you know that."

All he could do was nod. Then he was alone in his room.

"I scented my vowed today, Mom," he said, knowing she would not hear. After ten minutes of forcing himself to eat, his stomach protested. Then it was another night of fighting not only memories of Inanis the spirit, but now Alena's serpents too.

Trevin held Elodie close as they lay together in her bed. His arms were wrapped around her stomach as he spooned her. She was fast asleep, her arms loosely draped over his. Her heart rate was calm and steady. Last week had been rough on him and he had missed her so much. It was part of a newly formed vowed bond, his dad and Miles explained. Trevin was sure it would cool down eventually but right now he didn't want it to. Ensuring she felt safe, that she could trust him to be there without a doubt was a priority for him. Especially since Quinn didn't care to be there.

As he lay there with her, he couldn't help but recall earlier when they were getting ready for bed. They got ready for things that usually occurred before slumber found them. It had been a week after all. Yet he felt her body tense then a tremble took over her. As if a chill seized her spine. It made her eyes water and she said pain radiated inside her before it was gone just as fast as it had come on. The absolute despair in her eyes was something he hated seeing on her.

"The Old Giants are sad yet silent," she'd said.

His dad had reported nothing wrong; no one had felt anything. Then when he suggested that Nightswift send a raven out, she grew worried and instantly told him not to. Next week was going to be so hard for her. Cyrus would likely ignore her even more than Quinn did. Not that he was entirely upset with him staying away from her.

That wasn't a good thought pattern to have and he knew it. She needed to feel comfortable with Quinn and Cyrus. She needed to be able to trust them as much as she trusted Greenthistle. Building that trust was Quinn and Cyrus's responsibility. He couldn't force them to all be best friends.

Not wanting to dwell on those thoughts, he carefully removed one arm and grabbed his phone to send his dad a message.

Nothing was reported to Nightswift by the ravens?

Nothing at all. I asked Bracken. Want to send them out to search?

Trevin sighed and looked at Elodie again, fast asleep. She had told them to send no ravens. They still scared her. He told his dad no and set his phone down.

Just as carefully as before, he resumed his original position and kissed her shoulder softly. "I will do everything I can to ensure you are safe, Little Mink." His voice was low and gentle.

He lay there until he too found sleep.

CHAPTER 16

With a slow start to the day, Elodie and Trevin packed their things and headed off to Greenthistle for the week. Her lessons would cover everything she had learned at Ashdale Estate and more. Twice this week she would be expected to return to her house and back to Greenthistle estate alone. The second time she would be timed so as to determine how quickly she could get between houses. Trevin would be busy most of Monday with drills. On Tuesday and Thursday, they would be working opposite since he had night shifts with State Parks and she had lessons during the day. Echo had gone over the schedule with her as Trevin sat by her side. He inquired about their bargain and naturally she did feel dejected.

"While I do have to uphold the bargain, please do not take this as a complete loss. This will be good for you, Trevin, and Cedar get used to the dynamic. I will have Autumn step in as well and allow Trevin to observe. Overseer duties and all."

"Understood," Elodie reluctantly accepted.

"That said, you didn't fail, nor should you feel as though you did. You tried on the first day and it was Quinn who didn't seem to give you a chance after. In all honesty that raises my concerns that he might need a tighter rein after all."

Elodie slumped down in her seat.

"He disregarded his assigned tasks. Our heirs know better. Have known better long before you. Big responsibilities are nothing new to them. One as simple as spending time with a friend should have been effortless for him. You tried, Lady Elodie. You did not fail," Echo explained.

To her surprise, she felt less upset about the situation. Ashdale would be a concern later. Her focus this week was Cedar.

They had two lessons that afternoon involving target practice with her vines, followed by more response exercises. Despite things coming easier to her, she still felt that she needed improvement. Echo and Trevin offered her plenty of encouragement though.

When it was time for dinner she sat at the table. Autumn and Cedar were present. It certainly was another dinner with family yet some part of her had strayed further into the ocean of doubts. She didn't feel comfortable voicing any of it yet because she didn't understand what she was feeling, so instead she glanced towards the window, looking at the redwoods. They watched her back but didn't say anything, as though waiting for her to go sit with them.

She knew there would be time this week. Maybe she could ask them how to ease the self-doubt away. Trevin's hand took hers and when she shifted her eyes, she noticed Echo watching her. She cringed at his inquisitive look. He was always assessing.

"Did they tell you something?" Trevin asked softly.

"No." Her response was short and her cheeks heated.

"Lady Elodie," Echo said calmly.

Elodie brought her eyes to meet his. "Yes, sir."

"Don't get lost in all the thoughts. I encourage you to voice them to any of us."

"Of course, sir. I am grateful for you all and to be accepted." A small smile formed and she looked down, reaching for her fork despite feeling everyone's eyes on her.

"There's plenty more to drink if you think that will help," Cedar laughed. "I am happy to get you some of Dad's expensive stuff."

Elodie heard the warmth in his tone and something in her swelled. A cry halted in her throat but it was not out of sorrow. She was grateful for Greenthistle. For giving her a chance. One she hoped to not mess up. The cry came out as a small, strained laugh.

"Thank you, Cedar. I am alright though."

"Well maybe after one of our lessons?" He took his glass in his hand.

"Maybe," she laughed and squeezed Trevin's hand. "I hope I don't annoy too many mountain lions this week."

"Nah, they're all curious about you," Cedar laughed

"I'm not sure if that's a good thing or a bad thing?" Elodie laughed again.

"It's a good thing. They're happy an Earth Blessed aligned with us, with them," Autumn chimed in.

"Go easy on me tomorrow. I'm slow and weak as I found out at Ashdale."

"No, I've seen you, you're amazing. Don't even worry about times or errors," Autumn insisted. Elodie smiled.

"It is all true, Lady Elodie. You are doing remarkably well. Ashdale reported you did last week as well."

"Thank you, sir." Her smile was a bit bigger and some of the doubt had been erased.

Trevin leaned into her a bit.

She leaned back into him and continued to listen to the conversation, still not eager to lead it.

As Monday morning came, Trevin kissed her so many times that he was nearly late for his drills.

"Trevin! Miles is going to be livid. Go to drills. She's perfectly safe with Autumn and I today," Echo sighed, clearly unamused.

"I know, I know," Trevin huffed out before he changed into feral and made for the door.

"Lady Elodie, I'm sorry to have to send him off for the day. It is a lesson in itself that we can monitor his level of control and drive. Know that on your days and nights away from each other he began to resemble his old apathetic self, but he certainly has a fire inside him now."

"I understand why we have some time apart. I actually haven't had someone so attentive before. It helps that he seldom has to guess what I am feeling." She laughed nervously.

"It does make things easier. I must say it is a shock to see him so attached, but that is what a vowed bond will do. Next month, when your Ashdale week begins, you will be at drills with them. Miles, Bracken, and I will all be present as well."

"Does that mean all three heirs will be at drills too?" she asked nervously.

"Yes, it does. On your week off, we will have drills at Nightswift and resume the rotations which will line up with your week at Ashdale."

"Understood, sir." Elodie took a deep inhale.

"You will be alright, little cub. Now let's proceed to today's first lesson."

Elodie ran through more of the reaction drills. Autumn joined, helping with her agility. Then they moved onto sparring. Echo was in charge of coaching and Autumn was her partner. They both assured Elodie she would not hurt Autumn. After some hand-to-hand combat, they incorporated her vine and eventually merged everything they had done today. Elodie got the hang of each individual drill with the exception of winning a match against Autumn. But when she merged everything, she couldn't focus and the frustration began to grow. She would miss targets, stumble over her feet, hesitate when Autumn or Echo jumped out unexpectedly. She hadn't mastered much at Ashdale either.

During one of the runs, she was trying to focus on everything and the doubts poured once again. When Autumn lunged out, she stumbled backward down the rocks she had just climbed. As her body fell, she felt an impact on her rib and cried out. Echo was by her side in the blink of an eye.

"Elodie! I'm sorry," Autumn rasped, running up to her.

Echo's hands hovered over Elodie's body. "Shhh, I'm going to place my hands on your side to heal it, okay?" Elodie nodded and firm hands touched her side. She felt his magic mending the bone, making the pain decrease, yet the tears still continued to fall. "I don't need Trev's gifts to see your fears and doubts. You are wanted. You are loved dearly. I am sorry for ever putting you both in a position where you had to question that." Echo's words were soft and soothing.

Listen to him. You are home, you know this.

Sit with us.

Elodie watched the trees and the ferns, eventually pushing herself up to sit.

"Any pain?" Echo asked.

"No, sir."

"Good. I think that is enough for drills today. We will resume tomorrow. Ari and Olive will be over tomorrow morning to help you learn about high estate life. Autumn will join. Then Trev and I will monitor Cedar's lesson on communication. Then some conditioning ending with you running to your residence and back." Elodie nodded and glanced at the trees again. "Go get cleaned up and relax until dinner."

After getting up and assuring Autumn it wasn't her fault, Elodie went to Trevin's room. Their room she had to remind herself still. Once she was bathed and in clean clothes, the backyard was the next destination. A spot seemed to beckon her to sit, ferns arched over her and an Old Giant within arm's reach.

She wasn't sure what she was feeling, and why it all felt so heavy. It was everything all at once. It was the sheer love from Greenthistle accepting her, this family that she belonged to now, this world she was part of. She felt a sense of remorse for what had been lost, longing for her parents, and even the familiarity of Marin at times. A sadness hit her too that the three heirs were so divided, then a fear of next week at Nightswift gripped her after that. There was also a hint of rejection that Quinn hadn't really been there when she needed him. It almost struck her as odd that Cedar had been around for her more than Quinn, though she was certain that was because he felt he had to be.

Do not discredit the youngest cub. He truly feels remorse.

He misses his brother, and wants you to know he is here for you too. Look into his eyes next time you see him.

Elodie nodded and asked more questions, but also shared some hopes for this week. That she was excited to meet mountain lions, to overcome that fear of them and establish a mutual respect for each other. She almost asked about the words and visions she got when she opened the tome, but was too scared of the meaning, Instead she asked if the Old Giants would be there next week for Nightswift. She had a solstice to get through, and a house that probably didn't think much of her.

There is never a place where you will feel our absence. Even when you are beyond our groves, you will know we are here.

Now, chin up little cub. Your vowed is eager to see you.

"Thank you." Her voice was soft and meant for the earth alone.

As she walked back towards the deck she saw Trevin, who looked relieved to see her.

"There you are. I was worried. My dad didn't see you come out here. Are you alright?"

"Yes. They want me to sit with them. I started doing it last week at Ashdale."

"Do you talk to them, or is it more meditative?" Trevin asked. He must have just gotten back, his clothes and hair a mess.

"Both? They answer some of my questions, tell me it's normal to feel everything all at once like this. They're sharing a lot of knowledge and it's a heavy weight. They have strong sturdy trunks to hold it all. I have emotions, so they tell me what I can hold now."

"Are you feeling alright?"

Elodie paused and met his eyes. He raised his eyebrows in question as he scanned her.

"What are you seeing right now?"

"Curiosity? Hesitation. There is sadness and a general sense of doubt? You are questioning a lot. There is some happiness there too though. Dejection as well but also more confidence." He paused. "You're growing and you want this role but you're still unsure?"

Elodie nodded, knowing there was no use in denying any of it. He could see it all. "How do you see those things? How do you see emotions? Do they take a shape or a color or something?"

"I see into someone as though I am on a path with multiple gates I could push open. Some are locked up and closed off. Those feelings are usually the ones the person is most scared of revealing. Other gates are lit up, others wide open. Over time I have pieced together a connection between some emotions."

He then laughed softly and took her hand. "When we first locked eyes at that party, I could see your attraction and curiosity. When you looked at Autumn and Charles talking, I thought for sure I'd see your jealousy that your friend was fawning over Autumn, but I didn't. Instead, I saw endearment and you smiled at them."

Elodie smiled and felt her cheeks heat.

"Now I see the gate light up that you are embarrassed or bashful. When I was delirious with floss flower oil, I ignored all the gates that lit up. Your eyes were all I focused on. When I finally heard your words, telling me to wake up, I saw the path and I saw how terrified, sad, and distraught you were."

She nodded and squeezed his hand. He pulled her into a hug then went up to their room. As Trevin cleaned up, Elodie asked about what Cyrus's gates looked like, and Quinn's. Everyone had similar gates as everyone had some emotions that were universal, but some gates he only saw in her, or in others. If the gate was opened and empty, or the light was off so to speak, it meant the person was not feeling those particular emotions. He used the example of her lack of jealousy towards Autumn and in fact, the only time he ever saw jealousy in her was after she had seen the picture of Alena and him. How he hated it too because he never wanted to be in that position to begin with.

When Elodie compared this to what she had seen in others so far it was different. She didn't see gates, but rather felt the word was the best way she could explain it. Elodie figured it was the same as assuming as people usually did. It wasn't Trevin's gift at all. *Maybe I didn't get anything when we vowed ourselves. I already have the Old Giants in me. I don't think it's fair that I have both powers.*

When they had dinner with his siblings and dad, Elodie couldn't help but notice Autumn was a bit nervous, and again Elodie tried to focus on how she was gathering that information. When nothing was mentioned on Autumn's nerves, Elodie knew calling her on it would likely make the situation worse. So she dropped it and enjoyed the night with Trevin.

Chapter 17

The next day she insisted Trevin sleep before meeting Olive and Ariyanna. They covered Nightswift's, Greenthistle's, and Ashdale's domain and how the regional and local councils worked. She learned about how mortals drew the county lines and what that meant for the high estates of those now defunct counties that had to integrate with the now existing counties.

She ran more sparring and agility drills and continued to work at merging everything together with Echo, Autumn, and Trevin. Cedar was present but remained silent until leading her through a communication lesson with mountain lions where Echo and Trevin observed.

Elodie felt frustrated not being able to communicate with the mountain lions but was able to run between her house and Greenthistle Estate. It was almost like second nature to her. She took the victory and knew she would keep working hard.

The nights Trevin was working, Autumn and Cedar were there to keep her company. Cedar had asked it was okay if he hung out with them but understood if she wasn't. Elodie could tell he was trying and she didn't want to deny him the chance. Yet she was also grateful Autumn was there too. They told her Trev had found out about her fractured rib when he was reviewing notes on her reaction times.

"He was in the study while you were with Olive and Ariyanna," Cedar explained. "When he saw the log he snapped at Dad, who assured him that everything stopped and he had healed you in seconds. Dad is the strongest healer in the territory after all."

"He didn't take any anger out towards anyone right?" Elodie's concern grew. "I hope they weren't talking about my inability to communicate or on the course."

Autumn just laughed as though her brother's anger were no big deal. "Trev was angry but he knew it was an accident. All he did was just glare and told me to be more careful and stormed off to wait to smother you with affection. No one is disappointed in you either."

Cedar laughed. "He's ridiculous. The vowed bond is something else. I've never seen him so ready to fight everything."

Elodie frowned. That pit was forming in her stomach again. Her mind pacing from one damning thought to the next. All these disruptions she didn't know how to fix.

"El? What is it?" Cedar asked, setting his glass down.

She tried to compose herself. "Nothing. I'm fine."

"Don't lie, you clearly are upset and have been for some time. We have all noticed it and we want to help you. All of us. Even Cedar," Autumn prodded.

"What the hell?" he laughed. "But seriously. Speak freely with Autumn and I."

Elodie smiled genuinely this time instead of the one she forced a few seconds ago. "Thank you both. It's nothing you said, Cedar." She paused and looked down. "I love Trevin so much but I don't want him to feel like he has to fight his family over me. To throw away everything he is working towards."

"El, Trev isn't going to have to fight any of us for you. We have all sworn to you and him that we are here for you," Autumn explained. "I'm not scared of my big brother's wrath, and neither is Cedar or Dad. So he has been a little neurotic, it's expected, especially given what he is," she laughed.

"There is a reason I train with the guard so much more than he does. Empathic Seekers can get irate, it's why it is imperative they have the balance and a guard that can stand up to them. I am here for you both. Even when he is being moody and you are overwhelmed. All of us are happy to have you here, as a Greenthistle."

"If only I could communicate with more than one mountain lion. They all stayed so far away today. The bears didn't."

"They sense you are overwhelmed and still scared of them. They are giving you space. You will connect with them. I am willing to bet it has something to do with the dynamic you have with Connor versus me. Connor is so soft spoken and quiet compared to Quinn. You started from scratch with Connor. You're starting from a very bad start with me and it's my fault entirely."

"But I do trust you, Cedar. I trust all of Greenthistle. And Quinn wasn't even there for the lesson with Connor, either of them. Just Lord Ashdale."

"I heard," Cedar groused. "What an ass. Don't worry if it takes you all summer to connect with mountain lions. You are not doing anything wrong."

"They will still keep you safe, El. They all know you are so important in many ways," Autumn said and leaned against Elodie.

Over along Avenue of the Giants in Humboldt State Redwoods, Trevin worked his shift with his intern, Austin. He knew he shouldn't be annoyed or angry that he had an intern to oversee or that he was working, but Elodie was at Greenthistle, and he wanted to make sure she was comfortable. Though he had no doubt Autumn was keeping her company.

He knew this was coming too; it wasn't as though he hadn't worked nights since he and Elodie had become a thing. It just felt different this week. Accepting that it was going to be a long trying summer for everyone, a loud sigh escaped him.

"You stressed about something?" Austin asked, causing Trevin to roll his eyes.

"Just a lot on my plate."

"Home stuff?" Austin asked, almost a little too eager for Trevin's liking.

"Stuff. Have you finished reconciling those campsite logs?"

"Not yet," Austin laughed and got back to his task.

A chill had passed over Trevin suddenly, causing him to instantly look towards the window. He fixed on them and tried to sort what he had felt. The sensation stirred a tension in him and yet something told him all was well. He wasn't sure if it was a whisper or a sensation or what, but it did confuse him. Wasting no time pulling his cell phone, Trevin sent a text out to Elodie then to his family asking if she was alright.

"So, you married or got a partner? Kids?" Austin's tone grated on Trevin. It rubbed him wrong that such questions would even be asked. He turned and saw Austin grinning at him. Trevin really was finding it difficult to not hate Austin already.

"Engaged, no kids," he said shortly knowing he had to answer.

"Oh, congratulations." Austin's tone softened, now a little less grating.

"Thanks," Trevin muttered and looked at his phone. Elodie messaged saying she was fine. Autumn and Cedar hung out with her on the patio and they had wine by the fire pit. Then another text said she was in bed and bundled up. A relieved sigh came out of him.

"What does your fiancé do for work? How did you meet?"

Trevin looked up, seeing Austin again looking right at him with a smile. *Damn. Is everyone going to test my nerves as of late?* "She's in education. And we met at a party."

"Teacher? Nice. She is off for the summer. I take it?"

"Yes." Trevin took a deep inhale, fixing his eyes right on Austin who stared right back with that grin. "Given what she does, I don't tend to share a lot about her. Safety and all. So get back to sorting those logs. We got to do rounds when you are done."

"Of course, understood, Mr. Greenthistle."

Trevin broke eye contact when his phone buzzed. His dad said all was fine. It was a quiet night, Elodie did well on her reaction drills and he would be changing up the drills to try to catch her off guard. Trevin could not shake this feeling about Austin. He supposed it might be his general irritation and stress but he was not going to take any chances now. He promptly messaged his dad.

Can you grab a full file on someone?

Why? And Who?

Intern is giving me an uneasy feeling.

Could be the vowed bond, but I will pull it and go over it with you tomorrow.

Austin set the stack of paper down and sat back in the chair. "All done, sir."

Trevin looked at him again with that smile. Again he looked at Austin, seeing nothing more than eagerness and curiosity. Another sigh slipped out of him. "Alright, good. Let's do the rounds and ensure everything is good. We will do that again at two and five. Afterwards I will show you how to prepare the check-out form for the morning shift.

"Sounds good," Austin said, standing up. "So, were you born here?"

"Yes." Trevin's answer was short.

"Travel a lot?"

"Enough," Trevin answered as they walked out of the office.

"Fiancé born here or?"

Trevin sighed again. "Generally this is quiet time, so we tend to keep it down on night rounds. People are putting out their fires and putting their food in the bear boxes so keep an eye out to make sure that they are doing it right and the dark campsites have no smoldering embers."

"Got it," Austin said, eager as ever.

The remainder of the night went much the same and Trevin was running out mindless tasks to give Austin. He savored the quiet peace when it was his break or Austin's and was eager for the shift to be over. Usually Trevin talked to Elodie on nights he worked. They would video call for a bit and text a bit more until she fell asleep. However, Trevin wanted to be extra cautious now.

Finally, the end of the shift came.

"Good job tonight. I will fill your report out on Friday morning and leave it in your box."

"See ya Thursday, Trev." Austin grinned, causing Trevin to glare one last time.

Then Trevin headed off to his truck and drove it back to another site then bolted off into the forest. Relief flooded him when he scented Elodie and part of him wanted to just crawl into bed with her before she got up for his lessons and sleep for a few hours until her agility lesson in the afternoon.

Instead, he went into the study and closed the door. His dad slid the folder forward.

"He is a mortal from Shasta. Transferred last year to CalPoly Humboldt and if he stays on track, probably has another three semesters to go in their forestry program. Did you see anything nefarious in him?" Echo asked.

"No. Just eagerness and curiosity, but his smile and how much he watched me made me uneasy," Trevin sighed and sat back. "Maybe it is just the vowed bond, paired with Cyrus's damned grin. Austin's isn't the same but still it is just outright annoying. Then he kept asking about Elodie even when I told him to stop."

"You didn't reveal anything about her, right? We need to be careful especially with the warnings she got."

"No, he guessed she was a teacher but I changed the subject after that."

"Well what I got from Shasta was pretty boring. Average grades in school, no issues with law enforcement. Played football. Parents are still living and working in Redding. I admit I didn't dig as deep into his family tree as I did Elodie's but no traces of fae blood in the last four generations."

Trevin slumped back in his chair. "Damn it. Of course I had to get an annoying intern who just doesn't shut up."

"Just stay alert, I cannot imagine Shasta would send anyone to try to gain intel on her. Word obviously has spread that you are vowed. I have to put it in the report to the council too," his dad explained.

"I know. I'm sure they will all see it immediately. I'm just relieved Marin stands with us. I was worried for a moment they might actually try to take her back."

"I know, son. It always was a fear of yours. But she is home." Echo picked up the folder and put it aside. "She isn't talking much, nor is she calming down as much as I had hoped."

Trevin's shoulders slumped and he frowned. "I know. I sense her growing doubts. I know she trusts us, but what more can I do aside from insisting we both quit our jobs and smothering her?"

"There is nothing else you need to do; you are doing everything I hoped you would. But I am worried she isn't going to be ready. Miles expressed concerns with it too."

"Quinn didn't help. That bastard," Trevin muttered.

"No, he certainly didn't."

"I will see if I can get her to open up. No one is going to take her though. I'm not the bait either, that's why I wanted this file."

Echo nodded then took an inhale. "Trevin. Bracken informed me something happened to Cyrus on Saturday night when he was off house arrest but he will not talk about it. He said he just came home and they found him screaming in a scalding hot shower huddled on the floor."

Trevin sighed in distaste. "What am I supposed to do about that? If he doesn't want to talk it's not my problem. He better not hurt Elodie next week."

"I don't think he can hurt a blade of grass in his current state. It's going to be a rough week, but it is necessary."

"I'm going to go to our room." Trevin stood up. He certainly was feeling stress.

Echo nodded and Trevin left the study.

Chapter 18

By Thursday, Elodie still felt some lingering sadness but it didn't feel as heavy today. This was a sign that she was beginning to find a rhythm, at least she hoped. When Trevin left for his night shift, she went out beyond the backyard for her lesson. It was then when the nerves and doubts crept back in.

Cedar wasn't here yet, so she waited for a bit. Leaning against one of the Old Giants, her eyes traveled up to the sky. The stars, framed by the crowns of the Redwoods, shone bright. Elodie had a sense they were watching too, only it was something other than the Old Giants. Then she realized the stars had some life force yet to wink out of existence. For a moment her mind began to wonder why the spirit showed a white void. There was a certain stillness in the dark of night and yet that white void had been eerily still. She could tolerate the quiet stillness of night, she even found solace in it these last few nights because she knew she was never really alone. An estate that had done so much to make her feel accepted was only a few yards away. Yet that stillness of the void wasn't something she ever wanted to encounter again.

Elodie suddenly realized the Old Giants hadn't spoken to her, they just watched. Then she realized how long she had been just standing there staring at the sky and that Cedar still wasn't here. A blood-curdling scream made her tense and flex her hands, ready for whatever may be out there. Something rustled behind her and she spun around not seeing anything.

Mountain lion. That scream was a mountain lion shriek, she thought and inhaled.

"Okay, relax and do your best to communicate with it, until Cedar gets here."

She still hadn't seen it. Surely one wouldn't attack her at Greenthistle. That was absurd. A low growl sounded behind her, causing her to spin around, yet she did not see it. Recalling everything they had taught her on Tuesday she tried to call on them, to connect with it. Deep breaths came from her as she tried coaxing it forward or to chuff. She had her dagger and Trevin's scent all over her.

When her eyes scanned the forest, she stilled. One had its eyes locked on her, watching.

Come on, chuff or look away. Drop the predatory gaze. I'm Trevin's vowed, I'm Earth Blessed. Please. Her heart hammered against her chest and then impulsively, she looked towards the house, hoping Cedar was coming. When she looked back at the animal, it had begun stalking towards her with focused eyes. These were not the familiar green she had grown accustomed to. These were an amber color. No chance of it being Autumn either.

Then she noticed another watching her just beyond the one stalking. It too began towards her with a growl. Four more came out of the shadows. All of them fixed on her with various growls and shrieks, making her jump.

"Please stop! I'm aligned with Greenthistle. I'm Earth Blessed."

One shrieked and Elodie's eyes shifted to it for a second, something was more familiar about it than the others. She looked to the one nearest her and tried tapping into it. Her eyes fixed on the familiar one and she gasped, taking a step back. She had seen this one before.

"Cedar," she choked out. It chuffed in acknowledgement and stopped its stride.

"Good, you can recognize me, El." His tone was warm and relaxed. She noticed the other mountain lions stopped where they were, watching as one of their heirs now strode up to her. He nuzzled her hand, letting a chuff slip out.

"Communicating with me is a little different but I could see you applying what we did on Tuesday. They sense your fear and see it as resistance. Trust them and trust in yourself. Letting them see you interact with me like this will help.

We sometimes referred to them as keget, which is the Yurok word for them," he explained.

"Oh," she choked out and rubbed his head.

Cedar walked around beside her as her hand ran along his fur. "Besides, if Trev was here tonight there would be no way tonight's lesson would work. Trust me and trust yourself," he said with a laugh. He then crouched down right in front of her and bared his fangs. Her body was tense and she took a step back. "Relax and trust me. Let them see how you might come to trust them. I know I'm not your favorite, and they know that too. That's why I was the best option for these lessons."

"What are you doing?" Elodie asked.

He let out a chuff. "A little game of cat and mouse. Only I don't know who's who," he laughed. "Trevin would have me pinned on the ground so fast if he knew this was in the lesson tonight."

"Cedar?"

"I know you won't hurt me. Even when you were consumed with despair and I was the cause of it, you told me to stay with you, so I will. Humboldt's keget will stand by you if you ask them to. They know what you did, they all do. How you saved Quinn and Autumn, how you pulled Greenthistle's heir and Nightswift's heir back from the brink of death."

"I did what they asked me to do. I did what I had to," Elodie said, taking more steps back.

"Now, keep doing it." Cedar then lunged at her.

Elodie ran and tripped, falling forward on the dirt. She could feel Cedar land right beside her. "Let's try that again."

"I thought your dad said we weren't sparring partners?"

"We aren't sparring. We are playing a game," Cedar said, trotting off. "Get up."

"How does scaring me help me communicate with them?" She pushed herself up and got to her feet, not bothering to dust herself off.

"Ask them."

"I'm not going to turn a bunch of mountain lions on you, Cedar." Elodie took a deep inhale.

"I would be impressed if you did," he laughed. "Watch them, show them you rely on them. That you want to. Use them to detect where I am. Then when I lunge, apply what Trev, Autumn, and my dad have taught you about defense. I know you won't hurt me," Cedar said and she heard a twig snap to her left. She turned and looked at the mountain lions laying nearby. Their heads moved and so did their ears. Her eyes caught sight of a tail twitch as she moved her feet to follow the subtle movements of the mountain lions.

When one of the mountain lions' ears swiveled just as her eyes glanced over, she stopped and watched intently.

Then she saw one stand up and gaze at her intently. This one had been lying near where Cedar had vanished into the foliage. It came to a crouch, which confused her. *Why would this one be crouching facing me if Cedar was behind it?*

It was facing her, but its eyes were not on her. They were just past her. She spun around just in time to see Cedar crouch and lunge at her again. This was the very image of him she had seen before on her first night over here. When he was lunging at Trevin.

Elodie stepped back and tripped this time, falling flat on her back seeing Cedar leap in the air coming right for her. Instinct brought her hands up, shooting her vines out and flipping Cedar right over her. Realization hit her that he was going to land on his back, so she ripped the vines back just in time for him to twist his body, landing him on his hind leg.

He bounced up to his feet just in time and chuffed.

"That was awesome! Let's do it again. Ask them to show you where I am coming from," Cedar directed through their mind link.

Once he disappeared into the foliage, Elodie stood watching the mountain lions. *Keget, guide me, please. I want to serve Greenthistle. Always.*

Then she noticed a mountain lion to her left look past her. She turned to find another one sitting up as its eyes trailed the foliage line. The ones nearby swiveled their ears and she watched until suddenly one snapped its head in the opposite direction. She turned to face Cedar lunging again at her, only this time she held her ground, eyeing the animal as it closed the distance between them with its descent.

She jumped back on a graceful step, followed by two stumbling steps until she stabilized herself on another mountain lion. Her eyes shot wide as it fixed its eyes on her.

Thank you. Elodie tried to slow her breathing. Then it chuffed at her and her smile grew wide.

"Excellent. Again," Cedar said and they repeated the exercises a few more times, where the mountain lions responded more to helping her. Every time Cedar would lunge, she would either use her vines or scurry out of the way and each time she got surer on her footing. Until he charged her.

Her eyes shot wide and she stumbled back, tripping once more and restraining Cedar.

As soon as she caught her breath, she retracted her vines and sat up so fast that she felt slightly dizzy.

Cedar stalked right up and stood nearly nose to nose with her.

"I knew you'd get it. No patterns next month," he chuffed again.

Elodie swallowed hard and then noticed someone walk out on the deck.

"Mother above, Cedar, are you trying to make your brother more neurotic? You two better not fight in the house," Echo lectured.

Cedar changed back into fae and laughed. "It worked. But be sure you shower really well and take your clothes to the laundry room. Trev is going to be pissed."

"Yes, go get cleaned up before you get into bed tonight. I started watching when I noticed the teal flashes. Very impressive, Lady Elodie," Echo followed up.

"Thank you, both."

Once Elodie was cleaned up and had a small meal, she curled up in Trevin's hoodie and nodded off. The magic use still left her pretty tired, but she was happy things were finally starting to come easier to her.

CHAPTER 19

When Trevin walked through the door the next morning, he went into the study and pulled out Austin's file again. His eyes scanned the same documents he had seen on Wednesday. A birth certificate that matched with his age, enrollment forms with the university, and his job application to state parks. When he scrolled over his statement of qualifications, the section for interested locations made him pause. Humboldt State Redwoods and Grizzly Creek, Trevin's assigned locations. Sitting back in his dad's chair, he mindlessly tapped his fingers on the desk, staring at the documents. Movement in his peripheral shifted his focus to the doorway.

"It is not often I see you in that seat. I think the last time you did, your mother was reading folktales that would one day come to life in the form of your vowed."

Trevin looked up to see his dad walking into the study. "How did the lesson go yesterday?"

"Cedar took a different approach than we were trying on Tuesday, and it worked. She hasn't emerged yet this morning."

"I knew she would get it," Trevin beamed. "What approach did Cedar try?"

His dad laughed. "Oh, just an approach you'd never have approved. She can recognize him really quickly of the ones outside though."

Trevin let out a disgruntled sigh. "So he scared her?"

"She was fine and stood her ground as strong as any Greenthistle. Cedar behaved perfectly. You know she could easily end up in a situation where it won't be in our backyard with your brother running a drill."

Trevin sighed again and glanced at the folder. Something about the two sites on Austin's letter of interest made him wonder.

"Did something happen last night I should know about?" Echo asked.

"Just more questions that were borderline prying. Where my fiancé was from, if my parents were from here. If I had any places I frequented. When he asked if El had found any favorites, I told him to never ask about her again. Then I started asking him where he was from, why he chose Humboldt, what his parents did. All the same shit he asked me. He just smiled and answered them all like an idiot with that unnerving smile, but his emotions were just genuine answers. All matching what's here. Nothing I asked seemed too personal for him."

"If you are not sensing any malice in his emotions, I am not really sure what else there is, Trev. We'll have to just keep an eye on it."

"He said he has a girlfriend who lives in Orick with her parents, she is a commuter to the university." Trevin looked at his dad.

"I can't start pulling files on everyone who comes in contact with the kid? I'd have files on the entire campus and every state parks employee. Besides, if his girlfriend's family lives in Orick, then what? They probably have been here awhile. It's a small town. Look, I'm not trying to dismiss any gut feelings you have but you also have to consider the stress you are dealing with. It's a lot to handle. I get it," Echo noted.

"I know. I just want her safe, but I can't keep her locked up here at the estate."

"She is safe. He is a mere mortal, and unless she has told anyone about what happened to her, everyone assumes she is mortal too."

Trevin just sighed and glanced at the letter again. A faint scratching sensation deep in his core, as though an itch was nestled deep in his mountain lion's flesh.

"Next week is going to be really hard on you, I can tell, but you are going to have to trust Nightswift."

"I do trust Nightswift, but Cyrus cost them power. None of us can forget that." The bitterness was heavy in Trevin's tone.

Echo sighed. "Well, not much can be done to avoid it. Go see her and get some sleep."

"What happened to him last weekend?" He glanced at his dad.

"He still won't talk about it. I told Bracken it might be best if Dee opens the revelry but he is still holding out that Cyrus will. He is terrified of the precedence it's going to set."

"Cyrus still has his tongue. If he isn't going to talk about anything then how the hell is he going to remain heir?" Trevin could hear the anger in his own words.

Echo's shoulders slumped. "I really don't want to see Bracken and Ari lose him but I also hate how dark the path ahead is. How much we still have to do and not much time to do it," he said with resignation then as if exhaling it, Echo stood taller. "Go on up to your room. Breakfast will be sent up soon."

Trevin tossed the file back in the bottom drawer and went up to their room. All his irritation left the moment he saw her asleep and curled up with his hoodie. Quietly he removed his boots and uniform then slipped under the covers, wrapping his arms around her.

The faintest whiff of Cedar lingered on her and his anger spiked. He then pulled her closer as he nestled against her to override the scent. Trevin knew he needed to get these emotions and this territorial urge under control. He trusted her and he did trust his brother. Then he realized he didn't know exactly what the lesson had entailed other than somehow scaring her. He felt her heart rate pick up then she nestled into him more.

"Morning, Little Mink."

"I do love waking up next to my keget. Your hoodie is okay, but I much prefer you," she laughed then turned around. "How was work?"

Trevin nuzzled her. "Fine, a few people at the campsite got a little rowdy and I had to break up a fight, and the intern was annoying as usual. He seemed to enjoy the action. Of course I couldn't let him break up the argument."

"Were you okay?" she asked.

With a laugh he responded, "Of course. Drunk mortals are easy to handle."

"Well, good. Now you can sleep."

"I will when you head down for your morning lesson. I will be there in the afternoon though. How was your communication lesson?"

"Good. I was able to get them to help me detect where Cedar was," Elodie beamed.

He smiled and rubbed her head. Breakfast was sent to their room and Elodie got up to sit at the table. When Trevin turned around after setting the tray down, he noticed her walk with the slightest limp.

"El, why are you limping?" He clenched his fist. She took his hand.

"Cedar was so careful last night. I stumbled a few times at the beginning of the lesson and then at the very end it wasn't the most graceful landing."

"His scent is on you. It's faint."

"Don't get mad at him. His scare tactics worked."

"Mother above I'm going to kick his ass. He scared you?" Trevin hissed. "I trust you entirely. Please tell me about the lesson."

"Well, he stalked me and lunged at me a few times." She began to say then went on to recap the lesson. "But it worked. He didn't injure me and you know that wasn't his intent. Plus your dad watched the lesson too."

"He is still an ass, but I know. I am glad you can call on the keget," Trevin exhaled and eventually crawled into bed for a few hours while she went to her lesson.

Later when Trevin had woken up and headed back downstairs he saw his brother. With a glare he gave Cedar a shove. Naturally he didn't budge, instead he just offered a smug grin.

"Go on, Trevy, get all your frustration out on me. I will be around for it all next week," Cedar laughed.

"Don't remind me. And you are such an asshole."

"Tell me something I don't know and let me tell you something you already know. Elodie will be safe with me. Nothing worse than the expected scrapes at drills will ever happen to her while I run the lessons."

Trevin blew an audible guest of air through his nose then nodded. "I will probably take you up on sparring or runs next week. Between my annoying intern and how Quinn treated her last week, next week is going to be maddening."

"I honestly expected so much more from Quinn. I haven't talked to him or Cyrus though. Gaining hers and your trust is my top priority."

Trevin sighed and looked his brother in the eyes. "Thank you, Cedar. It sounds like you have her trust. I am relieved you have been there for her. You have mine too."

Cedar gave him a brimming smile then ruffled Trevin's hair, laughing. "Looking forward to seeing what frustration does to you."

Trevin sighed in annoyance and fixed his hair as Cedar laughed, walking off towards the kitchen.

CHAPTER 20

Sunday arrived and with some stalling from Elodie and much reassurance from the Greenthistle family, she and Trevin headed out the front door.

The trail took them north, each step growing heavier. Maintaining a steady breath and heartbeat was proving difficult for Elodie. Not because she was winded, since this trail was actually very easy for her she found. It was what awaited at the end of this trail that made walking it hard.

Nightswift Estate.

All she knew was that Cyrus had been mostly confined to the estate, hardly left his room, and had panic attacks day and night. All of Greenthsitle and even Lord and Lady Nightswift had stopped by to ensure she would be safe.

Elodie had learned their names. They had both offered them to her along with their mortal names. She found Lord Nightswift's name to be very unique and somehow fitting for him. Bracken, known to the mortals as Brian, certainly carried himself as the ever observant and watchful high estate lord of Nightswift. Last week was the first time she had seen him drop the focused intensity of his gaze and offer her a warm soft expression.

Lady Nightswift was pure grace and her name reflected it. Ariyanna, "Ariya" on the mortal side, was a mother who was watching her only son lose himself. She recalled Ariyanna thanking her at the Spring Solstice. The sorrow in her tone and expression made Elodie sad for all of Nightswift. It was those moments that really sat heavy on Elodie's conscience.

"El?" Trevin said, giving her hand a little squeeze. "What's troubling you the most?"

"I don't like this situation. Everyone says I'm safe, I know, but I don't know what Nightswift is going to be like. I've hardly interacted with them. At all."

"I know it is scary. I hate that I can't be there with you this week. I trust Lord and Lady Nightswift, though if that bastard tries anything, scream and do not hesitate to use the floss flower on him. Protect yourself." Trevin's disdain was apparent and that too hurt Elodie. Everything about it just felt wrong. Greenthistle was telling her it was okay to stab Nightswift with floss flower. Frowning, her eyes focused on her boots, her ears taking in the sound of the small crunch of soil underneath.

Eventually, they stepped onto the property of a large modern looking residence. A flat roof and massive windows surrounded by old growth redwoods. It was made of wood and had multiple levels of course. It reminded her of something she would see on the cliff sides of Monterey or Sonoma Counties and comparable in size to Greenthistle and Ashdale Estates. She could only imagine the training course, how impossible it would be for her.

The doors opened and together, hand in hand with Trevin, she walked inside and took a deep inhale.

She saw Lord and Lady Nightswift standing front and center smiling at her. Both of their daughters stood to the side of them. Dee eyed her up and down then rolled her eyes, causing Elodie's heart to tense even more. Poppy looked at her, wide eyed and nervous, stepping closer to her dad. Someone was sitting on the bottom step, staring at the floor. Elodie knew it was Cyrus without making eye contact. The realization that none of the Nightswift children liked her threatened to make her eyes well up.

They knew this would be the biggest challenge. I knew it too.

She glanced at Trevin who stared at Cyrus with confusion, shock, but also anger.

"As I assured you both, Lady Elodie will be safe and no harm will come to her. We look forward to the week ahead and she will be treated with the utmost respect as any member of Nightswift Estate would. We are in Lady Elodie's debt," Bracken said with reverence.

"Good. I expect nothing less," Trevin said sternly. He turned to Dee and Poppy. "I expect you both to guide her as needed. She's smart and eager to learn."

Poppy nodded diligently. Dee just smirked and fixed her eyes on Trevin and it reminded Elodie of Justine's disdain. Dee gave the smallest nod. Then Trevin turned to look at Cyrus. He still had not looked up. Elodie glanced at Lord and Lady Nightswift, who watched pensively.

"You know your orders. Dare lay a hand on her and I will not hold back this time. Be grateful I see the shame all over you," Trevin growled.

Elodie watched Cyrus tremble and look away. Tension gripped her body at the uncomfortable interaction.

"Yes, sir," Cyrus managed to whimper out.

There was nothing equal about this interaction. Cyrus was fully submitting to Trevin. Elodie worried about the dynamic. Their dads all seemed so equal in their dominance while somehow maintaining a balance. Yet that was not the case with their firstborns.

Quinn hardly seemed to care about Trevin's flaring temper and Cyrus could hardly look at anyone without cowering back. Her mind raced at how it could be fixed. This task seemed monumental, especially since she hadn't helped Quinn and Trevin.

"Master Greenthistle. If she so much as gets a rip in her clothes I will inform you. But know that drills will occur and injury may happen. Know they will not have been induced by anyone in the Nightswift household or the guard," Bracken said sternly. "Remember this is new territory for us all. Be better for your vowed."

Trevin forced an audible exhale through his nose. "See to it that stands true this week. I would love to have my concerns eased." Distaste lined Trevin's voice.

"She will be safe and sound. We give you our word Master Greenthistle. We will see Greenthistle early for the solstice, yes?" Ariyanna asked.

"Yes, we will be there. Her things will be sent early."

Elodie watched Lord and Lady Nightswift nod.

Trevin then turned to face Elodie and she forced her breathing to normalize. He pulled her into a tight hug.

"I am a phone call away," he said softly to her. "Learn from Nightswift, okay?" He sounded resigned. Elodie nodded and squeezed him tight. Trevin pulled back and cupped Elodie's jaw. "Take a deep breath, Little Mink. I will see you at the solstice then be back on Saturday afternoon." He gave her a soft smile as Elodie felt the calming wave.

"I love you," she said quietly.

"I love you too, El." Trevin smiled and then gave her a brief kiss. He took her hand and with one small calming wave washed over her before he let her hand go.

"Be strong, I am counting down once again," he said, then walked out of the estate.

Elodie didn't want to look up to see him go. Yet when the door opened, she glanced up to see him give her a smile before he was gone from view. As the doors closed, a pit formed in her stomach. She looked down then heard Bracken let out a long breath.

"That went better than I thought it would honestly. He has an abnormal level of control. Ever the rule follower," Bracken acknowledged.

"That would be Echo's doing," Ariyanna added.

Elodie still did not look up. Instead she focused on trying to keep her heart rate normal.

Ariyanna took a few steps closer to her. "Lady Elodie, I know this is overwhelming, let me show you to your room?"

Elodie heard Cyrus get up but flinched when his dad spoke.

"Cyrus. You have ten minutes then I expect you in that study," Bracken ordered. Elodie could hear his heartbeat echoing hers, both were pounding. She dared look at him and watched a chill take over him.

Instinctively Elodie took a step back and this action seemed to cause Cyrus to drop his head. She saw how much he was struggling to even stand up right, as though just breathing took all his focus. She recalled him chained down, screaming, how battered his body had been. Her mind questioned if this was how things had been for him the entire time.

Help him. He is part of the high estate.

Do not lose him. He is needed.

Elodie's eyes shot wide before glancing at the window then at Cyrus, not noticing everyone looking at her.

For a split second she locked eyes with him and everything stood still. Their heartbeats went silent and she was unsure if either of theirs were still working. Her eyes focused on something inside him. He had been feeling so much but beyond the severe weight of it all lay something else. There was a newness to Cyrus that had not yet surfaced. It reacted to her; she reacted to it but she did not understand what it was. A teal flash washed over her vision, causing Cyrus to gasp then promptly run upstairs, slamming his door.

Her thundering heartbeat crashed into her, along with all of her other senses as Elodie looked at her hand. "I'm sorry. I—I don't know what happened. My hand didn't illuminate right? No vines? I didn't feel them, I wasn't going to use them!"

Bracken cautiously approached her. Poppy now clung to her mother. "No vines came out. Just a flash of your eyes."

"I don't want to hurt anyone with this. I have been working every day to control it!"

"I know, I have seen it. Cyrus is still recovering from it all. He's been going through withdrawals."

"He's scared? Of me? Trev? I am not sure what happened," she said, taking a deep breath.

As she was about to explain what she had sensed in him she stopped herself. Was this something she wanted to tell them? Or was this something she should let surface on its own? The thought struck her and she looked at her hand again. When Elodie assessed what she had seen in him, it was not evil or malice, it was something new. Foreign. Yet it was nothing like her.

Dee let out a long sigh and walked past Elodie to the stairs. "Some Greenthistle," she griped.

"Delia," Ariyanna snapped.

Another sigh escaped the second born. "Now she knows my name. Thanks."

"She deserves to know it."

Delia scoffed and left.

Ariyanna lightly placed her hand on Elodie's arm. "My apologies, Delia can be standoffish at times. Now let's get you settled in. Poppy, come with us, please."

Elodie looked at the door with some small ounce of hope Trevin would come and pull her back to Greenthistle. Then she felt horrible for thinking that. How could she be the Earth Blessed if she wouldn't look at one of the high estates?

With that thought she took the first steps, feeling Bracken's eyes on her, but she did not look at him.

Once in the large room, which she realized was a mere door away from Cyrus's, she took in the decor. A queen size four poster bed, a small dining nook with coffee, tea, fruits and pastries were set out. A small refrigerator and carafe of water sat nearby. There was a large walk-in closet, a dark hardwood dresser and desk matched the bed frame. The floor was layered with dark hardwood with a plush area rug. Hanging on the wall on one side of the dresser was the Greenthistle crest embroidered into a tapestry. It was the tapestry hanging on the other side that really drew her in.

Her eyes fixed on the crescent moon below the redwood nestled between three ferns and the eight-point sun above it all. The sigil was black against a golden rod, white, and teal background. Elodie couldn't look away from it. This was her sigil, her identifier that she was home. Aligned with Greenthistle, always standing with them, but something else entirely different.

"Is that—" Elodie paused. "My sigil? Crest?"

"It is. Humboldt's Earth Blessed. The one chosen by the Old Giants that gives our lands life, and is loved by the Great Mother. The girl who walked among mortals, and ran with the fae. The girl who would save them both because this was her home. The one she chose," Ariyanna spoke softly. "Trevin's mother, Selene, had a book of folktales she would read to them often. It had the story of the Earth Blessed. It was an ancient folk tale of those who were granted many gifts, who would become the very embodiment of a territory, respected and loved by all the high estates." She paused and a bittersweet smile came over Ariyanna's expression.

"When I had heard what happened, the connection Trevin had made, I thought of Selene. That somehow she knew, or at least hoped one day you would find your way here and look after Trevin. I looked at your sigil carefully that night and realized that your arrival here was just waiting for the right circumstances. The sigil represents Humboldt at its brightest. The eight-pointed sun is said to be the estate children, its future and its beginnings. The Old Giant with three ferns, the three estates to protect their entity. Supporting it all is the one who holds it all up, the crescent moon bringing those tides and that life source of the mighty Pacific the Old Giants thrive on, our Earth Blessed."

Elodie's mind raced through the three estates, the families that made them as her jaw fell agape.

"Trevin was strong when I met him—I didn't make him strong. All I did was shatter dynamics between ancient estates that have protected this place far longer than I have existed. Even mortals are acting strange around me," Elodie said and looked away with shame after noticing Poppy looking at her with confusion. She tensed when she felt Ariyanna's hand rest on her shoulder.

"We know this may not be as easy a week as Ashdale was, but we do hope that one day you will see Nightswift as your home too. You are always welcome here. We will never stop serving and protecting you. You saved one of our fledglings, and we hope you know that you are part of our unkindness of ravens. Always."

"Thank you. I am grateful. Seeing the sigil, seeing Greenthistle's gives me comfort. I want to try, I am going to try," Elodie affirmed. Once again remembering what Echo needed her to do. *Try*.

"I know you will. Get settled and let us know if you need anything. Please head down the stairs in fifteen minutes."

As Elodie watched her leave she saw Poppy look at her with a stunned expression for a moment before running off after her mom. No words had been exchanged between the two but for some reason Elodie got the sense this expression was awe, shock, confusion, and maybe curiosity? A glimmer of hope? She was not sure why she thought all of these things when she looked at Poppy.

There was no denying that she had become so much more aware of the emotions those around her experienced, yet she never saw the gates as Trevin had described. She looked at the thin scar on her palm. How much of her power had been granted to him? Had he given her anything? Her mind went to Cyrus and all the pain and anguish on him. Trevin had said shame but Elodie did not think that was it, many emotions were all steeping under that shame. Yet Elodie couldn't grasp what it all meant. Nor could she grasp how else she could see it if not for Trevin's power now that she thought about it.

Cyrus had been possessed by a spirit that seized control of his body. He had fought it so hard too. The tremor in his fist was him trying to break those chains, to help her. To stop the chaos he had been trapped in from engulfing his friends.

With a sigh she unpacked her sketchbook and pencil pouch then set her water bottle down. After sitting on the bed to assess the plushness level, she got up and examined the tapestry. She had never seen it displayed so prominently. The thought never even occurred to her that she would have any insignia as they all had. Yet here it was.

Elodie turned and headed out of the room to go downstairs where Bracken was waiting for her.

"Follow me please." His tone was stoic.

Chapter 21

Once in the study, Elodie took a seat with a pounding heart and cautious movement. The calmness of the Old Giants pulsed from within her outward over the room. Letting out an exhale, her body relaxed slightly.

Cyrus remained still.

Bracken smiled warmly. "Truly amazing you are, Lady Elodie. I look forward to seeing all we may accomplish this week." He steepled his hands on the desk and took a slow inhale. "Cyrus."

Elodie watched Cyrus wipe his eyes when his dad focused on him. She wasn't sure what was happening.

"It has been nearly three months and you will not speak of anything that happened to anyone. You cannot keep this bottled up, son. You told us you wanted to tell her first and here she is."

Elodie's mind processed what he had just said. At some point her eyes shifted to the area rug following the intricate filigree pattern. She heard Cyrus sniff.

"Cyrus. Please talk." His dad's pleading voice snatched her gaze towards him. She saw his desperation, hopelessness, and fear in his eyes. No gates, just a word in her mind to place it.

"I'm scared." Cyrus's voice was so small and battered down.

Yet it broke beyond the thundering in Elodie's heart, calling her gaze. She assessed his inward posture, the tears he failed to wipe away. His body looked thinner, as though he had lost some muscle or weight. He never was as muscular as Trevin or Quinn, then again neither was Bracken compared to Echo and Miles. Part of their feral form she deduced. Regardless Cyrus had been toned, now he almost looked frail.

"I'm sorry." His words were small.

"You are not leaving this room until you talk to her. Acknowledge her at least," his dad said with a hint of sternness to him. Cyrus remained quiet and his dad sighed again, sitting back.

Elodie swallowed hard. She wasn't sure what to say or do.

Help him. He is still struggling and still trapped.

You saved the mountain lion, now save the raven.

Another wave of calm came over the room. Then Elodie felt a phantom shove push her towards him. Gentle but the intent from the Old Giants was clear. She had to try.

Lord Nightswift observed her. "My apologies Lady Elodie. I know this must be stressful for you," he said remorsefully.

Elodie stared at him, confused. It was stressful for her, but Cyrus was under a great deal more stress and it didn't take any special abilities to see that. This was Cyrus after Inanis, stripped away, and grasping the few remaining shreds of sanity it had left him. Trevin had said he was pompous and arrogant, but never malicious. Intelligent and hardworking but with a cocky nature. Trevin and Autumn had said Cyrus wasn't ever bad, people just had to get past his overzealous confidence.

Yet Elodie had only ever seen him with Inanis holding the lead. Their first interaction was at that bonfire, one week after that attack that left injuries on Trevin. Echo said he really wasn't sure if Cyrus would pull through and how that thing must have sped up his healing. She had seen him that night in the ruins. He was so terrified and exhausted as he screamed for help. The terror in his eyes, the terror she too had seen for mere minutes, he had seen for months.

"Cyrus," she said softly. He turned away, wiping his eyes. "You haven't told them what you saw? The—" She stopped herself from talking about the stark white void she had seen. The Old Giants burning, her home burning, and the earth screaming. A chill passed over her thinking about it. "No, I don't imagine it is easy to talk about, I don't like to think about it either. If it helps, they know, your dad, Lord Greenthistle, and Lord Ashdale know. I told them what I saw that night when they took me to Sequoia Community Park. How hollowing it all was to see."

"I let you see that!" he rasped out, covering his face with his hands. "I let it take over you. I'm sorry." He dropped them and finally looked at her, tears still poured. "I'm sorry, Elodie! You fell into that void. All the cuts and scrapes on you. I can't get the feeling off my hands, the taste of it out of my mouth. It sickens me that I caused that. Yet you still ripped those chains off me without a word or second thought. As soon as I was free, I couldn't comprehend anything and I just ran right back to those Old Giants. When I turned, I saw you fighting those chains with everything and realized what stupid fucking worthless coward I was! I heard Trevin scream for you. Quinn was too scared to let him go. Autumn and Cedar were so terrified.

"It plotted to do horrible things to you, Elodie. It wanted to make Trevin watch too, then do horrible things to him after he had given up. The second it saw him nuzzle you that night in Arcata Community Forest, it knew what you were and I knew you were vowed to him. I tried to fight it. I tried to tell him. I did! I tried making hints to Trevin about being vowed and I knew you were Humboldt's Earth Blessed, our only salvation to this thing I carried. Every time it made me touch you." He dropped his head into his hands again and swallowed hard. "The bonfire, at Solstice. I tried to fight it. I tried to scream louder. Hoped someone would connect that you were the Earth Blessed. All that needed to happen was a small incision be healed by Lord Greenthistle to bind it to you in a bed of ferns under the Old Giants. And every day that passed, I heard our dads discuss and debate what to do with you. I sobbed as it laughed in my face because they didn't know and it wouldn't let me tell you. I tried. And every time it just beat me down more."

Elodie's eyes welled up. Bracken gazed at his son, speechless.

"Would you—it—have tried to hurt me at the bonfire?" she asked worriedly. As if the realization of how long she had been in danger hit her.

"Elodie." There was so much pain in his voice as he looked at her once more. "It needed to let you bleed out, beyond Lord Greenthistle's ability to heal you. The beach would have been ideal. Your blood flowing into the ocean, Lord Greenthistle wouldn't have been alerted in time, couldn't have rushed there in front of a bunch of mortals to heal you. But you never gave in," he said through tears. "You looked for Trevin, I could see it, it could see it. Your heart searched desperately for him that night, and he searched for you as soon as you sent that energy pulse out. It was a distress call for him and it knew it would wait and watch." Cyrus took in a deep inhale. "I've never been so grateful for Cedar's stupid games in my life because I'm not sure what might have happened had he not kissed you and felt that tapping on the vowed bond. It was foolish, its namesake, Inanis. The more it watched the more you two had time to bond. The ward Trev put on your place made it impossible for me to enter unless you invited me in and I was so glad you never did," Cyrus said, finally looking at her.

"Did it—want Alena or was that you?" Elodie watched a chill overtake him at her name.

"It latched onto Alena for her malicious ways. I never paid any attention to her before." He shuddered as if remembering something. "I hate her. She is just that horrible. So it would use her because it knew how much I didn't like it. It urged Cedar to join, seeing his wariness of you and how much I hated being with Cedar in that way."

Bracken had gone sickly looking hearing all of this. "Son. You've kept this in for three months? Why?"

"I hurt her! She is terrified of me. I watched Autumn and her bond instantly. I watched Quinn stay near her enough to calm her down for Trev. Let her dictate their friendship as she was comfortable." Cyrus finally looked at Elodie. "I watched you and Trevin act like fools in love. He struggled with the right things to do even though he knew how much you loved him, and how if he lost you, he would never bounce back from that. It would be just like when he lost his mom all over again, but he can't handle that twice. He never handled losing her, and when he thought he lost you, he shattered. All the while I was the creepy one, I was the one who made you crawl out of your skin and in the end, I hurt you. I chained up your vowed and hurt him. He was once my best friend." Cyrus cried into his hands again. "I'm sorry. For the monster I became to you. Trevin hates me, will hate me when he hears all of this. I'm sorry."

"You could see everything that happened to me those days before the ruins. There was always a raven nearby. It was you that entire time?"

Cyrus nodded again. "It blocked all of Nightswift from seeing through them. I watched you fall deeper and deeper into your despair, thinking you had gone insane, thinking that he hated you, medicating just to sleep and gripping your dagger calling for him. Thinking that he wanted that monster Alena over you, his vowed. I saw the bear attack. I watched Trevin carry you in his arms frantically and cry out for his dad to help you. Begged him to do so. Lord Greenthistle healed you but you never touched the redwoods or the ferns after that because you were so petrified to even go outside. You had been stripped of even the simple things that brought you peace and I hated myself for not being stronger. I do hate myself. I'm sorry."

Elodie wiped her eyes and looked at the ground. She didn't say anything for a few breaths as she processed everything.

"I also saw you at the peak of Russ Park, when you found that book, you touched your sigil and you saw that word Inanis. You had these pieces to a puzzle you knew nothing about and gave them to Greenthistle but they couldn't figure it out either. I can't stop seeing it all play over and over in my head and it terrifies me."

"I'm scared too. But we are here. I want to be here. I want you here too."

"You nor the Old Giants should still want me. I will drive my estate into the ground because I was stripped of everything that made me who I was when you pulled it from me." He brought his eyes to meet hers and the emotions crashed into her.

It was pushing and pulling her core, nearly suffocating her. Fear, regret, self-hatred, shame, despair, yet he was pleading. So many things caused a chill to wash over her and she realized he was at rock bottom, still chained up with no hope of ever getting out this time.

"They still want you, the Old Giants," Elodie said, her voice nearly breaking. His emotions were so much to hold. He had carried this for months.

Help him. Pull him back up.

It is time to save the raven.

Cyrus looked at her, meeting her eyes and again all those emotions crashed back into her. This was almost unbearable what he was feeling. She had to break the gaze first.

"This isn't something you ever should have encountered."

"But, I want this, I'm your Earth Blessed." She looked at him again finally but he had turned away.

"I know you want this, I knew the very moment I saw you walking with them. You are still so lost and I am not going to ask you to find me."

"But they tell me to help you. To save the raven," Elodie pleaded.

Cyrus smirked as if her statement was absurd and shook his head. "Help the Old Giants understand they made an error with me. Inanis took me because it saw how easy I was to break. How close to a monster I already was. Focus on Trevin." He still wasn't looking at her.

That hallowing feeling struck her again. This would be another heir to ignore her all week. Yet the Old Giants warnings were different for Cyrus as they were Quinn.

Tears started to fall from her eyes. Pieces she thought she had put into place suddenly didn't fit like they had before. That feeling from Marin Headlands came back. She didn't know how to help any of them, of course Mt. Tamalpais didn't want her in Marin County. Nowhere had wanted her like this place did. Yet it felt as if she was letting it crumble instead of helping mend it. *Did Mt. Tam know this?*

Fight for Nigthswift.

Fight for your home.

You both were chosen correctly.

Her eyes fixed on the window and the trees.

This was the home she wanted, had been searching for, and fought for.

"Cyrus?" Bracken asked, concerned. He stood up.

Elodie's vision saw the teal pulse and she turned to see Cyrus clutching his stomach tight. Fear took over her. That thing in him that was reaching for her, and he was fighting it.

Neither of you were chosen wrong.

Pull the raven back up. Help him fly again.

We need you both.

"I don't know how yet, but I will not leave you this trail alone, Cyrus," Elodie said, trying to hold her voice steady.

Something like need and want flashed over his face before he masked it again with an empty expression. He was quiet for a moment longer then spoke. His tone was level and he did not appear to have to keep it so. "I expect nothing of you, Lady Elodie."

Her tears fell once more before she turned to leave, hearing Bracken exhale and sit back down. She opened the door but stopped to look back at Cyrus. His heart rate had increased.

"Cyrus, you can call me El, if you want, we are equals now and we will be when we get off that trail." Then she closed the door behind her and ran right back to her room. Collapsing on the bed, her hands gripped the pommel of the dagger tight as she allowed herself to weep.

"Hope you are proud of yourself, the most you manage to say the past three months is to push your Earth Blessed away," Lord Nightswift spat out with disgust.

Cyrus rubbed his eyes trying to stop the tears. Bracken saw him flinch again as if he had irritated a wound on his face.

"Am I expected to be there for her lesson tonight?"

"No." Bracken watched his son sigh in relief then tense as he continued. "As I said, you both have lessons this week. You lost a lot of muscle and are likely rusty. Come next Monday. You will be at drills with Trevin and Quinn."

"I can't," he whimpered.

"You will, so I need to run an assessment on you to determine what you are going to teach her tomorrow morning. Let's go, I expect at least forty-five solid minutes from you."

"I-I'm not ready." Cyrus panicked.

"Whatever front you are trying to put up from her is pointless. You know what she is capable of. Nightswift should not leave her crying and feeling alone. Get in the training room, now," Bracken demanded. He leveled his gaze at his son.

Cyrus sat there for a moment breathing hard then cut his eyes away

"Your Earth Blessed just stood her ground despite her fears. She told you she would not leave you behind! Learn to walk with her. You are running out of time. You can avoid eye contact, cry and scream in your room all you want, but you will be ill-prepared for that regional conference in September."

He watched Cyrus fight back a cry before pushing himself up. He was breathing heavily as he walked towards the door. He got up and followed, watching Cyrus take slow careful steps down the hall into the training room.

Bracken began running through the same exercises he was going to give Elodie and was relieved to see Cyrus could do them with ease. He then ran through the exercises he planned to give Elodie at the end of the week and those too were proving easy. So he moved to the last set of drills he had given Cyrus before the ruins and sighed when he faltered, unable to complete more than a quarter of it. His raven faltered too. After getting to Cyrus's new baseline, he told him he was done for the day and that dinner would be sent to his room.

"You should consider being at the table for breakfast tomorrow. Assess how your sisters interact with her."

"Maybe. May I have a sedative?" Cyrus asked.

"No!" Bracken snapped.

"I don't want her to see me like that."

"Tough shit, Cyrus. You don't want her to see you having a night terror, then don't have one. We do not sugarcoat things for her, we just make sure she knows she is safe. You should be showing her how to walk the trail, not the other way around."

Cyrus sulked out of the room and Bracken waited for Elodie.

He noticed she was somewhat ahead of where he estimated but as she reached tasks she could not complete, she grew frustrated and distraught. By the end of the lesson she was nearly in tears again and all he could do was sigh in defeated acceptance.

"Lady Elodie." His words were soft as she pushed a gust of air through her nose. "This is a baseline, I knew there would be things you could not do yet, but you will. Would you like to have dinner at the table with us?"

She wiped her eyes. "I'm not really hungry, sir."

"I understand. I will send a meal to your room. Please let us know if there is anything you need, anything at all and we shall do our best to accommodate."

"Thank you, sir."

"Chin up, little cub, you are a Greenthistle, if I have ever seen one." He smiled.

She thanked him once more and went back to her room.

Bracken headed into the kitchen where he saw his daughters and his vowed. They all watched him.

"They talked, I assumed?" Ariyanna asked.

"He dropped a huge bombshell on her. He is so lost and afraid but he is resisting her. As though he fears scaring her again."

"How did she handle it?"

"Like Greenthistle and Ashdale would. With all the valor and loyalty of their most accomplished sentires, but she is still scared too. She stood her ground, told him she would not leave him behind and he just told her no."

"She is perfect for Greenthistle. The vowed bond is still so fresh. It must be driving her and Trev wild."

"It is going to be a long week," Bracken said, sighing. "They are both staying in their rooms tonight for dinner."

Ariyanna nodded.

"Is Lady Elodie going to help him?" Poppy asked, unsure.

Bracken looked at his youngest and smiled, hiding his stress. "She is a very brave cub. She wants to help him."

"I hope you girls will welcome her; she is part of the family now. She is every bit a part of all our lives as Ashdale and Greenthistle are," Ariyanna said.

"May I have dinner in my room as well?" Delia asked. Her dad gasped.

"Why?" her mom asked with a stern tone. Bracken noticed Poppy looked worried.

"I just want to be in my room."

"You will accept her. You are part of a high estate. She is here to stay, Nightswift has as much of her blood on our hands as Greenthistle does. She saved our home and saved your brother's life. You owe her too, Delia. He is alive because of her," Bracken said sternly. Poppy teared up.

"I know. I need to prepare for my lessons with her. And it's pretty obvious that just because he is alive, does not mean he is okay. Nightswift is not safe. I know blind denial when I see it."

"You are excused, dinner will be sent to your room. I know ignorant fear when I see it too," Ariyanna hissed back. "She is just as scared of us as you are of her. Remember that and prove her fears false."

Delia got up and walked up stairs. Bracken leaned forward on the counter, bringing his hands to his head.

"Olive said Connor was unsure of her too," Ariyanna noted.

"Delia is much more head strong than Connor. Connor had Quinn to watch and interact with her, who Lady Elodie is friends with." He sighed, then looked at Poppy. "Please do not shun her. Get to know her. She could use a friend at Nightswift."

Poppy gave him a nod despite the unease on her face.

Chapter 22

E lodie sat at the table for breakfast rather sullenly. Trevin had called and asked how the first night went. She was too exhausted to recount it but she told him some of it leaving out all the emotions that were experienced in that room. Using the lesson as a reason for her sadness and her exhaustion she ended the call with him early. All it was going to do was stress him out more.

She smiled at Poppy, who returned with a small smile but remained quiet. So Elodie did too. Noticing Cyrus and Dee were absent, she figured it was for the best. Her stomach was already in knots and having to see them would just make eating impossible. Ariyanna sat next to Poppy across from Elodie and smiled.

"Did you sleep okay?" she asked.

"Yes, Lady Nightswift." Elodie left out the part where she cried after getting off the phone with Trevin until exhaustion overtook her.

"I am glad. Whatever happened last night please know that we want you here too. I do apologize for Dee and Cyrus's behavior. It has been a stressful three months and we had hoped to have dealt with it before your stay."

"I hope not to add to it too much," Elodie sulked.

"No, Lady Elodie. You are not any burden at all. I am looking forward to our lesson this afternoon."

Elodie offered a small nod and continued to force the yogurt and fruit dish down. It tasted divine and she wished she could quiet her nerves enough to enjoy it.

"Thank you for helping me with my mortal lessons, Lady Elodie," Poppy said but tensed when Elodie looked at her and cut her eyes down. It caused her to frown.

"Of course. Thank you for helping me with the fae world."

Poppy looked up at her and smiled again. Elodie did too.

"We wanted to put a Greenthistle banner in your room, so you always know we welcome and respect you. But it was Cyrus who suggested the Earth Blessed banner in those colors." It was Elodie's turn to gasp now. "So whatever happened in the study, know that he is grateful for you too."

"Yes, Lady Nightswift," Elodie said then went back to eating, ensuring she got all the granola and honey scraped out along with any fruit she may have missed.

It was a lighter meal and they had close to an hour drive into Six Rivers over the ridge. It was not an area she had explored much. Since Elodie didn't have the ability to run or fly like the high estates, they took a passenger van similar to what they had done as Ashdale. Greenthistle had stayed closer to their estate. The van ride made Elodie uneasy. Nightswift sentries were in the van as was Bracken. She had been informed that other sentries, one of the trainers, and Cyrus would meet them there.

Her mind thought back to the knowledge that he had been the one to suggest her sigil. Her sigil that was uniquely hers, for Humboldt. She appreciated the sentiment yet he didn't seem to want her help. All the thoughts leaping from one doubt to another led her in a downward spiral.

When they arrived, she took a deep inhale before getting out of the van and waited for instruction. Cyrus stood looking exhausted. She hadn't seen or heard a sound from him after she left the study.

"Hi, Cyrus," she said, her nerves ever-present in her tone.

He looked at her with a flash of shock then schooled his face again with a deep inhale and gave her a nod. He turned his attention away from her and pulled out his phone. Elodie felt a wave of sadness and was about to say something but all that came out was a small sigh and she looked at the ground.

Staring at the soil, Elodie noticed how much dryer it was over here. Then her eyes shifted to the trees, which were a mix of conifers and other species. A

Redwood here and there but a young one. Ferns sprouted up too. The ground was rockier and not as soft as the Old Giants' groves. She stepped towards a conifer focusing on it now. All the emotions she had felt a moment ago were gone, replaced by curiosity.

She felt foolish that she hadn't bothered to really listen to anything other than the Old Giants. She had in King Range with Trevin but nothing talked to her then. With a nervous inhale, Elodie brought her palm to it and listened. Life thrummed on her touch but no words or greetings from the tree. A wave of sadness came over her once again. She hadn't even considered trying to talk to anything other than redwoods. Of course they should remain silent.

Then she thought about Cyrus. She hadn't bothered to check on him, despite thinking about him and wondering how he was fairing. She hadn't even asked Cedar or Quinn if they had talked to him recently. Then her body went still at the thought, hadn't they talked to him? Quinn had seen him but she wasn't sure how often. She removed her hand slowly and turned to face him. He was still turned away from her. Elodie swallowed back the new realization that he likely had some resentment towards everyone, her included.

Bracken eyed her cautiously and stepped forward to explain the drills.

"We are going to start with some agility to get you both warmed up. Then Cyrus will lead Lady Elodie through some tracking exercises. A sentry will hide something and I want Cyrus to teach her how he would search for it as a raven and how to do it in fae form. The last test will be you two working together to find something hidden."

Then they set off for the lessons. She was panicking at how utterly silent it was and how remote this was, even when she was deep in the redwoods, she could feel them. Yet out here, there was no sound and the sun was bright in the sky where no clouds lingered. The fog had burned off early, but there was some snow hanging on from winter. When she glanced at Cyrus, who was off on his own course that looked next to impossible, she was shocked to find him appearing to struggle just as much. He looked so tired.

When the tracking lesson came he spoke only of tracking and nothing else. She wasn't getting it and was only able to track one thing with help. The last task again left her frustrated in herself and Cyrus gripping his stomach for a moment before masking his own frustrations.

After the lessons, Bracken told them to not let it get to them. He reminded them of the importance of working together. As soon as he was finished talking, Cyrus walked off a little way, changed into a raven, and flew off.

Elodie frowned and looked at the ground again.

"Lady Elodie, you have not done anything wrong," Bracken implored.

"Yes, sir," she responded.

"I hope that you believe it before the week is up." She remained quiet. "We do not expect you to fix things you did not break. If you are on separate trails then you are."

"I'm supposed to be the Earth Blessed but it doesn't feel like I'm very good at it."

"You are brand new to all of this and handling it all as valiantly as ever. Echo and Miles also agree."

"Thank you, sir."

Bracken rubbed her back. "Let's get out of this sun and back to the estate. Ariyanna and Poppy will have a much more relaxing lesson.

Elodie climbed into the van, not making eye contact with anyone out of sheer embarrassment they had probably heard that.

The afternoon lesson went smoothly, Elodie assured Ariyanna and Poppy that she would study up on her notes. Poppy assured Elodie she would do the same after asking lots of questions about the mortal world and beyond Humboldt. When she worked with Poppy she felt at ease, most likely because she found herself slipping into teacher mode. Ariyanna had let Elodie lead those lessons, sitting back to merely watch as Nightswift did.

Then came her communication lesson with Delia. Her mom was present while Poppy went with her dad to work on her glamour conditioning. Elodie was struggling to communicate with the ravens and ended up discouraged. She didn't get it. Again, her mind went back to how much she avoided the ravens, how little exposure she had to them. Despite what Bracken had told her earlier, Nightswift was not a place she felt at home.

Again, Elodie took dinner in her room and tried to think about how she was going to talk to Trevin without just bawling her eyes out in frustration, because she wanted to.

Chapter 23

"How was today?" Trevin asked Elodie over the phone.

"Um, it was good. I had a lesson with every member of the family today. Cyrus was in a morning lesson with me but we worked separately. Then he taught me, or tried to teach me tracking. He looks exhausted though and I'm really slow." She went on to talk about the rest of the various things she tried to do today.

"You are not slow, and you are doing fine. I'm sure it was eye opening for Lady Nightswift to see you teach Poppy."

"Poppy is very curious. Her eyes get bigger and she starts leaning forward but she is scared of the mortal world."

"Yeah, that sounds like Poppy. Her gift, if she has one, hasn't shown itself yet. What did you do during the drills with Lord Nightswift? I'm so used to changing a ton on drill days. Fae. Mountain lion. Fae. Mountain lion. Fae. I almost feel bad for Cyrus having to be so high up in the sky then swoop down and then pounding his wings to get airborne again. At least Quinn and I stayed on the ground. But Cyrus is really strong in his flight. He always was."

"We ran some courses in Six Rivers. I hadn't explored that corner much before today. It is pretty. I have only been on highway 299 a few times. The land changes so much, but I could still feel those Old Giants just over the ridge. He had a vehicle to take us—me—back. An inconvenience I assume."

"It's not El. We adapt to suit you. We all need you. This is why they want these weeks to see how we can all use our forms to benefit you. We always work in tandem and now that means in tandem with you."

Elodie looked at him. "I'm really happy this is home. That Greenthistle and the other two estates welcomed me as much as they have."

"We owe you everything and I'm just glad I get to be yours, as long as you will have me."

"Forever sound good?"

"It sounds perfect." Trevin smiled at her. She smiled back. "I love you, Little Mink."

"I love you too, Trev."

Suddenly a chill passed through Elodie and made her tense. Trevin narrowed his eyes and tilted his head slightly. "What's wrong?"

He needs your help.

He is still chained.

Elodie looked at Trevin for a second with worry then jumped at the sound of screaming.

"No! No! Please. Trevin! No! Elodie!" She could hear what sounded like Cyrus. She looked over towards the door, then heard other doors open.

"Cyrus!" She heard Lady Nightswift call out.

"No! Please! Somebody please help me. I don't want to do this!" Cyrus screamed again.

"El." She heard Trev say. "Are you okay?"

"I'm fine. I just. He sounds like he's in so much pain."

"Were you okay after you sealed that thing back up? You didn't have screaming fits like that. That sounds like that night." Trevin got a chill. "When the mountain lion, you know—"

"No I didn't. I honestly had more nightmares and fits like this the week before the ruins, but haven't had any after. Though the thought of what I saw happened, gives me chills."

"Please! Stop!" Cyrus screamed again. She heard more people rushing and giving orders.

"Get another sentry, he's thrashing too hard."

"Where is the sedative?" another called

"It doesn't do anything, damn it. Cyrus! Cyrus, wake up!" Bracken yelled. Elodie flinched.

Then she heard a knock at the door and jumped again. She swallowed hard and looked at Trevin again. He nodded and then Elodie got out of bed holding the phone by her side.

"Lady Elodie. I am so sorry for the disruption. I wanted to check on you. Are you alright?" Ariyanna asked. Her voice was strained and exhausted. Her tone reflected in her tired face.

"I am fine. Is—Is everything okay?"

Ariyanna sighed. "Honestly. Last night was the first quiet night we have had."

Elodie's heart pounded with sorrow.

"I know this must be overwhelming for you to hear."

Elodie looked at her. "It's overwhelming for him." Her eyes started to tear up. "He's been like this for months? Alone?" The realization hit her so hard. "Quinn and Cedar? They are there, right?"

A frown crossed his mom's face. "Master Ashdale has visited once, a few days after. We have not seen Cedar."

A whimper escaped Elodie now that her worries were confirmed. "What? No!" She wiped her eyes thinking about how many nights had passed since the ruins. It had been months and the despair threatened to rip a chasm in her heart. Everyone had turned on him and she knew what that felt like. It had ripped her away from all of them, but everyone had left Cyrus behind. This wasn't his fault.

"We have been trying. He refused to talk until last night. He went out once and we know something happened but he will not talk about that either. We just don't know how to get him to talk. We want him too. His father is really concerned about—" She paused and looked down. "Everything."

Elodie looked back towards the window.

Help him. Do not leave him behind. The lady begs for you to help him behind but she will not ask.

Elodie swallowed hard and for a moment the house was still and quiet.

"No! Please. I'm sorry," Cyrus screamed out.

"He's going to go into near cardiac arrest!"

"Cyrus, please. Relax, please! They are fine," Bracken begged.

Elodie looked over in the direction of the strain and then back to Ariyanna.

"May I try to help him?" Elodie asked softly, fear and hesitation apparent in her voice.

"Lady Elodie." The other female gazed at her bittersweetly. "I do not want you to be frightened. I am aware you held it too."

"Let me be the Earth Blessed. They gave me a task that night in the ruins and I never completed it. I thought I did. Lose the mountain lion, lose them all, but I didn't save the raven. Let me try." Elodie wasn't sure she could help him, but every second she hadn't helped him sooner frustrated her and made the guilt sink in further.

"You are so kind. Your heart is so big. Thank you."

"Let me put a hoodie on," Elodie said, running her hands down the robe she was wearing. Lady Nightswift nodded and closed the door a bit.

Elodie looked at her phone to find Trevin's face full of worry.

"Be careful please. I know you want to help him but you know how strong he is. Please let the sentries do what they need to before you get close."

"I will. I love you," she said.

"I love you too."

After she hung up, Elodie tossed her phone down and slipped into the hoodie and athletic shorts discarding the robe then hurried to the door.

"I am worried this will only upset Trevin more. Lord Greenthistle is growing concerned with his newfound anger." Ariyanna hesitated.

"I want to help them but I feel like I'm causing a disruption now," Elodie voiced.

"You are not a disruption. You saved us all. You bled for Cyrus. Nightswift is in your debt just as much as Greenthistle is."

Elodie nodded then stopped outside the door. She could hear Cyrus panting. She noticed Delia holding a wide-eyed Poppy back down the hall. Delia looked nervous.

"Cyrus, hun. Someone would like to see you. To help," Ariyanna said softly, walking in slowly.

Elodie saw sentries holding his arms and legs down, the covers a jostled mess. His hair stuck to his head with sweat. Cyrus took an inhale and cut his gaze right at Elodie, causing her to flinch at his sudden movement.

"No. Please! I'm sorry. I'm sorry," he cried out again, trying to fight the force with everything in him, his breathing was ragged. "Please."

"Stop!" Elodie pleaded. "Give him space. It's making it worse! The chains and the restraints." She stepped forward. "Let him go. He won't hurt anyone."

Cyrus started whimpering. Finally, his dad stood back and nodded at the sentries, who slowly let him go. Cyrus curled up on his side, burying his face in the covers.

She walked closer slowly. "I will not hurt you, Cyrus. You know this, yes?"

He watched her, still trembling from fear. "I can't stop seeing what it was going to do to you, what it did to Trevin, what it wanted to do to him. To Cedar, Quinn, and Autumn. Every single time I close my eyes. I hear you scream. I see Trevin beg Cedar to not get you. He cried and begged him not to get you. He was about to order him and that thing, my hands shot him, robbing him of breath."

"You didn't though. Trevin is okay. He's healed now," Elodie said, still taking cautious steps towards the bed.

"I hurt him. It made me touch you. Made me touch Autumn. It knew everything! Everything that you were, and Trevin! My hands. It used my hands to do all of that." He curled into himself more.

"It used your hands. Not you." She got closer. "I saw what it wanted to do with my body too. What it would have done to you and Trev with my hands once it realized my power. It would have kept Cedar and Quinn for their size alone. I know, Cyrus. It's haunting," Elodie said and started to tear up. "I'm sorry you've been stuck like this. I'm sorry I was so meek and scared. I did think about you a lot but was scared and for that, I'm sorry."

Cyrus tried to catch his breath and looked at her. She sat down slowly on the bed and looked at him.

"You are good, Cyrus. You fought so hard. I know you did and the Old Giants know it too."

"Everyone knows the power shifted and I'm too scared to tell you why, to tell Trev why." He looked away.

"And yet Nightswift still remains second, because the Old Giants know where Nightswift is strongest. We don't know each other very well yet, and I know that is partly my fault, but I'm here, Cyrus. Your Earth Blessed stands with you. I want to stand with you. You are good. Walk the trail with me please. You don't have to do this alone."

"I didn't want to hurt anyone. I hate this. I lost everything because of it and everyone knows I'm a monster."

"I know it hurts. You know that I know this. I'm here, Cyrus. I promise you that I am here and that you are good. You are not a monster. These Old Giants are with you. They know you fought," she said softly and held out her hand.

Cyrus looked at it, then looked at her.

"May I? If not yet a friend, then as your Earth Blessed?"

"What are you going to do?"

"Just a soothing touch. No tonics, no sedatives, just something to relieve the tension. I can't do what Trev or his dad can, but I can help soothe with my vines. No restraints I promise, just some relief that your Earth Blessed wants to offer you."

Cyrus hesitated and then reached for her hand. He gripped it tightly as if she were going to fall off a cliff and Elodie watched him almost exhale in relief. She hadn't done anything yet though.

"I'm sorry," he said softer. His breathing slowed. "I'm sorry for last night and today, Elodie. I just feel like you shouldn't have to do anything else for me. What you had to do that night, I'm sorry."

"You are okay, Cyrus. You will be okay. I want to be here as the Earth Blessed and for you. I accept your apology." Elodie's eyes flashed teal, then the vine and ferns crept up his arm as tension left his body. That thing she had sensed brushed itself along her vines but she couldn't explain how that thought had formed. She hadn't seen it; it was more a phantom sensation against her magic.

As his breathing slowed and returned back to normal, her vines slowly retreated back into her palm. Cyrus let out a big exhale and looked at the ceiling.

"How do you feel?" she asked.

"Calm. Tired. Quiet," he said, his voice not as hoarse anymore.

"You are no monster, Cyrus. You are Nightswift's heir. Tell yourself that, okay?"

He nodded. "Thank you."

"Anytime. Even if it is not my Nightswift week. I am here," she said softly and stood up, letting go of his hand. She glanced at his parents who were stunned at what she had done. "Would you like me to stay longer? I don't mind."

Cyrus shook his head. "No. I want to try to sleep. I'm sorry." He started to nod off as though the exhaustion had poured over him.

Elodie glanced at his parents. "You should go first. I will follow." She looked back at him. "Remember you are good, Cyrus." Elodie watched him nod once then closed his eyes. Quietly she left, pulling the door closed gently. His parents followed her back to her room.

"Thank you, whatever you did." Ariyanna's voice was grateful yet hushed.

"I hardly did anything. His heart rate slowed as soon as he took my hand. The vines were very minor."

"He nodded off on his own. Quietly. Usually he screams himself hoarse before exhaustion gets too heavy for him. This is two nights in a row he has been quiet."

"If he wakes up screaming and thrashing, you cannot hold him down." Elodie's eyes watered. "You cannot smother him like that. He was chained up and smothered for months. Give him space, let him know you are here for him." She wiped her eyes.

"Understood. He usually wakes up like he did tonight, screaming and thrashing still locked in his nightmares. We didn't want him to hurt himself."

"Being restrained is the very thing he is trapped in. Tell him he is good. Tell him he fought hard. He did, he sacrificed so much to give me a chance and it's so unfair he has been left behind." Elodie wiped her eyes again but the tears kept coming.

"Ever the Greenthistle, so brave and valiant," Bracken said as Ariyanna rubbed Elodie's back.

Elodie frowned and her shoulders slumped.

"Do you need anything? It is really no trouble at all," Ariyanna asked.

"No thank you, Lady Nightswift." Elodie's voice was solemn.

"If you do, please ask."

Elodie nodded and watched them head towards the door.

"I hope I can help him, help them all be like they were. Before me." She looked up and saw them both looking at her.

"You are the Earth Blessed. They all had their issues before you showed up. None of this was your fault. All we can do is move forward. Together," Bracken said.

"You are part of this family, Lady Elodie. You have our loyalty because you fight for him. We will fight for you."

Elodie nodded and wiped her eyes. "Thank you."

"Rest up. We have a lot to do tomorrow." Bracken gave her a smile and they left the room, closing the door gently.

Elodie looked at her phone and sighed, wondering how she was going to tell Trevin about this.

The self-doubt crept in despite what Nightswift had told her. She couldn't help but wonder where they would all be if she had simply not given into that pull. If she had just refused to. Who would Trevin be today? Who would Cyrus be? Would that thing have destroyed this place?

As silence filled a room usually filled with screams, tears now filled a once vacant room.

After another long day of training and lessons with both Lord and Lady Nightswift, Elodie was tired. It was a good kind of tired though, despite the long days and her missing the mortal world, she felt better today. She worked with Bracken on drills and Ariyanna today on reaction exercises. It was a lighter afternoon than it had been yesterday and she was grateful. Yet that evening as she sat by the firepit after dinner sadness crept over her. Ariyanna suggested she sit with the family, but Cyrus had remained in his room for what seemed like all day.

She started to mindlessly draw ravens, adding a little flower crown to one with dazzling blue eyes with her gel pens. As she drew and listened to Aryanna and Bracken talk about solstice, Elodie felt eyes watching her. She looked up to see Poppy watching her and eyeing her sketchbook.

"Hello, Lady—" Elodie stumbled over her words. "Forgive me, I am not sure of the proper way to address you."

Lord and Lady Nightswift had quieted, watching the interaction no doubt.

"Just Poppy is fine. I'm too young to be a lady."

"Poppy is a very pretty name." Elodie smiled.

"Thank you, Lady Elodie," Poppy replied and looked at her sketchbook again. "I like your raven drawings. Especially that one." Poppy pointed to one with a moon behind the raven wearing a flower crown. It was surrounded by stars.

"Thank you. I like to draw."

"That one looks kind of like my brother's raven. But I don't think I've ever seen him wear a flower crown."

Elodie laughed despite feeling sadness for Cyrus. All of the emotions he held, alone, were hollowing to her.

"Are you going to help him?" Poppy asked.

Elodie deflated and swallowed back the pain in her throat.

"Poppy, be mindful when you ask questions," Ariyanna scolded. "Remember to watch and read them first."

"I'm sorry," Poppy sighed.

Elodie looked at the girl, noting her fair skin and blonde hair. Her eyes were just like Cyrus's, a dazzling blue sapphire like their mom. There was no denying they were siblings. Her face markings were even similar, just with dots underneath.

"I really hope I can help him. I want to. Trev and Lord Greenthistle told me he's a very good brother to you."

Poppy looked down. "He was, until last year."

"I think he wants to be again, but he's a little lost right now. I am too, but—" Elodie fought the cry back again. "I will not leave him behind ever again." Her eyes watered.

Poppy nodded and smiled a little. "Thank you, Lady Elodie. I miss him, but I'm still afraid of him."

"You have nothing to fear from him. He would never hurt you. That thing is gone and locked away. It will never get him again. I will not let it. I promise you that too."

Poppy smiled wider and Elodie saw the hopefulness in her eyes. Elodie couldn't help but smile at it.

"When you are ready, let him know you are there. That you will show him the way too. It is a little scary for us both in different ways right now, but we will be okay. He is still your big brother." Elodie looked at Lord and Lady Nightswift who gave her a warm smile, and she saw the hope on their faces too.

CHAPTER 24

Cyrus arrived at his lesson in Six Rivers again with Elodie. This time he allowed himself to try to be friends with her. He did not come down for breakfast nor ride with them though. Dread was building in him and he was so terrified of tomorrow's solstice. He had told his parents he could do the opening but the realization that Alena was going to be present made him tremble. It got heavier and heavier on his shoulders as the lessons went on and near the end of the day, he was even messing up at simple tasks. Elodie had asked if he was alright and he wanted to break down but his dad and the sentries were all there. All he could do was say he needed to go and that he was sorry. Then he took off, running away like the meek little finch he was.

Evening came and Cyrus paced as he had done the last few nights in his room. The fear and the nerves were agony to him. He was so desperate for Elodie's hand again. Yet he feared Trevin would be livid. He would be here tomorrow, so would Quinn, Cedar, Autumn, and Alena. He had managed to ask Cedar if he was still with Alena.

'Yeah, I broke it off with her the day after I got out of the hold. She slapped me and I told her to leave us all alone. She is such a bitch.' He could hear and see Cedar scoffing and smirking. At least he had hoped that was Cedar's reaction while texting that. Yet there was no follow-up, no offer to stop by, to see how he was doing. Cyrus knew he deserved it. Cedar had sworn himself to protect Elodie now. If Trevin hadn't lunged for him a few nights ago, Cedar likely would.

Then a memory of that scent grabbed him. What if his vowed was there? Would they see him be a trembling heap?

He stared at the door and sighed. Elodie was here. She had told him they were equals, friends. Even when he tried to push her away and made her eyes brim with tears, she held her ground. Just as she had done for Trevin and for him in the ruins. A true Greenthistle, strong and brave. He envied her, wished he could do that.

"Try. One step. That's what she would say. I am good. I will not hurt her. I am no monster." He told himself over and over again.

With a loud sigh Cyrus approached the door and stepped out of his room. After finding her room empty, he ventured downstairs to see his dad at the kitchen and they exchanged a glance. His dad was going to hear how weak and feeble his firstborn was. Nightswift couldn't be led by a little finch.

His dad got up, causing Cyrus to cower back. Bracken stopped.

"Cyrus," he said painfully. "You are safe. This is your home."

He nodded and swallowed. "I-I was looking for Elodie."

"She's with your mom and Poppy in the den."

Cyrus nodded but didn't move. He wasn't sure he could do this but he was running out of time. Asking her for help felt like too much. Hell, even telling her was too much to put on her.

"You can go talk to her. She certainly has been trying to talk to you."

"I know."

"Then go on."

"Yes, sir," Cyrus stuttered and took a step towards the den. He could hear their conversation then he stopped when he heard Poppy speak. His heart sank. She couldn't hear this. The thought of her hearing any fraction of this made a tremble pass over him and he had to support himself against the wall.

"Cyrus, go," his dad insisted, causing him to flinch again.

With every step he forced himself to take, each one got heavier. He had no idea how he was going to get through tomorrow night. He heard his dad sigh and walk towards the den.

"No. Please," he whimpered. "Please." Cyrus was breathing hard. "Please."

Bracken stood at the entryway to the den looking at him. He heard the conversation in the room stop. His mom rushed out looking concerned.

"I'm sorry." His mind flashed to Alena laughing again, causing him to squeeze his eyes shut. A gasp made him open them to see Poppy, now hiding behind Elodie who had an arm around his little sister. Elodie looked concerned and he couldn't stand it. "I'm sorry," he whimpered, then turned to run.

"Cyrus. I'm here if you need it." Elodie's words made him freeze in his tracks. "You don't need to be afraid. He would never hurt you, Poppy." He heard her say softly and saw her kneeling in front of Poppy. His eyes met his sister's.

"I'm sorry. I need to talk. I'm scared for tomorrow, I want—I need help." Cyrus tensed and felt his insides shriveling up when his dad sighed. Elodie's heart pounded, causing him to look at her wide eyes. Scared, she was scared of him. If she only knew what he had done, what had been done to him. Maybe she would laugh at him if she knew. His parents would be ashamed. Poppy wouldn't think her big brother was very strong anymore. Not that he wanted her to know any of the details. He hated how trapped he felt. All he could do was beg for relief that never came because he was drowning in his own head with torment.

"Where would you like to talk?" Elodie's voice was full of concern. He met her eyes again and they were fixed on him. As fixed as Trevin would get when he was assessing people's emotions. The thought crossed his mind that they had vowed themselves. Had Trevin given her the ability? Would she see his shame, would she know everything he was hiding. His eyes went wide with fear. "Cyrus, I'm also nervous for Solstice, but we'll help each other through it. Right? I know what you saw. I know how terrifying it all was. To see all of this burn. I'm sorry you've been alone like this. But neither one of us has to do this alone," she said softly.

"I caused you to be left alone. I caused him to let you go, I let you experience all this and left you on this trail you shouldn't have been on. I'm lost and it's not fair to ask you to come find me." He turned away again.

"But you want to. You knew that night in Arcata Community Forest what I was. And now these Old Giants want you to know that they look after their own. I'm here because you are good and you fought so hard for me to be here. Help me find my way too. Please?"

He thought of the Old Giants, the ferns, and her cradling his raven in her arms, soothing him and calming him down. Only so she could break through to rip his chains off to take them on to herself. She was right, she did know. He sighed and leaned against the wall, letting his body relax. His shoulders heaved and he looked up, seeing one of the windows. The stars caught his eyes, not the Old Giants, but they too were watching him. He could feel it.

"Outside," he replied, then looked at Poppy. "I'm sorry, Poppy. I don't think you should hear any of it. I want to be there for you when you integrate. But I need El's help first."

Poppy nodded and stepped away from Elodie.

Once they were outside, Cyrus sat on one of the couches. Elodie followed and sat next to him. She was still tense but she had sworn to be there for all of them and Cyrus needed his Earth Blessed. He had needed a friend for months. Quinn had been pissed at Trevin for letting her go, but he hadn't been very loyal to Cyrus at all. He had grown more elusive as of late. As she began to process all that had changed between the three heirs, Cyrus began to speak and she gave him her undivided attention.

"I went out when my lockdown was over. I was too scared to call Quinn or Cedar. Trevin was out of the question because you needed him, and he needed you. I ended up at the tavern." Elodie tensed. She had not been there yet but Trevin had expressed his disdain for the place. "I didn't go to hook up with anyone or seek anyone out. I just, I just wanted to know that someone saw me as something other than a monster who hurt the Earth Blessed but they all said it. 'Monster, unstable, should be stripped of his title. Should be in the hold.' I ran out of there in panic and someone approached me and said I looked like shit. When I looked up, I saw Alena," he said, trembling now.

Elodie looked at him with such worry now.

He took a deep breath and continued. "She grabbed my hand and I tensed. She said we needed to talk and I knew I owed her that much. We ended up at some secluded patch of forest." His voice started to shake and he wouldn't look at her. "She started to run her mouth, to talk poorly about us all, then she—" He swallowed hard. "Started to grab me, kiss me, I told her to stop. I said no. I said it so many times! Her hands were all over my body and I was too scared to fight back. Scared if I did I would hurt her, I would be that monster everyone knows I am." He was sobbing now and Elodie brought her hands to her mouth in shock. A pit formed so deep in her core, and despair poured into her upon hearing what had happened to him. His entire body was trembling with his sobs. He had been so alone and Alena had dragged him through the dirt. She had invaded Trevin's space and touched him, but she had literally assaulted Cyrus in the worst way possible.

"She kept repeating all the horrible things that spirit had said using my voice and I snapped, finally throwing her off me. When I got back to my feet, she called me pathetic and slapped me and ran off. I fell down and cried for an hour before I came back here. I took a shower to try to get the sensation off. If I wasn't feeling your blood on me, I was feeling her hands on me, tugging my clothes. I wanted the water to burn my skin off."

"Cyrus, can I give you a hug?" Elodie asked, her voice riddled with shock.

He looked at her, equally as shocked. "Why would you want to touch me? I hurt your vowed. Hurt you."

"It hurt Trevin, not you. That wasn't you. Whatever fucked up maliciousness stews in Alena is her business, but she was wrong. You did not deserve to be touched like that. You are good and not a monster. You are so brave and loyal to all of us and fought so hard. I can tell you are so exhausted from it all. You have been so alone for so long and I am sorry. Know that I will not leave you behind. Ever."

He nodded. "Yes." She looked at him unsure for a moment. "I would like a hug."

Elodie did not hesitate. She wrapped her arms around him and he grabbed her tight, then began to sob as if he could not bear it anymore.

"No matter how heavy any of it is, it's not your fault. I will never let that spirit get you again, I will not let her hurt you either," Elodie said fiercely.

"I said no so many times. Some fucked up part of me felt worried when I threw her off of me."

"You did not hurt her, she hurt you and she was wrong for it." Elodie held him tight and rubbed his back. "Those Old Giants know what she did. They desperately want you to keep this title because they know you are good, you deserve it. Never let anyone tell you otherwise. She will suffer her consequences, if the high estates will not do it, the Old Giants will."

"I never thought I deserved your help, never had a right to ask for it. I just wanted some kind of reassurance from anyone that I wasn't a monster. I never wanted to become one. I never wanted to touch you. The act of it made me cringe and scream so much. If Trevin saw it he'd have attacked me. That vowed bond drove him absolutely wild and he is so territorial over you. Then he just let go. I'm so sorry, Elodie."

"I accept your apology. I hope you can rest now, Cyrus. You are safe. Anytime you need me, call me. When you can come back to the mortal side, come to my house, stay in the guest room to get used to that side again. Trevin will not hurt you. He will not hurt you at solstice either. Let me have your opening dance. Please."

"El," he cried again, still hugging her as though she were going to fall if he didn't. "I can't. The rumors and the gossip. Trev is going to be livid that we are hugging. Please don't tell him. Please. I'm sorry." Cyrus went to pull away but Elodie didn't let go.

"He will not hurt you. Let him see how badly you are hurting. Trevin means what he said about me being my own person. He will always be my vowed, the one that I chose. But I am choosing you as my friend, and my brother. I am here for you, and in time I think Trev will come back to you too. Don't carry this alone anymore."

Cyrus just nodded and wrapped his arms around her again.

"You are so brave Cyrus. You are Nightswift's heir." Elodie noticed his parents standing in the doorway. They looked so worried and she wasn't sure how much they heard. "I know this might be hard, but I think your parents should know. I think Trevin should know."

"They are going to be so disappointed. They already are. Trevin doesn't want me as his second. A terrified little finch."

"No. That is not true. Your parents love you; they want you to heal. I know they do. If they know, they can help more effectively. They can find someone who can help. You know Trevin is the empath, he doesn't want you to hurt or hold this in. He just needs to learn to process this anger."

"I don't want to see their expressions when I tell them. I don't want to speak it again."

"May I? I want to help you too. I will not leave you here."

"Okay." He sighed.

"I will not violate your privacy nor do anything to break your trust, Cyrus. Are you sure you are okay with me telling them? You have the right to tell me not to, no need to make a bargain."

He gave her another squeeze. "You can tell them. I don't want to be there though."

Elodie saw his parents nod and then turn to leave, silent as ever. Cyrus stopped crying after a few more minutes and exhaled. His body went limp.

"I think I want to try to sleep. I feel so tired."

"Of course," Elodie said. They walked back to his room and once more she let her vines soothe him. Elodie watched his breathing slow as his head fell to the side. Seeing him and listening to his deep slow breathing, she could sense something in him changing. Yet it didn't feel like the Old Giants. Again, something reached for her vines, reached for her. Her vines reached for it too.

After another minute she went to turn off the light and saw his mom standing at the door. Her body tensed.

"He likes the light dimmed. Not too dark, but not too bright." She smiled and turned the dimmer switch down. "This is the quietest it's been for months." Elodie frowned. "Would you be willing to come into the study?"

"Of course, Lady Nightswift," Elodie said with a deep inhale.

Chapter 25

Once they were in Bracken's study, Elodie slumped in a seat and buried her face in her palms. All the emotions she had been fighting began to spill when Ariyanna rubbed her back in a nurturing, motherly way. At this moment she missed her mom and dad comforting her. She recalled their concern when she had cut her hand so many years ago. Every emotion felt so heavy at this very moment and as much as it all hurt, something told her she was right where she needed to be. It was exactly where the Old Giants, the stars, and the earth had wanted her. It was where she wanted to be, where she needed to be.

Nightswift had been so thoroughly hurt by all of this and some small wound that had not properly healed was starting to fester with infection. Elodie didn't know how to heal it, but she knew that it needed intervention.

"Thank you for letting him do that. For being strong for him. I don't think he had felt comfortable just crying on anyone ever. We have never seen him this traumatized before," Ariyanna said softly, still rubbing her back.

"I thank you too. For reassuring him we are not disappointed. That we are concerned," Bracken said gratefully, yet his tone was stiff.

Elodie thought about his dad sitting there looking so displeased while his son just trembled. He kept pushing and pushing. Just as Echo pushed Trevin and Miles pushed Quinn. The difference was, Quinn brushed it off. Trevin had grown strong and knew he needed to fight back. Neither one of them had been left alone like Cyrus had. She took a deep inhale and leveled her gaze at Bracken.

"Stop pushing him! I know they all have such a big responsibility as heirs but he is trembling near insanity." Her throat burned, trying to fight back that breaking in her voice. "I'm sorry if this is out of line or whatever, but he's still trapped and I failed. I didn't do what the Old Giants told me to do in the ruins. I left him behind and then so did everyone else. Stop pushing him."

"You saved everything that night, after we had all but cast you out. You didn't fail anyone," Bracken expressed. "And you are allowed to tell us how you feel. We all want you to."

"I did fail though. I was writhing on my floor and those whispers became screams. Save the raven, save them all, lose the mountain lion, lose them all. I saw Trevin lifeless in a pool of blood and everything burned. I left the raven there and someone else hurt him, because that mountain lion and that bear were too busy being angry with each other and everyone was tending to me."

"Lady Elodie. That simply is not true. As I said yesterday, you did not cause this, you cannot be expected to fix everything that was broken. You needed to know Trevin was there. He needed to know you were there and we would not stand in his way. He needed to learn to trust us too, because for a moment, when we took you he thought he had lost you for good. You needed Greenthistle." Bracken sighed and looked down before meeting Elodie's glossy eyes. "What happened to him? We found him screaming in a scalding hot shower."

Elodie saw the flash of teal in her vision and the lord and lady of Nightswift tensed.

"Alena assaulted him. Far worse than what she did to Trevin. I hated her that morning when I saw that photo. Hated that she was in his bed. She hardly faced any consequences for what she did to Trevin and if he deemed it not worth his time to pursue then fine, he decided that. But she forced herself on Cyrus far worse and then left him half dressed in the dirt," Elodie snapped out.

"She violated him?" his mom asked, hardly able to get the words out.

"Yes." Elodie explained the story and both his parents looked ill. "She cannot attend the Solstice. She was a bitch to me at the spring equinox and you know she will be absolutely vile to him tomorrow."

Bracken sighed and rested his head on his head. "I am not sure rescinding the invitation would be wise. Elmbridge will make a fuss."

"She hurt your child!" Elodie snapped.

He took a deep inhale. "I will request her ban from Nightswift Estate. I will request the logs to see if Elmbridge lost power, but these things will take time. If I had known sooner."

Elodie felt the tears fall. Guilt and shame crawled up her spine, planting their worries along the way. "He didn't feel safe. Alena cannot attend, she can't."

"Lady Elodie. There are formalities to these things and the ultimate fear is if we bring this forward, they will bring Cyrus's actions to trial. Trevin will be brought to trial, Cedar and you will as well."

"She already threatened to bring him to one. Why are you not helping him more?"

"Cyrus cannot take a stand; they will grill him. I will also have to report it to the regional council in September and I am already nervous about that. You have done so much in just a few days but I fear we are just beginning the ascent. I don't know what their requests are going to be. Cyrus could be stripped of his title. Cedar sentenced to time, Trevin too might be in jeopardy"

"Why?" Elodie said in a low tone with a glare.

Bracken sighed again. "Cyrus hurt an estate heir, he hurt the Earth Blessed, the list goes on."

"He didn't do any of that!" She gritted her teeth. Elodie had no doubt they could hear her heart rate now.

"He did something on his own free will. Something that costs Nightswift power, and the fae can tell. Everyone on this side of the boundary knows that Nightswift lost. We are lucky it wasn't enough to lose rank. He has not told you what I assume."

"No, but that's not fair. If he touched me willingly it was probably because he was forced to play along. He didn't shoot Trevin with those arrows willingly and he didn't want either of us dead."

"We know it was more than him getting too close or scaring you. He told us he never wanted to do that, had no desire to do that, and he cannot lie. He did something else and unless he can tell us why, I cannot bring him in front of any jury. We would be unprepared to defend him."

Elodie sat back and felt like she wanted to scream. For a moment she understood Quinn's frustration with the power shift despite him acting poorly about it all.

"If I have to go on trial I will tell them. He is good, he fought for Nightswift and me, he fought to give Trevin and I a chance." That pain in her throat was back.

Bracken looked at her with a sad smile before he spoke. "You may run with the fae, but you are not fae. You have the ability to lie. Your word will mean little to them in a trial, they will interrogate you just to make us all writhe. They know how human your heart remains and they know how to taunt. All fae do."

"I'm the one who could have died! I'm the one who saved you and this estate, and this entire place. I am the Earth Blessed, the folk tale that came to life."

"You are still foreign and new. Not everyone likes fairy tales. Just as some mortals do not like fantasy stories, not all fae hold the lore to be truth."

"Odd. Just a meek little mortal with dirt and boundary line in my blood, not worthy of Greenthistle's heir." She wiped her eyes and felt her face burn.

"In time they will accept you but right now a great change has come about our world and none of them know what to make of it. We do though and we know you are observant, loyal and strong. Worthy of Greenthistle in every way. I know you are overwhelmed with emotion, I see it on you, and you are still pushing through it all to get to Cyrus," Bracken said. "That is why you are here, but this trail is so new for all of us."

"Why would Trevin be in jeopardy? He followed all the rules. He was so careful and ready to drive himself mad."

"They will pick apart the story of you two to see if he ever in fact broke a rule and swayed you."

"He didn't! I saw him at that Halloween party and he left me speechless by just standing there in his fancy clothes. Does merely existing count as swaying? He has never forced my hand on anything."

"I know, Trevin has never done that to anyone. But they will question every single step you have taken and any of it can be twisted that he swayed you. He followed you some nights to ensure you were safe. He went to that café to watch you and made himself known to you. They could argue that it was swaying you towards him." Bracken let out an exhale. Ariyanna looked down in sorrow.

"We are vowed! Did you sway your vowed to move here? Does Ashdale get a pass since they were both born here? Did Lord Greenthistle sway Lady Greenthistle?"

Lady Nightswift got a chill at that and Elodie looked at her.

"No. None of us swayed, but one did try to say I swayed Ari to being with me multiple times and I still have never forgiven Lord Stormbriar for it," Bracken muttered and Ariyanna nodded.

"It is a strained dynamic with my father and I. Bracken's actions that night likely prevented a war with Del Norte and Oregon's southern territories. It was clear the argument had little ground to stand on when they swayed me to leaving. It was an adjustment for me to step into this role. It was an adjustment for Selene and Olive too. Every territory has different ways of viewing vowed bonds between fae. Between mortal and fae is such a difficult position for us to be in and the rules are so much more strict."

"What about Earth Blessed and fae? Trevin didn't sway me. These Old Giants pulled me up here." Her words cut off. Mt. Tamalpais had never wanted her, but at eight years old but these Old Giants had. Was that what made Marin County so stifling to her? Was it trying to push her out? Had it known she needed to be here?

Bracken spoke, pulling her attention back to him. "We know you chose this, you fought for it. I am trying to avoid saying it, but they do not factor you in, they just put you through it. You have enough fire in you. You might convince them, but you cannot carry us all through this one. It is not your reaction to any of Trevin's movements they will question. It is his movements that will be scrutinized."

Elodie pushed air through her nose and crossed her arms. "They would treat Greenthistle's heir apparent like that? Any of their heirs? Strip them of their title for something they did in their forties? And to strip Cyrus of his after what he has been through? It was beyond his control. And no offense, but you mean to tell me you never led a hopeless mortal on in your forties? Your nineties? Your 200's? I assume you are near Lord Greenthistle's age?"

Bracken grimaced as did Ariyanna. "I am 418, Ari is 391."

"Not one stupid thing that could be questioned? If they are going to question Trevin for merely being present where I was."

"None of us are saints, nor do we claim to be. Remember that. Cyrus will not talk about what he did but it is no secret he broke a rule. The question is which one did he break."

"This isn't fair though. Why are you okay with your children being treated like this? All they want to do is make you proud."

"I know. I see it in them all. But it is how things operate here, Lady Elodie. There are other estates that would love to take our place. Some feel they would be better at our jobs, and maybe they would. Some would be far worse. Regardless, a high estate falling out of rank, is not something any of us wish to experience, especially after what happened to Cyrus that night."

Elodie sighed as she realized how tired she was from the night. From everything. "I feel helpless and I hate it."

"You are not helpless. You have been proving it to us since you moved up here and started watching your environment just as diligent as any Nightswift. Trevin could see it in you and he saw who he wanted to become as a result of your presence. He is well on his way to surpassing Echo in every aspect," Bracken affirmed.

"His mother always said he would make Greenthistle better than Echo ever had." She laughed but it did not sound gleeful.

Elodie gained that the estate spouses had been close. Sisters bound by duty just as their partners were all brothers bound by the same. Now she was growing sad, thinking about how she might not have that. Sure, Autumn would be there, until she maybe wasn't. Her vowed could be anywhere and she wasn't beholden to stay like Trevin was. Then again, Cyrus and Trevin were in jeopardy now. She refused to give that thought any more attention. They would remain, the Old Giants wanted it to be that way. She would ensure they stayed that way, even if she had to do something drastic.

"Calm your mind and soul, Lady Elodie. You have done enough today. Sleep please. We still have a long week ahead. We will send the order out and check Elmbridge's rank. Alena will not be welcomed over here going forward. As you know one repercussion she did face after the ruins was being banned from Greenthistle," Ariyanna said softly, watching Elodie.

"Is she firstborn? Is she going to take over her estate?"

"She is the third born. Her parents have both been pains in all our asses for decades," Bracken said.

"Alena is absolutely vile."

"Rest. If you need anything, ask. Autumn will be over early in the morning and I will send breakfast and lunch to your room for you all. Poppy asked if she could get ready with you, if that is alright," Ariyanna asked. Elodie nodded and stood up.

"Of course." Elodie smiled after releasing all the tension she had been holding. "After I leave, please remind him I am here for him. He doesn't have to wait three weeks to tell me things. My phone is always on, the house is always open. You all opened your estates to me and I may not be able to give everyone their own rooms, but I do have an extra room," she offered, and they both smiled at her in response.

"You are very kind, Lady Elodie. Lady Greenthistle would have loved you, she had a big heart too," Ariyanna said. "We'll remind him and encourage him to reach out."

Elodie felt a sting in her heart at the thought of Trevin's mom. As she walked back to her room she began to wonder, thinking about what life must have been like for Trevin when that happened. Wondered what he was like before. He was twenty, aware of life and the expectations of him by then. She had been young and still learning about her world when her mom passed. She walked to the window in her room and looked at the trees.

Some part of her imagined a mountain lion cub so overcome with grief as it looked up at the stars. She imagined the Old Giants feeling their heir's sorrow.

Suddenly a new pain hit her heart as her mind flashed to that night at her house, before her Greenthistle week. The sadness that washed over her that night. She sank to her knees, recalling how she had told Trevin not to send ravens out. Ravens who would have found their heir being hurt, screaming in fear. She leaned forward and cried into her hands. They had tried to tell her and she ignored them.

"I'm sorry," she whispered. Lifting her head she looked at the trees. "I'm sorry. I failed him," she cried. "Cyrus."

This was not your fault.

You could not have forced either cub to come for him, you still cannot.

All we ask is that you continue to guide him.

The raven's nest is quiet thanks to you.

He can rest. He will always remain loyal to you above blood or bonds.

Elodie dropped her head, feeling a calming wave pulse over her. Her shoulders slumped and she pushed herself up and got into bed, before noticing a text from Trevin.

Little Mink. It is late for an energy surge.

Elodie knew this was not a reprimand but a request to tell him if something was wrong. To let him know she was alright. A defeated sigh slipped out of her as she texted him back.

I am okay. Nightswift has been so kind. I fear I might let them down. That I already have.

El. What happened? Were you hurt during a drill? Did Cyrus hurt you?

No. I am fine, no one has hurt me. I just feel lost at times.

Do you want to talk about it, or wait until I'm over there?

When you are here. I have a few more days to find my way. I want to find my way. I am safe though, Trevin. I love you.

Love you too. Your mountain lion is counting down the hours.

She smiled briefly and after plugging her phone into charge, wept until slumber took hold.

Chapter 26

As expected, Greenthistle and Ashdale arrived earlier the next day. Greenthistle arrived for Elodie's sake and Bracken had summoned Ashdale for a meeting. Trevin had been anxious in Bracken's study, wanting to see Elodie. Then he felt something hollow in him upon hearing what Cyrus had told Elodie this week so far.

Emotions surged. He felt anger for dumping everything onto Elodie. As if she needed any more to overwhelm her. There was also anger at Cyrus not fessing up to everything. Pride too that Elodie was so strong, not that he needed any more proof that she was a Greenthistle. Then his thoughts shifted from her to Cyrus. How lonely that must have been for him. How vile Alena was to do that to him, to leave him there screaming in the dirt. She should be on trial, for all of Humboldt to see how horrible she was, yet that meant Elodie would be poked and prodded. It also meant Cyrus would have to relive it in front of so many people. Feeling the weight of it all, Trevin slumped back in his chair and looked up at the ceiling.

"It was confirmed Elmbridge did lose power. Naturally they have made no attempt to make amends. I am not sure if her parents know. I would hope if they did they would apologize. However the ban has gone through. It is advised that none of the estate children talk to or about anyone from Elmbridge Estate. We will handle it."

"Wretched and deplorable," Trevin spat as he stewed in too many emotions.

"I commend you for not letting your anger surge, but despair always seems to have it out for you, Master Greenthistle," Bracken sighed.

"I don't know what to do." Trevin ran his hands through his hair. He hadn't styled it for tonight. He seldom did anything with it for any occasion.

"You will figure it out, son."

"I hate her so much. I was so stupid," Cedar scoffed and leaned against the wall.

"Did she do anything to you? Or you, Master Ashdale," Echo asked.

"She tried to see how serious I was when I broke it off with her, I promptly pushed her back and I told her to never go near Cyrus, El, Trev, or me again. Clearly she didn't listen. I should have ordered her," Cedar explained.

"Nah, I never gave her a chance." Quinn sat back in his chair.

Trevin now felt his anger surge and leapt up, scowling at Quinn. "You think I fucking did? I didn't want her in the house! Certainly not my bed. That was always going to be El's place! Justine is rubbing off on you."

"Not another word from either of you," Echo snapped. "I will not have a ruined solstice on account of moody cubs in Nightswift's domain."

Trevin sat back down.

"Drop it, Quinn," Miles insisted then crossed his arms.

Ariyanna took a deep inhale. "At any rate we still have a solstice to get through."

"Trevin," Bracken started, now looking at him with a pleading gaze. "Please, I am begging you for the sake of tonight and your second in command, let her be there for him. She is the only one he feels safe with. The only one who can calm him down quickly."

Trevin sighed.

"This is the most progress we have seen out of him. He can sleep through the night after she talks to him. He now leaves his room with no trouble. Please, I hate asking this of you. I know she is your vowed, he knows it too. He is terrified you are going to rip him to pieces but if we can get through tonight, he will be that much closer to getting better," Ariyanna pleaded. "Please stay the night at Nightswift, in her quarters with her. We would never ask you to be away from her during or after any revelry, but he needs all the support he can get right now."

"Thank you for the offer to stay. I'm worried though. This is a lot for her and rumors are going to start. About him, about her," Trevin groaned.

"Trev. I told you to fix this, with her and your brothers. He has been a wreck. Let her be the Earth Blessed. You know you already have her heart. This is part of her role, you are her vowed, but a high estate needs their Earth Blessed," Echo explained.

Trevin exhaled as his shoulders sagged. "I know. I trust her. But I still don't know if I can trust him fully."

"He hasn't tried to do any of it. He honestly avoids her and I can see that too weighs on her. I have seen them hug once and he was so terrified you would murder him for that," Bracken explained.

Trevin's eyes narrowed and he took a deep inhale, reigning in his territorial urges.

"She asked if she could give him a hug. It was the night he told her about Alena and he cried so hard. He just needed someone to be there for him. She is not the one any of us expected to be there for him. That likely includes him too."

Trevin recalled him trembling on the stairs on Saturday. Then he looked over at Quinn, who had the audacity to look annoyed by all of this. As if he was in any kind of turmoil. As if Justine had a responsibility anywhere near as big as Elodie did. "You don't see any of this?"

Quinn looked at Trevin with surprise, then he scowled. "No."

"The one time he saw him did not end very well," Bracken said with some spite.

"One time?" Trevin growled. "Why just one time?" Then he realized Cedar hadn't either and looked at his brother.

"What? I was busy with work and trying to make amends to El. I'm sorry." Cedar put his hands up, clearly knowing he had messed up.

"You didn't see him either." Quinn rolled his eyes.

"I was busy making sure our Earth Blessed was adjusted. I was busy living in two places and dealing with a dumb nosey intern. Not only that, he shot me with floss flower! Forgive me if it took me a bit to be ready to face him. What have you been busy with?"

"Trevin," his dad warned.

Quinn spat, "Covering for all our asses. He just trembled the entire time he saw me too, he wasn't going to cry on me and confess his sins. He is terrified of you and now he has the audacity to cling to El?"

A sudden coldness shot through the room and Quinn's face contorted to shock. Trevin looked at him with confusion when he saw the fear in Quinn's eyes. He noticed everyone else tense up yet Trevin hadn't felt anything. He didn't think it was Elodie. Autumn was with her, as was Poppy. Yet something made him turn to the trees and it was an odd sensation of warning. He was, however, still livid.

"It is highly advised you drop this now. Let her be the Earth Blessed they chose. Show her what Greenthistle's strength and Ashdale's loyalty means," Echo hissed.

"Fine. I would like for my vowed to be at my side at some point during the night," Trevin huffed as he sat back down, annoyed. He knew the motion made him look immature and he forced himself to take a deep breath.

"She will be. She loves you. But she wants to be a Greenthistle for Cyrus. Let her," Ariyanna said.

"Understood. Cedar, Quinn, may I ask you to also keep an eye out for Elodie and Cyrus?"

"Of course, I am on it." Cedar nodded.

Quinn rolled his eyes. "Yes."

"Thank you all for agreeing to this," Bracken sighed. "Maybe you should go see him? I can send some wine up?"

Trevin and Quinn looked at each other for a moment. Then Quinn looked at Bracken.

"I think the three of us entering his room is going to send him into a screaming fit." Quinn sighed in defeat. "I don't want to stress him or El out any more than tonight will."

Trevin frowned. "Do you think I should? I wasn't exactly very friendly to him on Saturday."

Bracken's expression was full of remorse. "I have not been a very good father to him during these months either. He flinches around me still. If you apologize or even if you just try, he seems to respond."

"I think he wants to apologize to those he wronged. Lady Elodie has been so kind to him and I think if you all are he will know he is safe," Ariyanna said.

"I think you should be the next one, Trev. I think he wronged you equally as much as El." Cedar laughed then nodded towards Quinn. "I will keep an eye on that asshole sitting next to you,".

Quinn rolled his eyes and pulled his phone out as he stood up.

Trevin followed Ariyanna up to Cyrus's room. He was unsure what he might walk into, and the unease grew.

She knocked and called for her son. "Cyrus, I just wanted to see how you were do—" She was cut off abruptly as she walked into the room. Trevin's heart tensed as he stood outside.

"I'm sorry," Cyrus whimpered.

"You can't do this tonight, can you?" Ariyanna sighed. Trevin could hear the disappointment in her tone.

"Please. I'm sorry. I don't want to disappoint you or Dad. I'm trying," Cyrus cried. "Please." Trevin rolled his eyes in anguish. He really had no one. Of course he clung to Elodie, she was kind and cared so much about this place that had wanted her. She had wanted it and all of them included.

"Someone is here to see you."

"El?"

Ariyanna remained quiet for a moment. "No, she is still getting ready."

Trevin knew this was not going to get any easier for any of them. This was not something that would ever heal properly if it wasn't tended to. Quinn certainly wasn't tending to it.

With an exhale he walked into the room. Something fell and hit the bathroom floor. Cyrus started to panic.

"No. I'm sorry. I'm sorry!" he screamed. Trevin saw him in the bathroom; he was mostly dressed save for the overshirt and his diadem. The look in his eyes was pure terror as he was backed up into a corner.

"I'm not here to be angry, Cyrus. Deep slow breaths," Trevin said calmly. "I'm sorry for how I acted on Saturday. It was uncalled for. I could see you were struggling. Your dad probably made you sit there, didn't he? Your choice would have been to stay up here, huh?" Trevin asked softly. Cyrus remained wide-eyed and heaving. "I am sorry I haven't been there. That you have been like this. I want to try to move forward when you are ready."

Finally he took a hard swallow. "Why?"

Trevin was taken aback by the question. "Why? There are a million reasons, but all of them boil down to me needing to be better."

"I hurt you. I hurt her. I sowed seeds of doubt."

"Did you want to? Was it your intent?"

"What! No! I hated touching her, that thing forced me to watch her, and every time she screamed your name I screamed right beside her, hoping she would hear me, that you would, or Nightswift would. That anyone would hear me."

"My dad told me to fix it. With her, with Cedar, and with you. I fixed it with both of them, but now you and I need to rebuild our trust. I want my second in command back."

With that Cyrus finally stood a little straighter and gave the smallest nod.

"He will not hurt you. You can see it, just as well as I can. I will leave you two alone for a bit," his mom said and Cyrus gave her a worried look. "Just try."

Cyrus leaned back against the counter and looked down as his mom left.

"She's right, I am not going to hurt you, Cyrus." Trevin watched him stare at the ground. "I'm sorry too for what happened. You didn't deserve that. Alena is an absolute bitch. I was—still am—livid she isn't in the hold."

"I should be in there too," Cyrus said, still not looking up.

"I don't think so."

"When I see El, I will tell her to go to you after they announce her and all her titles. Don't worry."

"If she gives you solace, then ask her to dance."

Cyrus looked up, finally meeting Trevin's eyes. They were red and glossy. "No. The rumors are going to start. It's only been a few months and I know the vowed bond is pulling at you. It's worse because you spent so long fighting it." He deflated again.

"You knew the entire time?"

"Ever since that night she passed out in Arcata Community forest and you watched over her."

"Fuck. And you couldn't say anything." Trevin's shoulders slumped.

"I tried, I swear I did, consequences be damned."

Trevin thought about all their interactions over the last six months.

"You tried to tell me at the bonfire didn't you, after you freaked her out at the bathrooms?"

Cyrus nodded. "Yes."

"You just had to watch me act like a complete dumbass and get her to despise me for months."

"She never hated you, not for a single second. Elodie loves you so much."

"Yea, well, I'm pretty sure she loathed me before King Range," Trevin sighed.

"Not even then. She just walked out to a redwood looking lost and told her mom that the magic was real, and then she said you'd think she was stupid that the trees talked to her and laughed to herself. But it was obvious she was doubting herself. Then she sent that pulse out."

"That's what that was? All while I was sealing my fate as the Greenthistle Disappointment in the tavern."

"No, you aren't. You went to the tavern? You hate that place," he said, confused, then frowned. "It made me watch her a lot."

"Yeah. I was just so riled up from almost taking her on her couch," Trevin explained.

When it was nearing time for the opening of the revelry Trevin stood up from the chair as did Cyrus.

"Cyrus, it's going to take time for me to work through everything that happened, for this vowed bond to calm down in me, too. But I do miss you. I miss just having a drink and talking to you. I haven't done that with any of you in a while. El is here for you. She always will be. I want to be as well." He met Cyrus's wide-eyed expression.

"Thank you, Trevin."

Chapter 27

Usually the master of the estate was already in the room, socializing when they made the opening announcement. It was Elodie who had gotten the big reveal with the doors. However, Cyrus struggled to walk through them this time. Elodie's grand announcement had been made and she walked through the doors. Cyrus knew he had a few minutes until he was expected to appear.

Taking a deep breath, he walked into the light. The brightness of them blinded him and sent a pulsing headache through him. He fought a tremble after hearing people gasp. Something in him was ready to rip out of him. The urge to run nearly overtook him until she spoke.

"You are good," Elodie said softly. Her words were a reminder to take a deep breath.

"Announcing the arrival of Master Nightswift." With the words he knew he had to do the opening dance. All he had to do was get through this and he could shrivel up back to his room.

"You are good. You are Nightswift's heir," she said again.

Cyrus turned to her and took a small step, waiting for her to step back. She held her ground.

Another step, and Elodie offered him a nod. He could hear the murmurs start and he squeezed his eyes shut. She repeated the affirmation one more time and he gave in, quickly closing the remaining gap between them. He watched her reassuring smile and scanned for fear and unease. She was schooling it well, but her heartbeat was too fast to match her expression.

"Lady Elodie. May I have this dance?" He bowed slightly.

"It would be an honor, Master Nightswift." She curtsied and took his hand. As they started to dance the murmurs grew louder.

"He is still so unstable."

"Master Greenthistle is going to lash out."

"Do you think she is sleeping with him too?"

"Oh maybe."

All their words seeped into his ears.

"Cyrus, ignore them. You are good. I trust you. Trevin knows he can trust you too." Elodie's words were so soft.

He nodded. "I'm sorry." He nearly whimpered.

"I feel more comfortable that you are here, that you are asserting I am an ally to you."

"Thank you." Cyrus took a deep inhale. "Trevin stopped by my room before I came downstairs."

"He did?"

Cyrus went on to explain.

As Trevin watched while fighting his rage at first, the sheer torment on Cyrus's face snagged him. He could hardly hold his head up. Trevin had just sat in his room and told him he wanted to be there for his second. He knew the Earth Blessed wanted to be there for her high estates. Forcing his body to relax, his eyes scanned the gawking fae examining their emotions, from fear, to shock, to disgust; some even had a level of contemplation. A few glanced at him then quickly looked away. He knew he was glaring, yet one expression held his attention.

A tree nymph fae mix, with russet brown skin and hair that faded from teal to white. Trevin knew of her. He had never spoken to her, but he knew her name was Bryla, firstborn of Petalgrace Estate. She was in the majority that didn't cross the boundary and lived in Nightswift's domain. He sometimes would cross her path while working when state parks work took him closer to redwoods where she tended to land. They never spoke though, sometimes she looked at him almost nervously. He had seen her at the tavern a few times too. She always seemed to have a mix of shyness and longing in her when she would look at them in the tavern.

Tonight, however, she was fixed on Cyrus and Elodie. Despair, sorrow, and jealousy plagued her right now. Trevin glanced at Cyrus who took an inhale and tensed. Fear and nerves washed over him. Elodie watched him and then Trevin saw it. His eyes darted back to Bryla who still looked so hurt. She didn't understand what was happening, nor did Elodie. He likely wouldn't have understood it either, had he not met Elodie.

Bryla was Cyrus's vowed, and Cyrus knew she was here. He had scented her above everyone else in this room.

Trevin debated for a moment if he was in fact breaking a rule, but he wanted Elodie. He didn't want Cyrus to cling to her all night when his vowed was right here. A little encouragement couldn't hurt. Quinn had outright told Elodie and he gained. Trevin knew if Bryla was ever in trouble, he would run to help Cyrus despite everything. He certainly would shield Bryla from anyone else who saw the vowed bond. So he made his way over to Bryla who was so fixated on Cyrus she didn't notice his presence.

"Lady Petalgrace. Just who I wanted to talk to." Trevin watched her startle and look at him with wide eyes. She was still feeling all her emotions but now was mortified.

"Master Greenthistle," she gasped.

"Come this way please." He knew some people were watching. "I wanted to talk to you about the Old Giants. You work in Redwoods National Park, yes?" he said calmly.

"Yes, sir, Master Greenthistle." Her voice was laced with nerves. He led her to an empty corner, only two sentries within earshot.

"Not a word gets relayed to anyone save for Lord and Lady Nightswift. Understood?" Trevin exuded confidence and sternness as he eyed the two. They nodded in agreement. "Do your best to keep watch over Petalgrace too."

"Understood, Master Greenthistle," they said, standing at attention.

Trevin looked at a worried Bryla now and offered a soft smile. "You have nothing to worry about with him nor El. She's helping out her brother."

"Yes, sir."

"I assure you, she does not intend to pursue him."

"Master Nightswift and Lady Elmbridge are—close. Lady Elodie is vowed to you. I assume this is just formality?" Bryla said and looked down.

"Cyrus and Alena are done. Have been for months. He nor my younger brother have any interest in her. Regardless of what it looked like, she was not kind to him, at all."

"What?"

"If you are comfortable, you should be his second dance of the night."

"I can't." She shook her head.

"I think you can, easily."

"But, he is Master Nightswift. He is heir apparent to a high estate. Petalgrace is hardly of any kind of status to dance with him."

"During any deliberations in the future, I would much rather work with Petalgrace than Elmbridge. My dad would tell you the same. I think Nightswift and Ashdale would very much agree. You do have every right to associate with us all. I assure you."

"Lady Elodie is very pretty. She seems very kind. Strong. Seeing her in winter, then spring and now, hearing what she did for you all, she is amazing. Certainly worthy of you."

"And did you know she did most of that while she was still a mortal?"

"A mortal? Cut the cuff off you? Carried you on your back?" Bryla marveled.

"Yes. A mortal proved she was a Greenthistle and worthy of this. So, you are most certainly worthy of him. I think he could use a presence such as yours in his life. So could El."

Bryla gasped. "Master Greenthistle?"

"Call me Trev. You should be his second dance." He smiled.

"I will try."

"Let him see you."

She nodded and then moved to the front of the crowd.

Trevin did too, moving somewhat near Bryla.

Cyrus grew tense again, likely scenting her. Trevin wondered what her scent was. He knew asking Bryla what she scented would be pushing too much. He hadn't broken any rules. He had merely offered a suggestion.

When the song ended Cyrus let go of Elodie's hand and Trevin moved into place right in front of Bryla. His arms wrapped around Elodie's waist. She turned around and pulled him in for a kiss, then he promptly pulled her out of Cyrus's line of sight and the two locked eyes.

Bryla hesitantly stepped forward and Cyrus offered a lower bow then asked if he could have the next dance. She took his hand and Cyrus saw her expression shift now to a warm radiant bliss.

"Are—" Elodie began but Trevin pulled her into another kiss.

"Not here," he said, pulling her away from the crowd. "Too much could go wrong right now and I don't know what rules do and don't apply to you. But if you were going to ask if they are like us, the answer is yes."

Elodie gasped and smiled widely. "She is so pretty. Her hair is like a dream. Are those colors natural?"

Trevin laughed. "Yes. No hair dye."

"I'm so jealous. She watched me a lot at the spring equinox. I wanted to say hi to her, but when I smiled at her, she just vanished back into the crowd. Is she cautious of me?" Elodie's expression turned sad. "She probably is cautious of me, or hates me for being close to him?"

"I explained you were helping your brother out. That was not romantic. She has always been on the shyer side."

"I heard the rumors. So did he." Elodie lamented.

"That is all they are. Everyone will get bored eventually." Trevin took her hand.

"I hope so. I hope he talks to her," Elodie said softly.

"Trust that it will all work out for the best. They have time. Lots of it." He kissed her forehead.

"I am so glad we do too now," she laughed and hugged him tighter.

"Lord Nightswift is letting me stay here tonight. In your room if you are comfortable," he whispered into her ear.

"He did? Of course I'm comfortable with it."

Trevin led her back onto the dance floor. There was no sign now of Cyrus or Bryla. He hoped he had not interfered.

Cyrus had indeed confirmed who his vowed was. Bryla Petalgrace. He was mesmerized and petrified at the same time. Every single thought had crashed down on him all at once and he froze. They had locked eyes and he wanted to ask if he could court her. Suddenly he wanted to fight and kick and scream his way out of his own head and towards her.

"You look beautiful this evening, Lady Petalgrace," Cyrus managed to say. His voice wavered.

She looked at him, stunned. "Thank you, Master Nightswift." She hesitated. "You look very handsome. As always." Her cheeks shimmered with a blush.

He didn't understand why she hesitated. Did she not want him? Was she appalled it was him; did she even realize he was her vowed?

Her hands fell away and she backed up. His vision slowed at the sight of her walking away, until tunnel vision took her far, far away. He quickly hurried off towards an empty alcove and sighed. He did not dance with anyone else that night. Instead, he watched her like an absolute creep, too chickenshit to approach her. Though she seemed slightly saddened. Defeated. Surely she had to feel defeated if she had realized she was vowed to him.

When he saw another fae ask her to dance, he felt an insane surge of anger and needed to pull her into another dance. The sensation in him was anger and that caused him to still. He took a step back. Then another. She couldn't see him freak out again. She had seen it before. She had stood at the end of the alley, as Alena dragged him away.

Cyrus also realized he barely knew anything about her. Trev had time to watch Elodie before he realized. Had time to get to know her and casually insert himself into her life. Cyrus hadn't done that. He had not gone back for the half nymph, half fae with the beautiful ombre teal and white hair. The urge to run his fingers through it grew. The blush on her cheeks appeared as a gold shimmer over her darker complexion and he found himself actually smiling. Smiling at someone new. She was beautiful, yet he knew nothing about her.

"What is he doing?"

"He's such a weirdo."

"Why is he watching young Lady Petalgrace so much? I thought he wanted the Earth Blessed. Or Alena," a voice near him said.

Spinning around, Cyrus looked right at them, causing them to run off. Her scent was close again. He knew she was near.

Hesitantly he looked up to see her eyes once again locked on him. He stumbled back then frantically searched for Elodie, unsure why he felt the need to do so. He needed to prove he could do this, everyone was watching right now, watching him fail.

When he spotted Elodie, he frowned as he watched her with Trevin. The two kissed and smiled at each other. There was no way he was going to ask for her help now.

He had done his part tonight. He was not needed here anymore.

And so, Cyrus slipped off, back to his room, for what was his shortest seasonal revelry ever. He went right for the hidden sedation tonics he had swiped and jammed the needle into his arm, barely pulling it out, before slumber took hold.

Chapter 28

After many hours of revelry, Trevin and Elodie went back to her room. Once inside he looked around and took in all the familiar amenities he was used to. His eyes fixed on the Greenthistle sigil, before taking in the Earth Blessed tapestry. He walked up to it and smiled.

"These are your colors." He laughed.

"Yes. Lady Nightswift said it was actually Cyrus who suggested it, to make me feel more comfortable here. I teared up when I saw it. It was nice of her to put yours up."

"Did Ashdale do this for you too?"

"No. I mean the room there is about as big as this one, the cabin type cozy feel, reminds me of Lake Tahoe or something, except it's missing the green roof."

"Green roof?" Trevin asked, puzzled.

"A lot of the buildings and houses there have green roofs and have a cabin-like appearance to blend in with surroundings. I only see a few green roofs here though."

"I see. Never been over there. You did Desolation Wilderness? I have heard about it."

"Yea, a few dispersed camping trips. Always camped with friends though and never in winter of course."

"Snow is not your thing. I remember."

"No, but rain and fog are." She laughed softly.

"Well, I am glad Oregon nor Washington claimed you for their own." Trevin smiled then closed the distance between them to embrace her.

"Me too, Trev."

"I owe you an apology for how I have treated Cyrus. I am so sorry that I ever let him feel so isolated. I should have been there for him too," Trevin said softly as he rested his chin on her head.

"I feel just as bad. I honestly thought he was going to hate me for letting that happen, for not seeing it. I felt sad hearing your dad tell us about his condition."

"I know, I felt bad too. My dad told me so many times to fix it. Even the night of the ruins and I just didn't," Trevin sighed and rested his forehead on her shoulder now. "He was once my best friend. We were always a lot closer than we were with Quinn, not that the three of us weren't inseparable, but Cyrus and I just had something more. We don't talk about it much but we had a thing in our twenties until our dads put a quick end to it. Two heirs together in the same territory is not great for succession."

"What? You and Cyrus?" Elodie was shocked. Trevin let out a small laugh.

"Yes. A few months. It was long after him and Autumn. She found it pretty funny when she realized it, and said she saw him straddle me in the pool after we played grab ass all night."

"Oh," Elodie said as if deep in thought.

Trevin pulled back and looked at her. She blushed then looked at him worried. "Is that curiosity and lust I see in you?"

"I—uhh—maybe. Just curious, and imagining the visual. Who was dominant?"

"We traded off. Sometimes it was a power play that we enjoyed. Once our dads found out, they split us up for a while and made us agree to never pursue that. So we just stopped, the longing gazes stopped eventually and we went out to the mortal world more. He would flirt and sweet talk and I tried to do the same but I just never cared too. Connection goes a long way for me obviously. I couldn't stand the smell of mortals on him. He always was cocky and slightly arrogant but he became outright obnoxious with both fae and mortals. So I just didn't go out as much with them."

"So he's been with every Greenthistle in some form?"

Trevin laughed. "Yea I guess he has." He pulled her closer in his embrace. "That lust you have is him and I right, not just him?"

"Trevin," she said, pulling back to meet his eyes, she could see his doubt and hurt so she cupped his jaw. "You are the only one I want like that. Yes, the image was both of you. He is attractive, but he is not my type, you are. I would never do anything to betray you or our bond. Nor would I ever want to prevent him and Bryla from having a chance."

Trevin smiled with such endearment and kissed her hard. "I know, Little Mink. While we may not have our diadems, I certainly would be more than happy to undress my vowed before I bed her again." His voice was so seductive to her ear.

She ran her fingers through his hair, giving it a small tug. Trevin pulled one hand away and faced his palm towards the door, throwing up a sound barrier. Shortly after, all their clothes found their way to the ground.

Eventually slumber took hold of Trevin and Elodie after a number of rounds.

Trevin somehow found himself in the forest. Things were hazy and he was disoriented. A mountain lion lay dead nearby him, his own face slashed open and bleeding. The gut wrenching screams from Cyrus, his raven cawing out of desperation filled the air. "No! No! Please. Don't."

He wondered how he got here and yet his body felt sluggish. He recalled the memory clearly but things around him were blurry.

Trevin looked at the trees noticing how still they were, then thought about how much life Elodie brought to the land. For a moment he wondered if she was camping on the beach with the mortals and the last ten months were just a fantasy in his head. Hopefully she was safe and cozy in her tent. *Memory? Dream? Or is this happening?*

"Trevin! No! I'm sorry!" Cyrus screamed and writhed, pulling Trevin's attention back to the raven covered in blood and wounds. Echo stood next to him, looking at the bird without saying anything. "Elodie! No. I don't want this. I'm sorry."

A gasp from behind snagged Trevin's attention and he saw Elodie run up to Cyrus.

Elodie wasn't there. The thought struck him yet he couldn't move his feet.

"Cyrus! No!" She ran up to the raven. "You are good. Fight for Nightswift, We are here."

Confusion was clouding Trevin's mind. "Help him, Dad. Cyrus is hurt," he pleaded, still in his feral form. Changing into fae while injured was very unwise. Injuries could become much more severe while changing as flesh and bone reconfigured itself.

"I cannot help him and she has done all she can. It's your turn. Fix it."

"I don't want to be a monster. No! Please." The hallowing despair in Cyrus's voice sent a chill down Trevin's spine. "Please stop! Don't heal me. Please! Just let me die!" The cries and screams continued.

Trevin didn't understand what was happening, this wasn't how that night had gone. *It couldn't be happening all over again, could it?*

The ferns and redwoods flourished around Elodie kneeling at Cyrus's side. *No, there were no redwoods there, they don't grow on the border with Trinity,* Trevin thought to himself as his eyes shifted to the trees then up to the stars. They pulsed as if mimicking a frantic heart beat. *Elodie's?*

The mountain lion was saved, the raven is still trapped.

She is grasping at sand, little cub. Watch over them both.

Show them both they are home.

Whispers poured into his ears now as though he were under a small waterfall, filling his core and a flash of green washed over his vision. Elodie screamed, writhing in those ruins as shadows engulfed her and ravens fell lifeless around them. Then the shadows came for him but ferns pulled him back.

He fought to reach for Elodie who lay lifeless near Cyrus. He reached his hand out and noticed it was covered in blood. The image made him scream. He ripped himself off of the ferns' grasp and fell forward in the dirt.

He jerked his body up frantically only to realize he was sitting in bed. Not at Greenthistle or Elodie's. His eyes scanned the room trying to figure out where he was.

"No! No! I'm sorry! Please. Trevin! Elodie! No!" The screams dragged a tremble out of Trevin's body. A gentle hand on his back caused him to jump. With a gasp he turned to see Elodie.

"You are okay, it must be his screams triggering something in you. I'm here, you're safe," she said calmly, embracing him. "I need to check on Cyrus."

Trevin could hardly make his head nod. He swallowed hard and it hurt with how dry his throat was. "Let me go with you. I-I can try to help too."

"Are you sure? You are spooked." She hastily got dressed. "I don't think I have ever seen you have a nightmare before."

"You are used to this, that?" Trevin motioned towards the door with his hand, he saw her with a Greenthistle shirt on, but with Nightswift's emblem on the shorts. He thought about the mixed matched assortment of clothes she had now.

"Yes," she said, heading for the door. "I think it would mean a lot to him for you to be there."

Trevin nodded and jumped up to grab clothes out of his bag.

When they got to Cyrus's room, Elodie tried to open the door but it wouldn't budge.

"Extra ward. Always up in our rooms during revelries. I think I can release it," Trevin said with sorrow in his tone. Elodie watched him hover his fingers over the door jamb, trace a symbol then tap his fingers in a sequence. The lock unlatched.

As soon as Trevin opened the door Elodie ran inside towards the bed.

"No! I'm sorry. Please! Please. Stop!" Cyrus screamed and writhed.

"Cyrus. You are good. It is not real. You are safe." Elodie tried to hold her voice calm but she was panicking.

"Has it been like this every night?" Trevin asked, walking to the foot of the bed. His eyes fixed on Cyrus, who was locked in sleep paralysis.

"Yes, he said he just didn't sleep the first night I was here. His parents said this is most nights for him."

Trevin watched her vines flow through her fingers to Cyrus's hands. She was careful to not wrap them around him. Cyrus's fingers were flexed out and his hands trembled, though he would not grab onto her vines.

"Please don't shoot him. Trevin! I'm sorry. Please someone, help me!" Cyrus screamed again.

Trevin thought back to his dream and wondered if Cyrus's screaming triggered it. That night was absolutely gut wrenching to witness. To know this had been Cyrus's life for months, to see Elodie trying so hard to keep her home together. Yet that dream was not how the night went. Elodie was never there. She was here now though, as ingrained into this place as any of them were. Recalling the whispers in the dream, his eyes went to the window. The trees stood tall and proud as they watched him. *Watch over them both.* Trevin turned back to Cyrus and Elodie.

Suddenly it occurred to him why Elodie clung to Cyrus too. They were both going through a rebirth. One had woken up in a new life and the other had been ripped from his old life, desperate to find his way back. *Show them both they are home.*

Power had shifted though and only Cyrus knew why. Trevin couldn't help a surge of anger at that thought, but he knew he could not dwell on it if he was going to fix it. Cyrus needed to fess up, and right now that meant Elodie would have to bear the burden whenever that confession happened.

"Please. Somebody. Just see what she is," Cyrus sobbed.

"This is the first time he hasn't woken up for me." Elodie panicked. "I don't want to grab him or shake him."

Even with the anger still simmering inside him, Trevin did not want to see Cyrus in this condition. Drawing a deep breath in he looked at his second in command and released it.

"Cyrus. You are Nightswift's heir. Wake up," Trevin said in a calm, confident tone that almost mirrored his dad. Elodie looked at him, slack jawed, just as Cyrus shot up and gripped his heart. He was leaning forward heaving. His other hand instinctively clutched Elodie's vines.

With a gasp, Cyrus tensed, pulling his hand away from Elodie to straight at Trevin, who had begun to pull the fear and terror off Cyrus; he could see the shame still there though, but it was far away. Every gate abruptly shut on Trevin.

"Don't pull this off me! I won't let you." Cyrus buried his face in his hands.

"Cyrus, breathe deep. It's okay." Elodie rubbed his back.

Cyrus trembled away from her. "Don't. I'm sorry."

Trevin let out a slow exhale walking over to the opposite side of the bed and as he held his hand out, Cyrus flinched and trembled. "If I couldn't bring myself to punch you then, I certainly can't now. Just a calming touch, I don't have vines and I'm not going to cuddle you in bed. This is what I have."

Cyrus glanced at him for a second then back down.

"Trust goes both ways. Let him help you too," Elodie offered.

"I hurt you so badly, Trevin. You only ever took care of me and that thing made me go for her. Made me do all those things. I'm sorry. The betrayal on your face when you found out what I told Alena to do..." His hands gripped the blankets tightly. "The night of the mountain lion attack, when your dad went to heal me, I was trying to beg him to let me die. I knew healing me would bind it to me and letting me die would kill it too. If I was stronger I would have been able to tell him," Cyrus cried. "There's been nights I wished he had let me die. I hate all of this so much."

Trevin felt his eyes well up. *His screams were him begging for mercy? Of death? My second wanted to die?*

"Cyrus, I forgive you. It did hurt, all of it hurt. Losing her and thinking it was for the best was horrible. But trying to rationalize how blood and bond could have turned on me, because I loved a mortal. After everything she did for me, how could I not love her? I knew you better than that, I knew you weren't acting right. It still hurts, but I forgive you, Cyrus. It wasn't your fault. You don't deserve this. Let me help you."

"Please. I just need more time. I'm sorry. I know you and Quinn hate me for it too."

Trevin sighed. "Please let me help?"

When Cyrus placed his hand in Trevin's, he pulsed a calming wave over him.

"Thank you," Cyrus managed to heave out. His body had relaxed. "I don't deserve any of you."

"You didn't deserve that mountain lion attack. I am sorry too," Trevin followed up. "I cried on the walk home, seeing your dad hold you. I felt as though it was my fault because my mind kept wandering to Elodie, that dormant earth magic in her trying to bind itself to her or the vowed bond, both kept snagging my attention. I felt like I let it happen to you and I was too much of a coward to look at them, too scared to pull any emotion off them. I was scared. Cyrus, I don't want anyone else as second. You are going to be there with Quinn and I. Fight for Nightswift. We are both here for you."

Elodie smiled and wiped her eyes. "You never told me that part, Cyrus. I am glad you are here. That we became such good friends."

Cyrus looked up at Trevin again. "You saw it with Bryla, didn't you?"

"Yes. What is her scent?"

"Sage and fuschia," Cyrus sighed and dropped his head again. "Why now? She is going to see that I am so unstable." He trembled again and Trevin pushed more into him, Cyrus gripped his hand tighter. "She was there that night in the tavern." He went on to explain how Bryla had stood at the end of the alley as Alena pulled him away.

"Vowed want the best for each other. They don't run when it gets scary or too dark either. When you are ready, talk to her. She will be there," Trevin insisted.

"Thank you," Cyrus said. "Sorry I interrupted your night together. I think I can get back to sleep."

"Are you sure?" Elodie asked.

"Yes."

"We are here. You are good, Cyrus. Remember that."

Trevin watched him nod but pulsed one more calming wave over him before leaving with Elodie.

Chapter 29

The next morning after Trevin left, Elodie went off to her lessons to finish the week. Then Saturday rolled around and Trevin was there once again to meet Elodie.

Cyrus recalled last night when he sat next to Elodie on the patio. Ever the watchers that Nightswift was, he had noticed Elodie getting frustrated with herself all week and not being able to communicate with ravens was eating away at her. Dee had not warmed up to her, making the lesson more stressful. When he noticed her walk by his door well after midnight, he decided to inquire if she was alright since she had done that for him countless times already.

Upon seeing her on the patio wiping her tears, he swallowed his worries that he might scare her or come off as overbearing and sat next to her. Then it was her turn to cry on him.

Cyrus listened when she expressed her feelings. She cried over how much Quinn ignored her, and how nice Cyrus's parents were to her and that she felt as though she failed Nightswift by not doing more sooner. He himself could not fathom why she felt that way but he let her sit and speak what she needed to. They had sat under the Old Giants and the stars, the raven and the mink who were both lost but now not so alone.

Now as he waited for Trevin to arrive, Cyrus stood away from his parents and sisters. Dee naturally appeared annoyed, as though she couldn't be bothered.

Elodie walked down the stairs with his mom. He noticed how much more relaxed she seemed. He wanted to believe it was because she had found a friend she thought she would never have, someone who knew what she was going through because he had gone through a similar feeling.

Yet Cyrus knew they hadn't gone through the same things. Elodie had not done anything wrong. She had been brave and kind to all of them. Cyrus had been a coward who toyed with so much, tampered with things that never should have been tampered with. He let out an uneasy exhale as he dwelled on it. The sound caught Elodie's attention. He almost couldn't stand her concern. He didn't deserve it nor anything Trev had given him.

All those things he had been forced to do sickened him. Yet now it felt as though the things he was hanging on to were only getting heavier. In some way it was far worse now that he had unloaded some of this weight, the things that truly terrified him only got heavier. The more things he hid somehow made every individual thing all feel equally as suffocating.

"Cyrus. It's going to be alright. Remember what I said, I'm here, you don't need to wait three weeks to talk to me alright," Elodie said softly.

Slowly his eyes rose to meet her and his vision grew blurry with tears. The stress made the thing in him pulse and drift upwards from some hidden well that had formed inside him. The spirit had formed it and he was so scared it was somehow permanently tethered to him.

He quickly cut his eyes down.

"You will be there too, right? I want you to be," Elodie asked with hope in her voice.

He didn't want to keep this weight tying him down but if he released either truth that scared him, he would likely be in the hold tonight. He glanced at his dad who watched him with a contemplating gaze. It made his heart pound and his breathing heavier. Everyone was staring at him and when the door opened, Trevin's scent grabbed him.

Cyrus took a step back and squeezed his eyes shut. He hated the choice he had made; it was going to absolutely crush not only Trevin but Elodie too. When he made the choice, he was frantic, and circumstances were growing dismal. He wanted to be free of it all.

He felt Elodie take his hand and the vines brush against that well, that thing buried deep inside it, brimming against the thinnest barrier, trying to get out.

"No!" Cyrus pulled his hand away and backed up against the wall. Elodie looked at him with shock. Hurt.

Trevin glared but remained where he was.

"Cyrus, I'm sorry. I should have let you know I was reaching for your hand. I just want you to know you are safe. I'm here. I promise you." Elodie then stepped away from him. He didn't look at her. Couldn't look at her.

"It was a good week despite everything. I think we made great progress, but we have much to do. I will give your father a detailed report. He, Miles, and I will be going over how to best assess the next set of lessons with you all now that Lady Elodie has had a week with all three high estates."

"Understood. I thank you all for making her feel welcome and teaching her how to be a Nightswift. I will be over here on Monday morning with my dad," Trevin said with that tone again. Cyrus could hear the high lord command of it, it reflected Lord Greenthistle so much.

Envy grew in Cyrus and he wanted so badly to do this, to be there as Trevin's second in command, to not leave any question as to what his own title would be in the future. From Master Nightswift to Lord Nightswift.

He heard Elodie thank them all and watched as Dee rolled her eyes. It made that thing stuffed in that well seethe, made *him* seethe. Here Elodie had just shown she'd be there for Cyrus and Dee was trying to push her away. When he saw Elodie lean down to hug Poppy, he couldn't help but feel a sense of gratefulness and love for her. Poppy would miss Elodie likely as much as he was going to.

That thing swirling inside him was pushing him to try, to not let them walk through that door without trying. The fear was tightening the noose around his neck, stealing the breath from his lungs. He knew the conference would prod and poke at Elodie with their gazes and words. If he had to admit what he did in front of the entire regional council, there would be very little his dad, Lord Greenthistle, or Elodie could do.

Cyrus watched Elodie give him a hopeful smile then take Trevin's hand. That thing rattled inside him as if snared by a trap. Ice slunk down his spine with each step they took closer to the doors. One of the remaining secrets was going to break out and he did not want it to be something he could not control. He could use his words; he had control over his tongue.

"Wait." His voice was a rasp. A mere chirp of a finch in front of the crashing waves of the mighty Pacific. Not the steadfast caws of the ravens. "Please."

Shame forced his head low, and his eyes on the ground.

"I—I want to—" His shoulders rose and fell with every labored breath. "Say what I did to cost Nightswift power." He heard Elodie, and both of his parents gasp. "But I'm scared."

"It will be alright, Cyrus. You are safe." Elodie's voice was gentle, and he wanted to believe so badly. He knew though if the sentries, or his dad hauled him away, no one could do anything for him. Maybe, she would at least visit him in the hold he hoped.

He didn't respond, nor look up.

"Into the study then. I must summon Lord Greenthistle, and Lord Ashdale. If Lady Elodie and Trev are present, you know Quinn should be too. We cannot exclude each other," Bracken explained.

He knew they needed to be there as much as Elodie did, his choice had eventually affected all of them, though the thought of Quinn and Trevin glaring at him, and Elodie doubting even more made him want to crawl into a hole.

Dee stormed off as his mom and Poppy headed into the kitchen. They would be informed later. This was official high estate business after all. Ariyanna's worried expression was not missed on him though. Elodie and Trevin had remained where they were, having a silent conversation. So he walked into the study and took his chair again, just as he had on last Sunday.

When everyone began to trickle in, Bracken sat at the desk, the other two high estate lords remained standing near him. One quick glance at Quinn told Cyrus he was in a foul mood. He slumped down on a window seat near Miles. Elodie took the same seat she sat in last Sunday and Trevin stood behind her with one hand on her shoulder.

"Quinn, drop your attitude. We were not summoned here for tea and scones, whatever you think is more important that this is not," Miles spat then crossed his arms.

Cyrus had no desire to look at anyone. *Why did I open my mouth? I don't want to face them now.*

"Go on, son." Bracken nodded.

Cyrus just shook his head now and looked away. If he told this truth, the other secret would likely drown him with how heavy it was.

"Would my vines help?" Elodie asked softly.

"No!" Cyrus snapped out and wiped his eyes.

"Okay." The smallness of her voice tugged at him. Everyone's eyes grated on him. Their presence was stifling in the study despite never having felt this before with them.

"Master Nightswift." Echo's tone was stern and serious, bringing a tremble up his spine. "If we know what caused the power shift, we can prepare that much more for the conference. We can go in with a fighting chance if we know everything instead of just something. The courage is there in you, find it again."

"I—I don't have courage. I have cowardice. I don't have strength or valor. I wasn't very loyal or kind to anyone," he sniveled.

"But you watched at least, right? You must have analyzed those observations, right?" Elodie asked.

The room was silent save for Cyrus's and Elodie's hearts.

"The Old Giants' message has never changed. They still tell me to lift you up, to help you fly again. They know you are good. So, I think whatever reason you made that choice, was because the risk of not making it was far greater than the power loss. That sounds like being a Nightswift to me," Elodie said.

Cyrus still couldn't stand to look at anyone.

"It's not that simple. I really don't know where any of us would be if I hadn't taken that chance. I took a gamble and didn't really consider what it might be like if I survived. I couldn't see that far ahead." Cyrus rubbed his eye with his palm. He purposely pushed hard enough to see colors; he was so frustrated with the situation.

"The Old Giants ultimately did decide to take power from you as well as Nightswift. Now it's time you let us know why. Never in my years of living in and ruling a high estate have I heard of the cause of a power shift going unknown for so long. The council will frown upon the leeway we have given you," Echo explained. His looming stress was apparent. Cyrus tried to lift his head up but still couldn't bring himself to look at Elodie and Trevin.

"Basically what he is saying is that if you don't talk, you are doing far worse than costing Nightswift power. You are making all three high estates of Humboldt look weak," Quinn muttered.

"Please don't, Quinn. He's trying. It was a lot to handle that night." Elodie's words were small and nervous. The little mink they all thought was timid and full of nerves but she never let any of it stop her.

"I know. I saw what you did with my own eyes. Everything you had to handle was on account of those two. At least one of them can own up to his fuck ups." Quinn stood up and headed for the door.

Cyrus finally looked up and watched him, also noticing Elodie wiping her eyes. That doubt was going to crush her for so many reasons and he wished he could take it all away, wished he could rip it off her, just as she had ripped those chains off him.

"Quinn, you will sit back down. We are not finished," Miles growled. Quinn clenched his fist and stopped walking.

"To just sit here and allow him to cower back? I owned up to fucking with their vowed bond. I didn't get a pass. Hell, Trevin got rewarded for his multiple fuck ups."

Cyrus watched Trevin glare with that mountain lion-like intensity at Quinn for a second before he knelt down by Elodie. "You did not cause this, Little Mink. Quinn is right, I fucked up horribly with you. But I will keep pushing myself to be better for you and our home."

Quinn scoffed and leaned against the wall with his arms crossed.

Trevin pressed his palm to Elodie's nape and sent her a calming wave through her, causing the tension in her to release. Then he turned to face Quinn.

"You should be grateful you got out of that as easy as you did. You fought hard that night, you held me back from an impulsive possibly fatal error, I thank you for that. But while those two were fighting within inches of their lives, I had to experience those moments knowing my time with her had run out. So stop acting like you cannot be fucked with your duty as an heir apparent," Trevin declared. Cyrus watched Elodie look at Trevin with awe at his confidence and tone. He also glanced at the three high estate lords behind the desk. Miles and Bracken maintained their serious expression, but the corner of Echo's mouth tugged up to the side slightly as he watched his son.

Trevin was becoming exactly who he never felt confident enough to be. A year ago he'd never have exuded that demeanor, then again a year ago, Elodie was not here. No one had any idea what was going to happen or that the brave little mink would grant them this day, would grant Cyrus this chance. A year ago, he himself had no clue a brave little mink would grab his hand and walk this terrifying trail with him, refusing to leave him behind.

He couldn't bear it. That thing inside him didn't want him to bear it either, if for Cyrus's benefit or its own, he could not be certain. The thought of uttering this confession before the region would be disastrous. Echo was right.

Wiping his eyes one final time, he took a deep breath and brought his eyes to Trevin. When he met the emerald-green eyes of this person he had shared so much with, he began to speak.

"Quinn wasn't the first to tamper with your vowed bond," Cyrus said, watching shock cascade over the room. "I also hurt a high estate heir that same night too. By my own hand and my own free will."

Chapter 30

"What?" Trevin gasped as if he had just been struck in the chest. "I don't understand. Quinn told her she was my vowed the night of the ruins. She didn't know that before, did you?" He looked at Elodie, who shook her head

Confusion overtook everyone and Cyrus had to take a few heavy labored breaths to form the words.

"It was long before the night in the ruins, I had little control over anything by that point. It was back in November." He paused and watched them all process his words. "Mere days before Elodie went to Marin on her break."

Trevin's eyes shot wide with realization. "You put that cuff on me? You wanted to?" Trevin spat. Quinn looked at Cyrus with such disgust he shuddered. Horror and shock took hold of Elodie. She was still trying to piece it all together.

"Why?" she asked. "What did you hope would happen? Anyone could have seen him before a raven did," she asked, staring at him with that gaze of someone who was about to plummet in a sea of doubts.

Cyrus swallowed hard. His throat had gone dry and it made the motion hurt. "It was also my choice to ensure no ravens did see him, that would put you in a very dangerous position, El. I—it watched you camp the weekend before, it saw you write out plans for that Monday of your break and then in a split-second decision I placed Trevin in your path. I followed your car and watched you strain, throwing everything you had into cutting that iron cuff off of him. All while I kept the ravens away until Trev got you inside to make the bargain with you."

He watched Trevin's expression race through the events of that day.

"You sedated me after we left Ashdale?"

A chill took over Cyrus as his eyes glossed over. "It was going to jump on you. It knew it needed El gone and you were too close to her. You hadn't been away from her for more than a single day since that bonfire. A raven couldn't take her down fast enough but a mountain lion—"

"Instead I told it how much easier it'd be if I dropped you in town, Elodie's savior hauled away, the towns' distrust of all of Greenthistle, Nightswift, and Ashdale. It would have the attention both mortal and fae and it could do as it pleased. But the only thought I ever managed to keep from it was that I'd put you in your vowed's path. Hoped that she felt the bond even if she didn't understand it yet. Pray that you had bonded enough to do whatever you both needed to do to help the other." Cyrus let out a long exhale and dropped his head in his hands.

"How the fuck did you weld iron on him?" Quinn snapped.

Not looking up, Cyrus took another deep breath and explained. Let the words slowly trickle off him, allowing more of that weight to lift. That thing inside was calm, it was no longer a spooked animal snared in a trap, it was just resting as if it too felt his exhaustion.

Cyrus had dragged Trevin across the boundary to a welding shop in town, had wrapped Trevin's hand and arm as best he could and wore gloves himself then as he explained it, watched every spark fly along with any love and trust Trevin had ever held for Cyrus. The spirit had increased Cyrus's healing and so he was able to say he had healed faster the night of the iron cuff, letting them all believe he too gained power.

"I think the reason for the power shift after the spirit was sealed up, was because I could not bear the responsibility while it held me. I might not have been strong enough to hold it off as long as I did either. When it realized what I did, it beat me down so hard. I could hardly move."

"Not only did you gamble with El's life, but all of ours too!" Quinn growled. "You had your moments where you fought, where you had your tongue, I saw you exhausted and nervous but you just stayed quiet? For months? While you creeped on El?" Quinn began to pace.

"I tried. I did! I know you saw it, Trevin," Cyrus pleaded, lifting his head to meet Trevin's still shocked gaze. "I wanted to, I screamed it in my head for months, at all of you, to just figure out what she was," he whimpered.

"The day after that mountain lion attack, when Quinn and I saw you in bed, you had sentries in your room with us, outside your door, round the clock care, you could have said something early on. El had no idea what any of us were at that point either. It was the safest you would have been." Hurt laced Trevin's tone. "She would have had a chance to still leave."

Cyrus tensed and cut his eyes to Elodie. He caught Echo tense in his periphery too. Elodie slowly turned her gaze to Trevin, somehow looking more hurt than she had prior.

"El, he didn't mean it like that," Cyrus implored.

Trevin remained frozen either too hurt, shocked or a combination of too many things, Cyrus wasn't sure. However what he did know was that every second Trevin remained silent, Elodie's doubts grew.

"Tell her what you meant, Trevin," Echo stressed. "That is an order."

What seemed like an unexpected chill shot up Trevin's spine as if he snapped out of whatever hold gripped him and dropped to his knees once more in front of Elodie.

"Seeing you hurt, having to do any of that, being scared, letting you think I didn't want you, thinking I wanted a different outcome than having you forever isn't something I would ever choose for you, Elodie. But you chose this and I am so incredibly grateful for you. Please never doubt that I want you."

Elodie looked at him so intently. She was so still. Her chest hardly rose and fell despite how loud her heart was thundering. Cyrus was worried she might pass out from holding in the tension.

"Would you choose to have your trust broken? Your faith in blood and bonds shattered?" Elodie asked with a broken voice.

Cyrus heard a gasp from Trevin then spared a glance at the three high estate lords. Their expressions were varying degrees of apprehension.

He could not put into words how much he hated feeling responsible for all of this. Trevin's trust and friendship hurt to lose but knowing what this was going to do to Elodie hurt him in ways he never imagined his heart could hurt.

"Elodie, do not doubt for one second he wants you. He wants this life with you. I took a risk, I am sorry." He looked at Trevin and Quinn. "I made a mistake that day after the mountain lion attack. I was scared and didn't know what it was capable of. It forced me to get up in the middle of the night, and inflict half those wounds you saw on me just to prove how little power I had. I wish I had told you or my dad, or anyone that first day."

He looked at Quinn. "It has been absolute and utter hell since I felt its fangs snap my wing. When she pulled it out of me, it was a small gasp of air before the landslide of guilt and nightmares buried me again." Cyrus then looked at Trevin. "That night it prodded you and Cedar to fight downstairs, when I told you that I sent Alena home with Cedar, I wanted you to punch me out. I was begging for you to just leave me unconscious. I saw it in your eyes how much you wanted to and you still didn't. You just let the despair swallow you whole."

Exhaustion now took over Cyrus and he slumped down into his seat. He heard the chair at his dad's desk slide back and tears began to roll down his cheeks.

"I'm sorry. I'm sorry. I was scared. I didn't know what else to do. I tried. I didn't want to scare her, I wanted her help. She makes Trevin so happy. She is good and I wanted to give them a chance, give you all a chance. I'm sorry." Cyrus cried into his hands. He saw his dad now standing in front of him.

Nightswift remains second. You are good Cyrus. You fought so hard. I hope you can rest now. Elodie's words played in his head. Cyrus was so tired of trying to claw his way above the rubble and rot he had caused. Slowly he lifted his head to meet his dad's eyes.

Coldness washed over him but it didn't worry him, it reminded him of flying at night against the stars, above the crowns of the Old Giants. He felt the faintest smile form on his lips as his heart rate finally slowed down. When Cyrus closed his eyes, everything went still once more.

Echo watched as Bracken caught Cyrus's limp body as it fell forward. "Cyrus!"

"Lay him down," Echo instructed and rushed over to check his pulse and eyes. "He's steady, likely just exhausted after what just occurred."

"So he confessed," Miles said, walking forward. He looked at Elodie and Trevin then Quinn. All three looked worried. "What now?"

Echo stood up and looked at everyone. Ultimately he would make the call. "I suppose we assess where we stand. It's the end of June, that leaves us a little over two months until the conference."

Miles let out an exasperated breath and paced back towards the desk in defeat.

Echo looked back at Elodie and assessed her for a moment as she sat on the edge of the chair, hands balled up into fist on her knees. She looked away. "Lady Elodie, tell me, where does Trevin stand in your life?"

Trevin went to say something but was interrupted. "I told you to never speak for her, Trevin. Not a single one of you was to ever sway her. We drilled it into your heads for years. Yet you all did." Echo glared at Trevin and Quinn.

Elodie spoke up in a small voice. "I have never wanted a place to be home so badly before. I want Trevin more than anything but it feels like this is just sand slipping through my fingers. Mt. Tamalpais could have chosen me, but it didn't want me, nowhere I went wanted me. But this place did and I feel like I haven't done enough and all the entities knew I wouldn't be able to. I don't know how to help any of you." Her voice broke.

"You know we can't tell lies. We are not omitting anything or twisting our words. We mean it when we say you are a part of these three high estates. Greenthistle is your home. The door will never be locked for you, it is not your job to fix our mistakes," Echo said softly.

Elodie nodded then wiped her eyes. "What are you going to do with Cyrus now?"

Echo and Miles glanced at each other. "Well I suppose this is a good lesson for you three, what do you think we should do with him?"

"Does it matter what I think? Because we know the tie breaker will follow his vowed," Quinn muttered, earning a sharp glare from Trevin.

"Then let's hear your stance. I have enough faith in Trevin to make a sound judgment considering all the factors," Miles hissed.

Bracken slumped down in the seat Cyrus had been in, absolutely defeated.

"Lady Elodie, what would you find suitable in this situation?" Echo asked.

"His room. If he is exhausted he should be able to recover, sir." Her voice was soft. Echo had known this would be her request. Ever the big heart for them all but never feeling as though she had a place with them.

"Master Ashdale?" he asked.

Quinn remained leaning against the wall with his arms crossed. "The hold. He welded iron onto Trevin then left him in town. So many things could have gone wrong. Never would I have even considered putting that battle cry out there using Trev." He ran his hand down his face in dismay.

Echo noticed Elodie look at Quinn with such hurt in her eyes as she opened her mouth, as if to say something but closed it instead.

"Go on, speak your rebuttal," Echo encouraged. Trevin was obviously torn and Echo could only guess what this was doing to him. A situation between duty and bond against your vowed was a heavy one. But if he was going to prepare them for this conference, this was as good a situation as any.

"You just saw him break, you've seen him break for months. I saw his hands tremble and his face contort in pain when he held that spirit and tried to fight it. I was only near him a handful of times, you both were around him weekly if not daily," she pleaded.

"The iron cuff is an assault on the entire estate. Especially when it's the heir. If he wanted to prevent that thing from jumping into Trevin there were so many other things he could have done," Quinn explained. He was trying to be softer with his anger towards Elodie.

"How? If he couldn't talk, then what? He simply does not show up to drills on Monday? Him doing that likely was the catalyst for getting Trev and I to talk while I was in Marin. We probably wouldn't have, Trev probably would have found out from Cora that I'd even gone out of town," she expressed, reflecting on it all. Trevin tilted his head slightly, as if thinking about it too. That was the moment Trevin deemed himself her overseer after all. "Cyrus admitted his intent was to throw the vowed bond in front of us, and he did, through a very serious offense, Trevin explained the iron cuff to me. But it wasn't as though I didn't already think about Trevin more than I should have at the point. I had scented him long before that too. The only difference after the iron cuff was I knew there was at least one mountain lion out there that would watch out for me instead of see me as prey."

A slight smile formed on Trevin's face and he placed a hand on her shoulder. His first touch since snapping out of that haze earlier.

Elodie glanced towards him then down at the ground in thought. With a deep breath she looked at Echo. "If the verdict is to put Cyrus in the hold for tampering with a vowed bond, then what is keeping Quinn and Trevin out of the hold?"

"What?" Quinn growled.

Trevin gasped.

"Explain," Miles commanded. His tone was stoic. Bracken too kept his composure despite his stress. Echo raised his eyebrows, waiting for Elodie to continue. She swallowed hard.

"The iron cuff is no light matter. But what other choice did he have to not put you all on high alert? I think Cyrus has been kept in isolation long enough if you deemed a punishment beyond what the Old Giants did." She took a deep breath to try to maintain a calm voice. "Quinn threw the vowed bond in my face by outright telling me because he didn't know what else to do either. He was desperate to get through to Trevin and me. So he swayed me, therefore breaking a few rules too. As far as Trevin goes, he could have remained hidden after that party but then what would that have done to me? His absence would have swayed me the other way and that was not what the Old Giants wanted obviously. I don't want any of you in the hold, ever. But you can't keep pushing Cyrus closer to the breaking point if you want him to walk into that conference with his head held high. This isn't how you help him."

Elodie was breathing hard and her eyes remained glossy but the tears didn't fall. This was exactly who Elodie had always been, scared, overwhelmed, and likely clueless about what she was walking into but still moving forward regardless to search for that small ray of hope that only she could see. Every day it only got clearer why the Old Giants had wanted her, and why it had been Trevin to see it. How they truly were made for each other. *Mother above, Selene, I hope wherever you are, you can see her,* Echo thought to himself.

Quinn and Trevin both looked at Echo with worry. "Your rebuttal, Master Ashdale?" he asked calmly.

"No." Quinn crossed his arms again.

"Master Greenthistle?" Echo turned to his son.

Trevin remained quiet and looked at Cyrus who still lay unconscious on the floor. Then he took a sharp inhale. "In his room." Trevin's words were something between regret and anguish.

"Point proven," Quinn snorted. Echo watched Trevin heave in anger and for all the strain on their friendship this was doing, he actually wanted Quinn to keep stoking the flames in Trevin. He needed to see the absolute fire and the control Trevin had over it. Elodie needed to know it too because despite being as magnificent as she was, doubts would always be her greatest danger.

"I didn't outright agree with her because she's my vowed. I would have said the hold, but then you and I should be in there too, because El is right, and you know it. You took a risk just like he did. You broke rules the same as I did. We got rewarded for it, he got punished for it."

"Can I go now?" Quinn rolled his eyes and looked at his dad.

"You are excused, not a word of this to anyone, outside of this room. That is an order, Quinn. Do you understand?" Miles demanded.

"Understood," Quinn said and left the room in a hurry.

"We will get Cyrus to his room and have him monitored. I will let you know when he wakes. You two should go home though, enjoy your week off Lady Elodie. Thank you. I'm grateful he has a friend like you. That they all do," Bracken said with a soft warm smile.

Elodie nodded and stood up. Echo watched the interaction between them. Trevin was now almost hesitant to touch her.

"Would you like to head to your house?" Trevin asked softly.

She paused and looked at the ground for a moment then at Trevin. "Um—can we stay at Greenthistle tonight?"

A sigh of relief escaped Trevin and he smiled. "Of course."

Echo too couldn't deny he too felt relief despite the tension Elodie still held. He watched them walk out the study, Trevin looping his pinky around hers.

The three high estate lords looked at each other. They were all exhausted.

"We are not going to be ready. Unless that girl can work a miracle in the next two months while overcoming her own worries," Bracken stressed and stood up to pick up Cyrus gently.

"It's this power imbalance. It's messing with all three of them on top of what occurred. Trevin nor Quinn know what to do with the extra power," Miles said.

"We add scenarios to their Monday drills starting this week. Elodie will be introduced to them next Monday when she joins. There is no more room for exceptions. We accommodate recovery as best we can," Echo asserted.

The other two nodded.

Chapter 31

As Trevin and Elodie walked home the silence in her was twisting his stomach in knots. He asked himself why he said that she could have left at least a dozen times. Then shock and despair just locked him in a coma until he snapped out of it with his dad's order.

"Elodie, I am so sorry about what I said. I didn't mean that I wanted you to leave. It just, it hurts sometimes thinking about how everything happened. It feels as though Justine was right. I might have chained you up." His words felt heavy and he wanted to hold her close.

"I'm sure I said some startling things too in that study. I know that you want me here. This place feels like home and I want it to be so badly, yet it feels like I may not be able to help you all when you need it. You say you all serve me but what if I can't serve you all?" Her shoulders deflated.

"You are still learning, we are still learning. There's things you do that we've never seen before. Everything we know, we had to learn. It wasn't that I wanted you to go, I hated even thinking about you somewhere else out there in the world, but I also hate that you had to go through it, experience it. I'd never have wished it on anyone." Trevin watched her and for a split second, he was so tempted to pull the emotions off her. But there were so many reasons he knew that would be far worse than what they were experiencing now.

The doors of Greenthistle opened and they walked in. Autumn beamed at the sight of them then frowned as she noticed their demeanor.

"What's wrong?" she asked.

"Cyrus confessed. Quinn is still pissed and I said words I regret."

"Trev, it's not your words that make me feel this way. I have felt this way for a while. I just need to work through it. I want to."

Trevin just nodded, holding a frown.

"Do you mind if I sit with the Old Giants for a bit? Alone?"

He let out a slow unsteady exhale from his nose before replying. "No. Do whatever you need to do. I'll be here, of course."

"Thanks, Trev." She took his hand and gave it a small squeeze. He wanted it to be reassuring, but it did little to ease his fears. Watching her walk towards the backyard, he felt his throat dry out.

Once she was out of sight, Autumn whirled on him. "What did you say? Why did you say it?"

"It's a long story," he mumbled.

"Well, can you tell me about it in the kitchen? Since the backyard is off limits right now."

Trevin didn't reply, still feeling bewildered. He wanted to be near Elodie. She had felt so distant but he knew smothering her now would only hinder them.

"Or you can go sulk in your room? I'm sure she will be done by dinner time." Autumn smiled, trying her best to comfort her brother. She had always tried to cheer him up.

Begrudgingly, he dragged himself to the kitchen and after taking a glass of wine, he began to tell Autumn what happened.

"You are not the best with your words sometimes." Autumn shook her head.

Trevin was slumped over on the table by now. It exhausted him to recap what happened.

"I know. Add this to the list of dumb shit I have said to her." He mindlessly rubbed his wrist, recalling the iron.

"She is fine. I highly doubt this is the only spot she can have a sit with them. Hell, she could have just stayed at Nightswift and used their yard."

"Please don't remind me. I'm happy she is here. I hope she wants to stay the night. But we were supposed to be at her house," Trevin lamented.

"You will be there tomorrow night." Autumn topped off his glass and emptied the bottle as Echo walked in. He raised his eyebrows in question at the sight of his cubs.

"Don't tell me Elodie went home after all?" Echo asked in his unimpressed tone.

"No. She's in the yard, doing her tree thing in her quiet time spot," Autumn explained.

"I am glad she has claimed a quiet spot for contemplation here. It will be good for her." He nodded slowly. "Trevin, stop sulking. You said something that struck a nerve. She was very much mortal and words sit heavy on them. Work past it."

"I know." He gulped.

"Then sit up. How are you going to treat Cyrus now?"

"Cautiously." Trevin brought his eyes to slowly meet his dad.

"Make sure it is not with anger. Keep it nice."

"Yes, sir." Trevin finally sat up and took a sip of the wine.

As predicted, Elodie did return shortly before dinner. She found Trevin and Autumn on the couch. Autumn got up to get Elodie wine despite insisting she could wait for dinner. Trevin looked at her then let out a shaky breath again when she sat down next to him.

"I'm sorry I worried you," Elodie said calmly and took his hand.

"I am sorry I said what I did and didn't explain."

"It's ok. I know better. I know you will always be my mountain lion. So brave and so beautiful." Her smile was genuine and he was so relieved to see it.

He pulled her into a hug and held her tight. She too returned the embrace just as tight. "Did you find what you needed?"

"I did," Elodie answered, running her fingers through his hair. "I still don't know what is going to be expected of me, or how I'm going to prepare for it, but they reminded me of something your dad told me back in March. You and I had plenty of chances to let this go and we still have that choice but neither of us wants to. You and I both know we are always better together. So I should probably start believing in myself if we're going to figure it out before the conference." She pressed her lips to his neck gently.

"Your mountain lion will be there every step of the way, Little Mink," he murmured in her ear, sending a chill down her spine. "With sound barriers ready."

Elodie laughed and playfully gave his hair a slight tug then tensed awkwardly when Autumn returned.

Later that night Cyrus eventually crawled back into bed after pacing for nearly an hour trying to convince himself he could sleep. His dad told him what had happened after he had blacked out.

"I am good. I am good. I am Nightswift's heir. I am good," he repeated to himself. Elodie had done so much for him this week. He had gotten most of the weight off his chest and yet, there was still one more secret he was terrified of.

This secret was one he did not understand. He had known about Elodie's dormant power because of that spirit, yet Cyrus did not really understand that spirit, nor this thing that remained inside him. Elodie had pulled it off him but something had altered him. That much he was certain of.

He was so scared they would chain down again or lock him up. Cyrus was still worried that he'd lose everything, and Elodie would stop reaching for him. That his vowed would be so appalled that she was stuck with a monster. "Bryla," he whimpered. "I am so sorry. I can't find my way to you."

As he rubbed his eyes the sudden coldness in his hands caused him to flinch. When he inspected for any discoloration and flexed his fingers, shadows started to emerge from his palms. A scream nearly broke free but shadows lashed out, muffling him. His eyes shot wide and panic took over.

"Remain still and silent," a voice that sounded like his own said. A whimper slipped out of Cyrus. He didn't know what was happening. Squeezing his eyes shut, all he could do was tremble. "Relax. No chains, no whips, but you cannot scream." Slowly he opened his eyes, expecting to see the spirit. Instead he saw his raven sitting on his chest. Confusion overtook him, stopping his shivering. "You knew something had been forming in us. It has evolved."

"How are we both in the same plane of existence? At the same time?" he asked in his head. His raven watched him.

"You were altered, so was I."

"What is this?" he asked.

"I don't know but you should embrace it."

"No." Cyrus trembled. "Not again. Please."

"You have been in control ever since the Earth Blessed ripped your chains off." The raven tilted its head.

"Please just let me sleep," Cyrus begged.

"Follow this. Learn it."

"I don't want anything to do with it," Cyrus pleaded as tears flowed down his cheeks falling right through the shadows. "Please."

"Embrace this. Just as our Earth Blessed has."

"No. She is good. The Old Giants chose her." Cyrus shuddered.

"And she said we were good. Do not scream. They may throw you in chains if they see it."

"Stop it please."

"The Earth Blessed has to learn and contain hers. We have to do the same. Let it guide you just as those Old Giants guide her. Do not scream." The raven peered down at Cyrus.

The shadows slowly released his mouth. When he turned his hand, the shadow swirled and moved with him.

"Let it show you what it wants us to be," the raven said then vanished back into him.

Cyrus sat up then lifted his hand up and down, the shadows followed. Gently flexing his fingers out, he watched the shadow flow like a wave. So he tried a quicker movement and flicked his fingers out. The shadows went faster and further than he anticipated and he knocked things off the medical cart left at the foot of his bed. The clang of things falling startled him and he pulled the covers over him and watched the door. He listened for anyone stirring in the house but it was silent. He looked at the clock and saw it was around midnight. After staring at the door for another ten minutes, waiting for any movement, he pulled his hand out from under the blanket. With his palm facing up, Cyrus watched the shadows slowly emerge again. As he watched the shadows closer, he observed what appeared to be midnight blue feathers hovering around the stream of shadow. Elodie's vine with the ferns came to mind.

"What is this?" he asked the empty room. His attention turned to the window now and focused on the trees. They were silent, but he got the sense they were watching. He could not tell if it was with fear or curiosity though. Something beyond the tree line caught his eye. A star was shimmering, then he realized all the stars almost looked brighter tonight. They shimmered and colors appeared brighter in the night sky.

He had stargazed plenty, perching high up in the crowns of the Old Giants. He had even flown higher than Hyperion, said to be the tallest tree on the planet yet never had he seen the stars quite like this. Then he looked back at the shadows hovering by the door as if it were waiting.

Carefully, he walked towards the door and drew the shadows back to him. After ensuring there was no movement in the hall he opened the door, following the shadows. They led him right to Elodie's room.

Her scent lingered despite staff having cleaned the room. The bedding was changed, floor vacuumed, and surfaces wiped down, but still he could scent her. Her Earth Blessed banner hung on the wall proudly. He spotted a few personal effects in the room, a notebook, a few pens, a book, and a water flask covered in various stickers of places near and far.

As he stood in the center of the room, the shadows flowed in between the nightstand and the bed. Then he saw it, a teal hair tie on the floor. He motioned his hand to pick it up and sure enough the shadows did, setting the hair tie on the nightstand. Again his eyes moved to the window. The stars were almost pulsing and the Old Giants remained watching.

Cyrus knew Elodie had sensed this thing in him. They had locked eyes and he knew they both saw the same thing. They were staring at a mirror but the reflection was different and yet had the same energy. He got so scared it would send her running out that door and a mountain lion would be in his face. As soon as her eyes pulsed teal, he ran, terrified it would come out of him. Given how his parents had reacted to everything else he knew they'd likely fear this.

He walked over to the bed and sat on it, staring at the hair tie. The realization that he didn't know what this was and didn't know how to tell anyone about it set in. His body slumped forward and he buried his face in his hands.

"I don't know what to do."

Elodie had been there for him; she had reached for him. She would fight for Nightswift despite how cold it had been here in the beginning. She had even brought Trevin back to the start of the trail they were on. Bryla was now here too. Everything still felt so daunting.

"Master this. For now, simply rest," his raven said softly in his head.

With a nod he stood up and looked at the hair tie again. He chewed on his bottom lip for a moment then grabbed it before heading back to his room.

After crawling back into bed, Cyrus fidgeted with the hair tie a bit before sliding it on his wrist. A small reminder Elodie knew he was good. Even if he didn't know who he was, he wanted to be good. This week hadn't been anything he expected.

And as if the Earth Blessed were still there, he nodded off to sleep on his own accord.

Even though one room would sit vacant for a few weeks, rest had found its way into the usual chaos of another room.

Chapter 32

Now that Cyrus was off house arrest he was expected to be back at Monday drills. Today they would be at Nightswift so he made his way downstairs, anxious as ever. It would be a crash course to contain his shadows. Succeed or he would be in the hold by nightfall. His frown grew with every step.

Next week Elodie would start with them on Mondays at Ashdale. He hadn't messaged her, she hadn't messaged him. *Just as well,* he thought. She was off this week, he didn't expect her to be on this side of the boundary much.

Once outside he glanced at his dad.

"Greenthistle and Ashdale are on their way."

A sigh escaped Cyrus. "El hasn't had any slip ups with her teal pulse right?"

"A very minor one when confronted with Quinn's mortal interest. From what I gather she can be a bit much but no one saw anything. Why?" Bracken eyed his son with curiosity.

"Just wondering. We are all here. Trevin will be here and not with her."

"She is rather independent on her days away from us from the sounds of it. I am sure she is sleeping in, it's her first day free of lessons from us. Hopefully she will relax some and return a little less overwhelmed," Bracken laughed. Cyrus nodded and remained withdrawn. "You and Trev seem to have made progress."

"Yeah." Cyrus sighed and dropped his shoulders.

"All we can do is move forward. Together. He is trying and so are you. Did you talk to Quinn at the solstice?"

"No." Cyrus looked down.

"In due time they will come back to you. For now, you know you have Lady Elodie," his dad said. Cyrus was waiting for him to bring up Bryla but he remained silent. It was a small relief for as much as he wanted to seek her out, he knew he was too scared to leave the estate.

Trevin and Echo walked in and Cyrus observed how Echo appeared relaxed while Trevin appeared cautious. Despite the tension, Trevin approached and offered a simple short greeting.

"Well, this should be an interesting day of drills," Echo said. "Are we all recovered from the revelry?"

"I'd say so. Cyrus even asked to sit at the table and we had a nice dinner as a family."

The two heirs glanced at each other. Then he watched Trevin look at the trees as if he were working something out in his head.

"El has been able to control her powers in the mortal world okay?"

Trevin's gaze fell back on Cyrus for a moment before he spoke. It made him uneasy and he started to mindlessly fidget with the hair tie still on his wrist.

"Yea. She has good control of her vine, but she still can't push it into her dagger yet. I've only seen it once when my dad made Cedar test her wits that first week."

Cyrus froze and looked at Trevin with horror. "What?"

"Yeah it was some exercise. Cedar had literally just apologized to her too, but Dad did it because she is too comfortable with Autumn and I. So he set up a drill to look like a trap," he explained.

"How did you know she could do that?"

"She told us about it. Cedar and Quinn were the only two that had seen her do it the first time. When she pointed it right at Cedar that night."

Cyrus dropped his face in his hand. "I'm so sorry."

"Cedar said it was like she snapped when she saw him. He couldn't believe what he was seeing then she pulled her dagger on him. Quinn caught up to her shortly after."

"I'm so sorry for all of it, Trev. I didn't know what else to do," he pleaded.

"You took a gamble, a stupid one, but you had no other choice. She won and we are all still here."

Cyrus nodded then took a hesitant inhale. "Do you know how she controls it?"

Trevin again looked at him then eyed his hands fidgeting with the hair tie, causing Cyrus to still. "We just tell her to breathe deep and relax. At first, when we returned to the mortal world, I would tell her to look down and close her eyes if she felt overwhelmed. Justine sure as hell made her uneasy. Still does but El holds her ground as valiant as ever. She defends you too. In fact, she has never once said anything bad about you."

This took Cyrus by surprise and just as he was going to ask about it, the front door slid open and caused him to tense.

Quinn was already looking uninterested in the day as Miles gave a nod.

"Guess we will see how today goes. For us and them." Quinn's apprehension was clear.

"They decide on a place?" Trevin asked.

"Redwoods. Justine said El had an aversion to Avenue and Humboldt Redwoods for some reason," Quinn said.

Trevin nodded and frowned. "I need to fix that for her. She gets really sad on southbound because it reminds her too much of leaving them. She'd camp there a handful of times in her mortal life and she always had to take southbound to go back to Marin County."

Cyrus frowned hearing that. "They were desperately trying to keep her here, her entire life."

"Did you know they were actually talking to her? Every time we felt that pulse?" Quinn asked.

Cyrus tensed and nodded. "That thing knew it. So I knew it. I can't hear them, but I could feel it. She'd always take a second and process what they had said."

"Let's get the drills started," Trevin said and walked towards the high estate lords who were looking over the drill plan. Quinn followed, leaving Cyrus sitting there.

Looking at his hand, he pleaded that the shadows would not slip out. He knew he would work with it tonight alone. When he looked up he saw his dad look at him with concern. Quickly Cyrus dropped his hand and ran up to them.

"We work together. In tandem. Not against each other. Let's start with the basics to see where we are at now and move forward. Always forward," Bracken said.

Then they began the drills. Quinn and Trevin snapped a few short snide remarks at each other. Cyrus was able to get back into the swing of things for the most part, but he would hesitate for a few times and feel his hands get cold. He would stumble and trip up, worried he would have to take flight and bolt up out of eyesight but he managed to keep the shadows inside him. Which took so much of his focus to do so.

By midafternoon, his wings flashed cold while in feral form. It was a battle inside him trying to clamp down whatever this power was. The spirit flashed in his mind. *No.* He imagined the spirit escaping and coldness numbed his wings, causing him to lock up.

"No! No! Please!" he begged as he lost momentum and started to plummet. The shadows were desperate.

"Cyrus! What are you doing?! Fly!" his dad shouted.

Fly or the shadows will save us, his raven said and that too startled Cyrus. He was the raven now yet it still spoke as if it were different entirely.

"Cyrus!" his dad screamed then took flight. "What's wrong?"

Cyrus cried out and the raven could be heard far and wide. He fought desperately to catch flight as his wings pounded. His muscles screamed at him all while he fought to keep those shadows down. Branches of redwoods scratched at him and slowed him before he crashed down into a soft bed of soil and ferns. The impact knocked the wind out of him since he had changed back into his fae form to avoid breaking his bones. He curled on his side, finally catching his breath with a huge inhale.

His body shivered and he heard his dad land next to him then changed back to fae. Echo and Trev arrived next followed by Miles and Quinn.

"Cyrus. What happened?" his dad said with a raised voice.

"I am good. I am not a monster," he repeated to himself as he found the hair tie still on his wrist. He fidgeted with it and tried to catch his breath.

"Are you alright?" Trevin asked calmly, sitting next to him.

With a deep breath, Cyrus calmed down. "Ye—yes," he stuttered out.

"Is that one of Elodie's hair ties?" Trevin asked after a few moments.

"Yes." With a sigh, Cyrus took it off to hand it back to Trevin. "I'm sorry. I found it after she left on Saturday."

Trevin looked at it and then at Cyrus. "She has tons of them, at both houses. Keep it if it can center you."

"It's weird. I shouldn't."

"It is what it is, I'm not mad or bothered by it. Put it back on your wrist, Cyrus," Trevin said gently.

He nodded and did. "I'm sorry. I'm not sure why that happened."

Not an outright lie. Just omission. He knew what happened and why he crashed, but not why the shadows were so anxious now. None of the drills were anything he hadn't done before.

"You have never had trouble in flight like that before," his dad said.

"I know," Cyrus said, sitting up. "I can get back to drills."

"I think we can call it a day?" Bracken looked towards Echo and Miles who both agreed.

Cyrus felt as though this were his fault. He started to get upset. "I can fly again, we can get back to drills. I'm sorry," he pleaded.

When the three estate lords looked at him, he flinched and looked away.

"Cyrus. It's alright. It's not that much earlier than we usually would be wrapping up." Trevin's tone was calm as he placed his hand on Cyrus's shoulder. He could feel the shadows looking at Trevin with great curiosity. It worried him.

"I'm sorry."

"Actually it might be good to end a little early today. We should all go over a plan for next Monday when Lady Elodie joins us," Echo suggested and everyone agreed.

The three heirs' phones all went off with a message notification and they looked at each other.

After reading the message Trevin smirked. "You want to reply or should I?"

Quinn shoved his phone back in his pocket and sighed.

Not far off a tremble had taken over Elodie and she looked at the trees abruptly with worry. Her steps had slowed as she watched her phone, seeing that Trevin, Cyrus, and Quinn had all read the message asking if everything was alright.

It is alright, little one.

They are all safe and free from harm.

"What's up?" Charles turned back to her. Cora and Justine turned too.

She looked at them. "Nothing. Let's keep going." They nodded and continued to walk. Charles lingered by her.

Her eyes scanned the trees for a raven. She hadn't gotten the hang of calling them yet. Lord Nightswift still had kept them sparse for her. Relenting, she sent Trevin a message asking if everything was okay. She knew they were all at Nightswift for drills. Nothing could hurt them at the estates. But something could hurt her if they were all busy. *No, Cedar would know. Autumn would, any of the guards would. I am safe and so are my friends.*

"Are you sure it's nothing?" Charles asked.

"Yea. I got a weird sensation and it's a little hard to ignore those now."

Justine glanced at her but didn't say anything. Elodie ignored it. Her main concern was if they were alright, especially Cyrus.

"I'm sure it's nothing. Trev is at work right?" Charles asked.

"Monday is drill day for them," Cora replied.

Justine turned back again and Elodie flinched. "What?"

"Yeah apparently, Trev, Russ, and Q run drills. Elodie told me that last year. I had no idea. They work out or do estate stuff or something," Cora laughed.

"So they are like just at the gym or something? Like all day?" Justine asked, confused.

"Well, they have a fairly decent workout room at their houses," Elodie said, then panicked. "At least Greenthistle does. I imagine Nightswift and Ashdale are the same." She was not about to open that can of worms that she had been to all three estates. Or that she had just stayed a week at each.

"That doesn't surprise me, they are all in amazing shape. Always were," Cora noted. "Anna and Caleb must use it too I assume?" Cora followed up.

"Yea, they work out throughout the week."

"Oh don't I know how good a shape Anna is in," Charles laughed.

Then she unlocked her phone and saw the message she had been waiting for.

Everything is fine. No injuries or anything. Cyrus had a mild panic attack but I spoke calmly to him. How about you? All safe?

Elodie stopped walking and typed out her reply to Trevin. She gave Charles a nod when he glanced at her and he went on to follow behind Justine and Cora.

> **Yes, everything is fine. I am staying alert and keeping my senses aware. I'm glad you were there for him.**

> **Good to hear. We ended drills a little early so we could come up with a plan for next Monday.**

Elodie sighed as she thought about it. She certainly was nervous about the drills with the three of them.

Now walking briskly to catch up to her friends, Elodie tensed upon hearing a scream, followed up by the growl of a mountain lion, then she ran.

Okay, you can do this. Just like Cedar taught you. It has to recognize what I am, and has to pick up Greenthistle's scent.

When she caught up to them, Charles put her arm out to block her.

"What do we do?" Justine panicked.

"Stay back, El. It's a mountain lion. I've actually never dealt with one before."

"I have encountered them before." Elodie inhaled deeply, stepping around Charles.

"Just be careful. If it attacks I don't know what to do," Cora panicked.

"Make yourself look big. Loud noises and do not break eye contact. Do not run or turn your back to it," Elodie said calmly while breathing hard. She clapped her hands and called it, getting its eyes to focus on her instead of everyone else. "Good keget. Eyes on me."

"What the hell? It's not one of your students, Elodie," Justine pleaded.

Elodie moved her hand to the hilt of her dagger which she had untucked from under her hoodie. She willed it to fix on her. To see what she was and who her vowed was.

"Go on, run along. It is not safe for you here." She tried to voice it calmly since her heart was anything but.

The mountain shifted focus to her dagger then began to sniff the air. It met her eyes again and let out a small chuff before running off deeper into the forest.

A huge sigh of relief escaped her, causing her shoulders to relax, unaware how tense she had been. *Thank you,* she thought to the mountain lion.

"Girl, how the hell did you just talk to it?" Cora gasped.

"Well, I clapped to get its attention. It might sound silly but your intention has a big impact on animals."

"Trev teach you that?" Charles asked with a hint of curiosity.

"Maybe."

"Why would he know?" Justine asked.

"He's a park ranger, probably encountered a few, plus it's on Greenthistle's crest for some reason," Charles explained.

"What? Why?" Justine asked, clearly still confused.

"Something with their family history. Ashdale has bears, and Nightswift has ravens," Cora explained. "You have never noticed it on their clothes sometimes?"

"No. I may be sleeping with Q but I'm not that invested in the family history," Justine replied, annoyed.

Elodie looked at her and frowned. *All this anger from her and Quinn just wants to be near her. Is he overlooking that Justine is not very serious about them? Have we?*

"I never asked Anna what the significance was. Has Trev told you?" Charles asked, turning to her. Elodie did know; it was part of her lessons, but she could use her own deductive reasoning for the significance. She could lie and say no, but then Justine or Charles might ask Quinn or Autumn and they would have to omit.

"Well." Elodie pulled her backpack around and pointed to a patch of the Greenthistle crest. "The three estates have traits they exude. Greenthistle is strength and valor, with ferns and Humboldt because that is their domain, and has been for generations. The thistle represents steadfastness. The redwood—" Elodie paused and looked at the trees for a moment. She knew they were watching but it was not a cautious feeling. It was almost a feeling of pride that swelled something in Elodie's heart. "The redwood was said to be a great entity, and a mountain lion because Greenthistle's ancestors were believed to be aligned with them. They have old stories of running with them, living alongside them." Elodie found herself smiling at the times she would lie next to Trevin in his feral form.

Justine watched her with narrowed eyes then glanced at the trees with disdain. "So Q's ancestors ran with bears? What are their traits?"

"Loyalty and kindness," Elodie answered but flinched when Justine laughed.

"So what does that mean for Nightswift? Being creepy and crazy or something?"

Elodie felt a sting in her heart for Cyrus. "Please don't, Justine. Russ isn't bad. He never was."

"You are cutting that asshole some slack too? Come on, El. He better not be at the next bonfire or party," she hissed and looked at Cora. "He is not welcome right?"

"I don't think he would be comfortable going. He did apologize but he is very lost, and he was hurt very badly. He really is a shell of his former self," Elodie interjected, not wanting to hear Cora's thoughts on Cyrus.

"You've seen him?" Charles asked, stunned.

"His dad made him apologize and the anguish in his eyes…It hurt to see him. He was so confident before, and now sometimes just breathing is hard for him."

"Maybe he shouldn't have done what he did then?" Justine spat. "You never said what their traits were by the way."

"Observation and analysis." Elodie hesitated.

"Oh good, glad it's not something creepy and a raven?"

Elodie sighed. "Please don't. This is Q's family too. You don't need to speak poorly of it. Learn to forgive. Especially when it didn't even happen to you."

"Fine. You know my reasoning though and that mountain lion just proves how dangerous this place can be. I just don't want something else to happen to you."

She looked at Justine and observed her emotions. In her mind she saw the words spite, frustration, fear, and worry. Elodie wasn't sure what to make of any of it. She could assume that from Justine's eyes Cyrus had done a very bad thing. Yet it felt as though it was more than that spurring Justine's emotions and opinions.

"I am safe here. Trust me," Elodie insisted. "Just like I can tell you that the rest of this trail is safe." Then Elodie proceeded to walk forward.

Elodie knew the move probably left it awkward but she wasn't sure what else to do. This was her home and being told it was wrong was not something she could ever accept.

"You okay?" Cora asked, catching up to her.

"Yea, I'm fine. It's just been a wild year. I'm glad I found this place though. Met everyone."

"I'm glad you are home," Cora beamed. Elodie smiled too and as they walked, she ran her hand through the ferns and felt their energy.

Chapter 33

When Quinn got to work at city hall the next day, he was a mix of thoughts and he did not want to be here. He had gone to Justine's last night, irritated enough by Trevin and Cyrus then Justine had told him about the mountain lion encounter. His heart nearly stopped before he felt a certain level of admiration for Elodie. She was doing her job as their Earth Blessed watching out for fae and mortal alike.

Explaining that to Justine, however, proved difficult. In fact, it was outright frustrating that he couldn't really tell her how Elodie seemed to "talk" to the mountain lion or why it had responded to her that way. He wanted to, though. She had also mentioned the feeling of the trees watching her which he did not understand.

The dynamic between Elodie and Cyrus too baffled him. She had defended him, which Justine certainly had opinions on. All and all it had been an exhausting night of trying to cover everything up.

The problem was he wanted more with her but that came with consequences he never wanted to face, consequences that had been instilled into him since he was young. Mortals were temporary. There was no magic to turn her fae, but Trevin somehow had found one of the special ones and she had saved everything.

He knew his loyalty would always be with Elodie without a doubt because of it. The truth was that one day Quinn would lose Justine.

He sat back and exhaled in defeat. Doubts easily took over Quinn and this was not the first time he questioned what he was doing as Master Ashdale. One thing he did know however was to keep this place safe for mortals and for Elodie.

"Lord Nightswift, sir," Quinn asked. Bracken looked at him as did his own dad. Echo merely glanced at him and went back to his report. "Do you have ravens watching any of the mortals?"

Bracken looked confused. "There's always ravens in town, you know this. But they are not watching any mortals specifically. They are just monitoring the towns for anything. Nothing has changed, with the exception of the occasional one passing over Lady Elodie's whereabouts to monitor the area. She recently informed me she is fine with it."

"Are you barred from any?" Quinn followed up.

"No. I'm not. What are you concerned about?" Bracken adjusted his posture to face him now.

"Is Cyrus monitoring them?"

This caused Echo to look at Quinn now while Trevin narrowed his eyes.

"No, he isn't back to his full workload yet. Unfortunately, the solstice took a bit out of him even with Lady Elodie's help."

"Okay."

"Why are you asking?" Miles looked at his son.

"Just want to make sure."

"Of?" Echo asked, setting his pen down and fixing on Quinn.

He rolled his eyes, unprepared for an interrogation. "Justine mentioned she felt someone or something watching her."

Trevin scoffed again. "Yeah, she thinks the trees are out to get Elodie. Thinks she should move back to Marin. Or anywhere but here really. The one place she is the safest."

"Look, I don't know what it was, I have gone to Sequoia Community Park a bunch and didn't sense anything. I just wanted to know if she was being watched, or if Cyrus was up to something."

Bracken sighed. "You know what state he is in. You just saw him on Monday, I've never known him to plummet like that." A chill passed over Bracken at the thought.

"Do you think it's Alena or someone associated with her?" Quinn asked.

"How would Elmbridge even know who your mortal is? And why would she care?" Miles asked.

"I don't know. She's made the rounds with two of us. I wouldn't put it past her to try. Or if Cyrus told her."

Trevin glared at Quinn now. "She never made the rounds with me. She is a wretched vile thing that inserted herself into my bed I share with El and only El. And you know what she did to Cyrus. Why are you blaming him? He's barely holding it together. I doubt Justine is any of his concern. She wasn't before the ruins, she isn't now."

"Yea, we all know who his concern was and is," Quinn retorted.

"The fuck does that mean?" Trevin growled, leaping out of his chair.

"Trevin," Echo warned, shifting his gaze. "Deep breaths."

Quinn watched Trevin's eyes narrow. "Odd that within a week, Elodie cares so much about Cyrus."

"What would you have her do? Not help him?" Bracken retorted, sounding almost wounded now.

"She was all nervous with me at spring equinox but she pretty much asked for his hand."

"Master Ashdale, while she is still overwhelmed, she understands her responsibility as our Earth Blessed. I would hope you understand it too, since Trev does. I as well as she would appreciate you not putting stress on that understanding." Echo explained, obviously highly unamused.

"Are you so stupid that you can't see why they formed the friendship they did?" Trevin asked. The two heirs leveled their gaze at each other.

"Enlighten me then, great and wise Master Greenthistle."

Miles sighed. "Quinn. Knock it off. Stop prodding him."

"Cyrus was there for her and he knew exactly what she was feeling because he felt just as lost. Not once did you just hang out with her or acknowledge her feelings when the entire point of these weeks is to get her to trust all of us. She needed a friend that first week at Ashdale and all of us thought for sure you'd be there for her. Treat her like your friend and not some shiny new toy whenever Justine isn't around."

Quinn looked shocked for a second then glared again. "You know that's not my intent with her."

"I know it isn't but it certainly doesn't appear that way to her. She felt rejected by you ever since your little display at spring equinox. Even Cedar made it a point to treat her as a friend. And neither my dad nor I had to ask him to," Trevin spat and sat back down.

"Because Cedar knows he needs to make amends," Quinn fumed. "It's hard to cover this up to Justine. You are not in this position, and you can't tell me Autumn is with Charles either because he is just so laid-back. Her gifts work a lot better on him than mine do on Justine. I can't cover up for Cyrus any more than El already has."

"Make a damned decision on who to be there for," Trevin snapped. "Be there for Elodie. I'm trying to be there for Cyrus, since we know you aren't."

Quinn sighed. "I'm sorry, I do not trust him anymore. I wouldn't trust him around Elodie, either. His vowed was right there in his arms, and he said like five words to her then let her go? Seems like you're both good at giving up on your vowed."

"Fuck you," Trevin spat out.

"Master Ashdale, this is not a conversation you should speak of," Echo said sternly.

Bracken exhaled. "I will post extra ravens in the Sequoia Community to see if we detect any presence or visiting fae. It may be worth looking into if she did sense something. Is she fae? You'd have mentioned it right?"

"No, she's mortal," Quinn said with some spite.

"I will see what I can find on her if anything. Maybe she had some extra sense or something buried deep in her," Miles replied.

Quinn noticed Echo and his dad glance at each other with a nod. Trevin let out a laugh at the situation.

"That should be a fun discussion when her entire background shows up in a nice little file." Trevin scoffed.

Echo just sighed and shook his head. "Whatever, I'm sure it's fine," he said. "Let's get these things wrapped up." Then he turned his attention back to his papers.

Trevin picked up his pen to get back to his notes. Quinn sighed a few times.

They both could not get out of the room fast enough and go their separate ways.

Elodie had gone to the café twice during her week off and hung out at Cora's. She hung out at her house with Trevin for a few nights as well before it was time to begin her second rotation at the estates. During her Ashdale week, Quinn had made it a point to hang out with her for two nights. Yet she noticed he was very engrossed on his phone and mentioned Justine a lot. She was becoming increasingly more aware of his level of want and yearning for her that it was harder to ignore it now. This realization saddened her.

After hearing about Trevin's words to him, she had no doubt they cut deep. What hurt her worse than Quinn's priorities though, was how unrequited it was. *One is overlooked and often overlooks.* The tome's warning came back to her and so she tried to think about what the warning really meant. To her surprise little had been unveiled about the Earth Blessed in the tome so far. It was part of her lessons with Lord Ashdale and Connor. Despite not really understanding how to translate the language, she certainly appreciated the knowledge she was learning from it about the area's history.

She had only talked to Cora about the future of Quinn and Justine a few times, since Cora saw Justine's side of it mostly. Her take on the situation was that Justine did love Quinn a lot but she wanted to deny it. Regardless of what it was, Elodie knew it would have to end, just as her time on the mortal side would.

By the end of her Greenthistle week, Trevin and Elodie went out to the usual Friday night festival in Old Town Eureka. There were street vendors and all the shops stayed open late. Walking hand in hand, Elodie enjoyed these times despite people-watching them. Sometimes Trev would pull her closer and smile wide. He would tell her how much he loved her, talk about how excited he was to marry her. On occasion Quinn and Cedar would be at the tables for their respective agencies. Trevin would stop by the state parks table and talk to coworkers. He always said he was too grumpy to be at the table so they never scheduled him. Sometimes they would meet up with Autumn and Charles and end the night at Elodie's house.

It was nights like these where she could at least let herself believe everything was alright, despite knowing it wasn't. The three heirs still carried tension and worry still clung to Elodie. At least on nights like this, she could set all those thoughts aside and enjoy the life she had built for herself. The life and the home she had fought for.

As they walked out of a shop, Trevin stopped short and gripped Elodie's hand tighter. Then she caught a familiar whiff.

"Trev, so nice to see you here," someone mused. Elodie took him in and realized it was the same one that had sat on the hood of his car. Then she saw Delia, annoyance plastered to her face. "And this must be Mr. Greenthistle's fiancé. Elodie is it? Trev, she is beautiful."

Delia looked at the male with some confusion and then annoyance towards Elodie.

"Elodie, meet Austin, my oh so curious intern."

This seemed to shock Delia.

"You know Dee, yes?" he said in a border line statement rather than a question.

"Yes, I have met Dee. It's nice to see you again and to meet you, Austin."

Delia rolled her eyes but nodded as if ready to leave.

"I have heard so much about you from Trev, El," Austin said with a relaxed tone.

"Oh." Elodie wasn't really sure what to make of this interaction. Trevin's tension and Delia's confusion screamed danger in her head. Austin's overconfidence certainly made her uneasy as did the use of her nickname.

"He seems happy tonight, usually he just scowls during our shifts," Austin laughed. "I always assumed Trev here had a miserable life, but now I see it must not be all that bad with someone like you around."

Elodie couldn't help but feel as though he was insinuating things.

"I don't have a miserable life, Austin. It is only miserable when I have to answer a million questions every shift." Trevin's tone held no sarcasm.

Elodie wasn't sure what to say. She glanced towards the direction of the Old Giants, not that there were a lot in this part of town. Something told her to be alert and when she turned back to Austin and Delia, his smile gave her a chill. It seemed off and the way he was so fixed on her as though he knew what she was...But then he would have to know what Delia and Trevin were and they would have said something. Trevin's demeanor caused her to worry.

"How did you meet Dee? Small world." Elodie laughed nervously.

"A party," Dee uttered. "You work with Trev?" she asked, turning towards Austin.

"Oh that I do. I was fortunate enough to be paired with this grump for my internship. They say he is the best though, so at least I know I'm learning a lot." Austin wrapped his arm around Dee's waist, pulling her close. "I saw Dee at a college party and thought she was beautiful so I had to chat her up. By the end of the night I was smitten and now I'm dating a Nightswift."

"That's cute. Trev and I met at a party too. But we really should be on our way. We wanted to get to a shop before it closes."

"Of course, I wouldn't dream of interrupting your date." Austin smirked and glanced at Trevin. Elodie just nodded and started to walk past him, but his hand came to her waist to stop her. "Hopefully you send him off to work nice and taken care of."

Elodie froze, unable to stop the blur in front of her. Trevin got right in Austin's face and pinned him against the wall. His glare burned a hole right into Austin.

"If you ever touch her again I will break your hand. Do not say her name or any variation of it, ever again."

"Of course, tough guy. My apologies. Enjoy your evening," he said and then guided Delia away as they kept walking, his arm around her waist.

Trevin and Elodie looked at each other and walked to a quieter block, letting out a breath.

"That was unnerving. He is a full mortal right?" Elodie asked.

"Yea. From Redding. I looked into it." Trevin took her hand. "Why?"

"Do you remember in May when I mentioned that guy vaping on his hood. That was him."

"Austin is in a world of hurt." Trevin clenched his fist. "He will not get to you. We will heighten your defense training. I will be damned if you get hurt here on our land, especially by a dumb ass mortal."

Elodie gave his hand a squeeze. "Did you know Dee was dating your intern?"

"No, and I hate that guy. I did not tell him anything, I didn't even tell him your first name. I swear."

"Maybe Dee told him?" Elodie suggested.

"I don't think she would. I've never known her to even talk about our families much at all. Her disinterested aloofness works well for us."

"Something about him seems weird to me. I feel like he is too curious, something in his grin. It's different from how Cyrus used to be." Elodie hesitated.

"I know what you mean. And he's dating Dee of all people. If Cyrus didn't mention it he may not know the connection," Trevin explained as he worked through his thoughts.

"I don't think he has spoken much to his sister at all. Should I ask him next week?"

"Yea. I don't know how calm I'm going to be if I ask Nightswift about this. If Dee is telling Austin things, I swear."

"I don't think she is, she seemed shocked at how he acted, plus wouldn't that cost Nightswift power? Their parents are so stressed as it is. Another power loss would add so much more. Dee has to know this."

"Yeah, you're right. I'll tell my dad about it. Tonight you are safe. We have until Sunday afternoon when my little mink is whisked away to the raven's domain for a week." Trevin laughed and kissed her.

"Let's hope I stop disappointing Dee and can communicate with them this week."

"You will get the hang of it soon. She holds a lot of resentment towards me still for what I let happen to Cyrus."

"You didn't let that happen to him. He knows that." Elodie took his hand.

Trevin smiled and they went back towards the crowd.

Chapter 34

It was the middle of her Nightswift week, when Elodie had just finished a book. As she set it down she eyed the bookshelf in the room. It did not have much on it. For a moment she debated leaving the book on the shelf. This would be her life for the foreseeable future, she could put books on this shelf, and the one at Ashdale, just as she had done at Greenthistle since they got her her own shelf in Trevin's room. She still had to remind herself it was their room and not just his anymore.

She had two lives to live now, just as they all did. They had adopted her into their families and considered her one of their cubs or fledglings. So much had changed and it hadn't even been a full year yet. Elodie thought about the good and the bad that had happened. And all that was still to come.

With a quick glance to the window she smiled knowing she was home, despite the unknown. The doubts always sat tucked away in the recess of her mind. These three estates had suffered a lot, even the mortals had seemed to struggle. The fear that she couldn't seem to find a way to help them nagged at her. She had figured out how to seal a spirit up, but she couldn't ease tensions between friends that grew up together?

All her life people had told her she was running away from things and it had left its mark on her. Not that she knew what she was running away from by leaving

Marin. She had tried, time and time again to find that part of her she was searching for there and elsewhere. It had been sitting here, in Humboldt the entire time, just waiting for her to wake up. Now that she had, she could not imagine letting go of this place for anything.

Quinn and Cedar had been the brothers she had never had. Autumn the sister she never had, Cyrus had been the best friend she never realized she needed. Then there was Trevin, who her heart would always yearn for. He had been so supportive every step of the way in this transition and he tried so hard to prove it to her.

Smiling at the thought she went to turn off the light but noticed her phone light up. It was a message from Cyrus.

Are you still awake?

                                        Yes. Are you alright?

I think so. I need to talk. Meet me in the training room, but we need to be quiet.

She tensed. That was certainly an odd request. Yet as she thought back to it, he had appeared to be struggling a lot during drills. That thing inside him was evolving. She replied with an 'okay' and threw her shorts and hoodie on. It was July and while some days had warm temperatures, evenings were breezy.

Quietly, she made her way downstairs to the training room and walked inside. Cyrus was already there.

"Close the door slowly," he said. Once she had Elodie turned back to him. "I need to show you something. Tell you something," Cyrus hesitated. "You have to absolutely promise you will not scream. I don't want to scare you. It's just, if someone sees it they might throw me in the hold."

Elodie nodded adamantly.

"I have been in here nearly every night trying to grasp control of it, but it's a struggle, especially when they glare or make their comments about me. I don't know what it might do and I'm scared it might want you but I don't know who else to ask about it."

"What is it?" Elodie asked with caution.

"Do not scream and please do not use your vines on me."

Her wide eyes fixed on him.

"Last month, after you left, I felt your absence. It was back to screaming and trembling when I tried to sleep. After my parents left I paced my room for nearly an hour, scared to try to sleep again. I felt like a failure. You had done so much and I felt as though I made progress, but it all came crashing down on me. When I tried to lie back down I got overwhelmed and went to rub my eyes, my hands were like ice. I examined them for any discoloration or anything—" He paused and brought his hand palm facing up.

Elodie watched intently. With a gasp she took a step back, seeing his eyes pulse with a royal blue shadow and then shadows drifted out of his palm towards her.

"What is that? It looks like remnants of the spirit but the feathers?" Her voice grew curious as they drifted closer.

He moved his fingers as if grabbing the shadows and pulled them back to him. Then as he made a wave motion with his hand the shadows did as well. "It's me. I'm in control of it. I am able to talk to my raven in my head, but it's not sure what this is either."

Elodie watched the feathers hover in the shadow, dark as the night sky. "It's beautiful." She smiled.

"This sensation started forming in me a few weeks before you stayed last month. I would be deep in a nightmare, and something was ready to come out of me, ripping me back awake. After your week here, it got too hard to contain so I've been working to control it. I've been scared it's going to slip out and they will throw me in chains. That first Monday back at drills was so terrifying."

"Trev told me about how you plummeted from the sky. How shaken up you were after that. I won't let them lock you up, Cyrus. I promise." Elodie raised her palm and slowly eased her vine out. He took a step back and retreated his shadows.

"I don't know what they might do to you, they are stronger around you. They reach for your vines."

"I know, my vines reach for your shadows. Is this why you have been struggling at drills, you are trying to hold it in?" she asked.

Cyrus dropped his head. "Yes. I'm scared to let anyone see it. That spirit was terrifying. I don't know what my dad might do."

Elodie paused watching his anguish. He took a step back from her in fear.

"Cyrus, I'm not going to let anyone hurt you. We will be alright. I am not afraid of you. I just want to see what happens when they merge, my vines have been reaching for you too, for these shadows," she said and watched him fidget with the hair tie on his wrist. "Trevin told me about the hair tie too. How you tried to give it back to him and he told you to keep it."

"The first night I discovered these, they led me to your room," he explained. Elodie smiled.

"I don't think it will hurt me. Let's just try."

Cyrus nodded and held up his palm. His body tensed as he let the shadow slip out. She let her vine show. Slowly and delicately as if in a synchronized dance they swirled around each other. Both sets of eyes transfixed.

He has awoken, by your kindness. But he is not like us and you.

The ravens were freed and they fought for their Earth Blessed, who swore she would fight for them. You saw what happened?

Elodie now replayed that night in her mind and her vision pulsed teal. A second later Cyrus's eyes flashed a dark blue and she could almost swear a galaxy pulsed in his eyes.

He looked at her worried.

"You are okay." Her voice was soft and almost ethereal now. "That night, ravens flew through the spirit, weakening it. Taking bits of it."

A chill shot through Cyrus. "Some of those ravens fell, I saw them, they were close enough to me that I absorbed their essence. You couldn't because you are not a raven, but we can if we are near enough to our fallen aligned animals. They held some of that thing?"

"I think so. The Old Giants told me that we were both chosen correctly."

"Am I night blessed? The stars pulse when I feel this." Cyrus looked confused.

"I don't know, is there lore about them?"

"Not that I've heard. I still have that spirit in me?" He panicked.

"Not the spirit but its power. Those ravens took pieces of it and gifted it to you," Elodie said. "Just as I control mine, you control yours."

Cyrus nodded and let his shadows interlace with her vine again.

As they watched the shadow and vine twirl around, both of their bodies pulsed. They were so awestruck they hardly registered the door open.

"Cyrus? Step away from her!" Bracken demanded.

"No. I'm sorry." Cyrus's eyes were wide with distress. He was trembling and Elodie saw his eyes pulse blue again. She heard the release of the gun.

Be a Greenthistle, little cub.

Impulse took over and she shoved Cyrus out of the way, feeling the pinch right in her neck. Everything felt heavy and she heard Cyrus cry out for her but he sounded far away despite him holding her. Everything was fading until she feel asleep.

"Elodie!" Cyrus cried out and caught her as her body fell limp. He started to hyperventilate. Sentries grabbed him and pulled him away. "Please! Please. I'm sorry. Don't lock me up. I didn't hurt her. I wasn't going to. I asked for her help. I didn't hurt her!" he sobbed and trembled. His mom ran in and gasped. "She's the only one who can possibly help me understand what happened to me."

"She moved faster than we've seen her move!" the sentry rasped out, dropping the tranquilizer gun and putting his hands up. "I'm sorry!"

"Do not move, Cyrus. Remain where you are," his dad said sternly. "Get her to her bed."

"What happened?" Ariyanna stilled as medical staff gently lifted Elodie.

"He has shadows in him, his eyes pulsed like hers except blue." Bracken paused and looked at Cyrus. "What is it? Don't bother trying to hide this, tell me, what is it? She took the shot for you."

The vitriol in his dad's voice made Cyrus tremble as he explained word for word what had occurred to his dad.

Ariyanna sighed and ran her fingers through her hair. "How high of a dose was that tranquilizer? Could it have sedated Quinn?"

"It might have slowed him some. It was a standard dose for a Nightswift, so less than a mountain lion and a bear. But Lady Elodie is none of those. I panicked when his eyes pulsed. His hands pulsed like hers," the sentry fretted. "But it was a shadow."

"We felt a pulse and the stars shimmered, the Old Giants shifted," Bracken said. Cyrus curled in on himself.

"I'm sorry," he whimpered. "I didn't hurt her; I didn't even touch her. Her vines touched my shadows. She always ends up hurt because of me."

Bracken's phone rang and he heard his dad sigh. "It's Echo. Take him to his room, ensure he does not leave. Post ravens at the windows, stand guard at his door. No one in or out except me," his dad ordered and looked at his son with disappointment.

Cyrus trembled and fidgeted with the hair tie. "I'm sorry," he cried out. "Why did she push me out of the way? I didn't want her to! I wanted her help. I wasn't going to hurt her!"

Trevin barreled into Nightswift Estate and caused half the room to jump. His heart was thundering.

"Where is she?" he shouted.

"In her quarters, asleep. She is fine. Just sedated," Bracken said, looking defeated.

"What!?" Trevin growled. "Why?"

Lord Greenthistle padded in at a more relaxed stroll though he was tense when he changed from mountain lion to fae.

"Something is still in Cyrus yet he appears to remain in control of himself. He said he could feel something in him change as his body healed. He thinks it awoke when she used her vines on him."

"Is he sedated?" Trevin snapped out. He was heaving.

"No. He's in bed trembling under the covers. She took the hit for him. We felt the pulse and the stars flashed brighter. I went to check on them, but their rooms were empty. When I checked the training room, I saw it with my own eyes. Her vine and shadows from him were intertwined." Bracken sighed and deflated in shame. "I got scared and didn't know what I was looking at, I was worried he was going to hurt her, that he wanted to. So I asked him to step away but his eyes flashed blue just as hers do and one of my sentries fired the tranquilizer. She moved so fast and pushed him out of the way."

"He caught her before she fell and screamed the entire time," Ariyanna repeated his words.

Echo looked at his son and crossed his arms. "Clearly she trusts him. The question is, do we?"

Trevin glared at his dad.

Bracken sighed. "I don't know what to do anymore. I want to remain a high estate, and want him to succeed me. But he's just so unstable. And the conference is in two months." He gave Echo a pleading look as if he could beg his friend to help.

"She doesn't seem to think he is unstable," Echo stated but he too sounded exhausted. Trevin slumped down in one of the chairs and dropped his head into his hands. "Something is going to have to give. They're going to rip him apart at the conference regardless if they see this, I don't know what they might demand. They're going to see the weak points in your armor, Trev. Quinn isn't going to be able to hold his wits either. Elodie wants so desperately to hold this together and she cannot do it if none of us are willing to budge."

"I know!" Trevin snapped. "I thought I had this under control, I thought I mastered it after Mom. I wanted to pull the grief off you, Autumn, and Cedar so I pulled it but it hurt more than I realized. Then that scar ripped open when I thought I lost El and it's still tender. I know Cyrus cares deeply for her. I know he needs her but he has to understand that if she is in danger it's only going to hurt him and Nightswift further. He has to protect her as much as she protects him. She took the fall for him. I don't even know if she had seen one of our tranquilizer guns. Would she have taken a bullet or arrow for him?"

"Do you doubt she would take one for you?" his dad asked.

"No! If she dragged me a mile out of an iron casket, I know she would do that for any of us, but they cannot lose her, they waited years for her. I can't lose her again."

"He calls for her during nights when the terrors get bad. He fidgets with that hair tie on his wrist, which he never takes off. He constantly repeats her words, 'I am good,'" Ariyanna said.

"I want to see her. Please?" Trevin pleaded to no one in particular.

"Come on, I will check her vitals just to see how her body processed the sedative," Echo said.

Chapter 35

Elodie was groggy when she came to. She saw Trevin sit up with his back against the headboard. He'd been looking up at the ceiling but turned to face her as she stirred.

"El," he said, his voice full of relief.

"Morning." She smiled weakly.

"Technically it is." He laughed softly and rubbed her head. "How are you feeling?"

"Tired. What time is it?" Her head pounded when she went to push herself up. She reached for her phone but felt Trevin's stomach instead. She realized he was on the opposite side of his usual place.

She looked at him with confusion before she noticed how dark it was. Her peripheral caught the banner on the wall and she realized where she was. Nightswift.

She pushed herself up and swayed. Trevin stabilized her.

"Calm down. Breathe."

"Nightswift. Cyrus! Where is he? Where did they take him?"

"He is in his room. I haven't seen him. Guards are ordered to keep him in and me out."

"He didn't do anything wrong! Nightswift's guard had a hasty reaction," Elodie spat out then heard someone approach. She turned and the headache flared. A small tremble took over her then a calming hand came to her back. She looked at Echo. "He's not bad. Tell his dad that. Tell his dad not to treat him like an abomination!"

"Lady Elodie, it sounds as though Bracken was startled as were his guards. We do not know what he can do."

"Then treat me the exact same way you treat him. His eyes pulsed blue and you locked him in his room. Mine pulse teal and you just leave my overseer in charge of holding me close?"

"This is new for all of us."

"Then let Trevin see how utterly terrified his second is! Stop treating me as the golden child and one of your own as the blight." Elodie nearly growled.

"Elodie. Breathe," Trevin said softly.

"He didn't hurt me, Nightswift's guard did."

"You jumped in front of him, the dart was meant for Cyrus, not you," Trevin explained. His eyes went wide at seeing her glare.

"He didn't need one! Cyrus needs to know the people who matter to him don't see him as a monster, he needs a hand to pull himself back up with, not to be chained down and yelled at then left in isolation." Elodie trembled and began to cry now as though the memory was too painful to hold. Trevin rubbed her back and pulled her close. "Help him, Trevin."

"I want to. But that risk he took. The iron cuff. Of all things. The shadows."

"You don't see his fear? His isolation pushes him closer and closer to the breaking point."

Trevin sighed. "I do see those too. Those gates are wide open. It still hurts though. This isn't a trail I want to be on any more than he does."

"Help him then. He has been fighting to keep this contained alone. Working every night to master it. It is not the spirit, it is Cyrus. We can help him and you all know this yet you do nothing? Look out for your own."

She looked over when Lord Nightswift approached. He offered a sad smile when Elodie glared at him.

"Stop keeping him chained up!" she hissed, noticing how Lord Greenthistle looked at her with shock. "I've told you so many times, stop treating your first born like the monster I saved him from. Or treat me the same way." Tears fell from her eyes.

"I don't know what this is inside him. Is it the spirit all over again?"

"No! It's Nightswift ravens that fell, making their sacrifice to weaken it so I could seal it up. They made the sacrifice to repay Cyrus for his fight. He will master this. He has been trying too. Let me help him."

"What if it is that spirit? Or it evolves into evil?"

"He asked for help and you punished him for it! He tried to show us and you locked him up. How do you think he turns evil?"

Bracken sighed in defeat. "We need to be cautious. We need to protect you."

Elodie went to get up but Trevin stopped her. She took a deep inhale, fighting the gut reaction to gust them all away from her.

"Let me go, Trevin." She gritted her teeth. Trevin gasped and removed his hand. She knew that command hurt him.

"I-I just want to make sure you aren't still groggy."

She stood up and stumbled back slightly but remained upright. Trevin stood by her, ready to catch her. "I'm sorry I said that, Trevin. Come with me please." He nodded and got up with her. Elodie took his hand firmly. "If that was an order, I rescind it. Don't ever let me go, please."

"I know, El. I'm sorry we are not helping. Slow your breathing before you walk into his room please," he said gently.

Elodie nodded then looked at Echo and Bracken. "Stay here and tell your guard to let us pass. Trevin will not hurt him."

"She's got a point, Bracken. You have got to start listening to her. We have to let Cyrus show us who he wants to be now. Let him know he is safe to be someone new because I don't see him going back to who he was before."

"Nightswift has hurt Lady Elodie so badly and she has done so much for us. That night still weighs on me as much as it does all of them. What we could have lost them both, how terrified she was, her injuries. His injuries. Some nights I can't even bring myself to look at the Old Giants for what we almost cost them and they still keep us in rank?"

"We all made mistakes with her. I would have cost you and her everything. She chose us all, let's listen to her, learn from her now."

Bracken turned to Elodie and, with a nod, stepped aside. Elodie and Trevin strode past them.

Cyrus had silently cried to himself for hours. The hair tie was leaving burns on his skin from fidgeting with it.

"Elodie. I'm sorry. Trevin." His voice was raw.

He began to wonder what would happen if he left. If he exiled himself.

You'd be an experiment or murdered. Your family would weep, your Old Giants would weep. You already know what would happen to the Earth Blessed. You already see what doubts and fears run through her head, that she will not voice.

She feels responsible for all of us. His raven told him even though he already knew it all.

Stay. We have to prove to her that is not true. Fight for her as she's fighting for us.

He continued to weep until he heard the door open. He scented Elodie and Trevin. A tremble took over him.

"No. Please don't. I'm sorry. I'm sorry," he cried from under the covers.

"Cyrus, are you alright, not injured?" Elodie asked softly.

He hated himself for his answer. "No! But you were. I can't do this anymore. I never want you to take the fall for me again. I'm so fucking exhausted. I never wanted any of this! All I am is a monster now. One who hurts his Earth Blessed he never deserved."

"That's not true, Cyrus," Trevin said calmly. "You do deserve her, and Bryla, and Nightswift. You are right, you never asked for any of this, but we will move forward. I'm sorry I am such a neurotic temperamental asshole right now. I'm trying to work it all out too."

"Bryla doesn't deserve to be vowed to a trembling little finch. She never asked for this either."

"She does deserve to see who her vowed is though. Then she can decide," Trevin said.

With a sigh, Cyrus wiped his eyes then threw the blankets off him. He finally looked at them. First he scanned Elodie, searching for any sign of injury. Then he looked at Trevin, searching for any anger. He found none on either.

"Do you think my vines woke you up?" Elodie asked.

"It felt stronger after that. I kept getting worried you would see it, you would know something was in me. What did you feel before you awoke? Was it the night of the ruins?"

He listened to Elodie speak of that brimming curiosity that had been inside her for decades. How she had felt it in her very core. When she had finally moved to Eureka, and began to go out and explore the trails, she would get scared but something told her it was safe. So further she went on them.

Trevin's gaze on her was one of such endearment. Cyrus could see so much love and adoration on his face for her. His brave little mink, who fought her way into Greenthistle. Cyrus smiled at the thought.

"I knew you needed Greenthistle to bind the magic to you," Cyrus sighed. "And I needed an Earth Blessed to pull me out of that blinding white void. But even when I was freed, I didn't know where I was, who I was. I still don't and it's so terrifying." Cyrus dragged his hands down his face as he let out a shaky exhale. "The whispers from everyone are not kind, their nervous or scathing looks, the disgusted looks directed at you, El. They are maddening. Alena's touch and words caressing my skin makes me want to rip my flesh off. The feeling of your blood on my feathers and talons makes me writhe. I just want it to end." He wiped his eyes. He flinched and turned his head away when Elodie sat on the edge of the bed.

"It will be okay, Cyrus, we will both make it off this trail. I still see how badly injured your body was in those ruins, it still hurts to think about you like that for months. But you can master this power, and that battle in your head is not over. That means you are still fighting, and you can win. We are here. Bryla is safe, rooting for you too, even if she doesn't know it."

Cyrus finally looked at her then worriedly looked at Trevin. They fixed each other for a second then Trevin stepped closer. A tremble passed over Cyrus, causing him to look away.

"The despair and insanity in your eyes is so heavy. I see it, and I know it's not my battle to pull it off you. But it is my battle to find both of you and bring you home, because they want you and El here to look after them. I want you both here with Quinn by my side. I want you comfortable and complete again, Cyrus," Trevin asserted and held his hand out.

Again, Cyrus looked at it then at Trevin. He hadn't flinched this time, he realized. With a hard swallow he took it and Trevin pulled him into a hug, causing Cyrus to tense for a moment until he allowed himself to collapse into him.

"You don't have to do this alone anymore. I'm sorry we ever left you behind." Trevin's words were soft.

Cyrus gripped his friend hard and cried into him. His emotions had crashed down on him all at once.

After crying on Trevin and catching his breath, he opened his eyes to see his parents and Lord Greenthistle standing in the hall, watching them. His eyes grew wide and he pulled away from Trevin.

Elodie's hand came to his back softly. "It's alright. They need to see it too. We are all in this together."

Cyrus nodded and then frowned, realizing Quinn was missing.

"That asshole will come back too, that is not your battle, it's mine and his," Trevin said.

"He hasn't been acting like himself."

"No he isn't," Trevin grumbled. "Not taking his duty seriously."

Elodie glanced back towards the trees for a moment and Cyrus knew her tells by now to know she was piecing something together.

"We will work on it. With Quinn. We will all help you find your way, Cyrus," Echo said.

Cyrus saw his parents nod. His mom wiped her eyes and smiled, looking hopeful.

"Trev," Echo called for his son who sighed again as he looked at Elodie.

"Counting down the hours once again, Little Mink." Trevin smiled and gave her a quick kiss.

"I love you," Elodie said quickly and smiled back.

"Love you too, El." Trevin then looked at Cyrus who cut his eyes down. "Show me the shadow thing on Saturday when I'm back here, yeah? I want to see it."

Cyrus looked at Trevin in shock. "Yes. I will."

With one last smile at Elodie, Trevin left and followed his dad down the stairs.

"It's been so long since I have hugged him," Cyrus exhaled softly. "I didn't deserve it."

"You deserve to have friends there for you. And to feel safe with your fellow high estates," Elodie noted.

"Quinn is jealous about more than just our friendship, you know."

"Is it the power shift? He has expressed he doesn't feel Trevin should have gained. His dad said the entire power shift was unmerited."

"It was merited though. All of it was." Cyrus frowned and sighed again. "He is jealous of what you and Trev have. I saw it in him over the months and weeks while I was trapped by that spirit. I didn't realize it at first but he grew far more attached to Justine than he should have."

"He knows better," Bracken interjected. "You all do. Even Trevin knew better and that's part of what is making him so temperamental now. He was struggling between a vowed bond pulling him in and following rules."

"I don't think she feels the same about him as he does her."

"All the more reason he should be acting like the Ashdale heir Miles raised him to be. Loyalty and kindness to our entity and Earth Blessed comes first and foremost. Then it comes to each other. He is lucky he retains the power gained from fighting for you, Lady Elodie. He better not cost them by ignoring his duty," Bracken hissed. "As it is Nightswift and Ashdale are far too close to switching rank and we can not let that happen. Meanwhile Greenthistle holds too much. I'm not sure we know how to fix it, but we all agree it can not shift again."

"Power shifted and now it's not balanced," Elodie stated. "I don't know how to fix it either."

"It is not yours to fix, Lady Elodie. It's ours to figure out. We were all given a second chance and so we serve and honor you. We have all felt minor ones here and there over the years, a sentry or staff aligned with our estates does something foolish, but it does not risk our rank since they are not of our blood. Now we have felt a major one." Bracken looked at Cyrus and put a hand on his shoulder, causing him to look away. "We will work past it. I just hope we are prepared for what awaits us all."

"I'm sorry," Cyrus said quietly.

"I am sorry too, son. Let us try to get some actual rest. It has been a long day and we have lots of work to do tomorrow. I suppose we will have to adjust lessons around to accommodate." Bracken looked at Cyrus, offered a small smile, and left the room. His mom followed.

Elodie placed her hand over his. "We will be okay. I will help you."

"Thank you, El." Cyrus was now smiling.

She smiled back and then after a few moments, she got up and left the room.

Cyrus flopped back on the bed and looked out the window. "They know everything, so why do I still feel terrified?"

As the week progressed, Elodie and Cyrus started to find their rhythm together. He didn't talk much and was still hesitant but they were able to complete their tasks together. They proved to be good sparring partners. She helped him with target practice and with some breathing techniques when he panicked, the way she had done with her powers. Some things worked and some didn't. Despite the dejection, she found that she didn't dwell on it much. Elodie was able to call on the ravens after enough time as well. Though Delia did not seem all that impressed. Poppy tended to cling to Elodie a lot and she even joined in on some lessons and drills conducted by Bracken and Cyrus.

When her week was up and Trevin arrived, he went into the training room to see what Cyrus really had in him. He was mesmerized by the way the two powers complimented each other. He also watched Cyrus perform similar drills to Elodie's and could see where the lesson focus could be.

Elodie too watched Trevin during this, sensing his emotions. Once again there were no gates as Trevin often described, but a feeling, a sensation, and a confirmation. She knew she should tell Greenthistle about this but she still wasn't sure she was actually seeing the emotions or had just gotten better at reading people. So she remained quiet.

Chapter 36

During Elodie's week off, the three high estate lords sat in Lord Greenthistle's office in the city hall.

"So. The dreaded announcement arrived. The conference. And it is earlier than expected," Echo said.

"How are we feeling about everything?" Miles asked.

Bracken let out a long sigh. "They have made so much progress and yet it just doesn't feel like enough. Cyrus is still nervous and those shadows now bring another set of problems. If I am being honest, I am petrified they are going to strip him of his title and keep him. They can't keep her but him, the night sky is everywhere."

"We just do not mention it," Echo said.

"Omission. Now let's hope they do not slip out or his eyes don't pulse. Getting her to control hers was one thing." Bracken nodded.

"Well according to Trinity County, word has traveled. There is talk of Master Greenthistle's vowed. Who was once mortal but is now, Earth Blessed. So they are all expecting to see her," Miles sighed.

"If anyone has seen Cyrus's shadows. Any of our guards broke their oath." Bracken began to fret.

"We would know about the guards," Echo explained. "We cannot cover Elodie up. Regardless, she was a mortal discovery, I also cannot cover up the iron cuff that led to that mortal discovery. Cyrus will have to stand his ground that he did the right thing. Elodie believes that he did. And Trevin is right, Cyrus needs to start being there for Elodie."

Miles sighed. "It just was too much happening in too short a time span. No other territory has dealt with this much in rapid succession, with heirs as young as they are. It's going to come down to their confidence and it's not Trev or Quinn's confidence I'm worried about." He rubbed his forehead.

"They both get uneasy with the whispers and murmurs here. He is still withdrawn, she still doubts her place," Bracken cautioned.

"I do not think she doubts her place here, I think she still doubts her worth. Trevin has done everything I need him to. This is going to come down to her and Cyrus," Echo said.

Miles sat back. "We should meet with her. Maybe this week, say in Sequoia Community Park? Neutral ground? Put her in a place where she may get nervous, that way we can see how she responds to the initial pressure? I know she trusts us, but she needs to start showing it."

"I will let them know when to meet us. But we will approach her in our feral forms and not give her comforts too quickly," Echo advised.

Braken and Miles agreed. As Echo began to fold the papers back up, Bracken pulled a folder out.

"May I request that we vote to end Cyrus's six month ban early? Ending it during Elodie's last week in her rotation?"

Echo and Miles looked at him.

"He seems to be doing much better, able to conduct lessons with her and run drills at his old level. His flying is stronger than ever. As though his shadows gave him more strength," Echo pointed out.

"If his first time back across the boundary to be put in a passenger van and driven hours away. I fear it will hinder our chances. Part of Elodie's lesson will be navigating to town from Nightswift Estate, to meet with him and she can monitor him in the mortal world. He can do a day at work then meet up with her and they can come back together," Bracken suggested.

Echo nodded but Miles appeared to be mulling it over still.

Bracken continued with a hint of nerves now. "Then we can repeat the same exercise where Poppy will join them. Maybe they can stay a night at her residence, so we can see how Poppy does in a safe space? Ariyanna will meet the girls in the morning to go back to Nightswift and Cyrus can return to his state work."

"Trevin is likely going to want to be there," Echo said with some unease.

"I encourage it. Quinn too."

"I do not foresee Quinn doing that. I still have my hands full with his defiance." Miles sighed. "It might be a bit cramped anyways. Poppy should have her space."

"I just need them both exposed to the mortal world and I thought we would all be able to help Poppy adjust. I don't want to hold her back any longer. My aim is to put her in Lady Elodie's class. If you are also in agreement."

"Nightswift sure has grown dependent on that girl," Miles said sternly.

Bracken sighed. "I know, she has done too much already, but she is our Earth Blessed. She is our liaison between the mortal world. Poppy and Cyrus are both close to her."

"Miles has a point, it might overwhelm her and claw at Trevin how much Nightswift is asking of her. But she is our Earth Blessed. We serve her, so that she may protect us and our entity. And I also agree, the conference should not be Cyrus's first time over the boundary, nor should the classroom be Poppy's first time. So, you have my blessing, Bracken."

"Thank you, Echo."

Miles remained silent for a moment then sighed with a smile. "You have mine too. We are in this together. Just as we always have been."

"Thank you. We will begin work immediately. I requested Cyrus to come up with some lessons to utilize his and Lady Elodie's powers during drills. As well as Elodie to help with control exercises for him."

The other two nodded and began discussing tactics for those lessons and more for the upcoming weeks.

That evening, Cyrus sat at the table alongside Poppy and Delia. As instructed, he was coming up with exercises for him and Elodie to try on their last week. The obvious choice was for Trev and Quinn to be the defense while he and Elodie merged their power. Elodie had gotten a grasp on her magic over the summer, but he hadn't been able to do the same. Echo had given Bracken some drills but Cyrus was not getting the hang of it.

As he sat at the table that afternoon he noticed Poppy drawing a flower crown on a raven. He took delight in seeing it. She looked up to Elodie so much. Delia could not be bothered and was scrolling through her phone.

"Your mortal interest is Trev's intern at State Parks? Who is this guy? You never scented Trevin on him?" Cyrus asked.

"I suppose Elodie told you all about the encounter?"

"Yes! You didn't tell him anything did you?" Cyrus eyed her.

"I'm not stupid. Of course I didn't. He just likes pushing Trev's buttons, I was bothered he acted like that too. He said he would cool it." Delia sighed and sat back in her chair. "Besides you used to push his buttons too."

Cyrus took a deep inhale. "Fine, we just need to be extra careful with El."

Delia sighed loudly again. "Of course we do. Coddle the little mink."

Cyrus felt the coldness in his hands but held his shadows in. "We are not coddling her. She's just got a lot to deal with right now and we want to make it easier on her."

"She could go back to Marin. Let them deal with her."

"Go tell that to Greenthistle, see if any of them agree with you," he scoffed and went back to his notes.

"I do not understand your aversion to her," Ariyanna said. "You really should accept her. It hinders her, and it hinders our estate."

"She is so nice. Why don't you even want to talk to her?" Poppy asked.

"Greenthistle wasted so much time on her, and she is slow. All this power wrapped up in so much anxiety is dangerous."

Poppy tensed, noticing a chill shoot down Cyrus's spine.

"She is not dangerous," Cyrus chided.

"Delia. Not a word more. You should be very careful how you treat the Earth Blessed. The Old Giants are aware of your sentiment," Lady Nightswift said.

Delia rolled her eyes.

The door opened and Lord Nightswift walked in. He had a big grin on his face and a file in his hand. After setting an envelope down in front of Cyrus, he then held the folder up. It had the name of the school district in Eureka on it and the name read 'Piper Nightswift'. His youngest sister groaned.

"Took care of enrollment paperwork today," Bracken said.

Cyrus picked up the envelope with an official Humboldt Fae Council seal imprinted on the paper.

"What is this?" he asked, growing worried.

"Open it. Why not read it aloud for us all to hear?" his dad responded with glee.

Cyrus cringed the whole time he opened it then began to read it aloud.

"As requested, upon reviewing his good behavior and ability to conduct drills and lessons, we the presiding council of Humboldt, with granted authority by Lord Greenthistle, Lord Nightswift, and Lord Ashdale, hereby release the six month ban of Master Nightswift entering the mortal lands. Dropping his sentence from six months to four months. Master Nightswift is to consider the ban lifted on the 15th day of August." Cyrus's eyes went wide and he looked at his dad who was still smiling. "What? No."

"Echo, Miles, and I all agree that this will better prepare for the conference which is happening before the school year starts this year," his dad replied. "Your lessons with Lady Elodie are going to be a crash course in how to handle it. And include you returning to work and evenings on the mortal side with Lady Elodie, and staying at her residence once with Piper."

"I'm not ready though," Cyrus gasped. "To go back to work? To sit in an office with Quinn? Trev? Then stay at Elodie's house. No." Any confidence Cyrus had shriveled up in that moment.

Lord Nightswift grimaced at his son. "I think you are plenty ready. Consider this me pushing you out of the nest, again, but to a much safer environment. You have to keep taking these steps forward. You know you have Lady Elodie's help too. Be sure she has your help when she needs it."

Cyrus let out a long and slow defeated sigh and sat back.

"I'm not ready for mortal school either. Everything could be shattered if my glamor slips," Poppy fretted.

Delia sighed. "Great. The heir apparent, afraid to leave his castle and the youngest following. The Earth Blessed doesn't seem to be helping a whole lot."

"Delia!" Ariyanna snapped. "This is how you cost us power. We cannot lose our succession rank."

"We will not lose our succession. And I will not stand for this family to not support each other. We all made a grave mistake with Lady Elodie and we will not do so again," Bracken demanded. His tone was stern. "Cyrus, you will return to your state job next week. I need you to show me you can do this, son."

"Can El be at city hall with us too?" Cyrus pleaded.

"You know we cannot swing that. She will be here working with us and the sentries."

Cyrus slumped back.

"What if I forget my glamour? Eight hours?" Poppy said worriedly. She glanced at Cyrus then at her parents. "What if I make a mistake and it costs us? Or Cyrus?"

"You won't. You know how to hold the glamour, and you knew this day was coming. We have been working on it with you. Try holding it when Lady Elodie is here. Drop it when she goes out on drills or lessons," their mom said.

"You are going to send me out with Poppy into the mortal world next week?" Cyrus panicked.

"Yes. We will arrange the meeting place with Lady Elodie. As I said it will be a different kind of week. We are too close to the conference and not near ready enough."

Cyrus sat back in his chair and looked up at the ceiling, thinking about everything he would have to adjust to.

Chapter 37

Cyrus was taking long deep breaths as everyone in the office had welcomed him back. Talking about how great it was that he made such a profound recovery. All Cyrus could do was nod. He wished his first day back was not sitting in a room with Trevin and Quinn. If this was last summer he would have been dreading a boring day instead being outside land surveying.

Once inside his dad's office, he stood and stared at his desk. A little onyx raven sat by his laptop. His hand was on the chair but he was having trouble pulling it out.

"Keep taking those steps, son," his dad said gently. "We are all here for you."

"I can't do this," he whined.

"You can and you will. Nightswift will not falter," his dad said.

After a few minutes of labored breathing Cyrus spoke. "It didn't feel like anyone was there for me." His eyes fixed on the raven trinket.

"What?"

"Months of being forced down by the sentries, by you, yelling commands to them. Then Alena." A chill passed over him. "Mom just begging me to talk in anguish, knowing how much I would devastate her. Dee hates me, Poppy doesn't trust me fully. Quinn wants nothing to do with me and Trev. Fuck, he is trying so hard but he still hangs on to that anger." He finally looked at his dad with glassy eyes. "And El. The one person who I expected to despise me, reached her hand out to me and never let go. Out of everyone, she's the one who helped me? She was the only one who began to wonder why Trevin would be friends with someone so vile. How I could break the pact and not face any consequences. No one ever questioned or thought to look at me?" He could feel the tears forming.

Lord Nightswift let out a deep sigh and bowed his head.

"I am so sorry, son. When Elodie told us what she saw, she cried for you. She told us how brave and strong you were to endure that. Learning about it all months later hurt your mother and I." He locked eyes with his son for a moment before speaking again. "But you can do this. Fight for it, fight for Nightswift. Fight for her. There may be a time you will be the only one who can get through her doubts."

Cyrus looked at the ground, taking deep breaths. With an inhale he turned and sat down at the desk opening the laptop. As he took in the day's assignment he sighed. It put him right with Quinn and Trevin in the conference room for a few hours. Then an afternoon presentation on the findings to the three estate lords. He once again thought back to any random day last summer, how easy this would be. The three of them would goof off more than they worked and still put together a decent presentation. He thought about how well they had worked together. Now it would be an uphill battle.

The hour passed much too fast as he read the assignment and the desired outcome, reviewing every policy and procedure change with the state transportation agency before it was time to face Quinn and Trevin.

With a deep inhale he opened the door and stepped inside the meeting room. Both Quinn and Trevin snapped their necks to look at him. Cyrus quickly cut his eyes down. He heard Trevin let out a small exhale.

"Welcome back to the mortal world," Trevin said with an inflection of a smile. Cyrus looked up and noticed Quinn roll his eyes.

"Back from your rehab stint?" Quinn asked, sitting back and crossing his arms.

Cyrus swallowed hard and nodded. "Good behavior and ability to conduct assignments according to the council. Approved by our dads."

"Your mom is working with Elodie today right, she's not just training with the sentries?"

"Yes, with my mom and sentries for some morning drills, then she is going to help Poppy with some mortal classroom things. She is starting school next month. Do you know about Elodie's lesson tonight?" Cyrus's voice faltered.

"No? What is she doing tonight?" Trevin asked. Cyrus ran his hand down his face. "Tell me."

"Why didn't your dad tell you?" Cyrus groaned. "She's to navigate her way on her own to Eureka and meet me somewhere in town to hang out. Then sometime before dinner I'll be watching her navigate back to Nightswift."

Trevin stared at Cyrus and the two remained fixed on each other before Trevin exhaled in defeat.

Quinn half laughed and then went back to the papers in front of him.

"Well take a seat and let's get to work." Trevin sighed and nodded at Cyrus.

Cyrus dreaded bringing up Poppy's slumber party and felt now was not the best time. Eventually he found a steady but unfamiliar workflow. Quinn didn't seem as responsive or engaged while Trevin was attempting to keep the assignment group oriented. It was clear he was growing agitated and it made Cyrus uneasy.

Finally the assignment was up and Cyrus read over Quinn's and Trevin's notes. All he had to do was present it later.

Before they headed back to their respective offices Quinn sat back. "Well that's over with."

Trevin nodded then looked over to Cyrus. "So you are off to hang out with El tonight?"

Cyrus nodded. "You can both come if you want. I'd almost prefer it."

"I got plans. Where are you going to go?" Quinn asked.

"I don't know yet. I don't think I can deal with Cora nor do I want to see Justine, yet. Probably should avoid Autumn and Charles too." Cyrus groaned and dropped his head in his hands.

Quinn grabbed his bag. "Justine does not want to see you either. She hardly tolerates Cedar and Trev. Sure got your work cut out for you don't ya?"

"I don't want to do this," Cyrus drawled out in a melancholy tone.

Trevin sighed. "I can't. I'm getting my case wrapped up to get rid of Austin being my intern. After his shit behavior towards El, I am not dealing with it. I'd advise Dee to end it with him but I know she's not going to listen to me."

Cyrus nodded. "I suggested it too but she's not going to listen to me either." He glanced towards Quinn. "Do you think she will listen to Connor?"

"Doubt it," was all Quinn offered before he zipped up his bag and headed for the door.

"Ask your brother, Quinn," Trevin said, eyeing him. "Your duty is to Humboldt, that includes Elodie."

Quinn stopped but didn't turn around and Cyrus grew more uneasy with the tension in Trevin and the disregard in Quinn. He could not understand what was happening between the three of them.

He could only imagine Elodie being here. How she would feel as though she hadn't done enough. This power shift was certainly the thing that would weigh on him the most. There was nothing Elodie could do to fix it. It was up to the three of them to simply move forward. He wondered if that was what his dad meant about being the only one to show Elodie this. Surely Greenthistle had told her.

Cyrus watched Quinn nod then leave the room. He turned to Trevin.

"What about after you wrap up State Parks stuff? Meet up with us?" Cyrus pleaded.

"Technically I'm not supposed to see her during these weeks as much as I want to. Just enjoy the night. My dad reminded me these weeks are as much a lesson for her as it is for us and besides this is her role as our liaison to the mortal world," Trevin noted then looked at Cyrus. "You will watch over her, right?"

"Of course. I never wanted to touch or scare her."

"Thanks. Be safe tonight. Both of you," Trevin said then got up and lightly put his hand on Cyrus's shoulder. Then he left the room and Cyrus was left with his daunting tasks.

After twenty minutes he walked to his desk and caught his dad's glance.

"How did it go?" his dad asked.

"Fine. I guess. Our dynamic changed. I never wanted it to."

"In due time it will smooth over."

Cyrus gave his presentation to the three high estate lords, all glamored to look mortal. He was nervous as they held their stoic expressions, occasionally writing notes. He knew none of the actual content was important. The entire day was a test to see how he worked under pressure.

They excused him from the room and he walked back to his dad's office and watched the seconds tick by. He knew they were debriefing, likely determining his fate as an heir.

He thought about Bryla. He had many times since June, not that he had seen her since that night. When the door opened, he jumped and saw his dad entering and took a seat at his desk.

"Well, the good news is that it was a very informative presentation, you did everything we asked as expected. What the three of us are worried about is the defeat in you. You know what the conference is going to be like. You have seen them drill others before."

"It's going to hurt to stand under their gazes and try to keep this in."

"We and Elodie will do all we can to stand by you at a trial. You know that right? Stand by her too. Please, I need you to."

Cyrus nodded then looked down.

"Go on and have a good evening," Bracken said, putting some folders in a drawer.

"El isn't going to be in Eureka for another forty minutes at least."

"I know, but I am leaving. I need to run by the school and take care of stuff for Poppy's enrollment then I need to work with her on her glamour assessment. She is still not as quick at it as I'd like. I think being around Lady Elodie is helping her though."

"Can't I just lock the door on my way out. Or like, leave through the window?"

Bracken rolled his eyes. "You have to leave the building, or everyone will think you are sleeping in here. Leave through the lobby. You are to return home with Lady Elodie, also I do not want to see either of you back at the estate before seven. Do you understand? That is four hours at least."

Cyrus remained sitting, not making any motion to get up.

"Cyrus, walk out that door."

With that order, Cyrus forced himself to take that first step.

Cyrus walked through the lobby, keeping his breathing steady and his hands in his pockets. He kept his eyes down avoiding anyone's gaze.

"Have a good evening, Russ," the receptionist said.

All Cyrus could muster was a head nod. His heart rate increased as he pushed the door open. One deep inhale filled his lungs and slowly his steps took him towards the historic part of town. He stopped at the block of Cora's café and stared at the door from the corner.

His phone buzzing grabbed his attention. He saw that Elodie had just crossed the boundary so he asked if he could order her something.

Hmm, iced mint mocha? I will pay you back!

I got it, El. Don't worry about it.

Cyrus put his phone away and glanced at Cora's café a little longer then walked an extra block to avoid walking by it.

Given that it was mid-august the air was warm and the sun was still bright. It certainly was warmer than he would have liked but the fog coming off the ocean helped cool his skin. He knew Elodie loved the fog and rain showers up here. Then again so did the Old Giants. They were one in the same after all.

As he walked his slow steps down these streets that were his home, Cyrus couldn't help but feel like a stranger here now. It was not that he didn't know where he was or where things were. No, it was rather the opposite. The streets were the same ones he had walked countless times. It was him that was different, he was now the new and odd one. He kept his head down as he rounded the corner, past the bagel shop that Elodie loved. He walked toward the bookstore with the white and red facade and paused for a moment. *Keep taking those steps,* he told himself as he walked in the bookstore.

He was greeted upon entering and his heart rate quickened. He nodded then cut his eyes down. The story of what had happened was told to him by his dad. He had been off at rehab for drug use, not an unlikely story for the area. It was an easy story to follow. While on a bender one night he wandered out in the forest and fought with Trev who was caught off guard. They both ended up injured. All true in theory. Luckily no one had asked yet.

After browsing the new release titles, he wandered to the middle grade books looking for a book for Poppy. She was burning through these ways too quickly and he figured a young adult would be fine. It was not as though she didn't already have some on her shelf. That section was upstairs so that is where he headed and found one with branches and a gold crown on the cover. When he rounded the corner back to the stairs, he bumped into someone. The impact didn't hurt him but he was stunned. Instinctively he flinched back a step, scenting mortal mixed with fae.

"I'm sorry." Words slipped out of his mouth quickly as he kept his eyes down.

"Russ?" Cyrus heard a male say and hesitantly lifted his eyes. A gasp slipped out and then he slumped his shoulders. "Holy shit you look like a ghost. You became one," Charles said, shocked.

"Yeah."

"Are you? Back now?" There was a hesitant pause in Charles's voice.

"Kind of. Back to work, yes, but I don't foresee hanging out with everyone again for a while. Life has been rough."

"Yea it sounded like it." Charles was quiet for a moment and Cyrus didn't look up. "You know, Elodie defends you a lot. I hope you never intend to pull that shit again. I told Trev I would kick his ass if he ever hurt her again, the same goes for you. I don't care how much training or whatever you do. And don't even think about pulling that shit with Anna. Don't even go near her."

Cyrus nodded, feeling the weight of this crashing down on him. He squeezed his eyes shut and told himself he was good. *The Earth Blessed said I was good, Elodie said I was, she forgave me. Trevin forgave me.* He swallowed hard and finally forced himself to look at Charles who took a step back in fear. Cyrus repeated his mantra again.

"I am so incredibly sorry for all of it. I look back at what happened and I hate myself for it. For what I did to her, and to Trev. Elodie has a big heart and I hope nothing ever shatters it again," Cyrus said, feeling the sharp sensation in his throat.

"Dude. You really haven't been doing good have you?" Charles asked. Cyrus remained silent. "I'm sorry. I was pretty pissed at you but seeing you now, damn. Take an inhale and breathe it out. I would offer you an edible but that's probably not the best idea. Your dad would probably kill me."

A small erratic laugh slipped out of Cyrus before he could stop it and it made him flinch. "I gave everything up. No alcohol even. I am actually just grabbing a book for my little sister. I gotta run," Cyrus spluttered out, stepping past Charles and running down the stairs. He paid quickly avoiding eye contact with everyone. After he was finished he turned for the door and his spine locked.

Autumn stared dumbfoundedly at Cyrus, causing him to swallow hard. He fought the shadows down.

"Russ," she gasped out.

"Hi. I gotta go, running behind," Cyrus gasped out.

Autumn nodded and stepped aside and Cyrus ran for the door, not looking back.

With deep breaths Cyrus slowed his pace and walked into the café. They had summer hours which kept places open longer. He ordered and grabbed a seat in the corner. Some people glanced at him while he messed with his phone for a bit nervously. Then he flipped through the book he had bought and took in his surroundings. There were black and white hexagon tile patterns on the floor and warm tones of the wood accents on the walls. Plenty of plants placed in the golden hour light casting through the large windows too.

Cyrus let out a low sigh and forced himself to relax. Setting the book down he cupped his hands around his drink and looked at it. As he took in the scents and sounds, his mind wandered to Bryla, getting lost on what if's and far off possibilities.

Thoughts of her sitting across from him passed through his mind. He wondered what she would order. Where they might go afterward. Maybe down to the waterfront to watch the boats and the sun set, or maybe they could go to one of the jetties and walk out to where the waves crashed. The thought of hugging her from behind as her hair blew in the wind made him smile.

Her teal hair was so beautiful. She had worn it in a braid crown at summer solstice, and the ferns that grew in her hair were the perfect accent. She could have been his that night, she could be his, if he could muster up the courage to talk to her. Then again he had been scared to sit in a room with Trevin and Quinn or to walk into his dad's office. He had been scared most of the summer to be near Elodie. She likely thought he wanted Elodie, thought poorly of her, like so many other people did.

One more thing he and Elodie had in common, mortal and fae alike thought poorly of them both. A sigh escaped him and then the scent cascaded over him. He looked up and tensed at seeing Elodie looking concerned for a moment then she smiled.

"Hello, Russ." Her tone was calm.

"Hi El. I got us some food, something to tide us over 'til dinner with the hike and all."

"I can hike five miles easily. But I'm a little hungry. Which one is mine?"

"Whichever one you want. I think I recall you like sweets, but I got a savory toast just in case."

"Can we split them?" Elodie asked bashfully. Cyrus tensed for a moment then nodded, glancing at the windows. "We don't have to. I can take one."

"I just don't want rumors here either. I came back from rehab to hit up Trev's girl."

"Do the opinions here mean as much as they do there?"

"Reputations and all dictate the role I will have for a time," he said quietly. Their table was far away from any patrons entering and it was not very busy. He watched her frown and looked sad. "El?"

"I was pretty overwhelmed that first week. Still am. Anxiety and all. Lord—Mr. Greenthistle said it was my story to tell so I worked one out with them. I think they were at a loss too." She took a bite of the savory toast with avocado tomato and egg on it. He observed her demeanor brighten up.

"It was totally plausible. It just means I am on my best behavior here." He watched her eyes shift to the book.

"Do you read those books?" she asked, confusion written all over her face. "That one is a new release."

"Not usually my genre, but fae are popular these days in books, yes?" He watched her nod then take a sip of her drink. "I got it for Piper, but I was also trying to stall for time when Dad kicked me out of the office," he sighed.

"I think, Piper?" She paused and Cyrus nodded. "Will like that one. I love the author. Maybe I will see if I can borrow it after her." Elodie laughed.

"I am sure she will be fine with that. She asked if she could borrow the books in your room. She swears she didn't go in there though."

Elodie chuckled. "Of course she can borrow any of them. She will love my bookshelves at home."

"She loves you a lot. I noticed her drawing a raven with a flower crown last week. Maybe she will bring it on Thursday," Cyrus groaned.

Elodie slid the savory plate towards him and took the one that had toast with fruit, honey, and a cheese spread. Her smile grew even wider and Cyrus felt his lips pull up at the corners. His mind went to Bryla again and he wondered if she would be shy on a date with him.

"It will be okay, Cyrus. I will talk to Trev about it tonight. When your mom told us about the sleepover Poppy got nervous, but I think it will be good for you both. I want my house to be seen as the safe house for you all should you need it. Just as all the estates are for me." Elodie smiled and took a sip of her drink. "How has it been, being back?"

Cyrus let out a sigh. "Stressful and a bit terrifying to be honest."

"Want to talk about it? You don't have to."

"I wasn't expecting this for another two months. Quinn seems distant but Trev really tried. He takes his tasks so seriously."

Elodie gave him a hopeful smile.

Cyrus and her talked about their lives when they were younger and he learned about hers. He admitted how often he thought about Bryla and that he wanted to learn who she was. Elodie encouraged him to do so. She complimented Bryla's hair, not that it surprised him.

He finished off the toast and then began their drive north to Orick where Elodie went to the trail head and led them to Nightswift. Another one of Cyrus's tasks was to monitor her navigation skills. She even summoned a raven to get her keys and take them to a fae to take her car back to Sunny Brae successfully.

CHAPTER 38

There was another bonfire that Saturday. Elodie had just gotten Cyrus's text. He wasn't coming. She had invited him but he just wasn't ready to be back.

Elodie looked beyond the light and frowned as she scanned the beach. She let out a sigh and looked at the sand. Feeling eyes on her, she met Quinn's gaze. He gave her a small inquisitive smile. She returned it for a moment then looked down at her boots in the sand.

"You should cheer up before your mountain lion rushes to your aid. He certainly is concerned."

Elodie smiled and looked back to see Trevin and Cedar watching. They were standing with Charles, Cora, and Autumn. She gave a nod to them then looked back at Quinn.

"I shouldn't stress him out."

"If you asked him to bring the stars to your doorstep he would find a way to do it."

Elodie smiled wider. They were the only two at the fire pit. Justine was coming later, since she was hanging out with her brother and his family.

"And if he did bring the stars to my doorstep, would you say I deserved him?" she asked with a sly tone. Elodie figured she could fake the tone until she made it.

"Maybe." Quinn smirked. "You deserve everything your heart desires, El."

"Do you think I deserved him before that night in the ruins? Because my heart certainly had desired him long before that night."

Quinn was quiet for a moment and Elodie watched him glance over at Trevin. Then his eyes met hers. "That is a good question. One I never considered."

"Do you think he will do it again?" She stared at him, watching his confused expression wash over him. She was not asking about her future with Trevin, she was asking Quinn to tell her what she already knew about Trevin's character.

"You're asking me if I think he will let you go again, thinking it's for the betterment of you?"

"I am."

Quinn watched her for a moment longer then responded. "No. I don't think he will. I think the only way he will ever leave your side is if you tell him too. And even then, I think he would still leave stars on your doorstep, no matter where you went."

Elodie felt her cheeks heat and she couldn't help but laugh bashfully. She loved her mountain lion so much. He was home just as much as these Old Giants. "I bet he would, as a reminder that he would always be there." She smiled warmly. Then glanced beyond the light with a frown. "Why aren't you there for them? What are you hanging onto?"

Quinn sighed. "I don't know. You were so hurt that night. Knowing how alone you were, and then we could have lost you, we could have lost everything. It was like nothing had become more clear to Trev at that moment. He knew exactly the Greenthistle he needed to be. Russ played a Nightswift flawlessly but it shattered him because he had no valor. And I feel as though my loyalty and kindness got thrown by the wayside. Yet Trev got everything he wanted."

"It's been months. You say you saw me so devastated that night, but you saw Trev devastated. You knew what he felt because you had seen him do it before. You saw Russ shatter and slip into absolute insanity. I know what I did that night because I knew I had to. They chose me to do it and I will not leave any of you behind, ever. Yet where is your loyalty and kindness for Trev? Where has it been these last few months for Russ?"

Quinn sighed and looked down. Elodie continued.

"I hate knowing Russ still gets scared on that trail. Still gets trapped some nights in his own head. Trev showed him he has Greenthistle's valor. Trev needs to know he has your loyalty too. I look back to when I first met Russ and it hurts to think what could have happened that night, but it also hurts to know he's still so scared. I want him to know he is good and other people can see it too. I need him as much as I need you and Trev. He is the only one who understands what it feels like. They both miss you, I know you miss them," Elodie lamented, looking towards the ocean

Quinn looked up at the stars. "I do miss them. It's just so much happened and none of it made sense. Why here, why us?" He rolled his eyes and shook his head seeing her deflate. "I don't mean it that way, El. I'm glad that you came here, but so much was altered and none of us were prepared for it. It even caught our parents off guard."

"So accept that it happened and prepare with us. You are left out in a different way than Russ is and I do not think now is the time to be divided. Please? Try to be their friend again. You were the first one I thought I could count on. That would be rooting for Trev to get the girl. Yet it felt like once we got our happily ever after you wanted nothing to do with me. Be my friend too."

Quinn let out a huge sigh and met her eyes again. "Alright, El. I will try. I promise you, Nightswift and Greenthistle have my loyalty and kindness. You always had it. I never wanted you to feel like you didn't have my friendship or loyalty. Trev broke then he got you back and all was well with him, his level of control frustrated me. I was scared of Russ then sad for him. It was more than I could handle. Justine was a good distraction."

"We are going to be okay. We are going to be there for each other," Elodie said and looked at the stars again.

"I suppose your mountain lion will be running over here soon because his little mink is all alone." He chuckled and stood up. When Elodie frowned at him, he nodded his head towards the parking lot. She followed his gaze, and understanding dawned on her upon seeing Justine arrive.

Over at the university, Austin was on a phone call outside of a party nearby. His eyes watched the treetops for any movement watching for a certain raven.

"Greenthistle's firstborn basically had one too many buttons pushed and I'm not his intern anymore. But I got a perfect backup to gain all the intel I need on all of them. Nightswift's second born. As soon as you give the okay, Zuli, this plan is foolproof," Austin said with a smirk to himself. "You can assure Luke of it."

"How is it going with Bracken's second born?"

"She has too much loyalty towards Nightswift and Humboldt to betray them. She's worried about her brother's 'rehab attempt,'" Austin laughed.

"Nightswift is pretty fragile right now despite the firstborn's efforts. Approval granted. Go on and lock her in tonight. I will let Luke know we will have Hazelthorn's heir." Zuli's grin could be heard in his tone.

"Will do. I will call you later to let you know how it goes."

"Excellent. Enjoy having your own pet raven," Zuli added.

"I gotta run, just spotted her overhead."

Austin shoved his phone in his pocket and pulled out his vape pen. He heard footsteps and looked up to see Dee in a short blue dress and boots. He smiled wide at her.

"Well that is just the outfit that gets me hot and bothered," Austin purred out and let his eyes rove her body.

"Maybe I am getting to know you better."

"Is that so? I seem to remember you saying 'if you got to know me better, I might have a chance with you.'"

"Maybe I'm giving you that chance." She gave him a coy smile.

Austin wasted little time closing the distance between them and pulling her into a deep rough kiss. He maneuvered them so he could press her against the wall with his body and felt her tense slightly. He laughed softly. "Whenever you want it bad enough, name the place, Dee."

"Not against a wall outside a frat house," she said, kissing him softly now.

"I can agree to that. I think you should agree to something though," Austin laughed and kissed up to her ear. He gripped her hair and tugged her head to the side bearing her neck to him.

"What's that?" Her laugh was playful.

He smiled and kissed up her neck now. "I order you to be under my command, Delia Nightswift," he purred as she stilled.

When he pulled away, he grinned at her wide eyes.

"How do you know about me?"

"I have my sources, and yes, I am mortal, but I know very well you are not. So let's see what power I hold now. Drop your glamour, let me see the real you."

Delia dropped her glamour and watched his eyes travel over her face.

"Nice, put it back on."

She did. "What are you going to do? My dad is going to throw you in our hold for this," she hissed.

Austin merely laughed. "Your next order, Delia, is that you cannot speak of this to anyone. Not your parents or the other estates, no fae or mortals. Not the little cubs nor your trembling finch of a brother or little sister and certainly not the little mink of Greenthistle."

"What do you want with me?" Her eyes began to well up.

"I just need a little birdie to answer my questions, what better source than one who despises Greenthistle and the mink?"

"I don't despise them! I never did. You can't hurt them," she shouted.

"Shh Delia, no shouting, and that is an order. I have a job to do here and you are going to help me with it," he said softly in her ear.

"What job? You work with Trev." She paused and watched him nod with a wide grin. "You can't hurt either one of them. All three high estates protect her."

"I used to work with Trevin." Austin grinned wide at seeing her shock of using Trevin's name before he continued. "I'm certainly not going to hurt her, and I don't stand a chance against a mountain lion. Tell me is he always so temperamental or is it his vowed bond?"

"You have been playing us all for fools this entire time," Delia rasped. She gritted her teeth and tried to push him back.

"As I said, I am just doing my job. I have no desire to hurt you or take advantage of you, but you are going to be in for a world of hurt if you go against my orders. Not all counties keep their mortals in the dark about your existence. And that thief, Echo Greenthistle has something that isn't his. I give you my word, Delia, I will release this hold when my job is done. Tell them whatever you want when I do."

"Fuck you," she snapped as the tears brimmed in her eyes began to fall.

"Such loyalty to your family. It must make you writhe how much they love the little mink of Marin."

"I'm grateful for her. I never hated her. I just hated that everyone was so focused on her that they forgot about my brother, they forgot about my little sister. I didn't trust her at first but now I want to tell her I'm grateful for what she did. We need her." Delia wiped her eyes. "Please don't take her from them. You can't be ordered, you can stop this."

Austin laughed and pulled her close despite her tensing. "No I can't actually, but if all goes according to plan, she will be returned to you, so tell her then. Mortals are well aware of how heavy unspoken words can be."

"Mortals can also lie!" she spat, trying to pull away.

"I can tell you I am not lying, she will be returned to you, in what condition, I cannot guarantee. Now we can go to the party and maintain a front for Connor that everything is fine, or we can go sit in my car and you can start giving me information. Your call."

"I have to give you information anyways, don't I?" she seethed.

"Yes, but I don't have to ask everything on my list. I can let you pick what you give me. Consider this my humanity."

Austin watched her for a moment. Then she took his hand and led him towards the door.

"Excellent choice, Dee. Glad you gave me a chance," Austin chuckled and followed her towards the loud music.

Chapter 39

The conference was quickly approaching and Elodie had been trying to savor the last two weeks of summer break.

Early one evening as they lay in bed naked, Elodie looked up at Trevin, who was sitting up with his back against the headboard. They had done two rounds and Elodie remained lying on her stomach. He glanced at her with a smile and rubbed her head.

"I want to go to that spot again. The one with the small stream by the boundary, you know, the one you found me in before I opened that book," Elodie said randomly. The thought had no sooner entered her mind before she spoke it.

"Any reason?"

"Well, I think that was the moment things felt different, with the Old Giants. I sliced my hand open climbing up the rocks and braced myself on the tree but I had to drop to my knees because the woozy feeling hit me. When I heard the voices, I glanced at the tree and noticed the streak of blood and I just had a feeling bleeding on the Old Giants meant something my mind could not process. I want to know what it would feel like to touch it again now. The one I bled on."

"Would you mind if I went with you?" he asked softly. "Or called a raven to be near at least?"

"I want you to come and I don't mind the raven either."

"Do you intend to bleed on it again?" Trevin asked, unsure.

She laughed softly. "No. I don't want to. But I just want to see what it might feel like to go back, now that I'm awoken." Elodie sat up and watched Trevin's eyes go down to her exposed chest.

"And when did you want to go?" he asked, meeting her eyes again.

"Later," she laughed, then straddled him.

After two more rounds, they were on the trail. Elodie retraced her steps, and Trevin followed, letting her lead.

"I feel much better about you being out here, now that I know you have eaten and hydrated, and you know you are home," Trevin said. "I remember seeing your car empty and the energy in the air was anxious. I bolted following your scent as fast as I could."

"I'm sorry. I knew how foolish it was, but something was pulling me so strongly."

"I am just glad I got to you when I did. I think the bear smelled your blood, and since you hadn't woken up yet, it was just blood to the bear."

Eventually she came to the spot. It was golden hour now and the sun illuminated the raindrops from the shower earlier. A smile graced her face knowing she was home. This place had given her that fresh start she had been seeking. Then the smile vanished to a frown when she thought about all that she had lost, all that had changed. What had happened to nearly everyone in her life.

"Little Mink. What happened? You were so overjoyed," Trevin said softly.

She turned to look at him. Her vowed, the one who had come for her and she had come for him. "It's just, all the good and all the bad to get here. It's hard to juggle it sometimes."

Trevin walked towards her and hugged her tight. "I know, El. I am so happy you are here though. That you never gave up." She held him tight for a moment then walked up to the rocks. She pulled her sleeves over her hands then assessed her climb for a moment. They appeared dry enough.

She knew Trevin was watching her, ready to jump in if she needed help. It was one thing she loved about him. She always had felt safe with Trevin, he never was overbearing, just remaining there should she need him however she needed him.

Once on top she looked at the tree. Any remnants of her had vanished, but she knew it had become part of this place. An extension of the redwoods. With an inhale, she pressed her palm to the trunk and instantly felt their embrace.

Consider this your second birthplace. Marin's blood will always be in you, but we sensed your curiosity and wonder when you gazed at us the first time. When we knew you'd always remain true to them, to us. You tripped and we feared you'd forget about us, but you didn't. Instead you just watched that boundary line flow into you and looked at us again as if you knew something connected us.

When you bled in this spot, we knew the spirit and the raven sensed it. So we pressed more in you. When the cub brought you to Greenthistle we knew your blood fused with us. You spilled blood for this entire territory and proved your loyalty to all of us, and to them.

All we could do was drop the bread crumbs for you though, for even though we chose you, wanted you, it was up to you to choose us. To want this life. The cub pleaded with us to tell you to say it, to tell him how you felt about him and yet we could not sway you either. If we had told you, you may not have believed us, or believed you wanted it.

Elodie nodded and looked up to the crown.

What would have happened if I hadn't realized it? Would that thing have succeeded?

Yes. But we would have forced you to another territory if we thought our existence was in jeopardy. Del Norte or Mendocino. Even in Sonoma or Marin if needed. The great mother does not want to lose you. You'd have been hidden from everyone until a grove claimed you.

Thank you. I am grateful for this home, this life I was granted, with him and the high estates. Even if it appears as though I am struggling, I do want this.

Your struggle is expected. It is a big role and lots of responsibility.

Thank you again. She smiled and before she could remove her hand they spoke again.

There is much unrest, and you should all tread lightly.

Their words made her tense as she glanced up again.

Remember you were chosen because you are all three estates. Be well, and know that none of this is your fault. The bear has one last request. Nightswift's talents would be best suited. Be the Nightswift you already are.

Elodie's eyes scanned the area.

"El?" Trevin asked. She remained very still.

What bear? Quinn? The trees remained silent. Elodie pulled her hand away and rushed to get down, with much more agility and grace than last time. Trevin was right there ready to catch her.

"You are spooked. Why? What happened?"

"Ominous warnings." She cringed.

"What did they say?" he asked, then his body stilled. Elodie caught it a minute later. A bear groaned and staggered up to them. "Fuck!" Trevin stood in front of her as the bear approached. "Fuck!" he hissed out to the raven. "Get my dad and Ashdale now!" Elodie saw the raven fly off with speed.

"What's wrong with the bear? It looks sick. Its jaw is locked? Rabies?"

"Yes."

"What?! No. It's staggering and hardly able to stand though, it's not aggressive towards us."

"It's accepted its fate. It knows it is beyond our abilities."

"Can't you try? They said it had one last request," Elodie pleaded.

"I can't cure rabies yet. I can bring an animal to sedation with my powers and find the disease but only Dad knows how to extract it. This is too far along even for him."

Elodie felt her heart start to crack. It let a low growl out towards Trevin then flicked its head to the side. Then it locked eyes with her and Elodie could see the pleading. *A request. Nightswift talents would be best. Observe and assess.*

"I—I think it wants to tell me something. Stand by me."

"El, this is dangerous. I'm not going to subject you to injury or rabies."

"It will be ok. It is the same one as before."

Trevin stood by her side, taking her hand.

As the bear looked into her eyes, Elodie's own started to water. *I don't want to watch it die,* she pleaded but the Old Giants remained silent.

The bear took a step and then bowed. Her eyes caught movement and saw Lord Nightswift arrive. She noticed Cyrus remained up in the tree, watching with horror. Lord Greenthistle and Lord Ashdale arrived with Lady Ashdale and Connor stopping in their tracks. She was stunned that so many were here. Quinn was not though and part of her wondered why Cyrus was here but Quinn wasn't. Even Cedar and Autumn were standing with rigid postures.

"It wishes you to know it is sorry it scared you, and that you were hurt. It didn't know you were Earth Blessed," Miles explained.

Elodie took a step closer. Trevin remained where he was but did not release her hand.

"You can't cure it?" She looked at Echo desperately.

"No. Sometimes we lose our aligned animals to disease or illness. There is nothing I can do for it aside from sedate it," Echo said.

"It wishes for you to simply tell it that it will all be okay. It wishes to die a loyal death with it's Earth Blessed knowing this," Miles added.

Elodie fought back the cry. She noticed Connor and Olive looking sad. She glanced up at Cyrus's worried face as he scanned the area. Miles watched him too with a growing hint of anguish. Finally she glanced at Trev. He motioned towards the bear. So Elodie did and knelt down.

"It's going to be alright. I am grateful for the bears. I know that they are loyal and kind to their Earth Blessed, and so are you." Elodie's voice broke.

The bear got up, nudged Elodie's hand with a small hum, then staggered back and let out a pained cry that startled her. When the bear collapsed, Elodie heard its last breath shoot through her like a bullet. She cried as Trevin pulled her close.

And all at once in unison, roars of the bears could be heard. Elodie could feel it thrum through her veins.

"I watched it die," Elodie mumbled but was not sure why she said it since they all had seen it.

"We will make preparations to return the bear to the earth." Miles looked around at where they were standing. "This location feels sacred though? What occurred here?" He tilted his head in confusion.

"This was where I found El that night. She bled here then I brought her to Greenthistle and she was healed by the oldest ruling estate. The night before she opened that tome," Trevin explained, still holding Elodie. She was leaning on him. She had not been prepared for how much this hurt.

"It wanted to be laid to rest here. Where it was accepted in its final state." Olive spoke softly.

"You're going to bury a bear here?"

"No, we will spread its ashes here," Miles explained.

"Oh." Elodie felt foolish for being so clueless about these traditions.

"This isn't right!" Connor cursed, causing Elodie to flinch. She had never seen him so emotional. His eyes were glossy.

"We will address it later," Olive hissed.

"Whatever," Connor muttered and ran off. Miles sighed. She glanced up again to find Cyrus watching the scene with sorrow.

Bracken walked up to Lord and Lady Ashdale and bowed his head. "I am sorry for your loss."

"Thank you. Thank you both for coming."

"Of course. Let us know if you need anything," Bracken said then he changed and flew up to Cyrus. The two remained watching but clearly were in conversation Elodie couldn't hear.

"Greenthistle is here too for whatever needs to be done. Should you wish Lady Elodie's help, just ask her, no need to check with me or Trev. You know this." Echo put his hand on his friend's shoulder. "I'm sure there is a reason, Miles."

"There had better be. For his sake," Miles growled. Elodie tensed, knowing exactly who that was about. "Ashdale is good for now. I appreciate you all being here." He turned and looked at Elodie. Unsure what to do, she bowed her head. "You as well Lady Elodie, I thank you for being there for the bear, in this place. I can tell it is very special for you. The bear's soul will live on here and watch over it."

"Should we go to Greenthistle or back to El's?" Trevin asked.

"Santiago Estate. I think we should discuss. It is a part of our life she may not understand," Echo explained.

"Are you okay with that?" Trev turned to Elodie. She nodded.

"Cyrus should come too. Bracken will update Nightswift Estate," Echo said and glanced at Miles who nodded pensively.

Chapter 40

Once back in Elodie's house, Trevin sat near Elodie, and Cedar leaned against the wall. Everyone else was seated, yet all were tense.

"As you may have guessed, Lady Elodie, the loss of one of our aligned animals is always painful for us. They are a part of us as the Old Giants are a part of you. A shift pulsed through the air and we never take those lightly anymore. This shift though had a sense of despair in it. Being that Trev had sent a raven, Nightswift was made aware and they have the ability to send out messages much faster, being able to tap into all of the ravens. Where we can only call for one to carry a message, they can broadcast," Echo continued.

Elodie listened as Trevin held her hand.

"It is desired and respectful that the aligned estate be present, at the very least, the leader of said estate and the heir apparent. The last time we lost a mountain lion—" Echo paused and glanced at Trevin. Elodie noticed Trevin looking at Cyrus who was looking down and fidgeting with the hair tie on his wrist. "Well, Trev and I were present but it was not a situation I ever wish any of them to encounter again."

"Understood, sir." Elodie kept an eye on Cyrus.

"It is also one I carry the shame of. I have always tried my best to maintain my composure no matter the situation, but we all make mistakes. My brothers, Miles and Bracken too have done their best but Bracken has had a few trying encounters and I fear Miles is close to experiencing one. Tonight did not help Quinn's case."

Cedar scoffed. "He's acting like a dumbass."

"Sometimes some mortals just snag us more than others. He likes her," Autumn countered. Elodie noticed Cyrus sigh but still looked at the ground.

"I just don't understand why he is glued to her. It is growing dangerous for us and Quinn knows it. We all know it. All it does is put more stress on El to cover it up," Cedar said.

"Emotions are difficult for us—them." Elodie sighed. "Having the ability to lie is no blessing I assure you. It does hurt me that she thinks I'm in danger here. I can't fault her for seeing things that way. I ran off one night into the forest and came back a week later, different. So much has changed for all of us. She cannot fathom it because she doesn't understand. Can't understand. He is in a rough spot." As Elodie explained, Trevin rubbed her back gently.

"He has a responsibility to his estate, just as Cyrus and I do though. He wasn't there for you, or for Cyrus. He doesn't need to be there for me as a friend but if I cannot count on my third then we have a problem."

"He wants to though," Elodie countered.

"Your father had this discussion with you, Cyrus?" Echo asked.

He nodded and took an inhale before looking up. "Yes sir. He could see Connor's disdain for his brother's absence tonight and his parents' disappointment. My dad and I spoke more of Quinn's misguided loyalty. Connor's disdain is much like Dee's is with me."

Elodie frowned and looked towards the window, recalling their words earlier. *Be the Nightswift you are.* There were still empty spots in the puzzle but the pieces in her hand didn't even fit. No matter how she rotated the pieces to line them up they never snapped into place quite right 'til long after the fact. If it wasn't screaming in agony thinking Trevin never truly cared, it was Cyrus trapped in his own bed for months. So what was Quinn going to have to suffer through while she stared at the pieces trying to figure out how to be a Nightswift.

Shifting her gaze to her palm she recalled what the Old Giants had said. If they had told her outright she was to become this, to all of them, she'd still have to decide what was right. She'd still have to piece it together, yet they had chosen her, they wanted her to do this. They knew she could. She wanted so badly to help them but all she was doing was sitting and staring at these pieces instead of just figuring it out. She would be the cause of it falling apart now.

Suddenly her mind spiraled so fast as if everything they had told her after the night of the ruins crashed into her. Her jaw clenched and a tremor took over her hand.

"El," Trevin said, sending a calming pulse into her. "Take an inhale, relax your jaw. Whatever is running through your mind or whatever they say does not supersede breathing." His words were calm as if leading her to that deep breath in and out.

Her eyes now noticed Cyrus fixed on her, watching. The Nightswift. He knew how to be a Nightswift, why hadn't the stars told him this?

"What is it?" Cyrus asked her.

"Do the stars tell you anything?"

"They talk to me in the form of my raven. It's a little weird though and I haven't exactly figured out how since I am the raven but somehow, I can talk to it." He paused for a moment. "As if I hadn't been going mad already. Now I can talk to the voice in my head."

"It's not that far-fetched actually," Trevin said. All attention shifted to him. "I remember looking at the background on Austin. He requested the two parks I'm assigned to and it just strikes me as odd. I felt for a moment, something scratching, inside my mountain lion as if it wanted to talk."

"That is an interesting development to have not told me," Echo said, eyeing Trevin.

Elodie kept her eyes down, recalling that puzzle piece she had too.

"Quinn overlooks and is overlooked," she said, realizing now how the piece fit. So much attention on keeping her safe and now Cyrus's altered state. "The warning before the tome. One taken to lure the prize. One left behind and altered. One overlooks and is overlooked. Quinn is overlooked because of me and Cyrus. Justine is a distraction from not having to deal with it."

"Just because we have an Earth Blessed to protect, and Cyrus has powers similar to yours, does not give him the right to ignore the most basic estate expectations," Trevin stated.

"I'd have to agree. These are things they all learn as kids, and have experienced before," Echo noted. "Surely he has to understand that even if she were to stay and settle down, he could not stay with her. She is a mortal, she will age."

"They told me to be a Nightswift tonight. I don't know how though, I don't know what I am supposed to see that any raven isn't." Elodie frowned.

"You are all three estates, El. You already know this," Cyrus said.

"You don't think he wants to leave Ashdale, right?" Elodie worried. They all looked at her now.

"Not once has he expressed he doesn't want to be heir," Echo said.

"Besides, he enjoys the perks too much. He'd be exiled from the mortal lands, hard pressed to find fae lands elsewhere accepting of him. Justine would still age and he'd be left with very little. He may be dumb but he's not that dumb," Trevin asserted.

"He has to know better than that. He can't follow her," Cedar huffed out.

Trevin scoffed. "He better not do anything else stupid."

"I will try to talk to Justine. Or even him. We kind of have somewhat of a similar situation."

"Thanks Autumn," Elodie sighed. "I imagine it's hard for Quinn though. Trevin and I are vowed, Cyrus knows who—" She stopped when he met her gaze worried.

"Knows who what?" Autumn asked with curiosity. Cedar glanced at Cyrus.

"I'm sorry, I thought they knew," Elodie gasped and put her hands to her mouth.

Cyrus sighed and dropped his head. "It's fine. Not like I know what to do about it. She will realize it soon enough if she hasn't already and she will likely be so put off by it."

"Tell her, Cyrus. It is the one piece of advice Quinn gave me that I regret not taking. There are no barriers to being with her either," Trevin urged.

"Wait, what? Are you talking about his vowed?" Autumn asked, confused. "Who?"

Cyrus hadn't lifted his head. "Bryla Petalgrace."

"Petalgrace is your vowed?" Cedar asked.

"Yes. Summer solstice confirmed it. Sage and fuschia. I probably smell like disappointment and disgust to her."

"Damn, two of you vowed already?" Cedar marveled.

"So you can imagine how Quinn is probably viewing the situation," Elodie followed up.

"Especially given how close Trev and Cyrus were at one point," Autumn added.

"Well that's another thing, he's been an absolute dick to Cyrus. I know I wasn't much better but I tried to get back to normal." Trevin frowned. "He hasn't even made an attempt."

"You did try. I honestly was afraid of you; I still am in some regard but you are here and have been. Quinn wants nothing to do with me." Cyrus finally lifted his head, his hair a mess.

"He doesn't want shit to do with me either as of late," Trevin scoffed.

Echo sighed. "In due time he will come back. I will talk to Miles about the concerns and warnings. I don't foresee Ashdale needing any help, but regardless if he asks you to be present when they scatter its ashes, I think it would be good if you were there." He looked at Elodie.

"Of course, sir." Elodie felt sullen with the weight of this situation despite Lord Greenthistle's smile.

"I am going to head home. Don't impose too much on Lady Elodie, that goes for all of you," he said and headed for the door, closing it softly behind him.

"Bryla Petalgrace. She's hot. Her bright and curious doe eyes." Cedar followed his statement with a slight whistle. "I definitely considered chatting her up a time or two in the tavern," he laughed. Elodie watched him tense and catch the glare from Cyrus.

"Don't." Cyrus's tone was level.

"Oh my god. It is true!" Autumn exclaimed. "Vowed." Her eyes shifted to Trevin. Then to Elodie who felt her cheeks heat. "Wait, didn't you dance with her at the summer solstice? Like for hardly a rotation of a song? Why?"

"Because I'm a fucking wreck. She doesn't deserve that. She deserves someone who is kind and strong. A high estate, not a trembling little finch."

"So, I can pursue her then?" Cedar laughed out. Cyrus glared again. "I'm kidding. Calm down. As if I'd want to face off against you. Besides, her little nymph friend she's usually with is pretty cute too."

Cyrus sighed and deflated even more.

"Tell her. You watched me be a complete dumbass and lose El. You know better."

"Elodie wanted this place so badly, she needed it, and needed you. You needed her. Bryla doesn't need me or my night terrors."

"But she is your vowed," Elodie said. "I thought that was what vowed did for each other? You wanted to be the best version of yourself because of them, for them."

Cyrus sighed again. "It's difficult when you don't know who you are anymore. I can't go back to being who she saw in the tavern. I don't want to."

"Why not see who you want to be around her? After I found Trev, I began to wonder if there really was something out there I was looking for. I always thought it was a metaphor or something, but once we started talking, even before I found out what he was, I couldn't help but wonder if we crossed paths for a reason. Turns out we did."

"She is just so soft spoken. And bright. I imagine her being so gentle and—" Elodie watched Cyrus pause as a faint heat flushed over his fair skin. He groaned then put his hand over his face and she couldn't help but see the embarrassment and bashfulness. "I just don't want to scare her or make her question why she was stuck with me."

"Did it ever occur to you that maybe this is what you need? The reason you feel it now is because you need someone like her? Alena isn't exactly soft or gentle, neither were any of the other girls you went for," Trevin said. "Maybe she is your vowed because you are meant to be softer and kinder than you have been in the past? Certainly not weak, but softer? People show a different side when they don't need to be defensive around you."

"You always did go for girls with bright hair colors. Alena's was darker than your usual," Cedar noted.

Elodie gave Autumn a glance, noticing her hair color. She laughed.

"I had it dyed pink. They called it daddy's little princess phase."

"Oh," Elodie said. Then she looked at Trevin and heard Autumn laughing again.

"Yes he has always had a thing for your type. Curvy girls with stamina."

"I know what Tanya looks like. Beautiful."

"I was the anomaly," Cyrus groaned.

"Maybe he just likes the odd ones?" Elodie asked with a hint of a smile.

Trevin smirked and gave her shoulder a squeeze. Cyrus gave her a quick smile then frowned again.

"I don't know." Cyrus looked at Autumn then turned to Cedar. "I am truly sorry for that night. "I didn't want to do any of that. To any of you. I hated all of it. I still hate it all. I know it wasn't me, but somehow, I feel responsible."

"It was a shitty night. I think we can all agree to that," Cedar replied.

"Understatement of the century," Trevin scoffed. Elodie glanced at him and noticed he grinned, Cyrus gave a small one back.

"I was shocked to see you in the bookstore. Charles was upset, but I changed the subject. He doesn't know about our history," Autumn said.

"I'm sorry for that too. That was my fault." Cyrus dropped his head again.

"We were young and dumb. Maybe we still are. Let's just be there for Elodie. For our estates. Bryla should know, Cyrus," Autumn suggested.

"I will try. Maybe after this conference. One thing at a time."

They all decided to hang out and have dinner at Elodie's, and to her relief, Trevin suggested Cyrus stay in the guest room and Cyrus did.

Chapter 41

As Quinn made his way home, dread was building in him. He knew he needed to face whatever was awaiting him at home, he knew exactly what had happened. That sense of loss could only mean a bear had been lost. Justine was going to spend the night at her brother's house, plans she had made previously. Yet now he wanted to plead that he could stay with her. When the feeling had hit him earlier a chill shot up his spine, causing him to stagger back against the cabinet. Justine looked at him with more concern than he'd ever seen on her.

As soon as he walked inside the estate he saw his dad standing there with a very displeased look.

Quinn sighed. "I'm sorry, okay."

"What was more important than this estate?" his dad roared.

"Maintaining this stupid front we have to put on. If I had run out of there again, how would I have covered it up? I'm sorry, okay. I will help with the preparations."

"That's not the point. You know good and well why we maintain this front. So I do not have to drag your ass in front of the council after we drag Elodie and Cyrus in there trembling."

"I'm trying to avoid it. Besides, Cyrus should be helping her but all that's happened is her helping him."

"Yet he was there tonight, all of Greenthistle was too. Do you want to know who else was there?" Miles chided.

"Elodie? Why?"

"Because that was the same bear that Trevin saved her from, the same bear that caused him to carry her unconscious body to Lord Greenthistle to heal. It wanted to make amends to her. When it died, she felt that despair just as hard as any Ashdale. She cried into Trevin and Cyrus was there for her too, for us even though he wasn't sure how to help. He searched for you, I saw him, I could see his heart pulsing. You were not there. You haven't been there for any of them. And now, you were not there for your estate," his dad went on and Quinn sighed. "She watched it die, and heard its last breath leave this realm. You were not there for one of ours. This is your duty. We look out for our own."

"I'm sorry! I didn't know how to cover it up."

"You better figure out how you are going to start covering it up. You have a responsibility to this estate. Maybe it's best you begin distancing yourself."

Quinn narrowed his eyes but didn't look at his dad.

"Right and how do I cover up the reason I'm distancing myself from her? Lord Greenthistle suggested that Trev do that with El a few months back. Look where that would have gotten us."

"Your mortal is not Earth Blessed, nor is she your vowed!" Miles roared in anger. "I know it, you know it and so does everyone else. You called Trev a coward for not being there for Lady Elodie, yet you hardly were all summer because your mortal was more important than her?"

"Justine will leave eventually, I am just trying to ride this out. So don't worry about it. I'm sorry." Quinn scowled then went upstairs to his room.

He knew he should go see Elodie at the very least if not Trev and Cyrus. He should talk to his mom and brother too. As he leaned against the wall, a loud sigh escaped him then he pulled his phone out to find Elodie's number. He thought about her stays during the summer, about what Trevin had said. How anxious her and Cyrus were yet they always stood near each other. Cyrus, her best friend on one side, Trevin, her vowed who held so much power now on her other side. Their bond would never be broken again. Her and Cyrus had some divine earthly powers. Cyrus knew who his vowed was and had been too scared to talk to her, to try to court her.

Trevin and Cyrus had everything. The first and the second, who had been closer friends, who had even been intimate with each other at one point, now had Elodie in between them. He knew it likely would never evolve into anything more than her and Trevin vowed and in love, her and Cyrus, best friends with shared trauma. Yet, they had each other. And there was no room for him.

Quinn had been there for her the night of the ruins. The only one who was and he had been so angry at all of them for doing that to her that he had wanted to forget it all with Justine. He felt cast aside from them all so he had done it right back to them, he realized. He and Elodie hadn't gotten close or even furthered their friendship because he didn't take the time. Then there was Cyrus who had been cast aside from them all, screaming and crying. He hadn't been there for him either when he could have been there for him, with Trev being so consumed with Elodie.

Yet his time with Justine was limited. She was going to leave. She was all he had, they had all ended up so divided and his heart stung. Elodie had been trying with everything in her to hold the three of them together, to hold the mortals together too.

Quinn threw his cell phone across the room and walked downstairs to the backyard, not seeing any of his family. It was a small relief to him right now. He changed into his feral form and walked into the trees. Elodie's scent lingered and he followed it to a spot in the wild old growth part of the yard. He imagined her sitting there, the ferns making an arch behind her. This must have been one of her spots she spoke to the Old Giants, he figured.

His eyes fixed on the bark then traveled up to the crown of his entity, causing him to sit back on his haunches.

"I am sorry. I'm sorry for not being there for your chosen one this summer, and not being there for a brother. It was a lonely trail though, for all of us. Justine is all I have. What I want. You could have chosen her too."

Quinn thought back to the sensations of sharpness trailing up his spine he had felt before the revelry this summer. They usually occurred right after he had said some childish immature thing to rile Trevin up. Something told him this was a warning from his entity. Stress on Trevin would directly translate to stress on Elodie, and of course the Old Giants did not want that for her. He knew he was prodding Trevin to lash out and it frustrated him that Trevin had managed to control it all as well as he did. He had only gotten better at it as time went on, because he had Elodie. He had his vowed. Quinn wanted his vowed yet he certainly wasn't being better for his estate, because Justine wasn't his vowed. She was what he wanted though.

With a loud sigh of defeat, Quinn slumped on the ground and lay there at a loss.

Be better, so that if your vowed does appear, you are not too much of a coward to approach her. So you don't need to rely on the Earth Blessed to stand tall. Loyalty and kindness, Ashdale, he thought to himself. *I am heir apparent to a high estate. They do need me, if I had been around I could have helped them.*

With another sigh he pushed himself to his feet to head back to his room, thinking how to make amends. They were all about to walk into a shitstorm. He would stand with them. He wanted to.

Sure enough, Quinn found his first chance to fix what he had broken at Cora's weekly hangout a few days later.

"I am going to go inside and talk to Cora and Justine for a bit, need anything from inside?" Elodie asked Trevin, leaning on him.

"Nah, I'm fine. Enjoy your girl time, sorry Anna got whisked away too soon."

"I have a lifetime of girl time with Anna," she said in a hushed tone.

Trevin laughed then kissed her head. He gave her hand a little squeeze and watched her walk inside. His eyes shifted up to the stars for a moment and he noticed something in him felt different. Trying to process what had changed, he looked at the crowns of the Old Giants in the distance. Elodie was mere steps away, and the energy did not feel stressed. Thoughts raced through his head as he examined what he felt. It was her energy yet felt as though he could see it, or touch it. As though it was a tangible thing, not just a feeling anymore.

The sliding glass door pried his attention towards it and he saw Quinn walk out. His head hung low and his shame was apparent. Trevin narrowed his eyes upon seeing the emotion.

Quinn sat down on the seat nearby and met his gaze. Trevin remained quiet, waiting for him to speak watching his shoulders slump and a sigh escape him.

"You have become so much more intense. Apathetic mope to the fiercest mountain lion Humboldt has ever seen," Quinn said with a small smile. This caused Trevin's mouth to gape open and Quinn laughed. "I am sorry for the other night. I'm sorry I wasn't there for the bear or for her."

Trevin could see he genuinely meant it. There was no anger or spite laced in his tone.

"I'm sorry I haven't been there for you and him, that I wasn't there for her this summer. I just didn't understand any of it. I still don't. It gets so hard to cover this all up all the time. It was jealousy that kept my anger going. That you got to have her by your side and those looks she gives you. The looks she gave you before she woke up."

Trevin remained watching him. Not sure what to say, so he remained quiet.

"Hell, that look she gave you after you kissed her right over there on Halloween, and the look you gave her. It was written all over her face how much curiosity you sparked in her and you didn't know what to do with it. It scared the shit out of you, didn't it?"

Trevin looked at the spot he had kissed her at and smiled. "It absolutely terrified me what I felt, that vowed bond is like a net falling over you. I had no idea why she took over my thoughts so much. Everything she did for me." Trevin smiled for a moment. "I am sorry too, I got so angry. You were right, I was pissed that I had been such a coward. I did rob her of her fairy tale. Her prince should have told her he loved her on the winter solstice. All I ended up doing was taking her choice away."

"We all let you down, we let her down. I just couldn't fathom why you weren't running after her that night. She saved everything and told you she loved you. I hated seeing you, Greenthistle's firstborn give up. I saw her run for you and I knew she always would. I knew it'd be tangled bedsheets and longing gazes between you two. It'd be absolutely disgusting walking into Greenthistle from that point on. I wanted a fraction of that with Justine. I hate that she tried to talk Elodie into moving too. That she would do that to us. And she has no idea how much it would hurt El." Quinn leaned forward in his seat and rested his elbows on his knees.

"I'm sorry. I know how much it hurts and I feel like an asshole saying it because sorry doesn't help. Elodie really does value you though. She values Ashdale. You were there for her, she felt at ease with you when Russ and Caleb were mean to her. She has a different kind of bond with all of us, but they all help make her whole," Trevin explained. "She needs all three of us."

"She is made up of all three estates. It only makes sense she needs us in different ways." Quinn smirked then sat back. "I've always felt a bit out of place with you and Russ. Like something was wrong with me. Impostor syndrome, I guess. When you started to confide in me, even more than your sister, I felt like I did belong. But you just let go of her along with all your Greenthistle valor. And Caleb was such a gullible fool to blindly follow Russ. Yet you all ended up one big happy family. I had Justine, and she's great, but I had her thoughts running wild and rampant. Everything got so fucked and I guess, I want it all to go back to normal, but with El here this time," Quinn sighed.

Trevin looked at him then looked down at the ground.

"So, I guess what I am trying to ask you is can we be brothers again. Maybe hang out with Russ too. Like we used to? On one of your nights away from El of course."

Trevin looked at Quinn and then at his hand out then held his own hand out and they shook on it.

"I'd like that, Q. Despite what it looked like I did miss you. I missed the dynamic we had, Russ sure as hell wouldn't have asked his dad if she could come to a seasonal revelry. I could see how pissed you were when you might have had to take El as your lady. Was Justine the reason?"

"Yes. I just wanted one time. One revelry to see her dressed like that and the expression on her face. Elodie looked like a goddess that night. But I know I can't have it."

"You will bounce back this time just like before," Trevin assured.

"I know. I did think about her after she left. We texted the first few weeks she was in New York. Then she just stopped one day and I worried a little something happened, but what could I do?" Quinn spoke. He continued to talk about how Justine actually walked in on him making out with another girl at that Halloween party last year. He didn't even know she had come back, and she wasn't mad, just embarrassed. Quinn had gone outside for air and had seen the entire exchange between Elodie and Trevin.

"So you actually won the game that night, and I came in dead last?" Trevin asked, somewhat baffled.

"I'd say you won for sure that night, by a landslide. Her ex sounds like an absolute asshole." Quinn laughed.

"Mother above, I hate that guy. Never has punching anyone in the face felt so good. The second he called her easy I almost unleashed on him, then as soon as he grabbed my shoulder, I did. He's about as big as Caleb, less muscle though. He probably thought he could take me easily. Little did he know I could pin a bear. Sometimes."

Quinn chuckled. "So, the conference?"

Trevin let out a big exhale. "Don't remind me. She has made such amazing progress with everything, and he is doing better. I hate to discredit any of their work, but I think even if all of us worked double time, three months is just not enough time. I'm scared we are walking right up to the gallows."

"I know the feeling. They are going to watch us all too. I'm terrified of it this year. I broke a rule."

"We all broke rules. As my dad would say, none of us were saints when it came to her. I'm not throwing either of you under the bus though. For as much of a dick as you were all summer, I want you in the rank. Not your brother, not another estate."

Quinn smiled and nodded.

They both looked over when the door opened and Elodie's scent hit Trevin. She looked at him with concern for a moment then smiled at the sight of him and Quinn.

Small embers fell but for once they held hope. However, those embers were soon to be snuffed out.

Chapter 42

The day of the conference had arrived and the high estate lords, their heirs, and Elodie gathered in a large stone structure outside of Redding on the fae side of the boundary. Elodie and Cyrus stalled in going with the guard. They were informed upon arrival they would need to be placed in the holding cell prior to questioning. Trevin was none too happy and started arguing, and Cyrus started to shiver in fear. Then they threatened to sedate Trevin, to which Echo ordered him to stand down. Elodie sighed at the sadness on Trevin's face.

He ran up to her and cupped her jaw. "You will be safe, and you will be strong. You are a Greenthistle and you know you belong in Humboldt."

"I know. I will do this for my home." Elodie let out a shaky exhale.

"Cyrus, you are Nightswift's heir. Fight for Nightswift, we will always fight for you." Trevin looked at Cyrus who could only muster to take deep breaths.

"Both of you can do this. You have worked hard all summer," Echo said.

"You two will have each other. I'm glad you became such good friends," Bracken said. "We will all be okay."

"You both know your loyalty, deep breaths and stay true, right back to home with us." Quinn said as he looked at them.

Trevin took both Elodie's and Cyrus's hands and pulsed a calming wave over them. "Good luck." He then stepped back as a sentry approached with the tranquilizer gun.

"Best be on your way Master Greenthistle. Wouldn't want you to miss it on account of being unconscious."

A sharp glare from Trevin before he looked at her. "I love you, your mountain lion is here." Then he turned and walked off into the dimly lit corridor.

"This way." The gruff tone from the Shasta County guard indicated he had a low tolerance for everything. Elodie could hear Cyrus's heart echo hers as they followed. "Two pounding drums marching to their fate," the guard laughed.

Cyrus let out an uneasy sigh and gasped when Elodie took his hand.

The guard turned and looked at them, causing them to both stop. He grinned a sly little grin. "Well isn't that something."

Elodie narrowed her eyes. "I don't know how Shasta does it, but Humboldt looks out for their own."

The guard laughed. "Funny an heir apparent needs to be looked out for and you, odd little thing, are not one of their own."

Cyrus gave her hand a squeeze.

"Humboldt is my home." She scowled.

"Keep arguing and we will throw you in cuffs. Let them all see how unruly the oddity is."

"El," Cyrus said cautiously.

"The little raven does speak after all. Keep walking. The council needs to see you in that room. Before they begin."

They continued walking until a door opened to the room they were to sit in for an unknown amount of time. Both froze, gripping each other's hands tight. Blinding white lights lit up a large stark white room. Chairs were mounted on the floor spaced far apart from each other with restraints present. Both stood breathing hard.

"Get in and behave. We don't use the restraints if they are not needed," he said, giving them both a shove then slamming the door.

They stumbled and steadied each other as they sat on the floor close together against the wall.

"I don't know if I can contain this. They can't see it," Cyrus said quietly.

"You can. We will be alright."

"Remember how to listen and analyze. Your Nightswift training is going to be imperative along with your Greenthistle training," Cyrus said as though he were out of breath. "They do not have loyalty to you as we do."

She nodded.

"Every territory is here. Marin, Del Norte, Everoak. All of them."

"At least it's not the entire state. The most estates a county has up here are five right?" Elodie asked. "Plus their heirs?"

"Yes and two of their top guards will be there too." Cyrus's breathing was growing ragged. "They want you to bend. They want to make Trevin writhe. Remember that. Mortal trials are a mockery compared to this."

"Ok, I can do this. I promise you will be okay. I promised your parents, Greenthistle, and Ashdale."

Cyrus nodded and they both sat in silence for some time.

"I want to be out of this room, but I know when I walk down that hall what awaits. I'm scared they are going to demand a harsher punishment, they are going to do testing, that I'm going to be kept here. That they are going to keep you here, you cannot be away from the Old Giants for too long. You know you can't."

"We will go home together. I will not leave you. Humboldt will not leave you."

"I miss Bryla even though she probably thinks I hate her. I think about her at solstice, in her dress. I was so scared to even approach her. And now, I might not ever see her again," he wept.

"You will be okay, Cyrus. You will see her again. I will make sure of it. I will see to it that you go back home."

"I wish I was brave like you are. I still feel like these shadows control me at times."

"Keep your breathing calm. Remember you are good. Your entity knows you are."

The door opened and the guard from earlier walked in. Cyrus trembled and curled in on himself.

"Humboldt's Earth Blessed, please come with me." He looked at Elodie. She froze and her heart pounded. With a hard swallow she stood up then glanced at Cyrus. He looked at her terrified.

"You will be okay. We will be okay. You are good. You know you are." Her words were uneasy as the pit in her stomach grew. Slowly she stepped forward and out of the cell.

The door slammed shut and she glared at him. The guard smirked and pulled a set of handcuffs off his belt. "I can throw you in these faster than you can blink," he said then pointed down the hall.

Elodie did as she was told. "Do not cuff Master Nightswift."

"If he proves unruly then I have no choice. He should want to put his best foot forward. Like his Earth blessed is trying to do." He leaned in close and grabbed her arm. "I see your fear though. Try being the Greenthistle you want to be."

"I am a Greenthistle."

"Then prove it to all of them. Including your trembling vowed. We might have to throw him cuffs. Lord Greenthistle was wise to vow you two, but it is proving disruptive."

"Don't touch any of them." She fought to keep her voice from breaking.

"Orders are orders. Now go," he said sternly, giving her another shove as the doors opened. She could see a large dark room with a path of light to the center. Figures could be seen sitting around a circular auditorium yet she had no idea where anyone was.

As she walked into the path of the lights on the floor, each one blinded her. Each recessed floor light she passed winked out with a loud click behind her, as if herding her and her alone onto a pedestal to be gawked at. Finally she made it to the center. The light overhead was warm and just as blinding. A headache pulsed through her temples as she tried to let her eyes adjust.

"She's not ok," she heard Trevin rasp.

"Do not get up," Lord Greenthistle said with gritted teeth.

"Behold, the first Earth Blessed in 600 years," a booming voice said.

Conjuring up images of the Old Giants, the trail to Greenthistle, to Nightswift, to Ashdale, the café, her mind desperately tried to picture home instead of this place. With another deep breath, Elodie clenched her fist.

"State your name and title," a voice said.

She swallowed hard. "Lady Elodie Santiago, of Humboldt territory, Earth Blessed of the Old Giants in the North Coast, aligned to Greenthistle Estate. Vowed to Master Greenthistle," she managed to say with the confidence she was starting to feel.

The whispers began. "That energy is ancient, a mortal girl chosen to harness it? Now ageless, immortal? What makes her so worthy?"

"Your keepers are not to speak until spoken too," the voice stated. She felt a surge of anger, remembering Trevin on his knees.

"Oh poor boy is going to lash out. It is too soon for this stress on them. The vowed bond is too fresh, They are far too young to be vowed," others murmured.

Elodie took deep breaths and reminded herself that she had dealt with three revelries now, dealt with Humboldt and Marin seeing her. She could deal with this. *Prove to them that I am a Greenthistle. Lord Oakstone tested you for a reason.*

"They are not my keepers. They are my family. My friends. My guidance. In turn I will always protect them. I have been called to Humboldt since I was little, I awoke when my home was in danger."

"You say Humboldt is your home but it was not always. State your place of birth and last place of residence. You have quite the impressive travel history, vagabond."

"Marin for both."

"Yet you renounce it?"

"I was born there, lived there, worked there. I was called to Humboldt by their entity." *Marin didn't want me,* Elodie thought to herself.

"Lady Lillyleaf, rise," the voice said. Elodie's heart tensed. She was unaware they would ask anyone else questions. *Hadn't this been what I was trained for, to do it on my own?*

"Yes, sir." Lady Lillyleaf stood. The movement turned Elodie's attention. She at least knew where Humboldt and Marin sat.

"Marin never detected an occurrence?"

There was a pause. "Twice, Sir. Both times, she was accompanied by her overseer."

Some murmurs followed.

"Explain."

"Once in May when she met with us. We established our allegiance with her and asked that she walk Mt. Tamalpais, our entity, and see her connection with our redwood groves. My heir apparent and Master Oakstone accompanied her along with her overseer."

"The other time?"

Elodie's mind began to race. The only other time she was there with Trevin was for her dad. *What had occurred?* she wondered.

Another pause. "Before that, we felt an odd energy in the air in February. Faint, but there."

"Did you not investigate?" the fae speaking demanded.

"We did, and found nothing, sir."

"You said her overseer was with her both times, did you meet with said overseer?"

"Yes, sir."

"And did you inquire about the odd energy?"

"We did. It was a faint pulse but different. When asked, her overseer said they did not know what it was but had felt it before and concluded it was connected to the redwoods. So we agreed we would consult with Humboldt should we encounter it again." Lady Lillyleaf's tone did not falter.

Elodie was growing nervous now. The words odd and different weighed on her. This was a long drawn-out process and Cyrus was all alone in that room. *Please let him be alright,* she pleaded with anything out there that might be listening.

"Please be seated," the voice said. Some more whispers occurred.

"Lord Greenthistle, rise."

"Yes, sir," Echo replied and stood. Her eyes noticed Miles leaning over and nodding to Quinn, who sat forward.

"Humboldt had quite the busy year, no? Usually you have nothing to report. You have worked so very hard to ensure that, yet here we are with an heir's seat vacant and a rare specimen in your care. Internal affairs indeed."

"You know precisely where Master Nightswift is. And the one you refer to as a rare specimen, is my adopted cub, chosen by the entity I serve. Any stress induced on her is stress induced on our entity. As was evident by the energy when we left our territory."

"Do you swear by the report you submitted of the accounts of the Earth Blessed's arrival to be true and written by your own hand?"

"Yes, sir. Only myself, Lord Nightswift, and Lord Ashdale have seen the document you hold."

"It is very detailed in recalling all of the chaos that ensued."

"I provided an accurate statement as is my duty," Echo responded, remaining calm while Elodie grew nervous. She did not doubt that Lord Greenthistle had written the truth, he had to have, right? But she had not seen the report and did not know how things were worded. What if her story did not match his? She still had so much to learn and surely there was something they hadn't thought of or some little detail they hadn't had known or she didn't know. The dread festered in her gut and the pulsing headache from the light remained. She hated all the eyes she could feel but not see. This was no revelry where they had all gotten a bit buzzed before a night of sweets and celebrations. This was an outright interrogation.

"Is her overseer present? Or are you standing in?" The voice slithered up her spine.

"Her overseer is present," Echo answered, still calm. Murmurs started again.

"And who might her overseer be?" The tone of the voice indicated a smile.

"Master Greenthistle." Echo's tone had switched to defeat. Gasps and whispers took over.

"Oh. Her vowed. He knew, he swayed her. Greedy little prince wanted to keep her for himself," they all rasped. Worry gripped Elodie.

"No—" Trevin cried out but was muffled by Quinn who held him down.

"How wild your firstborn has grown, Lord Greenthistle. He was so obedient before, never once out of line, not even when we stood here for the passing of his mother," the voice teased.

"He is still obedient. Majority of this room would act the same or worse if their vowed of six months were in her position right now," Echo stated with reverence.

"As if a coward would know," a voice from a different side of the room sneered. Elodie flinched and fought the urge to find the voice. She was not sure what to make of the words. They were full of spite and malice.

"Silence," the voice snapped. "Do you feel your firstborn swayed her when she was a mortal?"

"No, sir I do not," he replied with a slight exhale and Elodie caught the nerves in it. If Echo was nervous, she knew they were walking a very fine line.

"State your reasoning."

"He never once told her what he was. He was simply asked questions in which he answered. She found him unconscious and pieced the iron cuff together when she touched his hand. She got it off of him when I would not have been able to, and he knew the severity of the matter. So he made a bargain with her. If anything, I would say that right there is proof enough he followed the rules, we protect those on both sides of the boundary. He protected her. In turn she protected him."

"So very admirable. Tell us then, when did he proclaim himself her overseer?"

"That same morning when he got home. After I demanded to know what happened to him since he missed his drill day. Nightswift and Ashdale can vouch for that."

"And why did he need to proclaim such a role? An odd little mortal girl frees the heir apparent of Humboldt's oldest ruling estate and we all know you were not going to simply let her be. What did you wish to do to her?"

She heard a sigh from where Humboldt was seated and Echo was quiet for a moment. She slowly lifted her eyes to meet Lord Greenthistle's. Trevin had said what might happen to her if she broke the bargain, but she had never known what Echo's preference was. Though she certainly had a hunch now.

"What my duty demanded. I ordered her to be brought to our hold. I could sense Master Greenthistle's curiosity as he spoke of what happened and my preference was to scramble her memory then drop her back in Marin. I will protect my cubs. But I did not raise a coward, I raised a Greenthistle who would protect his vowed." There was a reverence to his voice again.

Elodie swallowed hard.

There was another laugh from the direction of the new voice. It was a blunt laugh of absurdity.

"You may be seated. Master Greenthistle, rise and only speak to answer questions."

"Yes sir," Trevin said, his voice holding anger. Elodie now realized why Lady Lillyleaf gave him the order so many months ago in Marin Headlands.

"Did you make a bargain with her before or after you knew she was your vowed?"

"Before," Trevin responded confidently.

They continued to ask questions that Elodie answered in her mind as Trevin recited the answers aloud. It was all true, he continued to answer the questions with confidence.

"So when did you tell her she was your vowed?" the voice asked. Then her heart stopped. She knew this was now going to bring Quinn to questioning and Cyrus was still sitting alone in that cold white void.

Trevin paused for a moment, then he took an inhale. "After she freed my bound wrists with arrows stuck in me and floss flower working its way through my blood. When I saw her for the first time, I thought I was dead. She told me to wake up and tell her what she was. So I did."

"Very admirable indeed, little cub. Sit," the voice said. Trevin remained standing for a second longer then sat.

"Earth Blessed. Do you have any other statements you wish to make known?"

Elodie swallowed hard again and raised her gaze, she scanned the faint outlines she could see that made up the region. She had been through all of them at some point in her life.

"Humboldt is my home, it has always been calling me back. I fought it, ignored it, traveled far and wide. No one chained me up, I willingly chose it and would every time."

"Your entity may have wanted you desperately, but they didn't, they turned their backs on you. Your vowed let you go too," the other voice said again.

A sudden movement caught her eye from Humboldt's direction. Echo's hand against Trevin's chest holding him back. Quinn was holding him down too.

"No, your rules did. They reached for me with everything in them. Like they will continue to do." She took a deep inhale. "Your territories did not want me." More whispering but none spoke up as Elodie continued. "I have traveled, spent time, and lived in your territories and beyond. Always thinking back and longing for those Old Giants. This power has been in me since I was eight, and yet none of you felt it. Trust me, I too questioned if it was right for me to stay there, before and after I met him. He did not sway me. It became a battle of what was best for Greenthistle's future."

"One could say that it was swaying. His presence swayed you. You chose to remain and therefore made a selfish decision."

Elodie felt her hand pulse hot and saw the flash of teal. Gasps sound.

"Do not move," Echo growled at Trevin.

"This is quite a bond we have never seen before. Earth Blessed vowed to a high estate. Power imbalances are bound to happen," the voice said. "It appears as though they already have."

"Humboldt's entity chose me. I chose it. If you are all so convinced that any of them had any part in swaying me, read the report again. Plenty of factors led me home and plenty warded me off, on both the fae and mortal side. Go question your own entities before you question ours."

Whispers and murmurs occurred.

"Earth Blessed," the voice finally revealed themselves in the form of a tall fae as he walked up to the podium. He had fair skin, and looked around her age with short light blue hair and short horns on his head. He wore a suit with some smaller vine-like designs embroidered into the jacket and pants. "Such a rarity you are. State your age please."

Elodie paused, then opened her mouth but closed it again. She wasn't sure what her age was. She had a birthday, celebrated one, but the lore said she would remain at the age she awoke at.

"Thirty-six? Sir," she said, unsure. The fae narrowed his eyes on her.

"Humboldt high estates gave a very detailed account of all that has unfolded during your time there and it would appear Humboldt owes a great deal of debt to you. You spilled blood on account of at least two of their heirs."

"I chose to do so. I would for any of them again if it meant they would remain safe."

"Do you fully understand the weight of the choice you made?"

"I do." Elodie held her head high. "There are still many unknowns as we are all learning about the Earth Blessed. I am learning much about the fae world."

"Do you understand you will have to remain on their side of the boundary, giving up everything you had, for decades upon decades?"

Elodie swallowed hard as she thought about Cora, about the school and her house. Then she thought about Trevin, and Autumn. She thought about Poppy, Quinn, and Cyrus. All the high estates and maybe even Bryla. They would be there, they wouldn't leave, she would be living in their world.

"Yes, sir," she said, finding that confidence again.

"You know you could live anywhere right? You could live in the mortal world, and explore all the boundaries even beyond Northern California. You could move and be the nomad you started out as."

Some part of her thought about that too being able to see more things. Travel would be hard for her though, that she knew.

"I am aligned with Greenthistle," she said, looking him in the eyes with assurance.

"You aligned with Greenthistle, you are not bound to remain in their estate chained up. There are offers you know. You could rotate years, offering your gifts, learning from many more high estates."

"I am aligned with Greenthistle," she repeated. "I chose Humboldt. The earth granted me a choice. The Old Giants of Humboldt granted me their gifts. Humboldt is home. Do not try to sway me from choices I made for myself."

More whispers. "How bold she is for one so young. Word is she spent most of the last three months training hard with the three estates, spending weeks with them."

"So it appears the cub of Greenthistle does know control if he lets you stay with male heirs." The fae grinned widely. "For one as curious as you, you sure are shutting a lot of doors by remaining in one territory, beholden to one estate. Still thinking like a mortal, young and foolish."

"I can't be away from them for long."

"And is that fact? It has not been documented that Earth Blessed cannot freely pass as mortals do. We all see you, we all would like to see you grow and learn. To learn from you."

"Do you have any documentation on Earth Blessed since the coast doesn't?"

"No, we do not. Your best shot is Marin, but it seems you have gained what little knowledge they do have on the Earth Blessed as well as their alliance. Now, onto the matter of Master Nightswift, do you think his punishment was just, given what he did to you?"

Elodie pushed out an audible gust from her nose. "He served more than one soul should bear. He is still serving it. Leave him to Nightswift and me to handle."

"The report states he was the one who put an iron cuff on your vowed. Poisoned him. Attempted to murder you both."

The whispers and gasps picked back up and Elodie saw the flash of teal and this time her hands illuminated. More gasps and louder whispers.

"I know damn well what happened. Read the report." She was determined to let her Greenthistle valor show.

The fae at the podium grinned wryly. "Possessed by the spirit named Inanis. Chained and beaten by it, his body merely a puppet. Reading further states the only power that could stop it was an Earth Blessed."

A wave of exhaustion hit Elodie and her illumination sputtered out. She stumbled but remained upright.

"No—" Trevin pleaded. Her shoulders rose and fell and she saw Trevin straining under Echo, Quinn, and now Miles.

Elodie then noticed the fae turn his attention from Trevin towards Elodie with a smirk.

"Go on, order him to stand down, or we will sedate him."

"I don't order him, just as he does not order me," Elodie panted out. Her expression grew sad. "Trev, I'm okay. I promise."

Trevin stopped struggling but no one gave him much room.

"You do have an impressive leash on him," the fae said as the other voice laughed with some snark. "Lord Nightswift, please rise." He looked back to Humboldt's section.

"Yes, sir." Bracken stood.

"Tell the region what punishment your heir received. Power shifted, and he is guilty."

"No. He's not," Elodie argued. She was worried now.

"Silence, Earth Blessed."

Sentries moved closer.

Chapter 43

Trevin had seen her clamp down on her power, he had seen when it slipped out and watched the faces of those in other territories with shock, awe, fear, jealousy, and spite. Eyes turned to him all the same. He had seen her exhaustion hit her and the moment her confidence had fallen off, that boiling energy had stopped so suddenly.

Trevin had noticed mention of Cyrus seemed to spark that flame and he wasn't sure how to feel about this. Jealousy did not pass over him, he knew it was not that, but they had some kind of connection. They always seemed to know of each other's presence before she even woke up, and now they both had an energy of earth or stars.

Cyrus would be up here soon. While Elodie had been hard to watch, Trevin knew Cyrus was not ready for an interrogation under a spotlight.

"Lord Nightswift, please inform us of the punishment Humboldt deemed appropriate for your heir apparent."

Bracken swallowed and spoke with certainty. "We kept him confined to his room for two weeks, and on house arrest for three months. He only returned to the mortal world a few weeks ago and is supervised whenever he is in the mortal lands, yet he only goes to his mortal job before he returns home unless he is with Lady Elodie, Master Greenthistle, or Master Ashdale."

"How long was he in the hold?"

Bracken sighed. "A few hours, sir."

The fae narrowed his eyes again. "A few hours in the hold when he tried to murder the Earth Blessed, assaulted her, poisoned one heir apparent, injured another alongside the rest of Greenthistle's cubs?"

"He didn't!" Elodie insisted.

"If only orders worked on you. Silence, or we will be forced to remove you," the fae snapped out. Elodie clenched her fist but Trevin could see how tired she was getting. Her emotions were going wild right now. *Mother above, we focused on the wrong things this summer. We were so focused on her staying safe in Humboldt but it should have been from outside forces messing with her emotions.*

"Lord Nightswift, a few hours followed by nights in his room at his own estate? I question why the high estate of Humboldt deem that punishment fair."

"Sir, quiet nights in Nightswift estate are a rarity. He was left traumatized from the spirit and then he was hurt badly again. Night terrors, and months of near isolation. He still flinches away from us at times."

"It would appear as though Master Nightswift may struggle to hold rank for Nightswift. Power shifted."

"No. He is making progress, sir," Bracken pleaded.

"Hmm, sit. Let the council see Master Nightswift."

Elodie was escorted to a different stand and the doors opened as Cyrus walked in shaking. His eyes watered. The murmurs and whispers started to sound like near hisses. "Trembling little blackbird. Unstable. Shame and guilt is all over him. Blood is on his hands."

Trevin glanced at Elodie and he could feel his heart break at her shock and disgust at the words. She was realizing very little loyalty lay in this room.

"You are good. You are going to be ok," Elodie said softly. Cyrus kept his eyes down as he stood heaving.

"Master Nightswift," the fae said, looking down on him. Cyrus flinched and a chill passed through him.

"Yes, sir." He managed to say through a breaking voice finally meeting his eyes. More murmurs.

"Per the report provided by Humboldt, you have been served the sentence your high estates deemed appropriate. You have returned to drills, to your mortal job and have taught solo lessons to your Earth Blessed."

"Yes, sir."

"Yet here you stand before us terrified and heaving. I question what progress means to Lord Nightswift."

"I-I have made progress," he stuttered, but could not look anyone in the eyes.

"Last time we saw you, you were so bored out of your mind sitting in your now vacant seat."

"It's—not. It's not vacant." Cyrus's heart rate faltered slightly as if he'd tripped.

"I see you here under this light, I see Humboldt's three estate lords and two of their heirs. Last year they looked ready to fall asleep, while now they are both tense as can be. And the funny thing is, your Earth Blessed who only fully awoke into her powers months ago stands taller than you now. Now maybe we can attribute that to her ignorance on account of being so new but you are not. You know exactly how severe a situation standing here is. It would appear as though you have regressed."

Trevin heard the grating laugh again. It was from Everoak's section. He couldn't be bothered with the, not after what had happened to his mom. The grating laugh wasn't even their high estate leaders but one of their sentries. He noticed Elodie glance over at them and saw her shock as she connected the dots. When Trevin glanced at the sentry, he was met with a wicked grin daring him to lose it. Trevin rolled his eyes and looked back at Cyrus. He pleaded in his mind to control his shadows, that he would not reveal it. They would be better suited to reveal it next year. If they slipped out, Elodie would surely throw herself in front of him again. Cyrus had not gotten much control over them in stressful situations.

"Please. I'm sorry," he said, trembling harder now. He could hear all the hisses, the fear. "I am still Nightswift's heir." Cyrus lifted his head and looked at the room. He noticed Bracken's shoulders slump and he looked down. Cyrus was being absolutely humiliated under that spotlight with tears streaming down his face. Never had any of them imagined Cyrus's confidence diminished like this. They had all failed him and now Cyrus might not be able to help Elodie.

"This isn't fair. Elodie is absolutely disgusted with all of them," Trevin hissed out quietly.

"There is nothing we can do for him or her. This is up to him," Bracken sighed.

"Then have faith in him. He will do this," Trevin snapped out.

"The question is should you do this, Master Nightswift? We have a bargain to make but first let's be sure we all understand what happened." The fae spoke and walked closer to him. "The report states you held a spirit in you, that made you commit the atrocities to your fellow high estates, and your Earth Blessed."

Mother above this is not going to end well, Trevin thought.

"That is correct, sir," Cyrus managed to get out with a level voice.

"Yet you lost power for what the spirit did?"

"No, sir." Cyrus slumped again.

"Then enlighten us what on this egregious list of offenses did the heir apparent of Nightswift sully his hands with?"

Cyrus's shoulders rose and fell with every deep breath he took. He had passed out last time when he fessed up to this in front of family and friends. Trevin could not imagine what Cyrus must be feeling now.

"I—I put an unconscious Master Greenthistle in Lady Elodie's path," Cyrus explained, growing more frantic with every word. "It absolved Master Greenthistle of responsibility for the mortal discovery."

The gasps and murmurs made him recoil.

"A terribly big risk you took, Yet I suppose you had many factors beyond your control." The fae frowned as he looked over the report. "Your father states here that he feels it was the only one you had. The iron cuff. Such drastic measures." The voice cooed in mock condolence.

"That is correct, sir." Cyrus was still heaving as he awaited his judgment.

"Yet you held your tongue, took advantage of seizing control of the ravens from your father to weld iron on to the heir apparent of Greenthistle to tamper with his vowed bond? Big risks indeed." The fae sounded highly unamused.

"Yes, sir." Cyrus's voice was barely above a rasp as he looked down and squeezed his eyes shut.

"In hopes that her power would awaken and not kill her? That she would find it in her to save your own ass?" Anger took over the deliberator's voice as he now loomed over Cyrus. Trevin could see the tears forming through Cyrus's lashes.

"No. I wanted her to save him, and them. I didn't think about what might happen to me," Cyrus pleaded. "I tried to beg Lord Greenthistle for death. I tried."

"Did you know how she could save them?"

"Yes sir." Cyrus hung his head low.

"Explain how she could have saved them."

Cyrus looked away in shame and Trevin saw it as clear as day. There was no mistaking it.

"The Earth Blessed could pull the spirit off of me, taking it on herself. Or she could have ended me and ended it. The spirit can only truly be ended when it is tied to a host. Otherwise it is containment."

Trevin felt his heart stop for a moment and all the emotions hit him all over again.

The deliberator scoffed. "I would certainly say that was a lot of faith to put on one small little mortal. I suppose you had been watching her for months though, asking her to finish you off was certainly not something her soul was capable of."

Tears fell from Elodie's eyes now as she rubbed them. Cyrus looked at Trevin with so much remorse too.

"Tell us about what happened the night you were off house arrest. The matter that you still have not brought up against Elmbridge Estate." The fae continued to loom over a now trembling Cyrus.

"Please, I'd rather not talk about it," Cyrus begged.

Trevin watched Elodie closely, her mind was processing too much. He was terrified she was going to make a poor decision. This was no place to show her valor, she needed to be a Nightswift right now. She needed to assess every possible angle. He was trying to figure out what the council was getting at. Assault charges were hardly the regional councils concern, especially within a territory.

"Heir apparent of Nightswift, you were touched against your will, stripped and assaulted. Yet you seek no reprimand for Elmbridge even as you stand here a trembling heap? You should want justice."

Cyrus squeezed his eyes tighter. His hands balled into fists by his side.

Trevin knew he was seconds from exploding. Elodie was fidgeting. *Please let this end soon. Please be strong, Cyrus,* he begged.

"I need more time." Cyrus was near hyperventilating. "Please," he begged.

"Nap time in your own bed was not enough time? Now you get to tell us which terms of the bargain you would prefer," the deliberator demanded.

"Please," Cyrus pleaded.

"The regional council will determine your punishment for the iron cuff and tampering with the vowed bond to be served here in Shasta County, or you can return and offer the Earth Blessed to be loaned out for other territories as needed."

"No," Trevin seethed.

"How is that fair?" Elodie spat out. "I'm not an object."

"You are a commodity, an asset. A rare one. Do you have a preference, Lady Elodie?"

"No," Trevin said louder.

He noticed Elodie and Cyrus look at each other.

"Master Cyrus Nightswift, I order you to answer."

Cyrus was trembling and he looked down. "Please. Please. Please." He begged as he strained the order.

"We can wait as long as we need, until your body curls in on itself from fighting your order. We will remain until you wake. As long as we need to."

Cyrus wiped his eyes. "I'm sorry." His shoulders slumped down, as if he accepted his fate already. A chill shot through Trevin. "I'm sorry."

"You face our terms, or she agrees to ours. Your Old Giants yield resources to each other, do they not? Humboldt strives to be like them."

Trevin was straining under the rest of Humboldt's hold.

"Settle the fuck down before I sedate you myself!" Echo hissed.

"No—" Trevin cried out but his mouth was muffled again by Quinn's hand.

"Master Nightswift?"

Without looking up he answered, "I want to go home."

"Bastard," Trevin growled in anger as Elodie's mouth fell agape. Betrayal coated her face. *After all she had done for him.*

The deliberator turned to Elodie now but she paid him no mind, still staring at Cyrus. "Lady Elodie, what do you agree to?"

Trevin looked back at Cyrus who was near convulsing, gripping his heart. Elodie's voice made everything stand still, including Trevin's heart.

"Send him home for Humboldt to take care of. I will go, serve the territories as needed. On my terms. I'm not to be called for trivial bullshit or swayed into relocating for any length of stay beyond the required task. My mortal job still needs to be considered so that limits my time too. Master Greenthistle and or any of Humboldt is allowed to accompany me and they nor I are to be threatened. Otherwise your bargain is null and void. If you want them to loan out an asset, prove that they can trust you with me," she spat with all the Greenthistle valor anyone of them had ever seen.

Yet that was not what she needed right now. They had wanted her, this was a trial for Cyrus's merit and Elodie hadn't seen they were banking on her sacrifice. The fight had gone out of his body. His dad watched him sternly. His hand remained on his chest.

"Does the council accept the Earth Blessed's terms?" The fae grinned wide.

"Agreed," a unanimous chorus sounded.

"No," Cyrus whimpered as he fell to his knees. All the life and fight had gone out of him. "Thank you. I'm so fucking sorry."

"The territories will look forward to your stay, Earth Blessed."

Trevin deflated. "Fuck!" he muttered and sat back as the room began to clear out. He could feel people looking at him.

"He just let her walk right into that. He didn't fight back," Quinn said. "He proved the council right."

The high estate lords remained silent.

Cyrus looked away as Elodie approached. "Elodie," he cried.

"You are safe. Everything will be alright," she said softly, but her voice was full of fear and sadness.

"I didn't protect you, Elodie," Cyrus heaved.

"I'll be ok. I can't be gone for more than a few days. Trev will be with me."

Trevin felt his anger surge and pushed out of all his restraints. He glared at Cyrus watching him shatter all over again. Any progress he had made with Cyrus over the summer was not doing near enough to quiet the anger building in him.

If Trevin didn't leave, he would in fact break a rule. Willingly.

So he ran out the doors and right up to his room, barely hearing Cyrus whimper about how sorry he was. Trevin did not want Cyrus to be sorry right now, he wanted him to fight back, to at least stand his ground and demand something else. Anything else.

Chapter 44

Never had Elodie seen the level of anger in Trevin's eyes before. As if led by instinct she took a step forward.

"Give him time. All of you," Echo said, his voice heavy. "This was not the desired outcome of today and we were not prepared. We took the wrong approach this summer with you both."

"But I will be safe. Trevin and Humboldt sentries will go with me right?"

"They will, but you know what happens every time you leave. We all know it. It sits heavy on your heart and it does weaken you, every time you have left you came back exhausted. This is all so new for you and the summer was not near enough time to prepare you for this. Not to mention the precedent this sets." His eyes traveled down to Cyrus who was still on the ground crying.

"Is—Trev mad at me?" Elodie's voice started to break. "I don't want to hurt him."

"No. He knows full well what it means to be vowed to an Earth Blessed. He just needs some time to process it all. There were a lot of emotions in this room. There were forces beyond you both feeding into his anger too," Echo said with a hint of annoyance in his voice.

"I too wish we had prepared you better for this, but I thank you for you being a Greenthistle and an Ashdale today. For always protecting my son and my estate, no matter what it costs you. Going forward, things will be different, you owe Nightswift absolutely nothing," Bracken said, then he looked at Cyrus with such disappointment. "Get up."

"I'm sorry. I tried," Cyrus whimpered.

"Get up, Cyrus." Bracken's tone grew stern.

"Wait!" Elodie cried out, not understanding. "Stop."

She felt Quinn's hand on her shoulder along with that calming cozy feeling. "El," he said softly. She shook out of his grip.

"You can't just act like nothing happened this summer, that the effort he and I put in means nothing. It was my choice. It always had to be my choice."

"You made your choice, but it was an ill-informed choice. This was not the time for you to be brave, this was a time you needed to observe. We needed to teach you when to be each estate and we didn't," Miles said.

"I failed you this time, You needed to be a Nightswift today and I didn't teach you how," Bracken sighed.

"I'm sorry, El. I should have done more," Cyrus cried and pushed himself back up. He couldn't look at her.

"Cyrus, you are good. Remember that," Elodie said then she looked at his dad. "If you want me to be a Nightswift, then remember how his Earth Blessed treats him and be a better Nightswift yourself. We are not starting over," she demanded. "I'm still fighting for him and all of you."

Bracken and her fixed on each other for a moment and she felt her throat tighten but she fought the urge to cry. Bracken simply turned to his son. "Let's go, Cyrus."

"Come, let's get out here and back to our rooms," Echo said.

The four of them gathered at Miles's room which was adjoining Quinn's room. They wanted to debrief before confronting Trevin so Echo put up a sound barrier.

"I know what Trevin's feeling, I feel it too. Cyrus knows better than all of us how to weasel out of a shit situation. He always has." Quinn paced the room. "That's the advantage to line of sight and watching so much."

"That room they stuck us in was jarring. It was a stark white void of a room. Cyrus was in for over an hour, alone. Give him a break," Elodie rasped.

"El. I get that. This is nerve wracking for all of us. Do you know how quick I held my breath when they started asking when you found out about the vowed bond?" Quinn rubbed the back of his head and exhaled deeply. "Trevin had every right to make me go up there and the bastard still covered my ass. But I would have owned my actions with pride and shoved it right back in all their faces just like I did with my dad. Cyrus has seen so many trials like this but he froze and let you take the fall. Again."

"Quinn is right. This last year with you has been such a delicate balance and we were all tense. Never mind Trevin's vowed bond. Imagine how this looks to the region. You are here, you saved all three of them and we swore to serve you, they should all three be fighting tooth and nail for you, yet only two did today," Echo explained.

"I could see Cyrus struggling to hold it together though. What was the other option? He stays here alone. I at least get to go back with you all. Cyrus would have watched us all leave him." Elodie felt her eyes well up again. She hated crying in front of all of them. It felt like that was all she ever did.

"Cyrus was supposed to hold his ground just like you did. He has yet to do that. The sacrifice should never be you. We wouldn't have left him here. We would have negotiated terms, they wanted you, not him," Miles said with reverence.

Elodie frowned and looked at the ground. It had been a delicate balance and again, she felt she hadn't done enough fast enough. They had been fine, but now it was all shattering because she didn't complete the task. Not only had Cyrus been left on that trail for so long, she hadn't even found her way off it even with a three month lead and a bunch of support.

"I wanted to help him and wanted to be brave for you all. His shadows were going to slip out, I know you all saw that."

"El. You were literally dragged into this world and put in front of them today. Cyrus should have negotiated for himself when they asked him for his bargain. Hell, you gave them terms for it. He could have too." Quinn looked at her. "The betrayal when he said he wanted to go home spoke louder than anything. He didn't fight for you. Every single soul in that room knew it too."

"He didn't feel safe though. The guard told me to be a Greenthistle and I thought I was." She deflated.

"You are a Greenthistle, Northern California knows this," Echo said. He walked up to her to rest a hand on her shoulder. "I am honored you chose Greenthistle. You are so brave, but just as Cyrus didn't feel safe, you weren't the

Nightswift you needed to be tonight. We were so concerned with you staying safe in Humboldt we didn't prepare you for outside threats."

Elodie flinched and looked up at him. The image of her running across those dry barren rocks under the blazing sun flashed in her head.

"We serve you, always," he said softly and removed his hand. "Go see your vowed."

Elodie quietly left the room and headed down the hall. For a moment she wasn't sure if she was ready to have this conversation. Those doubts again that she couldn't do this. Doubt that she could not face her vowed, the thought made her scowl. So she pressed her keycard to the door and entered to find Trevin sitting on the edge of the bed with his head down. With an inhale, he glanced at her for a second then got up and pulled her into a tight embrace.

"I'm sorry. I just knew I'd do or say something I'd regret if I sat there any longer."

"I'm sorry I made you mad. Or jealous. I love you, I want you."

"El." He pressed her head into his chest. "I'm not jealous of him. I know you'd do all that and more for me, but that's the problem. I never want you to pull yourself away from your home you fought for to save me. Cyrus has got to at least find the way to follow you. You cannot keep his hand in yours the entire trail."

"I know but he's been treated like a monster for so long and—" Elodie paused and gripped him tighter.

"And you showed him he wasn't. I fought for him and defended him too. His vowed is there and he can't find the strength in him to be better for her, for you? I don't want to lose him, but I cannot and will not risk you. I need you to understand that. You showed me who I was supposed to be. I can't lose you again. I love you, El."

She nodded and cried into him. "I'm sorry, I want the three of you safe. I'm the odd one out."

"Elodie." Trevin's voice was almost strained. "Humboldt is your home. I hope there is no doubt in your mind of that. This was Cyrus's chance to fight back yet all he did was watch you sink when you always pulled him back to shore. That's why I had to leave the room. I don't know what else we can do for him."

"I love you, Trevin."

"And I love you, Little Mink. Let's get ready for the evening. After tonight, the gawking is done. You and I will walk into the Autumn Equinox arm in arm and we will be at our estate."

She nodded and kissed him hard.

Cyrus stood in the room, staring at the floor. The weight of what she had done was really setting in, and why he had let her do that.

Bracken walked into his room through the adjoining door and crossed his arms. "You cannot let her carry you anymore! It is not her job to take the fall for you every single time it gets too hard. I cannot continue to allow you and her to even have lessons if this is how it is going to be."

"I'm sorry."

Bracken sighed. "Then fix it, Cyrus. Stop being sorry and help her. She needs you just as much as you need her but this is turning into her taking fall after fall for you. Trevin has his limits, Quinn is hitting his. Fight back."

"It was humiliating up there. I was barely containing my shadows. If they had seen my shadows—I need more time."

"Tonight made a mockery of not only you and Nightswift, but of Greenthistle and Ashdale. I came this close to losing you tonight because you didn't fight back. You have seen her stumble through every fear, worry, and doubt all summer long, and yet you couldn't do any of that for her? Nightswift is just taking and taking from our Earth Blessed and she's going to keep on offering until she has nothing left. Until Greenthistle has to intervene. You have to prove you want this. You need to be ready for next year. You need to be ready to fight for her."

Cyrus deflated and wiped his eyes. "I don't want to go to the party tonight."

"I think that's likely for the best," Bracken said.

He couldn't bring himself to look at his dad. He couldn't look at anyone right now. "I'm sorry I'm letting everyone down. That I am not as strong as I thought I was. I want to be better, be stronger, like her and you, but I just don't know how."

"Start swimming back to shore instead of hoping she will keep throwing out lifelines. I know I haven't been the best at handling this and I am sorry son. I love you, I know you will lead Nightswift to greatness and carry on the legacy, but you have got to start putting in the work on your own. You are not to spend time with her until you can show me you are a Nightswift. Assess who you are going to be."

Cyrus nodded and sat on the bed.

"I will send a guard with sedation."

"Yes, sir."

After Bracken left, Cyrus climbed into bed and stared at the ceiling. "Bryla. Please know I am trying so hard to be better for you. I want to get to know you."

The next morning, when Elodie heard that Nightswift Estate had left before breakfast, she frowned, set her fork down, and sighed.

"El," Trevin said softly. Quinn set his phone down and looked at her.

"I thought I was doing the right thing." She started to tear up. "I never completed that task they gave me, now I don't know how."

"You did though. You saved me and Trev, you saved the raven too." Quinn stated.

"It doesn't feel like I did. He's going to go back to his room and spend nights screaming and trembling just like he did in the spring. He told me it was imperative I be a Nightswift and I thought I was. I know you both saw him trying with everything in him."

"El, you did everything you could. The problem is he didn't. You have done nothing wrong," Quinn assured. Trevin nodded.

"But I could have—" she began.

"You know how to stay safe on your lands, you can communicate with our aligned animals. Now, we work on your doubts. You know we cannot lie. We know you trust us, now trust yourself." Trevin took her hand and laced their fingers together.

"He was left alone for so long though."

"He was, and that falls on me and Trevin and the rest of his friends to make up for, and we will. We all have a responsibility to you though, Cyrus included. Let us help you both now. Lord Nightswift is right, you owe Nightswift nothing, you owe none of us anything. Let us ease your doubts," Quinn said softly.

"You can't carry us, Little Mink. We are so grateful when you do though, but we need to be there for you. Without question and without doubt," Trevin said, wrapping an arm around her waist. "Please finish eating."

Elodie nodded then picked up her fork and finished most of her plate. After a few more moments she looked at Quinn. "Do you want to go to the Sundial Bridge with us?"

"I don't want to intrude."

"I understand if you have to get back or are not interested, but it'd be nice to have you there."

They packed up and headed over to the Sundial Bridge. As they walked across it, Elodie eyed the glass surface and the giant white pylon with the steel cables creating the perfect balance. She watched the water flow off the Sacramento River, moving under them and looked west, to the direction that would take her home.

They walked up to the pylon and took a selfie in front of it with the bridge vanishing behind them. Trev and Quinn were glamoured of course. Rounded ears, no markings on their faces. And while their eyes were still striking, they were not as bright. *One of them was missing,* she thought to herself as they started walking back. Next year. She swore that next year the four of them would walk this bridge. That she would be alright and so would Cyrus. Trev and Quinn would be alright too.

With a sigh she walked over to the railing and watched the water flowing under her. It flowed east, away from home. The realization of what they had asked her to do, what she had agreed to do set in. They now had Trevin as bait to snare her.

All she could do was fight the tears at how she once again failed to put those pieces together correctly.

Chapter 45

As the week went on Cyrus made himself scarce. His dad noted that he almost seemed to vanish entirely after his daily tasks were done. He would always report to work and estate requirements but as soon as it was done, he would say he would be out for the evening. There were never reports of anything bad happening. At one point the Old Giants almost seemed to shield him from his dad's ravens. Bracken could read his son and his resolve. He knew he needed to trust him that he was not in danger. That for once being alone was what Cyrus truly desired. Yet it did not ease Bracken's worries that maybe he had pushed Cyrus too far. That his son would not find his way back.

"I will be out tonight, sir." Cyrus looked at his dad with a stoic expression. He was met with an inquisitive gaze.

"Again?" Bracken asked.

"Yes."

"Training as you call it?"

"I still do not have mastery over things and would like to keep working at it, so I may be better suited to serve Humboldt and our entities. So I may better serve my Earth Blessed." Cyrus was standing still and tall.

"You know at some point I need to see this progress, right?"

Cyrus nodded. "I have not made much. Regardless of where I end up in the future, does not change the fact that Nightswift will always serve her as will I. I hope to show you progress soon."

Bracken fixed on Cyrus for a moment then spoke. "You are being safe right? Watching that territory line? I do not need Trinity, Siskyou, or even Del Norte County reporting what we kept from the council so soon."

"Yes. I'll stay away from the territory line. I'll be safe and will keep a few ravens nearby to watch."

"Okay. See to it that you continue to be safe. I will see you at the office tomorrow?"

"Yes, sir. Then I will return for Poppy's flight lesson."

"Before heading out again?" Bracken leaned back in his chair, almost in defeat.

"Yes. If you would like me to do something before I will."

"No. Just give me a briefing on her lesson progress. Lady Elodie says she seems to be coming out of her shell more in school."

Cyrus smiled. "I'm glad. She is taking after El a lot."

"How so?"

"I know she still holds some fear of me, but she no longer lets it stop her. I think it is good for Poppy to see how to work through the doubts and worries. Poppy will learn how to do it from a Greenthistle," Cyrus said. When Bracken nodded Cyrus turned and left the Nightswift estate, taking flight east.

Bracken rubbed his hand down his face as he swiveled the chair towards the window where he fixed on the sky and the Old Giants. "Please keep him safe. I'm sorry I took his lifeline away from him. He clung to her and it didn't help him." He heard Ariyanna sigh from beside him and met her gaze as she leaned against the wall with her arms crossed.

"He is not Trevin and you are not Echo."

"I've never needed to be like Echo because he never acted like Trevin, to this day he has never acted like Trevin, the good or the bad."

Ariyanna walked forward and sat in a chair. "No he's not. Cyrus was altered from that night just as Elodie was. They do need each other."

"I know, I failed them both. It was my gut reaction to keep Cyrus from her. To make him understand the burden she is trying to take on. She must loathe me for it too."

"She doesn't loathe you. The poor girl is still overwhelmed and they all hold a special place in her life. The thought of losing any of them pains her. All she has done is cling to this home she found. You and Echo both can call yourselves fools all you like but the truth of the matter is, we all were. None of us, including our kids, were without fault. We all made mistakes with Cyrus too. We have two very unique souls in our direct care. We have to be better for them and make it as safe as we can."

"I want to, Ari. I know how special they are, but we have never dealt with something like this, never even seen or heard of this. How many mortals have tripped on those trails out there and gotten a scrape? How many in the Sierra? Near Mt. Shasta? Not a single territory has found one? Marin is the nearest report to an Earth Blessed we have and yet, they hardly know anything. Then Cyrus. My own child is something unheard of. We could have lost him twice now, if not to some evil spirit, then to the whims of the council but protecting him comes at the cost of the Earth Blessed. I don't know what to do. Ashdale and Greenthistle fight for her. I'm tempted to pull Poppy from her class just to stop hindering Elodie."

"You know that's only going to hinder Poppy and Lady Elodie. They all have to find their way. She stumbled her way in here then protected it even when she was shunned. Cyrus will find his way just like she did, so we keep the light on for both of them. We keep reminding them, they are good, and they are strong and loved. What else can we do?"

"Ensure they know the door is always open for them when they return," Bracken sighed.

Cyrus landed hard and rough, skidding across the dirt. It was dryer over in Six Rivers. He had spent the first two nights deep in Redwoods National Park, but now he wanted to try further away from redwoods protection. With only the stars, they were his true power source after all. Some part of him felt safe with the redwoods because he always felt safe with Elodie.

Yet he knew his dad was right. He no longer could walk the same trail as Elodie. For all the things they had been through together, and everything they had shared, they were not the same. He had been born here, had been placed in line to become a high estate lord alongside Trevin and Quinn. It was expected of him. Elodie may have been placed here but they all had hoped she would do it. It was expected he would and he wanted to meet those expectations.

He pushed himself back up and let out an exhausted breath. He flew up high again and tried lifting more rocks and fallen branches he saw on the ground with his shadows. As he strained to do it, his frustration only grew that he could not fully master it.

The conference replayed in his head. The stark white room. The way the interrogation drilled into him, his body trembled and his eyes welled up. That spirit flashed in his head. Laughed in his ear.

No, he snapped in his head. Elodie's blood covering his feathers caused him to falter. "Stop." Alena's hands all over him, laughing. *Monster, unstable, would have killed Trevin.* "No!" he screamed and the raven cawed loudly. The stars pulsed and he began to plummet.

He didn't fight this. There were no redwoods around, they were Elodie's. He drew no power off them, and they only coddled him. He was under his entity and they all watched him fall. Just like they did at the conference. How humiliated he felt. He couldn't bring himself to look his dad in the eyes for days.

As he fell he saw and felt Elodie pulling him into a hug, telling him they were friends, that he was good. He saw Trevin smiling and telling him was good too, pulling him into a hug. Cedar, Autumn, and Quinn reaching out for him. Poppy's excited face as she showed him drawings of ravens with flower crowns. Then Bryla, he scented her. Her smile warmed his heart. He wanted her to know, wanted her to choose him, yet why would she if all he did was crash and burn?

These were the things he clung to in the darkest of times that had brought him back.

Trevin and Quinn had fought for their Earth Blessed and their home. He wanted to stand with them. He had been born to do this.

"No!" he screamed and flung his shadows out under him. When he changed to protect his raven, he still managed to hold the shadows and land right on them, soft and cushioned as though he were on a bed of ferns and soft damp soil.

Panting heavily, he looked at the stars and smiled. He managed to break his fall. He hadn't been able to yet. Also being able to hold the shadows out as he changed was new too. "I will fight with you all. I am going to court Bryla Petalgrace. I want my vowed to at least know," he said and once again the stars pulsed.

Leaping to his feet he grabbed a rock the size of a softball and flung it up. With his shadows, he let it come back down to the earth gently. He tried again, repeating it until he tried lifting bigger rocks with the shadows. They hovered in the air and the stars pulsed again.

"No doubt everyone is feeling this, seeing the stars," he huffed out with a smile, but he did not stop. He kept going more and more. Eventually he slowly was able to lift things and hurl them through the air, discovering there was a weight limit. His raven could only counterbalance so much weight. He noted it and flew through a sequence. Over and over he repeated motions, slowly maneuvering gracefully through the movements.

"I am Nightswift's heir. Bryla, you are vowed to Nightswift's heir. One chance is all I ask for. To show you and everyone I will do this," he proclaimed to the stars. They responded with a pulse of light. He turned to a raven, still keeping the block up.

"Tell Dad I'm fine. Safe. Not giving up."

The raven cawed and Cyrus continued to push himself through the night. He would go until the morning blue hour of dawn and catch a few hours of sleep in a conifer under the stars.

Chapter 46

E lodie was breathing hard. Trevin held her hand as they sat in the study. She had felt the pulses through the Old Giants, and seen the stars repeatedly pulse.

Rest easy, little one.

The raven is well.

He has emerged.

Trevin looked at her, feeling them pulse as well.

This sensation pulsing through her connection to the Old Giants was different than she had felt before, it was strong, almost commanding. There was no way to miss it and Elodie could not imagine what was happening. She told Trevin she had to talk to Lord Nightswift. They had to send ravens out. Yet when Trevin realized none responded to him he worried. Echo did much the same.

"Cyrus will be alright. He has to be," Trevin said.

Echo dialed Bracken with a hint of nerves and the three waited for an answer.

"Echo." Bracken's voice was calm, yet remorseful.

"Care to explain the stars pulsing? It is a little hard to ignore."

Bracken sighed. "Well, I cannot deny it is linked to Cyrus, but I do not know why or what is happening."

"He's not in his room? Why are ravens not responding to Greenthistle?" Elodie asked.

"No, Lady Elodie, he isn't in his room. He hasn't slept in his room since we returned from the conference."

"What? Where is he?"

"I am not sure. East somewhere in Nightswift's domain, but this has been a nightly thing now. He informs me he is leaving and is safe. Says he needs to master these things and his ravens keep a barrier around him. I cannot tap into them. He alerted me that he was safe and well, nothing more."

"What?" Elodie whimpered. "He is out there all alone, trying to control these shadows? He was struggled with them at drills."

"Just as you told all of us, trust he is alright. He says he is safe and staying far away from territory lines, no hint of stress or fear. He cannot lie, so I have no choice but to trust him."

"But, he isn't talking to me." She wiped her eyes. "It's just like Quinn acted all spring and summer. I hope he nor you feel responsible for what I did at the conference. I knew it was a hasty choice but I just didn't see any other way to protect all of you," she pleaded, sitting forward in the chair as if needing to be closer to the screen.

"Our protection never comes at the cost of you, Lady Elodie. Never forget that. He and I are responsible for this situation you are about to walk into. We had a very serious discussion when we returned to our rooms that night. I could not allow him to cling to you anymore, nor could I allow him to push Trevin more than he has," Bracken stated.

Trevin's jaw fell agape.

"You forbid him from talking to me?" Elodie rasped.

"No, but your lessons with Nightswift are on hold until he can prove to me he wants Nightswift. He was asking us to watch you sink right alongside him, and yet you still pushed him back up. I have a duty to this land, and to you. Greenthistle and Ashdale serve you, Nightswift needs to as well."

"You stripped him of everything he had left!" Elodie wiped her eyes.

"This is for the best. It was obvious the codependency was forming. An estate ruler who cannot stand on their own, cannot rule," Echo explained solemnly.

"Did you all agree to this? You all knew he was ordered to not talk to me? And played dumb?" Her breathing was increasing.

"El, no. I didn't know. I just figured he was busy after work or wanting time alone. He shows up to work meetings."

"Trevin did not know. We purposely did not tell him. Quinn does know though, Quinn did come through and prove he was an Ashdale. This was told to him on stipulation he continues to be one," Echo said.

"You told me to listen to him. I watched him grow stronger and try, but I also could see the fear in letting your hand go. Trevin has a great deal of control, but everyone has a limit. I know Cyrus can do this, but it is up to him to prove to all of us he wants to. You can fight for us all you like, but we have to show you we want it first. Never forget that, Earth Blessed," Bracken explained.

She glared. Her mind debated on ordering Bracken to release the order on Cyrus.

He will find his way back to you.

Let the raven become who he needs to be.

He was so lost until you showed him the way.

Now he simply needs to walk the rest of the trail back to you.

Elodie deflated. After she wiped her eyes again, she looked at Echo and then Bracken. "Fine," she muttered, then got up to leave.

"Elodie," Trevin called out, standing up.

"Trev," Echo said. Trevin groaned and looked at his dad, struggling between the order in his dad's tone and Elodie's distress. "We didn't tell you because we didn't want to take you away from her. You know as well as we do why it had to be done. He will fight to remain your second. You know he will. Tell her this."

"Do you doubt I can do it on my own? If I didn't have her?" Trevin asked, slumping his shoulders.

"I never once questioned your desire to do this, it was that you lost your way after we lost your mother. That much was always clear to me. You standing here right now tells me you want this. Go to her and make sure she knows she always has you."

Trevin sighed then ran to their room to find Elodie sitting on the bed looking down wiping her eyes.

He knelt in front of her, taking her hands. "I'm here, I always will be. You know that right?"

"Yes. I just—I thought I was helping. I didn't know what else to do other than give them what they wanted."

"You did help him immensely, but they are right, he has to prove he wants his birthright because he has yet to show us he does. He may be doing better, but we need to know he *wants* to be better."

"I know. I had honestly hoped Bryla would be what kicked him into action. Isn't that what vowed bonds do?"

"While you made me want to prove myself to everyone, I was dealing with a very different set of internal battles than Cyrus is. I saw no possible way I'd ever be ready to face losing you. Or even pulling you from the life you built for yourself. I thought making Greenthistle better was the only way I could ensure you'd always be safe here. Cyrus obviously doesn't feel he deserves her. Feels he will weigh her down. And in reality, he had a lot to work out. I don't think it would have been fair to ask Bryla to handle that."

Elodie nodded with a sniff. "I just want all of us to get along, to be there. I just want to have one event or get together where we are all present and able to laugh with each other. Or I don't know, maybe I just wanted to weasel my way into your group of friends and pretend it's normal."

"You are part of the group. We will have a lifetime of those moments. An immortal lifetime."

Elodie released a deep breath. Trevin stood up and gave her a kiss.

"Sangria on the patio sound good? Since I don't get you this weekend?"

"It's like eleven pm."

"And?" Trevin asked in a sly tone. "If you're ready to sleep you can, but if you're ready to be lulled into a deeper sleep, I'd certainly love to oblige," he laughed into her ear. She smiled then hugged him tightly, using him to stand up.

Once in the kitchen Trevin opened the door to the walk-in pantry.

"Are those for the keg et outside? Do they come inside?" Elodie asked.

He looked up to see her pointing at a basket containing numerous packages of cat treats. Trevin let out a nervous laugh. "They don't normally come in the house, on occasion they lounge on the perches in the training room since those doors stay open." He looked at her confused expression and gave a tight light smile.

"But you don't have house cats around here do you?"

"No." He smirked. "I kinda never anticipated having to explain it to anyone, but um, sometimes I like to snack especially at work and the turkey ones are good. Cedar will tell you the steak ones are better though. Autumn prefers salmon."

Elodie's eyes widened. "Oh. What? You are embarrassed? You just haven't snacked on them around me?"

Trevin laughed. "Finding out your boyfriend turned vowed eats cat treats made me a little self-conscious."

She laughed and wrapped her arms around his waist. "I never anticipated what dating a shifter entailed."

Chapter 47

As promised, Elodie went camping with Charles, Cora, and Justine. That night, they sat around the fire pit in Six Rivers, Nightswift's domain, a part of the northeastern county that remained new to her.

"So it's your second night roughing it with us, Justine. Like it?" Charles asked with a laugh.

Justine nodded. "It's nice but a little unnerving how quiet it is out here."

"We are fine. It is a campsite. At least it is not one of the dispersed campsites. Those ones you gotta really know what you are doing," Charles chuckled.

"I have stayed at one before, but my thoughts ran a little too wild and I freaked myself out," Elodie added. "I don't know though, maybe I will try one again." She glanced out beyond the tents and thought about it. How close to Siskuyou's border they were. Even Trinity could prove dangerous. Echo and Trevin had emphasized she absolutely could not cross the territory line. "I'd do it in Redwoods National Park, but here, I don't know."

"You and those trees girl. You literally are attached to them," Cora laughed.

Elodie smiled and glanced west towards where they were. She noticed Justine smile at her. This caught her off guard. Usually it was eye rolls and narrowed eyes. Maybe some camping had done Justine some good. *If only it were that easy,* she thought.

"Have you and Trev done any dispersed camping?" Charles asked.

"Not since King Range. That was a wild trip." With the shake of her head, she explained.

"That's crazy you two did that. Anna and I have only slept in the van a few times. It's so hard for them to take off work."

"Q said they are always so busy, not just with their jobs but county stuff and then estate stuff. Did you know their families consider Q, Trev, and Russ, Master of the estate?" Justine chimed in. "He explained it to me one night."

"What?" Cora asked.

Elodie felt Justine's eyes on her now.

"You knew that didn't you?" Justine asked her.

"Yes. I asked Trev a lot of questions, like ever since we started talking really. He's so patient and answers all of them."

"So what does that mean? What does that make Anna?"

"Well, it just means that they are expected to run it. Own it I guess. It is a big responsibility so I think that's why they are not running it entirely on their own. Their parents want to ensure it stays intact. Anna is just Anna or Lady Anna. Lady Greenthistle was their mom. Lady Ashdale would be Q's mom. Honorifics are very important to them," Elodie explained.

"So, when Trev fully takes over, are you going to become Lady Greenthistle?"

"No! I could never. I never want any of them to call me that. It doesn't feel right to me. Mr. Greenthistle sometimes calls me Lady Elodie. It kind of weirds me out."

"You have sealed your fate. That's for sure," Cora laughed again.

"Seriously. Anna hasn't even mentioned me coming over," Charles followed up.

"Same with Q," Justine chimed in. "Just what is it like? Luxury mansion? They are all so loaded."

"Yea I'd say it's luxury. Very posh. Anna's room is bigger than Trev's and Cedar's. Her bathroom alone was like the size of my place in Cutten."

"And she chooses to sleep at my place?" Charles laughed.

"Come on, you know none of them are stuck up."

"Caleb and Russ used to act like they were. I think Caleb just has a big head, his job certainly doesn't help," Justine scoffed.

"You really haven't seen Russ, he was near trembling when I bumped into him at the bookstore. Wouldn't even look me in the eyes," Charles noted.

Elodie sighed. *He had been doing better. Now he's banned from talking to me.* She looked up towards the trees. There didn't seem to be any ravens near, then again, she wasn't best at calling them.

"You always get that sad look whenever anyone mentions Russ and then you look at the sky," Justine remarked.

"I know. I know he's doing better but he still has a ways to go. He didn't ask for any of what happened to him after that night."

"You don't owe him anything."

Elodie sighed and looked at her. "I know."

Justine smiled at her. "But you are a good friend. A really good one. You always have been. I'm sorry I gave you so much spite over the summer."

Elodie smiled at her now. "I know it was an odd situation. I know what it must have looked like." Elodie laughed and noticed Cora and Charles smile. She let out a sigh and felt like they might be alright.

"I guess what I am about to ask you is unfair given what you did for Russ, but." She paused. "Be there for Q when I leave?"

Elodie flinched and looked at Justine stunned. "What?"

"I'm looking for new places to move, Eastern Sierra maybe? I haven't told Q yet. I will, I promise, but just be a friend to him. Hopefully Trev and everyone else will be there for him too."

"Justine," Cora sighed.

"I know, I wanted you all to know first. It's just the longer I stay with him, the harder it is going to be to leave. I didn't anticipate falling for him like this, and I'm not sure he anticipated falling for me as much either. He has El, and Trev, and I guess Russ back now. Caleb and Anna. Charles is staying another year too."

"Damn. I thought for sure you had succumbed to his charm," Charles laughed. "Anna and I have too good of a thing to end now. El clearly found her home."

"I guess I have to accept two out of three isn't bad then," Cora said. "But we will miss you. Café is always open, you know."

"I know. I will drop by again, I promise. Please don't mention it yet to any of them." Justine looked at Elodie.

Her heart pounded. This was unforeseen and she had no idea how this would play out. Quinn had just come back, and had come through for her and Trev at the conference. Her eyes shifted to the sky hoping like hell that there was not a raven near to hear that.

"Please don't tell them. I promise I will do it," Justine begged again, pulling Elodie's gaze back to her.

She had kept her bargain with Trevin, she always would. Kept her word that she would keep all the estates safe. It was also her life now too that she had to be mindful of. If she could keep their secrets safe, she would keep Justine's safe too.

"I promise you, Justine. I will not tell them, and I will be there for him when he needs it. Trev and Russ will too. He will be okay. But we'll miss you." She laughed despite that tightness she still felt. *One overlooks and is overlooked. We are friends again though. I will never leave any of them behind again. We will be alright.*

Refocusing her eyes on them she smiled and jumped in the conversation they were having about hiking trails to do tomorrow. Charles had a map out. The app they used had shown little in the area and reception was minimal out here. However there were lots of trails all around them. Trails that Elodie had not done. Land she had not explored but was hers to care for nonetheless. Sugar pines and other types of conifers that would grow big and strong with hers and Nightswift's help.

Early the next morning Elodie awoke in the tent to chilly predawn air. The day would be warm, though, since it was late summer. She missed curling up next to Trevin but it was the mortal's only camping trip he had called it. They both knew she should go. She should cherish these moments with her friends. It was a fun night despite the stillness out here. When Elodie was closer to the coast, she always knew those Old Giants were near, but out here there were only a few small redwoods scattered around. Surviving even if its life source of the marine layer didn't often reach this far inland.

Her heart was still heavy with Justine's news from last night. With a sigh she got up and walked outside. The land was unfamiliar to her and that was unacceptable. Her mind went back to when she had lessons south of this spot. When Cyrus was so trapped in his own head, and the trees wouldn't respond to her like the redwoods did. How hollowing the lost feeling had been in her at the time.

The border of Siskiyou was fresh in her mind with relations between the high estates as tense as they were. She knew she wouldn't cross the border. Just to be sure, she had double checked the county lines.

There was a trail nearby she could cover a few miles easily and be back in no time. All she would do is get a feel for the land then she would return and nap until everyone roused. With her boots on, she stood up, ensuring her dagger was tucked close. Once she got out of her tent she heard another tent unzip.

"Why are you up?" Cora's groggy voice made Elodie grin.

"Just going to take a little sunrise hike. It won't be far."

"Are you sure that is safe, aren't wild animals active right now?"

"I will be okay. It is only a few miles. I got this too." She tapped the hilt of her dagger.

"If anything happens to you, Trevin is going to kill me and then keep you tucked away forever."

Elodie laughed and shook her head. "Want to come with me?"

"No way it's too cold. Just be careful, Trevin has been pleasant, I don't need him to get moody again."

With small laugh Elodie headed off along the trail. After a few miles she noticed the sky lighten. The air was nipping at her nose despite the layers.

Suddenly a twig snapped behind her, making her tense. When she turned, an unfamiliar man was watching her. Instinctively her hand went to her dagger tucked under her hoodie. A malicious smile graced his lips.

"You are an interesting specimen. What are you?"

"Don't come any closer," she hissed out.

"Aww why not? You look like so much fun." He approached her.

"Stop. I'm warning you."

He laughed and took another step. Then Elodie heard more twigs snapping and saw four other men who were all much taller and bigger than her surrounding her.

A whimper slipped out of Elodie and she gripped her dagger firmly. *Ok, this is why they trained you. Just don't let them head towards camp.*

Quickly she searched the sky for a raven as she pulled her knife out and held the vial of floss flower in her hand. She went to unscrew the cap with her thumb but she was tackled to the ground. Her wrist was pinned so fast before she could even react. Her dagger ripped from her hand.

"floss flower?" One said holding up the vial.

Elodie struggled to get free but one of them straddled her. She strained and her breathing increased. The first male she had seen held her in place and leaned over her with a grin and slashed the dagger right below her collar bone stealing the breath from her. She released her vines in a frantic movement causing them to all gasp.

"Tre—!" she cried out through muffled words. Then she saw someone else pour the floss flower into her wound and her vines retreated into her body. "No!" She cried out. They had never tested floss flower on her, it obviously had an effect on her now that she was no longer mortal.

"Her blood has iron in it, yet it glows teal?" one said.

"She's the thing they've been hiding. Let's get her across the territory line," another urged.

"No! Please! Tr—" a muffled sob came out of her. Desperately, she tried to summon a raven in her head. *Please, Nightswift. I need you now.*

Moments later she heard a raven caw as it took off into the sky, causing them all to still.

"Nightswift has been alerted!" one gasped. "She's aware of the high estates? She knows how to call them."

"They will be here soon. Get her across the territory line."

Suddenly a burst of air hit the ground behind them, causing Elodie to flinch from the force. Then she saw the midnight blue shadows lash out and wrap around the necks of all her assailants.

Elodie's eyes widened seeing the shadows and she pushed herself up, crying out at the pain in her shoulder. Cyrus had his hand out holding the shadows like ropes, with one around each of her attackers' necks. The glare in his eyes was ready to set the world ablaze.

"What the fuck are you two? We don't want any trouble."

"You fucking fools. You straddling her tells me you were looking for trouble."

"We're sorry. Please don't tighten these," one begged.

"Like this?" Cyrus tugged tighter and they all tensed as he tugged them towards him. "I am going to let you in on a little secret, that dagger in your hand was gifted to her by her vowed. I'm sure you know of him, his title is Master Greenthistle."

Her dagger hit the ground as the males tensed and Elodie finally managed to scoot back to sit all the way up. The pain from the wound ripped another sob from her.

Catching her breath, she met Cyrus's eyes. They softened on her, looking like the Cyrus she knew all summer. It was the first time she had seen him since the conference; he was like an entirely new person. No fear or despair.

"He will be here soon, El. Just breathe." His voice was soft and gentle.

Her eyes saw another raven land hastily. Lord Nightswift had arrived.

"Cyrus! What?" his dad gasped. Elodie wondered if his dad had even seen him do this.

"They hurt her. I serve the Earth Blessed." Cyrus narrowed his eyes on the men.

"Who sent you?" Lord Nightswft demanded, regaining his composure. They all remained silent.

Cyrus pulled tighter, causing a few to tremble. "Answer him! You dare walk into Nightswift's domain and try to hurt one of ours?"

"Someone passing through Siskiyou told us about a treasure doused in teal. We—" He went still as Elodie scented Trevin. The mountain lion stalked towards them with ears back and a fierceness in his eyes. Elodie noticed he paid no mind to Cyrus's power.

"They have only been vowed for mere months too. Her overseer takes his job very seriously." Cyrus let out a little coy laugh, still holding them in their restraints.

Trevin glanced back at Cyrus for a second and tilted his head. A faint chuff of approval slipped out as he resumed stalking forward. Quinn and Lord Ashdale arrived along with Lord Greenthistle, all shocked at what they saw. Trevin growled at the one that had straddled Elodie and stared him right in the eyes.

"Her scent is strongest on you," Trevin growled out. "You dare touch my vowed?"

"Please, please."

Trevin lunged for him and pinned him with a roar, baring his fangs.

"Trev," Echo warned as he knelt down to Elodie. Trevin extended his claws to the man's neck then glanced at his dad. His eyes softened when they met hers yet when Echo knelt beside her pain shot through her again. Blood seeped into her hoodie.

"Let me examine the wound. Mortals are far too close though. Try not to scream, I need to get your hoodie off at least." Echo said softly.

Elodie nodded and took an inhale as her eyes welled up as she let him remove the hoodie.

"Hear her cries, and sit under her Old Giants knowing they will not take pity on any of you. I have every right to slit your throat, but letting you rot is a far better punishment. Your tainted blood has no place on our soil." She heard Trevin growl.

"There's floss flower on your dagger? In your blood?" Echo noted.

"Yes. It made my vines retract. I tried. I tried to do what you all showed me in drills," she heaved, clutching the wound. "It has an affect on me now."

"Trev. Heal her," Echo said.

Trevin growled once more at the male and then hurried over to Elodie and shifted back into fae form. "I'm here, Little Mink."

Echo walked to the males still noosed by Cyrus's shadows. Sentries from all three estates as well as Humboldt's guard had arrived. Quinn walked forward with a clenched fist. Trevin remained by Elodie, rubbing her head.

"He is going to release the restraints but if any of you dare move, be very aware you have all three high estates that are sworn to protect that girl. If her vowed isn't the one to rip you apart, one of us will. Convenient that you waited until after the conference to pull this shit," Echo condemned, then nodded at Cyrus who retracted his shadows. The males remained still as sentries seized them and escorted them away.

Cyrus and Bracken both swayed forward and looked at each other shocked as ravens cawed nearby. Elodie knew the caw was one of glee.

"What happened?" Cyrus asked.

"Your raven is bigger?" Trevin noted he looked at Quinn who was equally as confused. "Your bear is the same size."

"So is your mountain lion." Quinn tilted his head. "How?"

"Nightswift gained," Echo said. "But Greenthistle, nor Ashdale felt any power loss. How is this possible?"

Elodie glanced west, in the direction of the Old Giants and her eyes widened as she listened.

We want the three estates to remain as they are. The raven proved himself today.

It is not perfectly balanced, but it is on its way.

To serve and protect you, Earth Blessed, is worthy of merit. Nightswift's heir is loyal, observant, and brave.

She relayed the message to the high estates and saw Bracken look at his son with pride. She noticed Greenthistle and Ashdale smile as well.

"I'm proud of you, Cyrus. Worthy of Nightswift in every sense," Bracken said.

"I didn't expect anyone out here. I searched desperately for a raven."

"I heard your call and flew as fast as I could, sending the alert out to Greenthistle and Ashdale." Cyrus walked forward. "You called them well. You do not owe Nightswift anything, you never did, but I will always serve you, my Earth Blessed and my friend. You offered me your hand so many times when I did not deserve it. If you call for help, Nightswift ravens and the stars will always arrive to support Greenthistle and Ashdale. I give you my word, El. If I am to prove anything to anyone, it is that I will fight for you."

"You vanished after we got back," Elodie said, her words lined with hurt.

"We may have been on the same trail for a time, but I had to find my own way back to Nightswift. I want to prove that I deserve it. That I am good. That your Old Giants do not have a weak heir."

"Let's get you back to camp, It's after sunrise. Take my hoodie, you can't go back to them like this," Trevin pulled his hoodie off. "I will take yours to Greenthistle to get it cleaned and mended."

"Would you like a raven posted nearby? Just until you return to town? It is no trouble and it will not be watching you or them, just the surrounding area for danger. I promise. I nor Cyrus will tap into them unless we are alerted of danger."

Elodie remained quiet and looked at the ground. She met Cyrus's eyes and spoke to him. "Yes, please. I would feel safer knowing one is near."

Cyrus smiled and nodded.

Quinn sighed, smirking slightly. "How is she enjoying camping?"

Elodie's smile faltered ever so slightly. "She said it wasn't so bad." Quinn's pleased smile made her gut twist with the tension. *We will be alright*, she reminded herself silently.

"I will walk back with you then once you are sitting I will leave. See ya tonight?" Trevin asked, helping her up.

"Yes. Thank you again, all of you."

"Trev will debrief you when you return to your residence," Echo said. "Enjoy the weekend and be safe, little cub."

Trevin turned to Cyrus and smirked. "I gotta say you can be pretty terrifying with those shadows. I'm so glad you came for her. Thank you."

Cyrus looked at him in shock for a moment, then smiled. "After what she has done for me, always without fail. She's my best friend."

Trevin's smirk flattened the slightest bit.

"I'm sorry. I just—I was so alone."

Trevin took an inhale and smirked. "I know, I'm sorry, I wasn't there when I should have been. Want to go grab a bite after I get her back to camp? Quinn? We can celebrate Cyrus's increase." Trevin looked at Quinn who sighed and then nodded with a smile.

Cyrus smiled too. "I will be overhead."

Once near the campsite Elodie gave her mountain lion a firm hug as Trevin chuffed her then nuzzled her head.

"Be safe, Little Mink. I will see you soon."

"I will remain alert. Enjoy breakfast with Cyrus and Quinn. I'm proud of you."

"I do miss them. I lost my best friend some time ago, long before that night. If I can't be his bestie anymore, I can at least be a good friend to him. Better than I was. I'm glad he has you now," Trevin said

Elodie gave him another squeeze then let go. They said one last loving goodbye then she quietly walked back to camp and crawled in her tent. She heard one last chuff laid down on her sleeping bag. No one had roused much to her relief.

Chapter 48

With September's arrival, it brought with it a certain kind of ease they had all been craving. Cyrus still hadn't gone out to the mortal world aside from work and to Elodie's. He, Trevin, and Quinn had resumed their usual workflow in the office with glazed over looks during meetings and goofed off in the conference room. The next task he needed to prepare for would occur with the change of seasons.

When the autumn equinox arrived, Cyrus scanned the crowd anxiously. He forced himself to keep his breathing calm. He could do what he needed to tonight, he was so ready to lock onto his target. Yet his focus was interrupted.

"Announcing the arrival of Master Greenthistle and his vowed, Lady Elodie Stantiago." This was the first time they were announced as vowed and once again the crowd were silent, then murmurs began.

Cyrus watched Trevin and Elodie walk out at the same time, arms linked, outfits complementing each other. They both wore the diadems from their first winter solstice together. Trevin had intentionally requested they reflect Greenthistle's colors. Even though it was fall, the green tones of the gemstones went nicely with their outfits.

He saw no fear in Elodie this time. Her heart was pounding alright, but her energy was so loud tonight, so full of confidence and bliss he hadn't seen her have, she was home. Trevin too exuded a confidence like never before.

When Cyrus stole a glance at Lord Greenthistle, he could see the genuine smile and pride in his expression. It made Cyrus smile too. He hoped he could see this look on his dad during spring equinox. He wanted to make his dad just as proud as Lord Greenthistle was of his firstborn tonight.

Realization hit him that Bryla hadn't yet arrived. She couldn't see this either. No one could deny Elodie and Trevin's bond tonight. He almost wanted to see the fool that challenged it. Trevin's confidence had reigned in his anger and held it poised and ready to strike.

He did not join any dancing, instead remained in the crowd. Various people came up to him and he did his best to put his best foot forward. Even when they asked about topics that grated at his core and caused him to grit his teeth. After two hours he grew exhausted. Elodie luckily had come up to him and talked for a bit. They toasted to the trail ahead and to Humboldt together, joined eventually by Trevin, Cedar, Autumn, and Quinn.

"Damn, talk about owning the place. You two may as well be king and queen," Quinn laughed. "You look beautiful, Elodie. You look like you are home."

Elodie laughed bashfully and Trevin smiled.

"You look beautiful too, King Trevy."

Trevin rolled his eyes but had a grin plastered on his face. Cyrus felt as though he had found his unkindness, his pack, his pride once again. He noticed Trevin looking at him.

"I'm glad you are here tonight," Trevin said, giving his arm a nudge.

"I am too, Trevy." Cyrus beamed when that scent permeated his nose. Bryla's scent.

He excused himself abruptly to seek it out. Yet he still could not find her. Finally he found her parents and approached them. The scent had only gotten a little bit stronger. As though she were upstairs or outside.

"Good evening, Lord and Lady Petalgrace, I hope your evening is going well," he said with nerves lining his tone. They looked at him, somewhat in shock. He bowed his head.

"Master Nightswift," Lord Petalgrace marveled.

"Sir, lady, if I may inquire as to young Lady Petalgrace's whereabouts? I would like to ask her to dance, to make up for summer. I had a moment of hesitation that has sat heavily on my shoulders ever since," he breathed out heavy words, traversing his nerves. *I'd very much like to court your firstborn...to ask her to give up her birthright,* he thought to himself and realized how big of an ask this would be, but the thought of ignoring this vowed bond and not seeing her was not a path he wanted to walk down anymore.

He noticed Lord Petalgrace let out a sigh of sadness. Her mom too looked so disappointed. *Something was wrong.*

"Master Nightswift, our apologies, I regret to inform you she will not be attending tonight."

His heart nearly stopped there on the spot. The tether was growing slack and he was trying to grasp it. "Why? Is she in some kind of trouble? Is she attending a revelry in another territory?" he asked worriedly. Why would she choose to miss a revelry? No one missed these, unless they were banned. He clenched his jaw and realized how close to breaking he must appear. Steeling himself again as much as it hurt to force himself into a tiny glass box, he looked at them. "My apologies, sir. Lady."

Lady Petalgrace offered him a small smile but she looked disappointed. In him?

"She's not in any trouble nor attending elsewhere, she is perfectly fine. She declined attendance. We insisted that she come but she hadn't budged and we were running two hours behind as it was. I am sorry, Master Nightswift."

Cyrus met Lord Petalgrace's eyes and there it was. Pity. They were offering sympathy. They could see what a lovestruck fool he was. He hadn't foreseen this setback, never anticipated it. Had she rejected him? Once again he forced himself up to the next grip on the cliff side and reigned in control of himself. That sting had hit right in his heart though and his hands went numb with a flash of cold.

"Of course, sir. I understand. Revelries can be a lot. Enjoy your evening," he fretted then hurried off. At first he maintained a normal pace then his steps increased, right to the bar where he downed a glass of whiskey, then ordered a glass of fae wine and downed that with quickness. *So much for giving everything up,* Cyrus thought. He hadn't even drunk anything with Elodie all summer. After downing two more drinks he left the revelry without a word or glance. He shifted into his raven and flew towards the town square, landing on that damned rooftop again. The square was quiet. The tavern was opened but he could tell it was nearly empty.

Her scent was here but it went off in a different direction. He spotted a raven and met its eyes. *If Dad inquires, tell him I am fine. I am safe.* The raven cawed then Cyrus took off west towards the boundary. Near Arcata Community. He was confused as to why her scent went in this direction. She could not cross into the mortal world and this was not near an entryway.

As he flew her scent got stronger, but so did another. Dread pooled in his stomach with this scent. His wings flashed cold and he ungracefully landed in a tree. He called another raven and asked it to land silently nearby and remain hidden. It obeyed. When he tapped into its line of sight, Alena and Bryla were sitting looking at the boundary. Cyrus wanted to scream. Wanted to rush down there and pull Bryla away from her.

"It's just a revelry. He will probably lose his title anyways and Nightswift will fall out of rank. Then who knows? Maybe we will be a high estate after Ashdale. My dad is pretty sure Elmbridge holds enough rank to fall into place. Then we can just ban Cyrus, Cedar, and Trevin along with his stupid little dirty mink."

Cyrus wanted to scream at her. He would never let that happen. Bryla sighed and wiped her eyes. *She's crying? And Alena is just sitting here doing a piss poor job to comfort her?*

"My parents were so upset I didn't want to go, I refused to get ready and they told me I was being foolish. My dad encouraged me to befriend Lady Elodie. And I had wanted to. I was hoping for Spring this year, but she was so overwhelmed, then I just felt so betrayed by them all in Summer."

No. Bryla felt betrayed by the high estates because of Cyrus. Elodie and Trevin had helped as much as they could. Trevin had taken a risk to push Bryla towards him, he knew that. Cyrus wasn't upset about it, even if it was just because Trevin had wanted Elodie back at his side. He was upset about the manipulation Alena was spinning though.

"You don't want to befriend her. Cyrus just clings to her. He used to fantasize about doing such unspeakable things to her. He probably secretly wishes he could. If they haven't already. Maybe Trevin is fine with it all. I mean, him, caring about a mortal? Even if she did become our Earth Blessed, it was only because Cyrus pushed her to. Not Trev," Alena laughed.

"Trev does love her though. I think he did before she awoke. Cyrus would never look at me like that. He looked like he was so uncomfortable with me when we danced together."

No! No, no, no! Bryla please, he pleaded. He was about to fly down there until Alena's voice slithered up his spine again.

"I wonder if Cyrus is uncomfortable with you," Alena said in a sassy tone.

That tone that slithered up his spine like a snake. That tone that made him writhe.

Cyrus could almost see that last chain holding him back snap and he swooped down to the ground, landing behind them.

They both turned and looked at him with wide eyes.

"Trevin does love Elodie, I would never touch her like that nor would I betray his trust. I never wanted to. Lady Bryla, you have never once made me uncomfortable, Alena does though for what she did to me, Trev and El."

"Why aren't you at the equinox?" Bryla looked at him with awe.

For a moment, all Cyrus could do was look at her, unsure of how to respond. *Am I really going to hesitate around her again?*

"I was hoping to have your first dance, to make up for summer," he said softly, reaching out his hand. He wasn't sure what would happen if she rejected him now.

Bryla's eyes got even bigger as she glanced at his hand then back to him. Cyrus watched the glow of her freckles against her russet skin. Bryla was the sun to his night sky. She always would be.

A slight sadness took over Bryla. "I'm not dressed for the equinox, though."

"It's alright. We can have a private dance elsewhere. Being by my side will garner attention. Nightswift's heir apparent and all." He glared at Alena. "Where I will remain in rank with Greenthistle and Ashdale."

"He is dangerous and unstable. You hear them. Careful, Bryla," Alena cooed.

It took everything in Cyrus for him to not tremble back but he would not be chained down again. He wouldn't let anyone else down, ever again.

"And you are a vile snake, Alena. You lost power. I fessed up to what I did to cost Nightswift power, you should tell her what you did to cost Elmbridge power. The Old Giants know, and the stars do too," Cyrus heaved out. Then he took a deep inhale and let his eyes pulse.

Alena and Bryla both gasped again.

"Lady Bryla, I will never harm you. I have thought about those brief moments with you ever since that night. They have helped me through some of my darkest moments."

He saw Bryla's eyes shift to the pulsing stars he not only saw around them, but felt as well.

"This is linked to you?" Bryla marveled.

"It is. I'd love to tell you all about it."

She looked back at Alena who glared at him.

"Horrible wretched monster," Alena spat out.

It made Cyrus flinch and sent a chill up his spine as he repeated his mantra again and again. Forcing himself to take a deep inhale, he lifted his head once more. Then to his shock, Bryla took his hand.

"If you are comfortable being seen with me, like this, I'd like to go, Master Nightswift," Bryla said. He could sense her nerves, but this was that one chance he was going to get, he knew as soon as they arrived at Greenthistle, everyone would shift attention away from Elodie and Trevin to himself and Bryla.

"I want everyone to see us, Lady Bryla, I have broken too many chains to be dragged down again. You always have Nightswift's protection." He smiled and then leveled his gaze at Alena. "Enjoy your night." He scoffed then led Bryla back towards the path.

His heart was pounding. Alena was unpredictable, so he called for the raven nearby and flashed into its vision as it watched she fled in the direction of the tavern. *Good. She didn't win, she won't win.*

Once they were about halfway to Greenthistle, he stopped and let out a huge huff of air. He was exhausted already and knew he still had to walk into Greenthistle, but with her by his side, he knew he could.

"Lady Bryla." He faltered as he took both of her hands in his. "You were there at the tavern, when she dragged me out of that alley weren't you?"

"Yes. Something told me to go to you, I didn't like what they were saying and I didn't want to believe it. I had seen her with others before that night and thought it was over, that maybe I could talk to you."

He brought her hands to his chest. "She hurt me that night. Badly. It is why she is banned from Nightswift. I don't want to spoil the night by talking about it, but I promise to tell you everything that happened. Elodie is like my sister, she is my best friend and I never once thought of her as anything beyond that. What

Alena said about me wanting her was what she believed, the spirit wanted to hurt Elodie, wanted Trevin to watch my hands do it too. I am having to relearn who I am, but I'd like to learn who you are too."

Her bright eyes looked at her hands and he knew she could feel his thundering heart.

"Master Nightswift—"

"Please call me Cyrus," he interrupted.

"Call me Bryla?"

A relieved laugh slipped out of him as he brought her hands to his lips. "Of course."

"You were waiting for me tonight? Your first dance of the night?"

"Yes. I want it to be with you. I want to attend with you, if you would like to of course, but I understand if you want to dance with others. Just one dance is all I will ask."

"But Petalgrace is hardly considered an estate of status, and I'm dressed so informally. You are Master Nightswift. The impression this will make on your parents."

"None of that matters. You matter, Bryla. I know the pressure my status might put on you and I'm honestly terrified it's going to be something that scares you off." Cyrus explained, he could feel his face and ears flushing red. She just looked at him with her brows furrowed.

"I would be honored to be by your side tonight," she beamed.

He couldn't help but smile. He also couldn't help but pull her into a tight hug and inhale that scent of sage and fuchsia. He was ready to drown in it.

She gasped for a second then wrapped her arms around him with a deep inhale. Cyrus wanted to ask what his scent was, but he needed to be smarter about this. Just like Trevin and Elodie told him, he had time, a long time. He would start small, just as he had been doing all summer.

"Bryla Petalgrace, may I court you?" The whisper of his words made her still for a moment before she pulled away from his embrace. His heart was still thundering.

"Master Nightswift wants to court me?"

All Cyrus could do was nod.

"Yes!" Bryla chirped.

Then to his shock and desire she pulled him into a kiss. Cyrus couldn't help but pull her deeper into the kiss.

The rattle of a chain sent a chill down his spine. Alena's coy little laugh in his head made him pull back.

Fuck. I ripped them off! I have Bryla! I want Bryla!

Her hand gently came to his shoulder. "I'm sorry. If that was out of line.

Cyrus just pulled her waist close again. "Let me explain it all later, it still hurts some nights. But I want you. I want to be better for you."

She nodded. "Alright, Cyrus. I'm here."

"Thank you." He exhaled and offered his arm. "Shall we? I promise I am ready to face that revelry."

Elodie noticed Trevin and Autumn both turn towards the door to the ballroom. She glanced to where Echo stood with some other fae and he turned as well.

"Who else is arriving? It's like three hours in," Autumn stated.

"Good question." Trevin grew tense and took Elodie's hand.

A silence took over the room at the sight of Cyrus walking in with his arms linked with Bryla's. Her dress was gorgeous but it was definitely shorter than everyone else's ball gowns. It was also a rich green and gold dress that appeared to be made of leaves with green straps tied on her shoulders.

Elodie couldn't picture her wearing anything else honestly. "Cyrus?" she gasped in awe.

Both he and Bryla looked nervous. The whispers about Lady Bryla's informal attire and what might have caused their late arrival circulated. Some speculated she had been in trouble, others said they might have been busy behind closed doors.

Elodie watched as the two descended the stairs arm-in-arm. Bryla clutched onto him tightly and he leaned into her, whispering something with a smile. Bryla nodded and they walked to the dance floor where people made way for them to join in the dancing.

"Is he trying to steal our thunder?" Trevin asked, confused.

"No! We already had our moment and danced hours ago," Elodie scolded him. "We saw the stars pulse and you heard how worried his parents were when he couldn't find him anywhere."

"I heard Bryla hadn't planned on coming. Cedar was dancing with Bryla's friend," Autumn said, watching with just as much awe.

"So he went and found her," Trevin stated more so than asked. "The new Cyrus is here."

Elodie grinned widely at the two then looked around to see Bracken and Ariyanna watching attentively. His parents' relief was obvious but she also saw pride on Bracken's face and hope on Ariyanna.

When the dance ended, Cyrus and Bryla just looked at each other with dazed smiles. As if they couldn't believe they had just done that.

Moments later they made their way towards Elodie, Trevin, and Autumn.

"I'd like for you all to officially meet Lady Bryla Petalgrace," Cyrus declared and Elodie smiled at how happy and excited Cyrus looked.

Chapter 49

The following weekend Quinn had convinced Justine to try a night walk in Sequoia community park. She relented, much to his contentment. He knew night hikes had never been her thing, but Quinn would not let anything happen to her.

"I guess it's not so bad, but maybe it's just safer with you here." Justine laughed and linked her arm with his.

Quinn smiled and they continued walking on the paved path in Sequoia Community. He never did figure out what that feeling of being watched that she mentioned. She said nothing about Elodie's little mishap on the camping trip either. He hoped she didn't even know of it. The assailants were in the hold and would be dealt with soon.

"Well, if anyone tried anything they'd be pretty stupid. It'd take a very bold individual to challenge me. Plus they'd be in such serious trouble given my name," Quinn proclaimed.

"That's why you walk around without a care in the world?"

"An attack on me or you is not a concern in this park. Trust me." He chuckled.

"I mean your family pretty much runs this town."

"Technically, Greenthistle does. If we were in Ferndale or Fortuna, then yes."

"Elodie talks about a hike she likes a lot over in Ferndale."

"Russ Park?" Quinn asked.

"Yes. She says it's one of her favorites. I considered it but the incline made me a bit hesitant."

"It's really not that bad. The view from the top is pretty amazing. We should go sometime."

"Maybe. Suppose I could squeeze another hike in with you sometime," she laughed.

"Anytime, anywhere, I will go hiking with you."

"Anywhere in Humboldt you mean." Her tone indicated some sass and a sigh slipped out of him. "I'm kidding. I know, I know, family responsibility and honor and all that jazz. El has explained it all before."

"She has?"

"Yea, she said it was common in some cultures to remain close knit as a family. It was common with a lot of Mexican families, though she said she didn't grow up that way. Then again look at her now. Shackled up to Greenthistle."

Another sigh escaped Quinn. "She isn't shackled up. She is happy here."

"Yes. She has said that too a million times. But she was like, tucked away in the forest all summer with him. It's weird."

"She hung out. It's not as though she never showed up to anything."

"Not as much as she used to. I mean she's happy, right? She chose this. I know. I am happy for her, but I just think there is so much more out there for her than here. The same goes for you too."

"I like it here too. It'd be hard to leave." Quinn stopped himself there. He wanted to explain, wanted to tell her everything, and show her. He had wanted to take her to a revelry, wanted to give her a dagger and a diadem, he had wanted to do everything Trev had gotten to do with Elodie and Cyrus was now bound to do with Bryla at some point. Though he mentioned he hadn't asked Bryla about the vowed bond yet.

Quinn began to think. The revelry and dagger was impossible but if she could just see him, know what he could do, even know his real name. Elodie had clung to this world with everything in her, she fought for Cyrus, fought for Trev and for himself. Then Justine would know, she would understand and maybe she would want it too. As he worked through it all in his head he knew he would have to cover up even more for Elodie given what she had agreed to. A call would come from some county soon and El had stated she would only go when it didn't interfere with work. That meant weekends and holidays when she should be with her mortal friends. He sighed again, pissed all over again that Cyrus let her do that. Had put all of them in such a terrible predicament.

"Let's cut over on this trail, I want to show you something," Quinn said, heading off the paved path onto a dirt trail.

"Is it safe? It is kinda dark."

"Yes. Do you know how many nights Trev, Russ and I have wandered here? Take my hand."

"Okay." She took it and he led her through ferns, down a trail. "I don't know how Elodie can do this at night, just out there. The trail by her house, I've looked at that park and it is huge. This park is in the middle of town and it's just trails everywhere. She does this alone too." Justine sighed.

"El is in absolutely no danger, anywhere in this entire county. She is always safe."

"What? How can you know that though?" Justine asked.

"I'm going to show you why she is safe here. She is certainly something special on her own but we will protect her too, our estates will." His words held an inflection of a smile. He felt good about this choice.

"You are talking weird, Q. Where are we going?" Justine asked. He led her to the very spot where Elodie had been told everything she was and the three high estates welcomed her. Secluded and tucked away.

"Almost there," he said and then felt her stumble. He moved quickly and caught her.

Justine froze. She had known he was strong, his secure grip on her reaffirmed that but she didn't realize how fast he was. She also wasn't sure what to make of his claims that Elodie would be safe all over this county. She severely doubted that. It was a large county, with a lot of open land. Mountains, forests, jagged coastlines. It wasn't uncommon for people to go missing in this area either. Yet Q seemed so sure of it.

Finally, they stopped in a little clearing. There was no way she would have been able to find this spot and she wasn't sure she could get back to her car.

He turned to face her with a smile and she definitely was feeling uncomfortable but she trusted Q. She looked around. "It's pretty. But it looks like the rest of the park." A nervous laugh slipped out.

Q smiled wide. "Justine, I want to be honest with you. Even if you are going to leave, I want you to know. I don't want you to be upset with me or El, or think she is wasting her life here, because she's not. Trev loves her and she loves him. They will always protect each other."

"Okay, I get it." Her heart rate was increasing.

"And I love you, so I want you to know," Q said, relaxed.

"I love you too." She looked down briefly and shifted weight from one foot to the other.

"Q isn't my real name. It's actually Quinn. Q is the name I go by on this side of the boundary."

Justine stared at him confused. "Quinn. Okay, Quinn. I figured Q was short for something but what boundary? What are you talking about?

"There is a boundary line, I live on the other side, we glamour ourselves on this side, the mortal side. I look different over there than I do here."

Justine was about to speak, until she gasped and saw his eyes brighten to a rich amber gold, his ears grew pointed and he had strange markings across the bridge of his nose. She took a step back as her terror grew.

"How?" Justine's voice was a mere rasp.

"I'm fae and immortal," he said, applying it again then dropping it. "See?" He took a step towards her, reaching for her hand.

She stepped back again. "No. No." She shook her head. "Stay away from me." Justine's eyes started to well up.

"Justine. It's okay. I'm not going to hurt you. I would never. El was scared too."

All she could focus on was her heart hammering in her chest. "I slept with you. With some creature?"

"What? No." Hurt flashed across his features. "I'm just fae. We do not hurt mortals. We can't lie either."

"Fae. Your ears. Your face." She took another step back. "You lied. This entire time." She started to weep. This was not real, some fake imaginary thing yet he was standing right in front of her. Then she looked at the trees and thought of Elodie. She recalled Trevin's attachment to her. "Trev. Anna? Russ! You all did trap Elodie here. No. No. All of you chained her up. His dad? Your dad?"

"No," he groaned. "None of us chained her up. El chose this and him. She belongs here with him, she is his vowed or mate. She's saved him a few times now."

"This isn't a fairy tale. It's actually a nightmare she doesn't understand yet. Her prince chained her up and you all helped. You want to do the same to me," Justine cried into her hands.

"That's not true. I will never chain you up and we all mean it, if El ever wanted to leave, she is free to go. But she's important to us. She loves this place, it's her home."

Justine felt his arms around her and she tensed then pushed him away. "Stop!" she cried out.

A raven cawed as it flew off and she watched him still. "Justine, please, please tell me you are okay with this, that you accept it." He panicked and faltered back, gripping his heart. Absolute shock seized his expression now. "Oh no! No!"

"No. I don't accept anything from you. I don't want anything from you. You monster. Please let Elodie go. Please," she begged.

Then she frantically pulled her phone out to find Elodie's number.

"Justine. Please."

She unlocked her phone then heard a deep voice.

"Master Ashdale. You have committed a very serious offense. You and the mortal are to come with us."

"What? Where? I want to go home," Justine pleaded with the male who also had pointed ears. She took in his clothes. A uniform with a Humboldt patch on the sleeve, yet he looked as though he were dressed from a different time period she couldn't place, or a different world. "Please, please let Elodie go, please." She was sobbing now.

The male looked at her, confused. "Lady Elodie is perfectly safe and is not held anywhere against her will, she is free to pass as she pleases. However, you need to come with us."

Lady Elodie... Justine recalled her Elodie saying Trev's dad called her that. He used such a formal title. As she was trying to process everything happening Q spoke. *Quinn,* she had to remind herself.

"Please, let me make a bargain, she will be loyal to us. Don't take her. I can talk to her. In her apartment." Quinn began to panic as though fear had taken over him.

"No! I never want to see you again. I just want to go home. I was planning on moving!"

"Let me try to make a bargain, Justine, please?"

"Look at what you are doing, Quinn. If you have to force or beg, you ought not to. She is not the Earth blessed, nor is this the same situation as Master Greenthistle. You know Lady Elodie would have been in the same situation too. Lord Greenthistlstle demanded it."

"Fine then, I proclaim myself her—"

Justine screamed as three men restrained and muffled Quinn.

"Ashdale lost. You are in no position to make such proclamations to be her overseer. Every aligned sentry felt that power shift. Lord Ashdale would not have to honor such a proclamation anyways. You know how it works."

"But—just let me talk to her!"

"You know that is against orders. You deliberately broke a rule. Under orders of Lord Greenthistle, Lord Nightswift, and Lord Ashdale, you are to report to the hold immediately. The mortal will be kept safe, until the three high estate lords discuss the next course of action."

"No!" Justine cried out and went to run, but more people with pointed ears grabbed her. She saw certain insignia on their patches with colors, Humboldt's outline, and a redwood. Some had a bear on their patch, some had a mountain lion or a raven. "No!"

Something small pinched her arm and things grew hazy, and her body felt sluggish despite her pushing away from them.

"Please. I'm sorry. Justine." She heard him say just before she fell unconscious.

The stars and the Old Giants were watching because they knew their chosen ones had not yet made it safely off the trail and now a tidal wave was about to wash everything out. Coyotes were watching, waiting, and ready with an arsenal of bitter secrets and truths.

That little mink had been clinging to the bear, the raven, and her mountain lion with everything she could. She was the high estate's cub and fledgling and they were her unkindness. Yet, she would soon learn it was impossible to grip sand slipping through her fingers.

And so Zuli sat patiently, waiting to carry out his orders from Lord Hazelthorn, awaiting a little blackbird to feed Austin a great deal of information. Then the coyote would wait for the right time to strike.

One had overlooked and been overlooked.

One had been lost and altered.

And all that was left was getting the bait for the desired catch.

Selenite "Selene" Hazelthorn

Trevin "Trev" Greenthistle
Autumn "Anna" Greenthistle
Cedar "Caleb" Greenthistle

Echo "Earl" Greenthistle

Ariyanna "Ariya" Stormbriar

Cyrus "Russ" Nightswift
Delia "Dee" Nightswift
Poppy "Piper" Nightswift

Bracken "Brian" Nightswift

Olive "Olivia" Fernsplash

Quinn "Q" Ashdale
Coral "Conner" Ashdale

Miles "Mike" Ashdale

Lady Lillyleaf &
"Tanya" Lillyleaf
of Marin County

Lord Oakstone &
"Jared" Oakstone
of Marin County

Alena
Elmbridge
of Humboldt
County

Bryla
Petalgrace
of Humboldt
County

Acknowledgements

You made it once again! Thank you so much dear reader for sticking with Elodie and the crew. This book was delayed due to many reasons but the most prominent one being the loss of my dad. While my heart was rooted in the coastal redwoods of Humboldt County, his was split between San Diego and the Eastern Sierra. I would frequently send him pictures of all my hikes, day trips and weekend trips wherever I ended up. It was a bit of a loss to stop sending those pictures. As is a theme in many of my books, processing the emotions is important, allow yourself time to feel and process things. The Humboldt crew would remind you of that.

While we are not finished with the trail yet, we certainly wouldn't have made it this far without some very important people. There are always so many people to thank and I could add so many more pages thanking everyone.

Many people have come and gone over the course of writing the first book, but some have stuck around since the early days.

To Sac Writers, Adalyn Grace, and Night Owls thank you for awesome discords too.

To my editors Brittany and Kai, thank you so much for your help on tackling this beast as well. This has undergone so many changes from the first draft. To all the editors I follow, thank you for your consistent posts with helpful tips. I swear I didn't save em' and forget em'.

A huge thanks to all my beta readers for putting up with my idiots trip and falling along the many miles of drafts. Sadia, TZ Krasner, and everyone for your input. It is always appreciated.

To Carly, thank you for being such a supportive alpha reader. I appreciate you so much with your wealth of knowledge. I am looking forward to seeing your book on shelves one day.

To Tegan Weissman, for your constant presence and all you do. It really has made a huge difference in my life. To all the crew in the discord, thanks for your constant support too. I love learning about your characters and our daily questions about them.

As always this book would not be here if not for National and California State Parks and the many inspiring, enchanted places this state has. A massive shout out to Eureka Books, Los Bagels, and all the comforts of Humboldt. I have to give a shout out to a few awesome spots in Marin too for providing the perfect day trips when I can't get up north. Mill Valley Coffee company and Mt. Tamalpais Watershed. Also shout out to the Sonoma spots where I did a lot of read throughs along a magical river surrounded by marine layer and crashing waves near Duncans Mills and Copperfield's Books.

A nod to A Seat At the Table Books, Rachel, Natasha, Jason, Alex, Emily, Shae, Arden, Bonnie, and the rest of the crew for the third space and friends.

To Yang, Linda, Marie, & Gil for being the best coworkers and listening to my ramblings about this over coffee, boba, and KBBQ.

Once again, I am forever grateful to my family who made sure I had the opportunity to travel as a kid, to my sister for instilling a further degree of wanderlust and opening the door to Nor Cal. To my brother for furthering my love for the ocean.

All my friends who have sat quietly and listened to me when I would not shut up about these silly books I write and hyperfixate on.

To Cindy and DK, thanks for being some of the best hiking buddies out there who listened to me talk about this even more.

To Danielle, for being the best bestie and also listening to me tell you the entire story over hikes, coffee, thrift stores and road trips to the trees and mountains.

Joe, my love, thank you for always accepting my hyperfixations. Your unending support to let me create and explore this area we call home and willingness to join in sometimes means the world to me. I am so lucky to have a partner like you.

And to you dear reader, thank you.

About the Author

Kelly Virens is a fantasy author with a love of all things trees, mountains, oceans, hiking, and storytelling. Born and raised in San Diego, California, with a two year teaching stint in Japan, she relocated to Northern California to find home in all the amazing areas nearby. When she is not writing, she is usually off hiking or exploring somewhere in the region where she finds inspiration. Following a hike, she always stops by a nearby bookstore and a coffee shop. Her imagination is usually dreaming and scheming new things to write, draw, or make. Follow along with her explorations on Instagram with her personal account @fireflirt and her bookstagram @KellyVirensBooks

Check out more Secrets of Old Giants & Enchanted Senses content below

linktr.ee/portfireflirt